*But her passion
will enslave
his heart . . .*

The Royal Brotherhood Series
One Night with a Prince

"Jeffries not only beguiles readers with scenes of passion and vivid characters but steadily builds the story's tension to an exciting conclusion. The details of gambling, mistresses, and scandalous conduct further enrich the tapestry against which this emotionally satisfying story plays out. Jeffries's readers will be royally pleased."

—*Publishers Weekly*

To Pleasure a Prince

"Jeffries's sparkling dialogue takes center stage in an emotional, highly sensual and powerfully romantic story. . . . All the characters have such depth they simply leap from the pages."

—*Romantic Times*

"[The] parallel courtships of the Tremaine and North siblings engages throughout. Readers will eagerly await the third brother's story."

—*Publishers Weekly*

In the Prince's Bed

"A traditional Regency told with sparkle and energy. . . . The chemistry among all the characters—not just the hero and heroine—ensures that there's never a dull moment in this merry romp. . . . Fans of historical romances will find the simple pleasures of this novel irresistible."

—*Publishers Weekly*

"Delightful, sensual, and poignant, Jeffries's latest brings humor and pathos to a richly peopled tale. This is a delightful start to a new series featuring a trio of heroes to die for."

—*Romantic Times*

Also by Sabrina Jeffries

The School for Heiresses
(with Liz Carlyle, Julia London, and Renee Bernard)

Only a Duke Will Do

Never Seduce a Scoundrel

One Night with a Prince

To Pleasure a Prince

In the Prince's Bed

Sabrina Jeffries

BEWARE A SCOT'S REVENGE

Pocket Books

New York   Toronto   London   Sydney

An *Original* Publication of POCKET BOOKS

POCKET BOOKS, a division of Simon & Schuster, Inc.
1230 Avenue of the Americas, New York, NY 10020

This book is a work of fiction. Names, characters, places, and incidents are products of the author's imagination or are used fictitiously. Any resemblance to actual events or locales or persons, living or dead, is entirely coincidental.

ISBN-13: 978-1-4165-1610-1
ISBN-10: 1-4165-1610-7

This Pocket Books paperback edition June 2007

10 9 8 7 6 5 4 3 2 1

POCKET and colophon are registered trademarks of Simon & Schuster, Inc.

Illustration by Alan Ayers/Lettering by David Gatti

Manufactured in the United States of America

For information regarding special discounts for bulk purchases, please contact Simon & Schuster Special Sales at 1-800-456-6798 or business@simonandschuster.com.

Acknowledgments

Many thanks to Sally Avelle, for her invaluable travel books and firsthand tales of Scotland. I used every single one doing my research.

Prologue

London
May 1822

Dear Charlotte,

I hear that your former pupil, Lady Venetia, has once again refused a perfectly good suitor. Speaking as a disinterested observer, I believe the lady may have taken your rules for heiresses too much to heart. If she isn't careful, it will gain her nothing but a lonely spinsterhood.

Your cousin,
Michael

Daughters are a plague upon men.

So thought Quentin Campbell, the Earl of Duncannon, whose twenty-four-year-old daughter was giving him fits. He'd hoped that Mrs. Charlotte Harris's School for Young Ladies would teach Venetia to be malleable, but it had just made the lass more impudent. Apparently she'd inherited not only her mother's lovely features, but also her stubborn temperament. And he'd damned near had enough.

He found her in the kitchen of their London town house, preparing that vile medicinal concoction she loved to pour down his throat. "How dare you refuse the viscount's suit after I gave him leave to court you?" he blustered.

Cool as a Highland loch, Venetia continued pounding a purplish flower into powder. "If you'd consulted me before you gave him leave, Papa—"

"Consulted you! And given you a chance to pick apart yet another fine fellow?" He stifled an oath. "What offended you this time? His charming manner? His too broad smile? His well-groomed appearance?"

"I don't like him," she said with her usual maddening half-smile.

"Don't like him! He's fashionable and handsome, with fortune to spare—"

"So is my reticule." She poured the purple powder into a glass of water and stirred. "Unfortunately, it also has more personality, and nearly as much intelligence."

This was the trouble—his daughter's wit ran men off.

"My lord?" said a voice from the doorway.

He glanced at his butler. "What is it?"

"A Mr. Sikeston and some other men are asking to see you."

He tensed. Sikeston and his men were *here*, in London? Something must have gone horribly wrong. "I'll meet with them in my study."

As the butler hurried off, Quentin shot his daughter an exasperated glance. "You've gained a reprieve, lass. We'll discuss the viscount further at dinner."

Concern shone in her eyes. "Are these men here about the Scottish Scourge, Papa? You know what the physician said—you mustn't let yourself be provoked."

"Physicians, ha! Fools, all of them. What do they know?"

"They know enough." She held out the glass. "You should drink your tonic before you see anyone."

"I don't want my tonic, damn it!" She was always trying to coddle him. He needed to be firmer with her, as he hadn't been with her late mother, but on days like today, when she reminded him so powerfully of Susannah, it was damned hard. "Leave the men to me, ye ken? And don't be worrying your head over them."

She turned stubborn. "At least let me help you up the stairs."

When she tried to take his arm, he wrenched free, horrified by the very thought of his pretty daughter going near the blackguards awaiting him. "It has naught to do with you, so stay out of it!"

His vehement protest made her wince. "Fine, do as you please."

He started to apologize, then caught himself. This was important. He couldn't let her stick her nose in his business this time.

Pausing every few steps for breath, he made his slow way up the stairs. Damn Sir Lachlan Ross and his shenanigans—why couldn't the divil leave him be?

He should have known he was in trouble from the day Ross first appeared in London. The young baronet had demanded what he thought was due his family and the Clan Ross, and Quentin had dismissed the laird's claim, determined never to reveal the ugly secrets of his past, to Ross or anyone else.

Since then, he'd paid dearly for his silence. The insolent young clan chief had begun riding the roads as the Scottish Scourge. Stirring up trouble, Ross was, trying to force Quentin's hand. He robbed Quentin's friends when they strayed into Scotland, telling them to turn for recourse to "Lord Duncannon." Though he'd repaid their losses, it was humiliating that he couldn't explain why the man might be robbing them, not without raising questions he refused to answer.

Quentin had endured five years of this, hoping Ross would eventually tire of the game. Then Ross had brazenly robbed Quentin's own factor on his way to deposit the rents. His rents provided half his income, for God's sake! At this rate, the man would bankrupt him. So he'd hired Sikeston, an action he already regretted.

Entering his study, Quentin surveyed the grim faces of the men assembled there. "I told you never to come here."

"We had no choice," Sikeston said. "We're fleeing for our lives."

That took him aback. "From whom?"

"Sir Lachlan's clansmen. They've been dogging us since we left Rosscraig."

Ross's estate. Damn. He should never have told them who he thought the Scourge really was. "You were supposed to catch him in the act and beat some sense into him so he'd stop this nonsense. Not waylay him among his own people."

"We tried, damn it!" Sikeston cried. "But he didn't take the bait, no matter how much of your gold we spent or how many inns we went to, bragging of being your friends on holiday."

"We think he has an accomplice," another man put in. "Someone in London who knows your friends and tells him who to attack and when."

"Or else he's canny enough not to fall for fools pretending to be gentlemen," Quentin snapped. He should have hired more sophisticated men, but how was he to find them? He'd had enough trouble finding these.

"We didn't have an easy time at his estate, neither. His clansmen don't seem to know that their chief is the Scourge," Sikeston said. "They worship the man and will go to the death for him. We couldn't even discover where he spends his nights, though it's not at Rosscraig. He's like a wraith, slipping in and out of that estate, always surrounded by his men—"

"That's why I haven't gone to the authorities. His clan would close ranks about him." No matter how convinced Quentin was that Ross was the Scourge, proving it wouldn't be easy. With Ross being Quentin's neighbor, the authorities would assume their quarrel stemmed from a property dispute. And if anyone started investigating and discovered the truth . . .

He shuddered. "So you couldn't lure him out."

"We did," Sikeston put in. "But only by blackmailing a clansman to find out where he'd be. Then everything went to hell once we caught up with him."

Quentin glowered at him. "Because he set his clan on you?"

"No. We gave him the beating like you paid us to do." Sikeston exchanged an uneasy glance with his men. "But . . . um . . . well—"

"Spit it out, man, for God's sake!" Quentin snapped.

"We killed him, my lord. Sir Lachlan Ross is dead."

It took a moment for the words to register. Then Quentin felt the room sway around him. Surely he couldn't have heard right. "You killed him?"

"It wasn't our fault," another man said. "When we jumped him on the bridge, he was armed with a knife. If Johnny here hadn't laid a cudgel to his head—"

"A cudgel!" Quentin thrust his face in Sikeston's. "I told you I only wanted him roughed up a bit!"

Sikeston glared at him. "Indeed you did, my lord, but you weren't there. Ross is built like an ox and fights like one, too. He also used to be a soldier, something you forgot to mention when you hired us."

Quentin had been afraid they would refuse the job if he told them. Biting back an oath, he stared at Sikeston. "So the blow killed him, did it?"

"If it didn't, then the water did. After the man was struck, he fell over the rail and into the loch." Sikeston's lips thinned. "He never even came up for air."

A chill chased up Quentin's spine. "And his body?"

"His clansmen were nearby, so we dared not stay to see if it was found, but he couldn't have survived. He was unconscious when he hit the water."

Quentin sank into a chair, overwhelmed at the thought of what his actions had wrought. The rogues had committed murder. In *his* name. For God's sake, Ross had a mother who depended on him, and a clan that needed him . . .

"I take it that his clansmen found out that you killed their laird," he said hoarsely. "And now you've led them right to me."

"No, my lord. We were careful not to be followed here, but we must leave London before they find us. So we'll need the rest of the money you owe us."

Quentin scowled. It went against his grain to pay the rogues after they'd committed murder, but he had no choice. One word to the Ross clan about who'd been behind their laird's death, and he was good as dead.

But at least the feud was ended. Quentin had kept his sordid family secrets, and Ross had carried whatever knowledge he had of the truth to his grave.

The Scourge would torment him no more.

Chapter One

❧

Edinburgh
August 20, 1822

Dear Cousin,

I worry about Venetia's trip to Scotland. Yes, I know what the papers reported—that the Scottish Scourge was killed three months ago in a fight with Sir Lachlan Ross that left both men dead. Still, considering the Scourge's mysterious grievance against the earl, I'd feel easier if someone could produce the villain's body.

Your anxious relation,
Charlotte

"Mama would have loved this," Venetia said wistfully to her aunt, Maggie Douglas, the Viscountess Kerr. They stood in line waiting to be announced at the True Highlander Celtic Society's masquerade ball, now near enough to hear bagpipes skirling from inside the Edinburgh Assembly Rooms. "Don't you just adore the tartans and strathspeys and costumes and—"

"—packed streets and wretched food and ghastly accommodations?" Aunt Maggie rolled her green eyes, the same shade as her niece's. "Not a bit. Unlike you—and my sister, when she was alive—I prefer the comforts of London. Why, I haven't had a wink of sleep since we arrived."

"So the snoring I hear nightly comes from our baggage?" Venetia teased.

"Mind your tongue, or I'll make *you* take the lumpy side of the mattress."

Venetia laughed. "Forgive me. You've been very good to put up with it."

Their lodgings truly were awful, but they'd been lucky even to find them. Every spare bedroom, garret, and cellar had been spoken for by the hordes that had descended upon Edinburgh to witness the first visit of a reigning English monarch to Scotland in nearly two centuries.

But Venetia didn't mind their miserable inn room. She'd waited sixteen years to return to Scotland, and she wouldn't let a flat pillow and a lumpy mattress—or a grousing chaperone—dampen her pleasure.

Venetia squeezed her aunt's hand as the line moved forward. "You can't know how much I appreciate your accompanying me. Otherwise, I would never have convinced Papa to let me come."

"I'm rather shocked that you did. However did you manage it?"

"Oh, Papa is easy enough to handle. I only had to make one tiny promise."

"And what was that?"

She cast her aunt a game smile. "To accept a proposal of marriage in the next year."

"That isn't exactly a tiny promise, my dear. And who is the lucky fellow?"

"Lord, I don't know. Anyone I can endure, I suppose." And anyone passing the inspection of Mrs. Charlotte Harris and the mysterious Cousin Michael, who routinely provided information about men in society to Venetia's schoolmistress.

"Papa worries I'll never find a husband," Venetia explained. In truth, she'd begun to worry the same thing.

"A lady like you will always have proposals," her aunt said with a dismissive wave of her jeweled fingers.

"It's not a dearth of proposals that worries him. It's my lack of interest in any of them." She'd promised her mother never to marry any man who didn't rouse her senses, whatever that meant. When Mama had elicited the promise, she hadn't said it was because of Papa, but Venetia often wondered . . .

"So have you any particular men in mind?" her aunt asked.

She blew out a long breath. "No, but I hope to find someone in Scotland, away from the fortune hunters and dull-witted English lords. I want a Scottish laird with a venerable old name, who lives and breathes the Highlands—"

"Like the fellows in those ballads you love to collect, I suppose."

Her aunt's contempt was plain. "Why not?" Venetia said defensively. "Why shouldn't I have a Duncan Graeme or a Highland Laddie who'll carry me off to his manor in the Highlands to live in connubial bliss?"

"Because you're about as Scottish as the Queen of England, my dear."

"That's not true!" she said, thoroughly insulted.

"You've got too many fine manners and too much English deportment for a country that thinks a good evening's entertainment is a jar of whisky and a rough brawl. You wouldn't last one day with a 'Highland Laddie' before you wanted to hit him over the head with the jar."

That might be the case, but she didn't feel any more comfortable in England. When she lost her temper, people called her "that Scottish termagant." Too much reserve, and they said she was a "haughty Scot." And when Papa fell into his heavy brogue, she always had to interpret it for others. As if he were foreign, for pity's sake!

Then there was the insidiouly superior manner of the English toward their "lesser" Scottish subjects, which even Aunt Maggie had adopted after her years married to an Englishman. She scowled at her aunt, who didn't even notice.

"You're certainly wearing the right costume for catching your ballad hero husband." Aunt Maggie lifted her white silk mask to survey Venetia's gown of simple worsted. "Highlanders practically worship Flora MacDonald."

"As well they should. She saved Bonnie Prince Charlie."

"Yes, yes, but it's a pity she had to dress like a farmer's daughter."

"She *was* a farmer's daughter." Venetia adjusted her own silk mask. "And I had quite a difficult time finding the right gown, so don't make fun." Fortunately she and Flora both had black hair and fair skin, so they resembled each other.

"At least the color is good. You look well in burgundy."

"So do you." Venetia bit back a smile. "Who are you supposed to be again?"

"Don't be impertinent. You should be glad I bothered to wear a mask. If not for that old fool, the colonel, twisting my arm, I wouldn't even be here."

Colonel Hugh Seton was one of the hosts of the ball and, unless Venetia missed her guess, quite enamored of Aunt Maggie, given how he'd tracked them down at their inn after their arrival. "He's rather forceful, isn't he?"

"Forceful?" Her aunt snorted. "He's mad. Why would the Celtic Society put a blustery cavalry officer in charge of a ball? Heaven only knows what nightmare of bad taste awaits us—he probably had them perch saddles on the chairs." She scowled at Venetia, who was laughing. "What, pray tell, is so amusing?"

"You!" Venetia choked out between peals of laughter. "I thought you liked him, given how you chatted about my old school yesterday. You told him his daughter is lovely."

"She is, but it's no thanks to him. Charlotte Harris is responsible for *that*." Aunt Maggie shook her head. "The fellow patted my bottom as we were leaving, for heaven's sake!" The color in her cheeks showed she wasn't as affronted as she pretended. "He illustrates perfectly what I mean about Highland Laddies. The impudent devil acts as if he's his daughter's age—"

Her aunt broke off as they reached the top, then whispered to the servant, who announced them as "Masked Lady" and "Flora MacDonald."

No one in the packed ballroom seemed to heed their entrance, except a tall man near the doorway who swung around to stare at them when their "names" were announced.

He barely spared a glance for Aunt Maggie, but

Venetia he assessed with a thorough, rather unsettling perusal. Then he lifted his glass in a silent toast.

Her "English deportment" demanded that she squelch such presumption from a stranger. But he was a particularly *attractive* stranger and she was in costume, after all. Besides, his Stuart tartan showed he was probably just playing Bonnie Prince Charlie to her Flora.

So she acknowledged his toast with a nod . . . and made sure to look him over. Despite his brawny build and the jagged scar marring his high brow, he captured the royal manner to perfection. He suffered a white powdered wig with regal dignity, and he kept his posture stiff and his bearing as aloof as any monarch.

But the rich chestnut-brown eyes gazing at her through the black silk mask weren't remotely aloof. They burned with startling fierceness. And they seemed oddly familiar, too.

Before she could wonder at that, Aunt Maggie was hurrying her to the receiving line and Colonel Seton.

"Ah, you've come at last!" the colonel exclaimed as he seized Venetia's hand, apparently recognizing the two of them despite the masks.

The widower looked rather dashing tonight in the tartan of Robert the Bruce. With his full head of steel-gray hair, his soldier's fit form, and his brilliant blue eyes, he cut quite a fine figure for a man well past forty.

With a furtive glance somewhere behind her, he said in his usually booming voice, "Delighted to have you here, Lady Venetia. Most delighted."

"Shh, Colonel," she chided. "You aren't supposed to reveal my true identity until the unmasking."

"Right, right, forgive me. Quite a blunder, what? It won't happen again, Flora."

She laughed. "I suppose it doesn't matter anyway. The place is probably filled with Flora MacDonalds and Bonnie Prince Charlies."

"No, indeed. We have princes to spare, but *you* are the only Flora." He leaned close with a conspiratorial air. "The other ladies preferred more ornate costumes." He slanted a glance at Aunt Maggie, then broke into a jovial smile. "Like the fine one your companion is wearing. And who exactly is she dressed as? You didn't mention her costume yesterday."

"She's a queen," Venetia lied.

"Which one?" he persisted.

"Come now, sir," her aunt said dryly. "It should be obvious that I'm—"

"Very pleased to be here," Venetia hastened to say. "We both are."

"Excellent!" He rubbed his hands together. "Have you asked her about tomorrow, the outing to Holyrood Park?"

"Yes, and she said she'd be delighted to go."

"'Delighted' wasn't quite the word I used," Aunt Maggie muttered.

"What?" Colonel Seton asked, bending nearer to hear over the din.

"She said, 'Thank you for thinking of us, sir.'" When her aunt snorted, Venetia went on quickly, "It's sure to be tedious in town tomorrow with no activities scheduled for the king, so we're grateful for the diversion."

"Splendid! But are you sure you don't want to visit Rosslyn Chapel?"

"No, indeed," her aunt cut in. "I promised Venetia's father we wouldn't stray from Edinburgh."

Venetia sighed. They'd arrived here by ship, so she'd

barely seen any of the countryside. But the specter of the Scourge still haunted Papa and he wouldn't take the chance of her running afoul of any "Scottish brigands."

"Then Holyrood Park it is," the colonel said cheerily. "We'll march up to Arthur's Seat after our picnic. The view is spectacular, though the climb is hard." He seized Aunt Maggie's hand. "I vow to help you every step of the way."

"I do not need your help, sir." Her cheeks pinkening, Aunt Maggie snatched back her hand. "Nor have I given you permission to be so familiar with me."

His jovial laugh showed he wasn't the least put off. "Indeed you have not, Your Majesty." He poked Venetia jocularly with his elbow. "I hope she won't order me executed for my impertinence."

"Don't tempt me." With a sniff, Maggie turned to Venetia. "Come, my dear, we're holding up the line."

Laughing, Venetia followed her. As soon as they'd left the receiving line, she said, "You've certainly made a conquest."

"Lord help me," her aunt snapped, although her eyes shone brightly.

"Oh, he's not so bad." As they skirted the room, Venetia gestured to the masked guests swirling in a wave of tartan and splendid gowns. "You see? Despite your fears, the ball is lovely—very festive and Scottish, but tasteful."

"No doubt the other committee members voted down his more boorish ideas." They halted near a pillar. "I only hope that he thought to designate a ladies' retiring room. I have need of it. What about you?"

"I'm fine. I'll stay here."

"Very well, I shall return shortly." Her aunt cast her a

teasing glance. "Perhaps one of your ballad heroes will float by while I'm gone."

Venetia frowned as her aunt walked off. Float by, indeed.

"Surely the dancing's not so bad as all that," remarked a husky male voice at her elbow.

Venetia turned to find the Bonnie Prince Charlie from earlier standing behind her. Speaking of ballad heroes . . . She tried not to stare, but he was even larger close up, a decided improvement on the original short and slender Prince Charlie. "Beg your pardon, sir, are you speaking to *me*?"

The corners of his mouth crinkled up. "Aye. You were frowning, and I wondered if it was the dancing that failed yer inspection."

"Not at all," she said with a flirtatious smile. "I adore Scottish dancing."

"Ah, then perhaps it's the garish excess of tartan. Too many kilts and such."

"Certainly not. The kilts are my favorite part. Every man should wear one."

He eyed her askance. "Every man?" He nodded toward a portly gentleman kicking his hairy legs up dangerously high. "Even *him*?"

She stifled a laugh. "All right, I concede the point."

"We should ask that fellow and the king to refrain from the fashion."

"Oh, I heard about the king's kilt! You must have been at the levee for the men. Was His Majesty's attire really as appalling as everyone says?"

His gaze grew shuttered. "I don't know, lass. I didn't arrive in town until yesterday, so I only read about it in the papers."

She sighed. "Me, too. But I heard that he wore flesh-colored pantaloons underneath his kilt."

His eyes gleamed at her through the slits in the mask. "So you prefer the alternative, do ye?"

What a shocking thing to say! Yet she rather liked his daring. It tempted her to be equally reckless, something she could never be with English lords.

"Not for His Majesty. Frankly, I think he should stay away from kilts entirely." Her gaze trailed down to her strapping companion's knees, bare below his own kilt. "But other gentlemen are certainly welcome to practice the old traditions."

He chuckled. "Glad to know you approve, lass," he said in a throaty brogue that melted her bones. He lowered his voice. "Now I can guess what had you frowning so fiercely a moment ago. You were trying to figure out which gentlemen were practicing the old traditions."

Torn between laughter and outrage, she said, "I certainly was not!"

"Were you imagining the king in his pink pantaloons?"

"No, nothing like that. If you must know, I was . . ." She cast around for a suitable excuse. "Trying to make out the tune the pipers were playing. I have a passion for Scottish songs—I gather them from broadsides and such." She added a trifle defiantly, "I hope to see my collection published someday."

He continued to stare out at the dance floor. "A lofty endeavor."

"You don't disapprove?" Most people said that well-born ladies shouldn't dabble in a vulgar business like publishing.

"I've no right to disapprove." He shot her a veiled glance. "Why? Does your husband give you grief over it?"

"I'm not married, sir," she said with a coy smile.

"Ah. Then your parents must be the ones giving you grief."

"Papa does think it's silly, but he tolerates it well enough." She flicked her fan back and forth. "I suppose you think he *ought* to give me grief over it."

"No. If anything, young ladies should have more freedom than they do."

"Really?" Mrs. Harris routinely warned against men espousing freedom for women, since that often meant they only wanted the women to be free with *them*. Yet he didn't seem like a fortune hunter. And he didn't know who she was, so how could he be hunting her fortune?

She smiled cautiously. "Do you approve of such freedom for your wife?"

"I would." He dropped his voice to a murmur. "*If* I happened to be married."

A little thrill shot through her. But how absurd of her to be attracted to an utter stranger. It was his stunning costume, that's all. In his kilt, he bore "the manly looks o' a Highland laddie," as "The Tartan Plaidy" put it.

But it wasn't merely that. His eyes, with their golden specks, still seemed very familiar . . . "Have we met, sir?"

"Don't you remember, Flora? You helped me escape the English after Culloden." His words were teasing, but his countenance wasn't. It held a seriousness utterly at odds with the whirling, laughing crowd around them.

"I mean," she chided, "have we ever met as our real selves?"

"I wouldn't know that, now, would I?" He bent near

to whisper, "Unless you tell me who ye really are beneath that mask."

"You first," she demanded.

"Och, no, lass." He laughed. "I'm not taking the chance that you'd order me to stop speaking with you, all because we lack a proper introduction."

Oh, he was certainly a sly one. "And what makes you think I'm the sort to follow the proprieties so stringently?" she asked in a voice equally sly.

"The way you speak and stand. Yer ladylike manner." His gaze fell to her mouth, and something flickered in his eyes that made her skin thrum. "The fact that talking to a man like me has got you so nervous that you can't rest easy until you're sure who I am."

"That's preposterous." She ignored the kernel of truth in his words. "If the colonel invited you, you must be his friend, and I doubt he has unsuitable friends."

"What if the Celtic Society invited me? Are you as sure of *their* friends?"

"Absolutely. I've attended the society's lectures in London, so I know them to be respectable." Her eyes narrowed. "Perhaps I even saw you at one."

"Perhaps." But his amused smile told her she was far off the mark.

"Or perhaps . . ." She stood back to survey him critically.

He bore too polished a manner for some country Scot, so he was either a gentleman or an officer or both. He did carry himself with military rigidity, not to mention his jagged scar . . .

"Might you have been in a Highland regiment?"

"No," he said with a swiftness that made her sure she'd hit upon the truth.

"That would explain where I met you," she pressed on. "Regimental officers attend London affairs." And his costume looked adapted from a uniform, its hardy leather sporran and its serviceable cross belts unlike anything the real Bonnie Prince Charlie would have worn.

"No, lass," he said more firmly. "Fine guess, but no."

"I'm back," Aunt Maggie interrupted as she broke through the crowd. She gave Bonnie Prince Charlie the once-over, eyes narrowing. "Excuse me, sir, but have we met? I could swear that we have."

"I said the same thing!" Venetia exclaimed. "He reminds me of someone."

"Sir Alasdair Ross," her aunt said. "Don't you remember, dear? The baronet who lived near your family? It's the eyes, and the square jaw. The man's been dead for years, but they could be related."

"We are indeed, I believe." Her ballad hero forced a smile. "He's a distant relation."

"Not too distant, I'll wager, for you look as if you could be his son." Aunt Maggie surveyed him critically. "He had a son, actually. Do you remember *him*, Venetia? I know you were only eight, but—"

"I could never forget Lachlan Ross." That was it! That's who the man reminded her of, the boy who'd dubbed her Princess Proud.

She'd thought of him often through the years. When last she'd seen the heir to the baronetcy, he'd been sixteen and too caught up in rebelling against everybody and everything to bother with a mere girl. So she'd preserved her pride by pretending not to care and making rude comments about his haphazard dress and country manners.

Secretly, though, she'd worshipped him. She'd adored his tall, rangy body and his untrammeled hair the color of burnt sugar, and she'd admired his wild bent.

Though that had probably got him killed. "He's dead, too, Aunt Maggie. We read about his funeral. That awful Scourge fellow murdered him."

Her aunt clucked her tongue. "Such a pity for one to die so young. I suppose, sir, that you heard—"

"Yes," he broke in. "So how do you ladies like Edin—"

"I don't know what the boy was thinking, to tangle with the Scottish Scourge," her aunt went on. "Did they ever find the villain's body?"

Their companion gave a pained smile, as if not liking to discuss such an unsavory subject with ladies. "He was washed out to sea after the skirmish, I believe. I doubt anyone could ever find him." He glanced over to the floor. "Excuse me, madam, but I was hoping to dance with your niece—"

"Oh!" her aunt exclaimed. "And here I am blathering away like some old fool." She looked him over, seemed to like what she saw, then said, "I suppose it's all right, but I'll expect a proper introduction after the masks come off later."

"Of course." He offered his arm to Venetia, that fierceness burning in his gaze again. "May I have the honor?"

A strange thrill swept through her as she took his arm. "I'd be delighted."

"Enjoy yourselves," her aunt said as she waved them off.

When they were out of earshot, he said, "I should warn you that it's been months since I've done this. My dancing is like to be rusty."

She gazed at him in surprise. "Then why did you ask me to partner you?"

"Because I enjoy a challenge, lass." He shot her a dark glance that thrummed through her like the piper's hum. "And I begin to think that you might be one."

With that intriguing remark, he led her onto the floor.

Chapter Two

Dear Charlotte,

Don't worry about Lady Venetia. The authorities are sure that the Scourge is dead. Rich friends of Lord Duncannon traveled to Scotland a month ago, and saw nary a hint of him on the roads. So your charge will be as safe in Scotland now as she would be in England.

Your cousin and friend,
Michael

Sir Lachlan Ross wished he'd had a more canny answer for the lass, but he couldn't admit that he'd really asked her to dance to tear her away from that cursed discussion. Unfortunately, now he had to suffer through an entire set.

The music began and he forced himself to move, forced himself to ignore the throbbing in his half-healed ribs and the ache in his once-broken thigh bone. Although certain steps proved a minor agony, it was better than listening to Lady Kerr talk of his family, unraveling his plans with each casual word. How in God's name had the viscountess seen the resemblance between him and Father? For that matter, how had Lady Venetia noticed it? He was wearing a wig and mask, for Christ's sake! Not to mention that neither lady had laid eyes on him in years.

No one must recognize him, or this would be over before it began. His mother and clan had worked hard to hide the fact that he was alive by holding a pretend funeral for him. He couldn't ruin it by appearing to have risen from the grave to dance a reel with Lady Venetia Campbell.

The bonnie Lady Venetia Campbell. God help him, he hadn't expected that.

When last he'd seen her, he'd been a gangly lad and she a pale-skinned brat. Prancing about in satin and lace, she'd looked down her nose at him, chiding him for not behaving as "the future laird of Clan Ross" ought. He'd rewarded her uppity temper by ignoring her.

He sure as the devil couldn't ignore her now. Even dressed as a farmer's daughter, the sensuous beauty would corrupt a saint. Sinner that he was, she made his blood run hot whenever she flashed him that sweet-as-seduction smile. Or stepped lively in the reel, twirling and skirling and—

Holy Christ, he was waxing poetical. It had been too long since he'd had a wench beneath him. Not that he'd ever shared a bed with a lass so bonnie as she. Camp followers and trollops had always been his lot and were like to be so until he chose a wife.

But first he had to settle things with Duncannon.

He came down hard on his bad leg in a turn, and pain jolted through him from knee to hip, making him grit his teeth. Worse yet, he could see Venetia watching him, trying to figure out why his dancing was so stiff.

Mo chreach, she wasn't only beautiful, she was clever as the very devil, with her assessing glances and her probing questions. She'd even guessed he'd served in a regiment! 'Twas a wonder she hadn't worked out his entire plot already.

He hoped this ball hadn't been a mistake. But

tomorrow wouldn't work unless she could be easy with him.

The plan had been simple: come here tonight and cozy up to the grown Princess Proud, who he'd expected to be a vapid debutante. Rousing her interest in him was supposed to make the kidnapping go easier tomorrow. Except she wasn't vapid, and the only thing he was rousing was her memories of *him*. And her curiosity.

He could handle vapid girls—and had, a few times, when he rode as the Scourge. That only required a firm voice and a stern look. The threat of a blunderbuss didn't hurt, either.

But cowing them was easy compared to snatching Duncannon's canny daughter from Holyrood Park, in the center of a city where half the lords and magistrates of Scotland were staying. The latter required more finesse.

He shook his head. How did her sort turn out as anything but vapid after prancing about at a fancy school, then swishing through polite society for years?

And why the devil had she grown so beautiful? He'd heard she was bonnie, but no one had warned him that her hair shone like glossy black silk beneath the candlelight, or that her lips had the sweet little bow shape that tempted a man to trace it with the tip of his tongue . . .

He swore under his breath, missed a step, then almost lost his balance when his bad leg buckled. It was a timely, though painful, reminder of why he was here.

This battle between him and her father had naught to do with the lass; she was only a means to an end. Best to remember that. Because once he threw off the veil tomorrow, she'd turn on him like a cornered wildcat. There could be no truce between him and Duncannon's family.

Thankfully, the set ended without his making a fool of himself. As they left the floor, he searched for her chaperone. Ah, the lady was standing with Colonel Seton. He should give the man more chance to work.

Lachlan slowed his steps. "Are ye from Edinburgh?" he asked.

"London. But I used to live in the Highlands."

"Why did you leave?" How much of the truth had her father told her?

"My mother died, and Papa couldn't bear to stay in Scotland without her."

So Duncannon hadn't told her a damned thing. Not that he was surprised; the man was too wily to let his daughter know he'd abandoned his responsibilities. "Then yer father didn't come to Scotland with you," he said, though he knew the answer.

"No. He vowed never to return and won't break that vow even for this. I had a hard time even persuading him to let *me* come. That's why I must return directly to England once it's over." With a sigh, she swept her hand to indicate the ballroom. "This is as close as I get to the real Scotland on this trip."

"The *real* Scotland?" He couldn't suppress a snort. "This is no more the real Scotland than I am the real Charlie. Walter Scott trumped up this daft nonsense for the royal visit, with Lowlanders wearing tartan and half the Highlanders banned from town for being too rowdy."

He stared out at the dance floor, his gut tightening. The very sight of the lairds dancing away in their kilts sickened him. Their people fled to America in droves to keep from starving, and the chiefs would only dance.

Bitterness laced his words. "Mustn't frighten the English king with a show of arms. Or alarm the London Scots who want only a taste of the old country."

She bristled. "Now see here, sir, you know nothing about 'London Scots.' If I had my way, I'd be living in the Highlands right now." Her tone turned acid. "But while you men can do whatever you want, young women can't go where they please. Not until they marry."

"Of course not, lass." Holy Christ, he was no good at cozying up to fine ladies. "Forgive me for speaking out o' turn. Sometimes my love of home tramples my good sense."

She accepted his apology, thank God. Then she ruined it by turning the conversation to him. "So you're from the Highlands, too?"

Damn. But since she'd already guessed it . . . "Aye. Highland-born and bred." He changed the subject before she could ask what part. "Looks like yer chaperone is arguing with Colonel Seton."

She followed his gaze. "I should rescue her. She claims not to like him."

"Claims?"

"I think the problem is that she likes him too much."

Good. That made everything easier. "Then we should give them time to work out which it is."

Dancing another set was out of the question; he'd barely endured the one. "If you like, I could show you the decorations for the Peers' Ball Thursday night." He gestured to a nearby curtain draped from floor to ceiling.

"There's a door hidden back there that leads to the other ballroom, which isn't being used this evening. Care to have a look?"

A well-bred lass like her would know she shouldn't go with him, but he could tell from her hesitation that she wanted to. If she did, it boded well for tomorrow.

Mayhap a bit of coaxing was in order. "I'll understand if those proprieties of yours are rearing their ugly heads. A fine lady like yerself—"

"Not at all," she said with a breathless little hitch that sent his blood coursing to the wrong places. She took his arm. "Lead on, kind sir."

Moments later they were in the next ballroom, watching servants drape tartan over chandeliers and position gold damask sofas on the narrow one-step-high stage built to surround the room, so the portly king would have a place to rest between dances.

"What a magnificent effect!" Her green eyes sparkled behind her mask. "How kind of you to let me see it before the room is packed with people."

She gave him a smile that would light up the barest crofter's cottage, and he reacted with a swift intake of breath, followed by a swift throbbing in his ribs. "I'm glad the ballroom passes yer inspection," he bit out over his pain.

His terse tone made her smile falter. "I can't wait to see it fully lit on Friday." She toyed with her fan. "I suppose you're attending that ball, as well?"

"No," he said baldly. *And neither are you, lassie.*

"Oh."

The sympathy in her voice made him regret his blunt words. Now she thought him too low to be invited, since only peers or those with titled connections had received the coveted invitations. As clan chief he would also have been invited, if they hadn't believed him dead.

His stung pride got the better of him. "I have to return to the north."

"Where in the north?" she said, suddenly alert and eager.

"No place ye'd ken." He had to get her off this dangerous subject. His eyes fell on the archway. "They removed the bow windows so guests could pass into the courtyard. Would you like to see what they've built out there?"

Her gaze turned sultry. "That would be lovely, thank you."

His heart began to thud. *Careful, laddie, keep a rein on yer urges. Mustn't frighten her off.*

Trying not to notice her delicate touch on his arm, he led her into the dark courtyard, where painted wooden pillars supported a tent of rose and white muslin. When they slipped inside, they found themselves in a very small and private space.

"A theater owner is having sets painted with pictures of the Highland countryside." Lachlan gestured to one end. "Then they can draw back the muslin to show the scenes."

He felt her gaze search his face. "You seem to know a great deal about the plans for the ball. Are you a friend of the theater owner?"

"I know people enough in Edinburgh," he said evasively.

Her voice turned sly. "I suppose you made many friends in the army."

He tensed. "I told you, I was never in any regiment."

"Nonsense." She planted her hands on her hips. "I'd swear that you adapted that costume from a regimental officer's uniform."

Devil take the lass. "I borrowed it from a soldier friend."

"I see." She snorted. "And that's why the coat fits you to perfection. Did you borrow your military bearing from your soldier friend, too? And your tendency to pepper your speech with talk of skirmishes and inspections?"

Mo chreach, he hadn't realized how he'd betrayed himself. Best turn the tables before she pieced together who he really was.

"I know why you're so eager to make me into an officer." He stepped closer. "Because you can't make me into a peer, and only an officer or a lord can be fit company for a lady of yer breeding."

She thrust out her chin. "I never claimed to be a lady of breeding. For all you know, I might be a milliner."

"If you say so, lassie." With a chuckle, he mimicked her earlier attack. "That's why you carry yourself like a queen and spend your days collecting ballads, the way milliners do."

A shaky laugh escaped her. "You've caught me, sir. I'm no milliner. But I could still be a gentlewoman of little means and fewer prospects."

"Which is why you're attending the Peers' Ball." He smiled. "Come now, why not just admit you're a lady of rank?"

"Not until you admit you're a soldier," she said primly. Then she caught her breath. "*That's* why you remind me of Lachlan Ross! He went off to join a regiment, too. I used to imagine him in his regimentals—"

He kissed her, a brief, soft kiss to shut her up. What

else was he supposed to do, damn it? He had to keep her from making comparisons.

When he drew back, her breath came quickly. "I . . . I . . . what do you think you're . . . doing, sir?"

"Proving that you're a lady of breeding." He slid his hand about her waist to draw her close. "Because there are certain liberties a lady would never allow me."

"How do you know what a lady might allow?" Her warm, spicy breath teased his senses. "Some are more reckless than others, especially when they're held in the arms of a strapping soldier—"

He kissed her thoroughly this time, sealing his mouth to hers, drinking in her hot breaths, enjoying the fine tremor of her body against his.

He'd been aching to do this all night. Not because she was Duncannon's daughter or because she held the key to his clan's future, or even because she'd grown into such a bonnie lass.

It was because she'd dressed as Flora MacDonald, even though it meant wearing a simpler costume than the other ladies. Because she collected Scottish ballads, of all things. Because she'd had the daring to hint that gentlemen should go bare-arsed under their kilts. It was impossible to resist such a female.

Especially knowing that once she found out he was her enemy, she'd only look on him with wild and furious hatred. So before that happened, he had to taste her . . . touch her . . . see how far he could tempt her.

Even if he suffered for it later.

Chapter Three

Dear Cousin,
I'm sure you are right about Lady Venetia's
safety. Lady Kerr is a responsible lady, so I am
probably worrying for nothing. I shall let your
assurances ease my mind.

Your grateful friend,
Charlotte

During her years on the marriage mart, Venetia had endured the occasional kiss. But none like this.

Lord save her, so *this* was what Mama had meant by rousing her senses. They felt assaulted from every direction ... the faint rasp of his whiskers against her skin, the woodsy scent of heather, the surprisingly soft lips that played over hers, molding, testing, tasting, until she thought she might die if he didn't stop.

Then he did, and she wanted to die even more.

"Ah, lassie, that *is* sweet," he murmured against her lips, sending her into a frenzy of need beyond her experience.

That was probably why, when he covered her mouth again, she let him do the unthinkable. She let him plunder her mouth with his tongue like some ballad highwayman stealing her gold. And oh, how strangely delicious it was, far better than what her married friends had described. No man had ever dared be so bold, and if he had, she'd have put him right in his place.

But with this fellow, she wanted it to go on and on ...

the reckless plunges of his tongue, the silky strokes
that launched her heart into a feverish pounding. The
champagne she tasted on his lips made it feel as if
she'd shared his glass and was now drunk on the heady
libation. Oh, such glorious madness.

Mrs. Harris's strictures whispered in the back of her
mind: never kiss a strange man, beware fortune hunters,
always keep your head about you in the dark. She ignored
them, counting on her mask to protect her.

She ached to be a ballad heroine, sneaking out to
meet her lover in the secret night, stealing kisses, rousing
the wildness that had clamored in her breast for so long
she was sick with the need to set it free. So she let him
drive his tongue deeply, tangling it with hers before
withdrawing, only to thrust again over and over.

Then he began to touch her, too, skimming his large
hands up and down her ribs with shocking possessiveness.
How thrilling! How dangerous. Oh, she would regret this
later, but for now . . .

Her knees grew wobbly, so she flung her arms about
his neck and arched up against him—only to steady
herself. That's all. Truly. No other reason.

He knew better. "Have a care, lass, or you'll tempt me
to be more reckless still."

More reckless? She wanted to know what *that* might
be, wanted to see exactly what she'd been missing.

Hussy! she chided even as she tightened her arms
about his neck. "I thought you officers had too much
discipline to be reckless," she breathed.

He trailed hot kisses along her chin and down her
neck. "Still trying to figure out who I am, are you?"
He tongued the hollow of her throat. "Can't leave well
enough alone."

Never. "I'll tell you who I am if you tell me who you are."

"I already know more about you than ye ken."

"You do?" She jerked back. So she *had* met him before! She *knew* she'd been right about that!

"I do." His eyes glittered through the slits of the mask. "You're a canny young lass who hasn't been kissed well enough or often enough to keep you from seeking out trouble. That's who you are."

The evasive answer sparked her temper. "That's not what I meant, and you know it. You, sir, are a teasing coxcomb."

She whirled on her heel, but he snagged her about the waist, drawing her back against his muscular form with a laugh. "I thought you decided I was a soldier, my lady."

"Plenty of soldiers are also coxcombs," she said loftily, trying to ignore the heat of his body plastered against her back. "And you continue to assume I'm a lady of rank when I've neither confirmed nor denied that assumption."

He chuckled against her ear. "No? Stalking off in a fit of temper is what a lady of rank does when she can't get her way."

The implication that she was some coddled aristocrat annoyed her. "Don't assume you know what I'm like simply because I let you kiss me."

His hand caressed her throat as his mouth brushed her ear, warming it. "I know this much about you—you enjoy taking chances." He hauled her back around to face him and lowered his head to hers. "So do I."

This time he kissed her with a fierceness that she more than matched. Dear Lord, what was happening to her? Some strange Highlander assaulted her with kisses, and she threw herself into it like a dockside tart.

She should return to the ballroom. She mustn't let the rogue think he could do with her as he pleased.

Except that he could. She wanted him to. And this magical muslin room seemed so unlike the real world that it felt right to indulge just this once. To enjoy herself just this once. Let him plunder her mouth just this once.

"Lady Venetia?" came a sharp voice from the ballroom. "Are you out here?"

She broke from the Highlander with a gasp. Lord save her, someone had found them. Should she stay silent? She wasn't sure she could, with her breath coming in furious gasps and her heart beating like a kettle-drum.

She was still hesitating when her Bonnie Prince Charlie stepped back and lowered his arms. Just in time, too, for the person who'd spoken pulled aside the muslin to look in, then lifted a candle. Light flooded the man's face.

Oh, fudge, it was Colonel Seton. At least he hadn't discovered them embracing.

The colonel glared at her companion, then settled a stern glance on her. "Lady Kerr has been looking for you."

"Bonnie Prince Charlie was showing me the decorations for the Peers' Ball," she said swiftly.

"You'd best return to yer aunt," Colonel Seton said with an air of command that caught her off guard. "I need a private word with this gentleman."

Oh, dear, she hadn't meant to get her Highlander into any trouble. "He did nothing wrong. It was perfectly innocent, wasn't it, sir?" She shot him a pleading glance, but that was a mistake, for his stare turned her knees to water.

"Yes, lassie, perfectly innocent." But he somehow made "innocent" sound more like "indecent."

Lord, she was being fanciful now.

"Go on, my lady," the colonel said. "I don't wish yer aunt to worry."

"Very well." She smiled at her Highlander. "Thank you for the dance, sir."

" 'Twas my pleasure." He lowered his voice. "My very great pleasure."

And with the delicious thrum of his brogue ringing in her ears, she fled.

Lachlan watched her disappear beneath the archway with his blood afire and his cock hard and heavy beneath his kilt. He must have lost his bloody mind, to keep kissing the lass so. But Holy Christ, she'd a way of making a man want her . . .

He swore under his breath.

"I agree wholeheartedly." Seton glanced back to make sure Venetia was out of earshot. "Was that wise of you?"

"Dinna fash yerself. I know exactly what I'm about."

Thank God the man hadn't witnessed the kiss, or he'd see that Lachlan was lying. That kiss had shaken his self-control. No woman had ever affected him like that, not even his former fiancée, Polly, who'd thrown him over for a rich man.

No, Venetia was naught like the demure Polly, to be sure. Despite being the most elegant female he'd ever known, Venetia had a secret, passionate nature as ungoverned as any Highland fling. It drove him into a dangerous carelessness.

But *mo chreach*, her mouth alone would seduce the dourest Presbyterian . . . and her body fit so well in his arms that he'd been sore tempted to lay her down right here and—

Don't be thinking that!

No matter how fine the lass's kisses, she wasn't for him. She could never be for him. And she'd be the first to remind him of it in the days to come.

"You almost gave me heart failure, you know," Seton said. "When you disappeared through the door with Duncannon's daughter and stayed gone so long, I thought sure you'd decided to snatch her tonight."

"With half a dozen magistrates in the next room and the city full of soldiers and constables?" Lachlan snorted. "Don't be daft, man. I'd be lucky to make it half a mile out of the city. But tomorrow the soldiers will be at Portobello Sands drilling for the review; that's when we'll do it."

Seton let out a breath. "I can't help thinking like an officer: strike while the enemy is at hand. I forget that the Scourge must be more careful—"

"Hold your tongue," Lachlan hissed. "The Scourge is dead, remember? And he must stay dead to all but Duncannon and his family."

"Speaking of his family, what did you hope to gain by alarming the gel's aunt?" Seton asked. "You put Lady Kerr on her guard, to be sure."

"And I gave you the chance to play the hero for her, as well. So the lady will be more apt to listen to you when her niece goes missing." He headed for the entrance to the muslin tent. "If anything, I made tomorrow easier for you."

He started to brush past Seton, but the man grabbed his arm. "I hope you're right. One false move and we'll both be hanging from the gallows."

Lachlan faced him grimly. "If you're having second thoughts, say so. I told you, ye don't have to do this."

"I'm not having second thoughts, damn it." He drew himself up like the proud old soldier that he was. "Unlike Duncannon, I keep my promises."

"You've repaid me a thousand times over—"

"For keeping that damned bastard from slitting my throat in Aviemore? How can that ever be repaid?"

"If you do what you promised tomorrow, that will be payment enough." He glanced into the ballroom. "Is everything ready? There's naught to tie you to me?"

"Don't worry." Seton puffed up his chest. "I took care of it. You'd think that by now you could trust me—"

"I do trust you, I swear. But it's one thing to wheedle information out of your daughter about when Duncannon's friends are traveling to Scotland, so you can pass it on to me. 'Tis quite another to aid in a woman's kidnapping. For your daughter's sake, your connection to the Scourge must never be found out."

"Don't worry about me and Lucy," he said peevishly. "Worry about yerself. Worry about Duncannon going to the authorities once he realizes you're not dead."

"And risk his daughter's life? He won't. Besides, he knows what he's guilty of—that's why he's never gone to them before. He'll try to deal with this himself, as he did when he sent men to murder me. Then I'll force him to admit his crimes."

"I still think you should have gone to the press with your claim—"

"So he can deny it? I have no proof, ye ken? He has

to swear to it before witnesses, so I can get back what's owed to me and my clan. No matter what I have to do." But Seton needn't know how far he was willing to take it. "If you decide this is too risky, I won't blame you. I can manage without you."

"I'm not going to change my mind." Seton clapped him on the shoulder. "Just send me some of that fine whisky you and your clansmen cook up, and I'll be content." He headed for the courtyard. "Now, I'm returning to my guests before they come looking for me. And it's time for *you* to vanish."

"What will you tell Lady Kerr and Lady Venetia about my disappearance before the unmasking?" Lachlan called out.

"That I ran you off for sneaking in without an invitation and bothering my important guests."

Lachlan snorted. "You think you can convince them of that? You're not the best actor, you know."

"I convinced Lady Kerr that I fancy her, didn't I?"

"Only because you *do* fancy her," Lachlan said dryly. "And from what I can see, your attentions annoy the lady. You've got to be more subtle if you want her under yer thumb."

"I don't want her under my thumb, I want her—" He caught himself, then scowled at Lachlan. "Oh, go on with you, you rascal. Don't you be worrying about me and Lady Kerr. You ought to be worrying about you and the little lass."

"What do you mean?"

"She's pretty as a picture, Duncannon's daughter." Seton gave him that officer's stare. "So what *were* the two of you doing out here in the dark?"

"Nothing for you to be concerned about," Lachlan lied.

Nothing he should ever do again, either. Because kissing Venetia could well become a dangerous habit. And he had enough danger in his life already.

Chapter Four

Dear Charlotte,
I perfectly understand your concern. The thought
of two ladies alone on the road with only servants to
attend them worries you, since you would never be
so unwise as to travel without male protection.
                                    Your cousin,
                                    Michael

The morning after the ball, Venetia was transcribing ballads from her newest broadsides when Aunt Maggie went to answer a knock at their inn room door. Venetia hadn't even heard it over the thunder of regiments marching off to drill.

After speaking with the servant, her aunt came to Venetia's side. "Are you ready to go? Colonel Seton is here to fetch us for our outing."

"May I finish writing down this last verse?"

"Certainly. I'll go keep him company." Aunt Maggie headed for the door, then paused. "Are you sure nothing happened last night between you and that Bonnie Prince Charlie fellow? I was horrified when the colonel told us he'd entered the ball without an invitation. The audacity of the man!"

She forced a smile. "No, nothing happened." Much as she longed to gain her aunt's advice about her secret encounter with the Highlander, Aunt Maggie would disapprove of furtive kisses in the dark with a stranger.

A rather bold stranger, according to the colonel,

though he'd claimed not to know the man. How odd. She could have sworn that he had.

"I only mention it," her aunt said, "because you seem rather glum."

"I dreamed about Braidmuir, that's all." She sighed. "I miss it so much. I wish we could at least visit." She hadn't returned to their estate in years.

Sympathy furrowed her aunt's brow. "I know, my dear, and one day I'm sure you will. Just not on this trip." She smoothed her blue muslin gown. "Well then, I shall go join the colonel. Don't be too long."

As she left, Venetia stared down at her ballad notebook. She *had* dreamed of Braidmuir. But more important, she'd dreamed of Lachlan Ross.

In her dream, her parents had been arguing, their voices so loud that she'd sought solace in the cool glen near Rosscraig, with the burn that Lachlan had always liked to fish. She'd found him there, too, but he'd changed—grown taller, older, more filled out . . . rather like her Highlander from last night.

She kept forgetting that her Highlander was a distant Ross relation. But that—and the resemblance he bore to Lachlan—was the only thing the two men had in common. Lachlan had always hated the Highlands—he would never have called it his home. And even if both men had served in the army, so had many Highland men—it had been the only way to maintain traditions like the wearing of the tartan during the years those traditions were outlawed in Scotland.

Although Lachlan had never been averse to draping himself in tartan, he'd always despised the kilt, calling it daft nonsense invented by—

Walter Scott invented this daft nonsense.

Her heart skipped a beat. Her Highlander had said that last night. What if by some miracle it *had* been Lachlan? What if the papers had been wrong? It would explain why he seemed so familiar, why she'd dreamed of him.

She shook her head woefully. She just wanted to believe it was Lachlan because she hated to think of him as dead. She and Aunt Maggie and the Highlander had even stood there discussing Lachlan's death—surely if the man had been Lachlan, he'd have revealed his identity then.

So her Highlander was probably exactly as she feared—some penniless foot soldier with no prospects and a bit of polish, who just happened to be skilled at kissing. A man in search of a fortune. She'd probably be disappointed if she met him by day and had time to assess his true character, so she must put him right out of her mind.

Once she went downstairs and they all set off for the park in the colonel's splendid little barouche, that became easier. Who could think of fortune hunters on such a summer day, with a glorious vista rising before them? As they approached the park, the Salisbury Crags shone golden in the sun, and the balmy breeze warmed her chilly heart. She began to anticipate their climb eagerly.

When they stopped beside Duddingston Loch for their picnic, her heart leaped at the sight. Arthur's Seat soared above them, a piece of the Highlands plunked down in the midst of Edinburgh. It was as close to home as she might ever get.

They dined on smoked salmon, creamy caboc cheese, and thick brown bread, laughing at Colonel Seton's tales of his adventures abroad. She noticed that Aunt Maggie wasn't entirely immune to the colonel's flirting, which Venetia encouraged. She desperately wanted a good husband for her aunt.

So when Aunt Maggie rose to fetch her walking stick from the carriage and the colonel's gaze followed her, Venetia had to smother her smile of delight.

"Your aunt is the finest woman I've e'er had the chance to meet," he remarked.

"Is she now?" Venetia tried hard to appear nonchalant for her aunt's sake.

"Do you think she'd countenance the attentions of an old soldier like me?" He looked for all the world like a commander plotting a campaign.

She bit back a smile. "You have a chance, yes." *More* than a chance, if he proceeded with caution. "But you must be patient. She's slow to warm to people."

"Will you help me? We rough fellows tend to forget how to behave around fine ladies. But I think if I could get her alone—"

"Of course. Whatever I can do."

"Splendid," he said, glancing up at the mountain. "Just follow my lead."

"What do you intend?"

He patted her hand. "Don't worry—I won't alarm her. But it's hard to court a woman when she hides behind her niece's skirts."

She laughed. "I imagine it is."

After lunch, they started their walk to Arthur's Seat. The birches around Duddingston Loch took little time to pass through, but the actual climb slowed their pace. Thank heavens she'd chosen her most serviceable apparel—a sturdy pelisse robe of merino, her Limerick gloves, and her leather half-boots—because they had to clamber over many a boulder. Still, the walk proved invigorating, and her wide-brimmed straw hat protected her from the bright sun.

They'd just crossed the last hill before the summit when Colonel Seton stopped short and cried, "Damnation!"

"What's wrong?" Venetia asked in genuine alarm as he sank to the ground.

He removed his boot to examine his heel. "An old war injury kicking up." He rubbed his stocking foot, then winced. "I should have known better than to attempt such a climb, but I did want you ladies to see the spectacular view."

"Just like a man, to be doing things he oughtn't," her aunt muttered as she went toward him. "Let me take a look."

"No need, it's fine." Casting her a determined smile, he put his boot back on and stood. Only to yelp loudly and drop back down.

"Stop that, you silly fellow," Aunt Maggie protested. "You mustn't go another step. Sit here while Venetia and I fetch the carriage."

He sighed. "The carriage won't make the climb. You'd have to unhitch a horse and lead it up here. Though perhaps if the two of you would let me lean on you, I could limp back down—"

"No, indeed," Venetia said hastily, realizing he was waiting for her to "follow his lead." "I shall hurry down for the horse. It won't take long."

"And I'll go with you," her aunt said.

"Certainly not. We can't both ride. I can fetch it myself. You should stay here and keep the poor colonel company."

Aunt Maggie looked torn, but practicality won out. "All right, dear. But do be careful, will you?"

"Of course," she said with feigned seriousness.

Venetia set off down the path in a hurry, then slowed her steps once she was out of sight. It wouldn't do to ruin Colonel Seton's efforts.

Fanciful thoughts of Aunt Maggie and Colonel Seton in some future marriage absorbed her as she strolled down the mountain. His daughter Lucinda would surely be happy about it. The wedding could take place in Edinburgh, and Venetia might even persuade Papa to let her come to Scotland again . . .

Spinning such delightful scenarios kept her so absorbed that she was near the bottom before she knew it. She'd almost reached the woods skirting the loch when a strange man emerged from among the birches, giving her quite a start.

Not that it was odd for people to be in the park today—they'd encountered several walkers—but something about the single-minded expression on his face gave her pause. Even his gentlemanly attire—the chocolate-brown frock coat, buff trousers, and polished Hessians—didn't assuage her discomfort.

Casting a nervous glance about her, she realized that this part of the park was presently deserted. Worse yet, the man seemed to be headed right for her.

Then she noticed his stiff gait, and her heart stuttered. He was tall, with the same chiseled chin as her Highlander. As he doffed his broad-brimmed beaver hat to her, she spotted the jagged scar on his wide brow. Relief flooded her.

"Good day, lass. I don't know if you recognize me without the costume—"

"I do indeed." Except that it wasn't the masquerade that she was thinking of. In the brilliance of a sunny day, with his mask gone, he looked even more like . . .

She caught her breath. The color of his eyes, the arch of his brows, and the shape of his features were the same. And oh, Lord, although his hair was shorter now, falling only to just above his shoulders, the particular chestnut hue was an exact match to that of—

"Lachlan?"

The stunned expression on his face told her she was right.

"Lachlan Ross!" she cried. "You really *are* alive!"

Chapter Five

⁓⊗⁓

Dear Cousin,
*   Once again, sir, you attribute to me notions that*
never crossed my mind. Why shouldn't two women
travel the country with only servants to attend
them? This isn't the England of your childhood.
Highwaymen are scarce these days. I daresay
women have more to fear from London pickpockets
than from good country Scots.

*   Your annoyed relation,*
*   Charlotte*

*D*evil take her, he had hoped the lass wouldn't put
it together so quickly. He'd planned to give her a false
name until he could lure her into the carriage by playing
on their acquaintance from the ball. That wouldn't work
now.

A shame he couldn't just toss her over his shoulder
and carry her off, but a party of walkers had emerged
from the woods, headed for the climb. The park was lousy
with visitors today—anyone might hear her scream and
come to her rescue.

He'd have to play along until he got her where
he wanted her. That meant he'd have to explain his
miraculous resurrection. Or avoid explaining it.

"Yes, I'm alive." He clapped his hat back on his head
and made a show of looking around for enemies. "Can
you lower yer voice? No one's supposed to know."

Such secrecy must have appealed to her, for she

dropped her voice to a conspiratorial murmur. "Why? And how can you be alive when the papers said—"

"I know, lass, I know." He cast a furtive glance at the party passing them. "Can we talk about this somewhere more private? Let's head for those woods."

"Oh, I forgot! Forgive me, but I must hasten to Colonel Seton's carriage."

As she continued down the path toward the woods, he followed along. She was playing right into their hands, she was. "Is that where yer friends are?" he asked in feigned innocence.

"No, I have to ride a horse back up the mountain for the colonel. We were walking to the top when he supposedly injured his leg, and now must ride down."

"Supposedly?"

She laughed. "I suspect he's only pretending to be hurt to get my aunt alone so he can court her. Since I heartily approve of the courtship, I must maintain the pretense by riding up to fetch them."

He shook his head. "You're not dressed for it, and it'll take time to unhitch a horse. Let me carry you up in my carriage."

"It can't make that climb, sir."

"Not on this side of the mountain, but on the other side is an easy road to the top," he lied.

"Really?" She stopped short. "Are you sure?"

Lachlan smiled. "Most people don't know about it. My equipage is just inside those trees; let me drive you up. The colonel may need me to carry him to the rig." He offered her his arm.

"I sincerely doubt that," she said with a laugh, but took his arm all the same. "But I suppose we should keep up appearances for his sake."

"Aye." Deliberately he covered her gloved hand with his. "Besides, I'll take any chance to be alone with you, even if only for a bit."

Her whole face brightened. "Oh, Lachlan, I'm *so* glad you're alive."

Guilt pricked his conscience. She wouldn't be thinking that for long.

"But you must tell me how—" she began.

"Not yet, lass, not until we're alone."

Which had better be soon. Already his body suffered the toll of the past week's travel. He couldn't wait to have the pretense over, even if it meant she would despise him.

Despite his throbbing thigh, he hastened his steps, ignoring the glance she slid at him as they walked. He was too busy scanning the area for any other strangers who might happen upon them. This mustn't look like an abduction.

"How did you know about the road up the mountain, anyway?" she asked.

"I attended school in Edinburgh."

"I forgot about that." She added in a teasing voice, "Probably because it did you little good. You returned to Rosscraig as wild as when you'd left."

The word "wild" scraped his nerves—he'd heard the accusation from his father a dozen times a day when he was young. "You can't possibly remember what I was like when I went off to school. You were only a wee thing then."

"True, but I heard stories. And I remember what you were like when you returned."

"Aye." He frowned. "You called me a dirty savage."

To his surprise, she chuckled. "Only because you were

so mean to me, telling me you had better things to do than coddle a 'silly girl.'"

"Are you saying you *didn't* think me a dirty savage?"

The pretty pink blush that stained her cheeks sent his blood pounding in his veins. "I thought you were wonderful."

Ignoring that bit of amazement, he said, "Ah, well, you were a girl. Girls get funny notions into their heads."

The impatience in his tone must have sunk in, for her hand stiffened on his arm. "Lachlan?" she asked, her voice suddenly wary.

"What, lass?"

"How did you happen to be here today at the same time we are?"

Damn, she was starting to realize the oddness of this. But they were in sight of the coach, thank God. He quickened his steps as he spun the tale he'd prepared. "After Seton tossed me out last night, I found out where you were staying. I followed you this morning, hoping to have a word with you, but then Seton arrived, and I thought it best to . . . catch you alone."

They approached his rig, and he let out a breath. "Here's my carriage, lass." He called out to the lad on the perch, "Look lively, Jamie! We're headed off!"

His long-term partner nodded and took up the reins as Lachlan helped her into the carriage, then leaped in behind her.

The team pulled off so quickly that she was thrown back against the squabs. He took advantage of her loss of balance to jerk down the window shades.

"Lachlan," she chided him, "you may not move in society much, but surely you realize I can't ride with you in a carriage with the shades down."

She reached to pull up the shade, and he caught her hand. "Leave it be."

Her gaze shot to him. "I cannot—"

"You can and you will. At least until we're away from the park."

"What do you mean?" she said warily. "We're going up to Arthur's Seat."

Releasing her hand, he pulled the shade aside just enough to look out. "Do as you're told, and everything will be well."

She stared at him as if he'd slapped her, but he had no time for coddling her. They would soon reach the entrance. Some guards had been lounging about there earlier, probably because the road went right past Holyrood Palace. Fortunately the king wasn't there today, so Lachlan hoped the lazy louts would let them pass after seeing the shades down. If not . . .

"Lachlan!" Venetia said in that imperious voice she must have inherited from her father. "I demand that you stop this carriage right this minute."

He glanced over to find her glaring at him. He considered trumping up some tale about how he was kidnapping her to marry her, but that was a level of deception he couldn't stomach. Time to drop the pretense. "Sorry, lass. I can't."

Venetia heard his words with a sinking in the pit of her stomach. She should have known something was wrong when he'd first showed up at the park. But like a fool, she'd been so happy to find him alive. "Why not?"

He tipped the shade aside to glance out again. "I'm surprised you haven't guessed it by now, given my miraculous resurrection."

Her heart began to hammer in her chest. "Yes, perhaps

you should explain how you came to be declared dead," she said hoarsely. "The papers claimed you were killed in a battle with the Scourge."

"That was a lie I had my clansmen plant. Truth is, my battle was with your father's men. They were the ones who tried to drown me in the loch."

"My father's?" she said, completely at sea. "But why would my father's men attack you? You've never done anything to—"

"Think, Venetia." The icy gaze he leveled on her sent a chill right to her bones. "You're no fool. Who's the only Scot yer father would want to murder?" His voice turned hard as nails. "The only man who'd dare to kidnap his daughter?"

The word "kidnap" froze her blood. She was going to be sick. Lachlan had always been reckless, but surely he couldn't . . . "*You're* the Scourge?"

He tipped his hat to her in a mocking salute. "At yer service, my lady."

Lord save her. All this time when Papa had complained about the Scourge, he'd been complaining about Lachlan. Lachlan had been the one to steal from him and torment their friends, lying to the world, and to her today so he could—

"You unconscionable blackguard!" she cried. "How dare you!"

She lunged for the door, but he grabbed her easily, hauling her onto his lap and clamping his arm about her waist as he locked her legs between his.

"I wouldn't do that if I were you," he muttered against her ear. "You can't leap from a carriage at this speed, or you'll kill yerself."

"That's what you're going to do to me anyway, aren't

you?" she spat as she struggled against his hold, knocking both their hats off.

"Don't be daft. And stop acting the fool, unless you want me to tie you up."

That stopped her short. She didn't want to be tied up, but neither did she want to be kidnapped.

Oh, how could this be happening? What a fool she'd been to think that the unruly Lachlan of her childhood would turn out to be anything but a scoundrel. And she'd given herself into his hands without a fight, too!

"Papa will find you. He'll hunt you down and tear your heart out—"

"What a bloodthirsty wench you've become," he taunted her. "But don't worry yer pretty head over it—he won't need to hunt you down, because I'm inviting him to Scotland to rescue you. Then we can settle this matter between us."

Her blood ran cold. "What matter? Why do you hate him so?"

A panel slid open behind their heads. "We're approaching one of His Majesty's Guard, sir," the man named Jamie said. "What shall I do?"

Venetia tensed. This was her chance to scream, to—

"Don't even consider it," Lachlan growled, as if he'd read her mind.

Suddenly she felt something cold and hard jab into her ribs. She looked down to see the end of a nasty-looking pistol just under her arm.

Oh, Lord. He had weaponry, too. She was done for.

Lachlan turned his head to the open panel. "Halt only if the guard demands it. If he does make you stop, keep him to the right of the carriage, and tell him . . ." He paused, then tightened his arm about her waist. "Tell him yer master is on his honeymoon and has no interest in the king's affairs."

As the panel slid shut, Lachlan shifted her across his lap so that her back was to the right-side window with the pistol shoved against her belly.

Fear snaked down her spine. "You would never shoot me," she whispered. "I'm no good to you dead."

"True." He slid the gun between her arm and her side, aiming it at the window. "But if you say anything to attract attention, I'll shoot the guard. Do you want *his* blood on yer head?"

Her chest constricted. He had her other arm trapped against the back of the seat, which left only the one that lay against the gun. She might be able to grab his arm, but it was thickly muscled, and she probably couldn't win that fight. Besides, if the gun accidentally went off . . .

"You wouldn't kill a fellow soldier," she said, as much to convince herself as him.

The carriage began to slow as a voice hailed the driver. "Are you willing to gamble a man's life on it?" Lachlan hissed.

As she hesitated, gazing at the implacable features of a man she no longer really knew, she heard the guardsman ride around to the carriage window.

Lachlan muttered an oath. Before she even realized what he was up to, he reached over to lift the shade on that side, then slid his free hand behind her neck to hold her still while he shoved his mouth against hers.

That was the only way to describe it. It certainly wasn't a kiss, for his lips were as rigid and unmoving as rock. But to anyone looking at them from the outside, they would appear to be in an intimate embrace, two people in love.

The irony of it made her want to weep. Especially when he tugged her hair free of its pins, scattering it down her back to create the impression that they were in the midst of . . . that he was in the midst of . . .

"Not a sound, ye ken?" he murmured against her mouth. "Or I swear the guard dies." He pressed the side of the gun against her ribs where her arm hid the muzzle from view. "If I don't kill him, Jamie will."

For a long moment they sat poised, with Lachlan's pistol lying beneath her underarm and his mouth against hers in a mockery of their kisses last night.

Kisses he hadn't meant. Kisses he'd given her only to lull her, to persuade her to go off with him today. Curse the wicked blackguard!

A horse snorted mere feet away and the guard's gaze bore into her back through the window. Suddenly, the guard laughed and called out something to Lachlan's accomplice. Then the carriage moved again, and her chance for any escape vanished into the wind.

It was too much for her. She bit Lachlan's lip. Hard.

"Holy Christ!" he spat as he drew his head back. "What the bloody hell—"

"Let me go!" she cried, ignoring the pistol. Elbowing him in the ribs, she struggled wildly against his hold. "Let me go, you scoundrel!"

As a string of Scottish oaths poured from him, he practically tossed her across the carriage to get her off his lap. She scrambled into the other seat and glared at him, surprised to see that he'd gone entirely pale except for the brilliant scarlet of the blood trickling from his lower lip.

When he wiped it from his mouth with a curse, she refused to feel any guilt.

He was in for a surprise if he thought she'd continue to go meekly along with this madness. So he wanted to destroy her father, did he? Fine. But she would make him regret kidnapping her every step of the way.

Last night she'd made the mistake of relaxing the habits and practices of a lifetime. That had got her here, so no more. As Mrs. Harris always said, a lady's weapons weren't made of steel, but they could still cause harm. It was time to embrace them, to use whatever she had to fight.

Because no one took advantage of Lady Venetia Campbell with impunity. Not even the Scottish Scourge.

Chapter Six

Dear Charlotte,
    Once more I find myself in the uneasy position
of having to apologize for an insult I didn't realize
I had given. You seem to take offense easily these
days. Is everything all right at the school? Or am I
the only one who annoys you?

Your concerned friend,
Michael

Lachlan stared at his captive, not sure whether to throttle her or applaud her. Princess Proud had a fierce little temper. Who'd have thought it?

Mo chreach, she'd bit him hard. And that was before her elbow to his ribs had made him see stars. "You've turned into quite the termagant, Venetia."

"At least I haven't turned into a thief! At least I don't prey on poor, defenseless women—"

"Defenseless? You bloody near bit my lip off!"

She glowered at him. "And if you ever try to force a kiss on me again, Lachlan Ross, I'll finish the job."

Force a kiss ... the woman was trying his patience. "Dinna fash yerself, lassie," he growled as he restored his pistol to the special pocket in his coat. "That kiss was purely for show." It infuriated him that she could believe he would take advantage of her. Or that he would *need* to. "I can have any woman I want in Ross-shire; I don't need to dally with the likes of Duncannon's daughter to gain my pleasure."

Her chin quivered. "And last night? Wasn't that a dalliance?"

More like a mistake. "It was part of my plan, that's all." He wasn't about to let the fearless female guess how badly he desired her. No telling what portion of his anatomy she'd destroy if she knew *that,* the little shrew.

But she didn't look like a shrew just now. With her rich mane of ebony hair tumbled down about her shoulders, she looked young and wounded and vulnerable, as would any lass whose sheltered life had been shattered in a moment. Her loch-green eyes glimmered with so much dark hurt, it made him want to draw her back into his arms and kiss that sweet, trembling mouth.

"I can't believe this," she said with a shake of her head. "I'd never have guessed that the Scourge is you, that you could be capable of such treachery."

"I only want what's owed to me and my clan," he ground out. "If you accuse anybody of treachery, it ought to be your blasted father."

"Oh? What awful thing could he possibly have done to justify this?"

"Aside from trying to have me killed? Aside from ordering his men to—" He caught himself. If she knew she could torture him with just the jab of her elbow, the rest of the trip would be a nightmare.

"To what?"

He'd tell her only the barest facts of that. "To drown me."

She stiffened. "Even if that's true—and I doubt it—you can hardly blame him, given how you've been robbing all his friends for no reason."

"No reason!" He snorted. Her self-righteousness

helped him remember she was a means to his end, nothing more.

And it was high time the wench learned why. "I'll give you a reason, Princess Proud. Your father is a thief and a liar. Thanks to him, my clan has been struggling since before I returned from the war."

That wiped the haughty expression from her face. "What do you mean?"

"Did yer father ever tell you about yer Jacobite grandfather, Wily Will Campbell, the third Earl of Duncannon? One of the few Campbells who didn't fight with the English at Culloden?" When she nodded, he settled back against the seat. "After the '45, Wily Will was stripped of his title, and his lands were forfeit to the Crown because he supported Bonnie Prince Charlie."

"I know." She folded her arms over her breasts... her too-ample breasts that were thankfully shielded from his gaze by that shroud of a purple gown. "Papa got Braidmuir back when the lands and dignities were returned to families in 1784."

"Not quite. The debts owing on the properties had to be paid first."

She shrugged. "So Papa had to pay some money. What does that matter?"

"What 'matters' is how much. Forty thousand pounds, it was."

The blood drained from her face.

He wasn't surprised. Duncannon had kept the truth from everyone else; why not his daughter, too?

He went on in a cold voice. "Yer father was young and didn't have forty thousand pounds, so he borrowed it. From *my* father, his closest friend, whose family stayed out of that mess and who owned a rich estate and fine lands."

Her fingers plucked distractedly at the fabric of her sleeve. "Papa said something once when I was a girl . . . about how I should be nice to you because we owed your father a great debt. But I didn't realize he meant it literally."

"Well, he did." His voice chilled. "And after yer mother died, he left Scotland and what was left of his 'great debt' behind him—thirty thousand two hundred and ninety-six pounds."

She was already shaking her head. "I'd be the first to admit Papa's faults, but he'd never renege on a debt, and certainly not such a large one. He has a strong moral sense."

Ah, yes, Lachlan had been on the receiving end of that "moral sense" years ago. "He reneged. My mother told me of it after I returned. She said she urged Father to press the matter with the earl, but he wouldn't."

"I-I don't understand. Why wouldn't your father—"

"Devil if I know, though I'll wager he was afraid of yer father's powerful friends." Gritting his teeth, he stared at her. "And we had money then to spare, fine crops, plenty cattle, and fat and happy crofters. I suppose since Father knew how hard Duncannon took his wife's death, he let the loan slide for a bit."

He balled his hands into fists. "He said it was only right to show Christian charity to a suffering man. He told Mother that the earl would pay once he finished his grieving. But then Father died and the war ended and the cattle—"

"I know. I heard that prices fell drastically after Waterloo."

He nodded grimly. "I came home to find Rosscraig in shambles. Yer father had turned his land over to sheep farmers, so *he* was sitting pretty down in London, but Mother and I refused to do that to our crofters."

Before she could ask what he meant, he leaned forward, planting his hands on his knees. "We *needed* the money your father owed, and he didn't give a bloody damn. I wrote him letters. He ignored them. I traveled to London to see him—"

"You did?" she said suspiciously.

He bristled. "You were at school then."

"But he never said anything."

"Haven't you heard what I'm saying? Yer father's a scoundrel—he'll not tell you that he threw me from his house for demanding that he repay his loan."

"I don't believe you. Papa's an honorable man; he would never do that."

Her persistent faith in her father, despite what he'd told her, infuriated him. "Ask him and see what he says."

"Let me go home and I will," she shot back.

"Oh no, lassie," he snapped, "you're not going anywhere until yer father repays that money. Until he looks my mother and my clansmen in the eye and admits that he took advantage of my father's friendship and the lack of papers—"

He caught himself, but it was already too late. Her pretty green eyes were sparking anew with temper. "Lack of what papers?" When he sat there mute, she said, "There's no proof of this loan, is there? If there had been, you would have taken the matter to the courts. Your desperate mother trumps up this tale—"

"It's the truth, damn you! Your father admitted it when I went to London!"

"Oh?" She folded her hands primly in her lap, the very picture of a lady who thought she was too good for the likes of the Ross clan. "What did he say?"

He stiffened. "That my father forgave the loan."

"There, you see?"

"And when I demanded evidence of it, he had me tossed into the street. Because he knew he was lying."

"Or he didn't want to deal with an irrational fool demanding money."

"Come now, lass, you're no idiot—do you really think my father would forgive a thirty-thousand-pound loan? Because *yer* father was grieving?"

She swallowed. Clearly even Princess Proud could see it was unlikely. "But you still have no proof."

"I have my mother's word. Father may not have told her where he hid the papers, but that doesn't mean they don't exist. Did you never hear how he died?"

Her eyes big and solemn, she shook her head.

"He went to help a crofter get his bull out of the burn, and the bull gored him. He was dead within minutes— nothing anyone could do." He gritted his teeth. "And no chance to tell my mother anything, either."

"But Lachlan—"

"If yer father isn't guilty of this treachery, why has he never reported me to the authorities for robbing his friends? He must have known I was the one, taking what I needed since he wouldn't give me what he owed. I *know* he knew—that's why he sent men to kill me."

Her expression hardened. "Even if I believed this tale about the loan, I couldn't for one minute believe Papa capable of plotting murder. Why should he, if he knew who you were? Why wouldn't he just have you arrested?"

"Because he knew what wrong he'd done, damn it!" Fury seized him. "Devil take you, lass, I promise you he sent men to kill me. Why do you think I can't—"

He caught himself before he admitted his physical difficulties. Bloody hell, she was like a priest, she was, wheedling more from him than he should say.

"Can't what?" she asked.

"Nothing. It's between me and yer father."

Her eyes turned cold. "Clearly, it's not just between you and him, or I wouldn't be here."

"Blame *him* for that. If you'd been *my* daughter, I would never have let you set foot anywhere near the highways where the Scourge rode."

Her lower lip trembled. "He thought you were dead."

"And now he'll know I'm not, won't he?"

She jerked her head away to glance blindly out the window. "I suppose you'll send a message to summon him to Scotland."

"Aye. He should receive it in a few days. And there's a note for yer aunt in Seton's carriage, as well."

"My aunt!" Her gaze swung back to him. "Oh no, she's stuck on that mountain with the colonel! They'll be waiting for me to come, and I won't—"

"They'll get down one way or the other. At the very least, Seton's coachman will go look for them when they don't return."

She got dangerously quiet, clearly working through something in her head. "Colonel Seton is part of this, isn't he?"

Holy Christ, she was too canny for her own good. "Are ye daft? I'd be a fool to conspire with a king's soldier, wouldn't I?"

"*You* were a king's soldier." Her eyes narrowed. "I'm sure that's where you met the colonel."

"I was with the Ninety-third in New Orleans, and he was with the Seventy-third on the Peninsula. So how the devil were we supposed to meet?" Of course, once the war ended, they'd both returned to Scotland, but he wasn't about to point that out.

"Besides," he went on, "a man like the colonel takes his service to England seriously. I just wanted to escape the Highlands. Joining the regiment seemed the best way."

After a childhood of Father's admonitions—to control his temper, swallow his pride, do as the kirk preached, and not drink whisky or consort with whores—it had seemed a relief to flee from home.

Especially after Father's betrayal.

No, he wouldn't think of that.

Besides, in the end Lachlan had returned.

After the Battle of New Orleans, where he'd watched hardened soldiers call out for their families while they bled out their lives on the field, he'd realized how fragile life was, how important things like home and hearth really were.

Tired of the wenching and gambling and empty pleasures he'd pursued whenever he wasn't drilling or fighting, he'd sworn to live a better life, a steadier life. Tired of yearning for the Highlands, of missing the heather and the glens, the cry of the curlew on the moors, he had pledged to return to the Highlands and his clan. To make peace with his father.

He'd never had the chance. Father died before Lachlan reached home, and his vow to live a steadier life vanished in the wake of the disaster his father had left behind.

It was either save his estate and clan, or watch his

crofters flee to Nova Scotia or Virginia like the others who could no longer scrape together a living in the Highlands. He should be thankful that his rigid father hadn't lived to see him running illegal stills. Or riding as a highwayman to get funds for the equipment and barley. Or dragging an upstanding fellow like Colonel Seton into his activities.

"Colonel Seton isn't part of this," he repeated, determined to convince her. "He's too good a man for that."

"Then aren't you worried about him sending the army out after you?"

"He can send out whomever he pleases—they won't find us."

"Then my father will send—"

"He won't. Not when I have you." He settled back against the seat. "And even if he does, I'm a hard man to kill, lassie. God knows yer father's men tried. Best remember that the next time you want to sink yer teeth in me. Between the war and yer father's treachery, I've no soft parts left. I'm rough as old timber, with a head solid as stone. Try to hurt me again, and I'll make you regret it."

She blanched, but didn't yield. "Oh, don't 'fash yerself,' sir," she said, her tone heavy with mocking. "You've made it quite plain that the Lachlan Ross I knew, the one who would never hurt a woman, is no more. The Scottish Scourge killed him and took his place. And that scoundrel is capable of any villainy."

The word "villainy" raised his hackles. He'd known she would react this way; he'd known she'd be as stubborn and sure of her lofty place as her father. But it still rankled to have her act as if he was in the wrong.

"Aye," he said coldly, "I'm liable to do anything, my lady. As long as you realize that, we'll get on just fine." He leaned forward to fix her with his fiercest gaze. "Because you're not going home until I say ye are. And that won't be until yer bloody father comes to Scotland."

"I tell you, something's dreadfully wrong," Maggie said as she paced the path beside where the colonel sat on a boulder.

He mopped his brow with his handkerchief. "See here, my lady—"

"Don't try to deny it again. Venetia should have returned long before now."

His frown seemed to concede the point. As well he ought—the sun sank lower by the moment, and they were still trapped on this cursed mountain.

At first, she hadn't minded it. After Venetia had left, the colonel had grown surprisingly quiet, less outrageous than usual. He'd scarcely even flirted with her, and since he'd flirted constantly since the day she'd first met him and Lucinda at Mrs. Harris's school, it was refreshing to have him refrain.

Well, not entirely. Try as she might, she did feel a twinge of disappointment.

What was she thinking? His flirtations were absurd for a man his age. The only reason he was behaving like a gentleman now was because of his pain.

She slanted a glance at his pale face. He must be suffering greatly. He'd allowed her to examine his heel, and she had cringed at the wicked scar that cleaved his flesh. A ball had shattered his heel, he'd told her, so the bones sometimes gave him pain if he stressed them too much. Why, it seemed a miracle he could walk at all.

Maggie sighed. How she wished they'd never gone on this outing. She didn't want to know about the colonel's suffering; it made it harder to dislike him.

And now Venetia was missing. "Do you think she has lost her way?"

"There's only the one path. If she lost her way, she's a fool."

Maggie strode to the crest of the hill to look down again, but she saw nothing of her niece. "I shouldn't have let her go alone," she said as she came back. "If she doesn't return before dark, she'll never find us without a lantern."

The colonel uttered a heavy sigh, then stood. "If it's that worried ye are, then we should try to go back."

"You needn't come along. I'll just go myself."

"No, you won't." He wavered unsteadily on his feet. "If you'll let me lean on you a bit, I can hobble down. I've had a long rest now—I should be all right."

She hesitated, but she really didn't wish to descend the mountain alone, especially when she wasn't certain what had happened to delay Venetia. "Very well." Hurrying to his side, she let him drape his arm about her shoulder.

It had been years since a man had done so, and the pleasure she took in the feel of his fit body astonished her. Alarmed her. Heavens, she was softening toward the old fool, and that wouldn't do. She had no desire to wreck her perfectly comfortable life as a widowed countess by taking up with an aging soldier.

As if he'd read her mind, he said, "It was good of you to wait with me. I'm sorry I couldn't be better entertainment."

"Nonsense. I don't need entertaining. I'm a grown woman, for heaven's sake." She actually liked him better when he wasn't trying so hard to amuse her. Usually, he did everything to excess.

They'd been walking in pained silence for an hour when they were met by the colonel's coachman. He was alone, which struck her right to the heart.

So did the man's cry as he approached and spotted his master's limping walk. "God save us, sir, what has happened?"

"Have you not seen my niece?" she asked, her stomach sinking. "She was supposed to be fetching a horse for the colonel, who has injured his foot."

The coachman shook his head. "I fell asleep on the perch, but I could hardly have slept through her taking a horse." He reached into his pocket. "When I got worried about you and went to see if Lady Kerr's walking stick was still gone, I came upon this. Perhaps it's a note from the girl. It's addressed to Lady Kerr."

The colonel reached for it, but Maggie snatched it first, opening it hastily. What she read there made her blood run cold.

Mindful of the coachman's curiosity, she pulled the colonel aside. "The Scottish Scourge has taken Venetia," she whispered. "Or someone claiming to be him, anyway. He's supposed to be dead."

"Yes, I read that in the papers. But the papers are sometimes wrong."

Her chest hurt. "I should have known such a devil couldn't be killed."

"What else does the letter say?"

She thrust the note at him.

The colonel scanned it quickly, then met her gaze. "He won't hurt her as long as you don't speak to the authorities and send no one after her. He says he only wants what Duncannon owes him."

"And you believe him?"

"Surely even a scoundrel like him wouldn't kill a lady."

"He doesn't have to kill Venetia to destroy her life. Once people hear of this, she'll be ruined. She'll never be able to marry."

"Then people mustn't hear of it, must they?"

How could he be so calm and controlled when her niece was in such danger? Who knows what horrible things Venetia was suffering even now?

"You must send men after her," she said hotly. "I don't trust the Scourge not to hurt her. We must ride into Edinburgh at once and gather soldiers—"

He grabbed her by the shoulders. "Stop, lass, and think. They say the villain has eyes all over Scotland. If you amass an army to go after him, you only risk her life. *And* her reputation." A frown knit his brow. "Thanks to my trouble on the mountain, he has quite a start on us. By the time we could reach town and organize soldiers, he'll be halfway to the north."

"The north? What makes you think he's headed there?"

"I . . . well, people claim he's from the Highlands."

"Only because Lowlanders think *all* thieves come from the Highlands," she snapped, then wondered why she bothered to defend her childhood home. "Do you really think that's where he took her?"

"Damnation, lass, I don't know. In any case, it doesn't matter. Going after her could get her murdered, and I know you don't want that. If it's ransom he's wanting, then he'd be a fool to hurt her. He says he's sent a letter to London for Duncannon. So we should wait for the earl's arrival in Scotland."

She gaped at him, part of her convinced by his argument, part of her outraged that he'd even consider standing by and doing nothing. "I thought you were a *man*. What man refuses to act when a scoundrel has kidnapped a woman?"

Steeliness entered his gaze. "A smart and careful one." At her expression, he muttered a foul oath. "Fine. If you want me to try getting her back, I'll arrange for men to search secretly, without telling them what girl they're looking for. But I'll pick the men myself." He squeezed her hand. "Will you trust me to do that for you, my lady?"

What choice did she have? He was right about the risk—the Scourge had murdered Lachlan Ross, so why balk at murdering Venetia? But the colonel had resources beyond her, and he *had* seemed eager to please her.

"Yes," she breathed. "I'd be most grateful."

"Good, I'll arrange it at once. You go back to London, and—"

"I shan't budge from Edinburgh until I know my niece is safe."

His face clouded over. "You can preserve her reputation easier in London—tell people you left her at her father's estate."

"No. I'll claim that she's ill—that's good enough. No one in Edinburgh will pay attention to the absence of one woman with all that's going on right now."

"Now, lass—"

"Absolutely not." She jerked her hand from his. "I'm staying here, and that's final. So you'd best get used to having me around, Colonel. Because I mean to make sure that my niece returns in one piece, no matter what it takes."

Chapter Seven

❧

Dear Michael,
Lady Venetia, who's been sending me daily
accounts of the king's visit, has stopped writing. I
know she's probably just too busy, but it isn't like her
to be so lax. I worry she has met some unsuitable
Scottish fellow she won't tell me about, and that has
made me snappish.

Your woefully peevish friend,
Charlotte

Venetia had spent the past few hours in silence, hoping that the carriage motion might lull her companion to sleep and give her a chance to escape.

No such luck. Lachlan sat like a soldier, rigid and alert, keeping his gaze trained outside the window. What he was looking for, she couldn't imagine. Enemies behind every bush? Lord knew he was cracked enough for that.

Him and his tale of abandoned debt! Papa was gruff and proud, but honorable. He would never renege on a debt, and he'd certainly never let his friends be plagued by the Scourge if he could stop it.

She scowled at Lachlan. To think she'd actually cried over his supposed death! Devious devil.

He'd always chosen the most reckless path. Running off to join the regiment when he was barely old enough to shave, riding the roads, and now this kidnapping. He didn't think things through.

Did he really believe that nonsense about an unpaid loan? Or did he simply resent Papa for making his own estate profitable by improvements while the Ross clan slogged along in the old ways?

And even if Lachlan was right about the loan, how could it justify what he'd done? Why, his first kidnapping had been of her best friend Amelia and Major Winter, Amelia's husband—another attempt to get money from Papa. If not for the major's clever escape, who knew what might have happened to them?

A glance at Lachlan's grim face made her shiver. Who knew what might happen to *her*? He said he wouldn't hurt her, but could she believe him? He wasn't the same man she'd once known. He had a fierceness, a chilling resolve about him. His willingness last night to use kisses to further his plan showed that.

She had to escape him. But how?

When they'd stopped to change horses, he'd made her sit as before, with the pistol aimed at the only window whose shade was open. The threat was always that if she gave an alarm, someone would die.

She wanted to believe it an idle threat, but dared not risk it. So her only alternative was somehow to seize his firearm. If he'd just fall asleep . . .

By the end of their next stop, she wanted to scream. As soon as they left the coaching inn yard, she threw herself across to the other seat with an oath.

"I don't know why you insist on going back over there," he said calmly. "I'll just have to make you move again the next time we change horses."

"How long do you mean to continue this nonsense?" She couldn't see the sun setting, since the shade was down on the west-facing window, but it must be nearly eight o'clock on this long summer day. "Do you mean for us to travel all night?"

"Aye."

The terse word sounded the death knell to her hopes for escape. If he didn't stop at an inn longer than to change horses, how would she ever get away?

And if she couldn't get away . . .

The full ramifications hit her with a force that knocked the breath from her. If she traveled alone with him for more than a day, she'd be ruined. No one in society would care that it was a kidnapping. He was a man; she was unmarried. That would be enough.

"This means the end of my reputation," she whispered, half to herself.

For the first time in hours, he really looked at her. "Not if yer father and yer aunt heed my instructions to keep this quiet. They're sly enough to invent a tale for your sudden absence. And once I settle this matter with yer father—"

"How do you mean to do that?"

His expression grew shuttered. "Never you mind how."

This only grew worse and worse. "You're going to kill him."

He returned his gaze to the window. "I didn't say that."

But he hadn't denied it, either. She rubbed her clammy hands on her skirt. "If you kill him, you'll be hanged, for it will come out that you're the Scourge."

"The Scourge is dead, and I mean for it to stay that way. That's why I told yer father and yer aunt not to risk yer life by saying otherwise."

"And if Papa refuses to play your game? Do you really

think he'll hand over thirty thousand pounds to you without a fight?"

"He'd better if he wants his daughter back."

"But what if he doesn't?" she persisted.

His gaze swept down her body in a slow, heated glance. "Then I get to keep you, don't I?" he said, his voice husky.

The provocative comment shot a thrill through her before she could stop it. A thrill of fear. Yes, it had to be. Surely she wasn't fool enough to still find him attractive. He was her enemy, not the Lachlan of her dreams. He was the villain behind the ballad hero who'd taken her mouth so sweetly in the dark.

So why were her mouth and throat suddenly dry, her hands suddenly shaky? And why, when his gaze darkened to jet black, then fixed on her lips, did her skin come alive, her pulse quickening?

Curse him for that. "Keeping me is not a choice."

That seemed to jerk him up short. Swiftly, he yanked his gaze over to the window. "Yer father will come for you. Don't worry about that."

Her stomach knotted. Lord save her, now she had something new to worry about. Lachlan might despise her for being her father's daughter, but he wanted her, too, in the way that men wanted women.

She'd seen that heated look on the faces of society men who'd danced with her, and she'd never let it bother her. Unfortunately, it was hard to ignore it with a man who had complete power over her. A man who'd kissed her passionately only last night.

Not that she would let him kiss her now, no indeed. If he so much as tried it, she would make good on her threat to bite him.

He pulled aside the shade, then frowned. "If you've got any sense, you'll sleep. We've a long trip ahead of us."

She *had* to escape. She had to convince him to let her leave the carriage the next time they stopped. Suddenly an idea occurred to her. She did have certain physical needs; he'd have to stop for *that*. "It's not sleep that I require."

He raised his brow at her clipped tone. "I've got plenty of provisions—"

"I'm not hungry, curse you." She was starving. It had been a long, *long* while since her last meal, but asking for food wouldn't get her out of the coach, would it?

How could she explain this to a man delicately? "I need you to stop the carriage."

He gave a harsh laugh. "Not bloody likely."

"It's most urgent that I . . . Sometimes a woman . . . or anyone . . . has to—"

"Drink something? Is it water you're needing?"

"No!" How could he be so dense? "The *last* thing I need is water."

The light dawned. "Ahh, you have to piss. Why didn't you just say so?"

She glared at him. "Because I'm not as vulgar as you."

"No, you're too lofty for pissing." A sardonic smile twisted his lips. "I could make a ballad of that for your collection, if you want: 'Princess Proud hates to piss / She thinks it's something crass. / And when she goes to ease herself, / Someone else must wipe her—'"

"That's enough." A blush heated her cheeks. "And that isn't remotely a ballad. It's doggerel, and bad doggerel at that."

He shrugged. "Suit yourself." He slid open the panel

behind his head. "Jamie, we need to stop. The lass has got to piss."

"Aye, sir," the young man said, and instantly the coach slowed.

"Not here!" she protested. "At the next place we change the horses!"

Lachlan arched one thick eyebrow. "You said it was urgent."

"I can wait until we stop where there's a . . . well, you know."

"A privy?" He eyed her with cool calm. "If you're thinking I'll let you parade through an inn complaining about your abduction, think again, lassie. It's here or nowhere."

Ooh, how she wished she could slap that calm from his face, then shove him out of the coach with a satisfying thump. What had Aunt Maggie said? *You wouldn't last one day with a 'Highland Laddie' before you wanted to hit him over the head with the jar.* How sad that she'd turned out to be right.

As the carriage halted, Venetia stared out the window. No trees or bushes for miles, just fields everywhere. "I can't . . . you know . . . out there, for pity's sake. Anyone could see me!"

"No one's around to see. Make up your mind—do you need to piss or no?"

Casting him a foul glance, she reached for the door handle. "Must you keep using that vulgar word?"

He gave her a wicked grin. "I find it most entertaining to watch you get your dander up."

"You really are a blackguard," she grumbled as she climbed out of the carriage. "Clearly you've been riding the roads with ruffians far too long. You've forgotten how to behave like a gentleman. *If* you ever knew."

To her horror, he stepped out after her and took her arm.

She snatched it free. "You can't possibly mean to accompany me!"

"I can, and I will. You're daft enough to try running off over these hills, and I'm in no mood for running after you."

"Lachlan, please, give me some privacy—"

"We won't watch, I promise. But I'm not letting you more than a few feet from me, so you might as well get used to it."

With a sigh, she relinquished her hopes for escaping him here. But despair dogged her steps as they left the carriage. Why must everything be his way?

The beast halted beside a shallow ravine. "Down there you'll be out of sight of the road. I'll put my back to you, but you have to talk to me the whole time. If you're quiet more than a moment, I'll turn around. Understood?"

Gritting her teeth, she nodded, then descended the few yards to the bottom.

She'd barely found a place to stand when he barked, "Talk to me, lass."

She cursed him soundly.

He chuckled. "That'll do fine, it will."

Lifting her skirts, she scrambled for something to say. "Are we headed to Rosscraig?"

"A place near there. It's where I've been living ever since your father sent men to kill me."

"Someone may have tried to have you killed, but it wasn't Papa. A man like you probably has hundreds of enemies."

"None who proclaim their connection to yer father right before they—" He broke off suddenly.

"Before they what?"

"Nothing," he snapped. "Just do what you're supposed to, will you, Princess Proud? And hurry it up."

"I would appreciate your not calling me that." She finished relieving herself. "We aren't children anymore, after all."

"That's for damned sure," he muttered, almost to himself.

She glanced at him in alarm, but he still had his back to her. Perhaps there was some measure of civilized man lurking inside him, after all. Perhaps she'd been going about this all wrong, fighting him when she should be cozying up to him, lulling him into lowering his guard.

She walked up the ravine. "I'm done. And I do appreciate—" She broke off as she cleared the top. "Oh, my word."

Lachlan glanced over at her. "What?"

The sun set over the mountains far beyond, casting the heights in plum-hued shadows of regal beauty. With the shade down in the coach, she'd missed this glorious view. Lavenders spilled into pinks that spilled into sunbursts so vibrant, they stung her eyes. "I haven't been home in so long," she whispered. "And there it is, smiling at me from the distance."

His gaze followed the direction of her hand, and his face softened.

"The tall mountain there is Ben Lawers."

She let out a breath. "It's like looking at a dream. A haunting, ancient dream that has teased me ever since I left. It's so very lovely."

"Aye, that it is, lass."

Glancing up at his face, she was surprised to see pleasure shining there. "You always said you hated the Highlands. You couldn't wait to be away."

"I was a fool, too full of myself to recognize what's important."

"And what is that?"

That fierce look stole over his face again, and he looked the very picture of a Highland warrior. "Home. A man's kin. It's where I belong, and that will ne'er change." Then he took her arm with impatience. "Back to the carriage, my lady. Move along."

She walked beside him in silence. What had she said to upset him? As a boy, he'd been capable of laughter. This surly Lachlan was a stranger to her.

As they climbed in the carriage and she settled into her seat, Lachlan ordered Jamie to drive on. She reached to lift the other shade, wanting to keep the view in her sights as they traveled, but he stayed her hand. "Leave it shut."

"Why?" She struggled against him. "We're miles from anywhere. No one will see."

He held her hand in a crushing grip. "Leave it shut, or I'll tie you up."

She stopped fighting him. She'd never be able to escape if he bound her.

When he saw that he'd won yet again, he released her. Throwing herself back against the seat, she struggled to restrain her temper. Getting angry hadn't worked very well so far.

Once she could trust herself to speak evenly, she said, "All I wanted was to see the mountains. Surely that isn't such a—"

"You think I don't know what you're about? You with

yer fancy words about the Highlands ... you're trying to soften me up so I'll let you go." Crossing his arms over his brawny chest, he scowled at her. "Turning me up sweet won't work any better than baring yer teeth at me."

The brooding look, his belligerent stance ... for a fleeting second it seemed like so much bravado, the sort boys showed when forced to do things they hated.

What was she thinking? This man had robbed innocent travelers without a thought, kidnapped her friends, and lied his way into her good graces so he could kidnap her, too. He might have a boy's selfishness, but the will behind it was a man's. And that man could very easily ruin her life forever.

But that didn't mean she had to let him.

Throwing back her shoulders, she took on the superior posture she'd learned so well at Mrs. Harris's school. "Since being nice to you offends you and biting you is out of the question, how should I proceed? Insults? Polite conversation? Tears? Is there anything I can do that will *not* annoy you?"

She could probably have cracked ice on his stiff jaw. "Keeping quiet would do the trick, lassie."

"No chance of that, laddie," she shot back, aping his brogue. "The least you can do after kidnapping me is allow me a way to entertain myself." She flashed him a syrupy smile. "Perhaps I shall sing. I have a rather extensive repertoire of ballads." And they did say that music soothed the savage beast.

"No singing. I remember yer singing. It's nothing I care to hear again."

Oh, of all the obnoxious insults. "I was six years old when I warbled that silly tune you're thinking of. I assure you, my singing is vastly improved."

"You want entertainment?" Jerking a knapsack from beneath the seat, he rummaged through it, then tossed an object at her. "Eat something. At least it'll gain me a few moments peace."

She tossed the paper-wrapped packet back at him. "No, thank you." She wasn't about to give him any peace.

His eyes narrowed. "I know it's not fancy fare, but surely even a fine lady like yerself won't turn up her nose at roast beef sandwiches."

Her stomach growled, but she ignored it. "If you want me to eat, you'll stop this coach and give me a proper meal."

"Oh, a proper meal is what the stiff-necked lady is wanting, is it?" He sat back in the seat, opened the packet, and pulled out what looked to be a very good sandwich. Waiting until he had her mouth watering, he held it out to her. "We're not stopping for any proper meals, so get that notion out of yer head. And starving yerself won't get you away from me either, so you might as well eat."

"I shall not eat until you return me to Edinburgh." She crossed her arms over her chest. "And there's nothing you can do to make me."

He stared at her, then began to devour the sandwich. "Suit yerself, my lady."

For a moment, silence reigned in the carriage as she fought to ignore the tempting aroma of roast beef. And was that mustard she smelled?

"I probably shouldn't feed you anyway," he finally said.

She remained silent.

"The more famished you get, the less trouble you'll give me."

She glared at him.

"With you too weak to run off or fight, I should be able to—"

"Oh, give me a sandwich, curse you." Leave it to a beast like him to call her bluff. And to hit on the one reason she *should* eat.

Eyes gleaming with triumph, he handed her another packet, then continued searching his knapsack. "There's apples, too."

She removed her gloves, unwrapped the packet, then laid the paper primly out on her lap to use as her plate. He stopped rummaging to watch as she meticulously tore the sandwich into more manageable pieces.

"What the devil are you doing?" he asked.

"Eating the sandwich."

"No, you're not. You're dissecting it."

She popped a piece in her mouth, chewed it ten times, then swallowed. "This is how I eat a sandwich, sir."

"Why?"

Years of habit. Mama had taught her to eat that way because of her tendency to wolf her food. But why tell him that when she could annoy him instead? "This is how civilized people eat. But of course, a man like you wouldn't understand."

She had to suppress her smile when he scowled. "In case you hadn't noticed, you're being abducted. It isn't the time to be worrying about yer proprieties."

"Good manners are always appropriate. Indeed, the true measure of a lady is how she behaves in the most difficult of times." When he snorted, she said, "I assume you were taught something similar in the army, to cling to discipline no matter what. Though you've clearly ignored *that* training in recent years."

"Ah, yes, discipline," he said with clear sarcasm. "The English word for 'stand and be killed if we say so.' "

She eyed him askance. "Isn't that what all soldiers do?"

"Soldiers fight. But when there's no way to fight and your commanding officer—" He cursed. "You wouldn't understand."

"I could try," she pointed out.

He sat back and changed the subject. "So that's what they taught you at yer fancy school, is it?" He flicked a hand to indicate her makeshift plate. "How to eat a sandwich like an English lady?"

With a sigh, she picked up a piece of sandwich. "Among other things."

"Like what?"

"How to sing," she said pointedly. "How to address one's betters, how to walk, how to speak French—"

"How to catch a husband."

She arched one eyebrow. "How to catch the *right* husband. Mrs. Harris was determined that we learn to distinguish a scoundrel from a gentleman." Her voice turned bitter. "Though apparently I didn't learn that lesson very well."

He stared at her, something almost like guilt crossing his features. When she grew uncomfortable and broke the glance, he returned to hunting through the knapsack. As she finished her sandwich, he set an apple atop her improvised plate.

But when she reached for it, he caught her hand. "You did nothing wrong, you know. Yer father should have warned you about me. It's not your fault."

"Are you trying to soften *me* up now? Because it won't work, laddie. I'm too 'stiff-necked' a 'fine lady' for that."

Bile rose in her throat to choke her. "Contrary to how it must have seemed to you last night, I generally don't allow flattery and sweet words to sway me from what I *know* is proper."

"Lass, I mean it," he said more firmly, closing her hand in his. "You did nothing wrong, ye ken? Neither last night nor today."

A heavy breath escaped her lips. "I should never have persuaded Papa to let me come to Scotland. He said it was too dangerous, but I didn't listen."

"It wouldn't have mattered." He stared down at her hand, then traced her thumb with his, almost absently. "I would have kidnapped you even if I'd had to risk going to London to do it. Once your father sent those men to kill me, the battle was set. Your coming here only made it a mite easier."

The unexpected kindness was too much to bear. Just when she wanted to hate him, he did something to remind her of the man he'd once been. Curse him for that.

Drawing her hand from his, she sat back in the seat and met his gaze squarely. "Then I'll just have to make sure the rest of it isn't so easy, won't I?"

Chapter Eight

Dear Charlotte,

I've said it before, but it bears repeating. Your husband may have been a fool, but that doesn't mean all men are fools. A pauper may love a princess and still not be a fortune hunter.

Your cousin,
Michael

Three hours passed, during which Lachlan came damned near to going mad. When the lass wasn't reciting her schoolmistress's tenets, she trilled every song she knew. He could have endured it better if she'd had a bad voice, but she sang like a nightingale, the notes silky and smooth as honey. It made a man want things he shouldn't, feel things he shouldn't.

That wasn't the worst of it, either. It was *what* she sang that spoiled his temper. No rollicking drinking songs and no heroic tales for Princess Proud, oh no. She sang of women who'd been seduced and abandoned by soldiers, or forced to marry the wrong men, or treated cruelly by their husbands.

When she was done with those, she turned to ballads about highwaymen. They always came to a bad end, too—hanged or shot down or betrayed by their true loves. She even managed to drum up a sprightly ditty about some idiot highlanders who kidnapped a girl, only to have her make fools of them by escaping.

Lachlan let her have her fun, partly because it kept

her busy and partly because the only time he tried to stop her, Jamie protested. Apparently the lad lacked any better way to pass the time while he drove.

But Jamie didn't have to watch her as the dusk bled into the moonlit night, to watch that lovely neck arch in song and those ample breasts lift every time she filled her lungs. Jamie didn't have to fight the urge to lean forward and kiss her throat, tongue the hollow there, drown himself in her flowery scent . . .

With a curse he jerked down the shade, blotting out the moonlight, so he didn't have to suffer the pain of looking at her and wanting . . . wanting . . .

Devil take the woman. She made him want too much.

Between her singing and her sighing over her Highland home, she was twisting him into knots. This afternoon, as she'd stared at the sunset . . . God help him, but he'd ached to catch her up and kiss her just for missing the Highlands.

Except that she didn't. Not really. She was remembering a place that no longer existed, if it ever had. She'd covered her childhood with roses, as girls were wont to do, forgetting how used to London ways she'd become, how used to living high and free off her father's ill-gotten money.

These days only the very rich of Scotland, the dukes and marquesses, lived that way, and they only managed it on the backs of their crofters. Once she saw how harsh life had become there, she'd recoil from it like his former fiancée had.

And who could blame her?

Silence finally descended over the carriage. He prayed that she'd sung herself hoarse.

"Lachlan?" came her voice out of the darkness.

He bit back an oath. "You ought to sleep."

"You're not sleeping, so why should I?" she said petulantly.

"I don't need to sleep." He'd purposely slept until noon today so he could make it through most of the night without.

"Oh, fudge. Even a scoundrel like you needs sleep." She paused. "Unless guilt over your many sins is what keeps you awake."

She never relented, did she? "More like that nasty discipline you said I lacked. Soldiers on the march go for days with only snatches of sleep. I've done it many a time." But he'd been younger. And he hadn't been recovering from a beating and a fever that had nearly killed him.

Blessed silence. But 'twas only for a moment.

"Does your mother know you're kidnapping me?"

Holy Christ, the lass certainly knew what questions would bedevil him. "No."

"Does she know you're the Scourge?"

"She doesn't know any of it," he snapped. "Why?"

"Surely she's noticed the extra funds and the disappearances—"

"A clanswoman learns early on not to pay such things any mind. Many a Highland man has to resort to dangerous or illegal work, like reiving or distilling. If his women are wise, they'll take whatever he brings in and keep quiet about it."

"And if they're not wise?"

"Well, then, he'll sew their mouths shut," he quipped. "Do you happen to have a sewing kit in your pocket, lassie?"

"Very amusing." She paused. "You make Highlanders sound like thieves, but I'm not some Lowlander to believe such prejudices. Certainly your family wasn't like that when I knew them. And you *are* a baronet, after all."

"Aye, and a lot of good having a title has done me. Or my mother."

She softened her voice. "I remember her well. She was always a practical sort, always busy. Come to think of it, she was also rather outspoken. I can't see her keeping quiet. At the very least, she's had to pretend you were dead for the past few months. Surely you had to give her a reason for *that*. What did you say?"

He could think of no reason to hide the truth, and mayhap if he gave her answers, she'd stop bedeviling him long enough to fall asleep. "I told her the Scourge's men ambushed me after I killed their leader. And I was so outnumbered, I had to pretend to drown to keep from being killed myself."

That's what he'd told her once he'd been conscious enough to speak, which had taken days. "Then I said that since I'd seen their faces, I'd best keep up the pretense until I could hunt them down." After he'd recovered his strength enough to fight back.

She chewed on that a moment. "Why wouldn't you just tell her the truth?" She added, in an arch tone, "She of all people should realize your cause was just."

"I don't want her having any part of it. If something happens and I'm taken, I want no blame falling on her. Bad enough that I had to confide in some of my clansmen after the attack. I never involved them before. I always felt that since I was the one choosing to risk my life, it should be my life alone."

"And Jamie's," she pointed out. "And the lives of the people you robbed."

"I never hurt any of them, and you know it," he ground out. "Ne'er did anything but take a bit of what yer father owed my family."

"What you *think* my father owed your family." When he cursed under his breath, she added hastily, "And what about Jamie?"

"Jamie and my other two companions came from my former regiment. They returned to Scotland to nothing—no homes, kin, or work. So I told them I'd share whatever we took if they helped me rob yer father's Scottish friends."

He frowned into the darkness. "Unfortunately, Sean and Robbie got greedy and decided to ride the roads on their own. Pair of fools got themselves murdered robbing a merchant with a blunderbuss. But Jamie's got good sense." His voice hardened. "And he's been loyal to me ever since joining the army as a drummer boy, so don't waste yer breath trying to convince him to help you escape."

"What a fine idea," she shot back. "He looks too young to have had many sweethearts. I'd wager that if I smiled and—"

"I mean it, lass," he growled, "leave the lad alone."

"Or what? You'll sew my mouth shut?"

"No, but I sure as the devil will gag you with my stock."

"You'd have to hold me down to do it, Lachlan Ross," she vowed. "And believe me, I'd make sure you didn't enjoy it."

A devilish impulse made him snap, "Oh, I don't know about that. At the moment, I'd give a great deal to have you beneath me." When he heard her soft gasp, he added, "So don't be tempting me to anger with talk of flirting with Jamie, or you and I'll have a right fine tussle."

That shut her up. Finally.

But now he had pictures to torture him, of laying her down in a grassy field and covering her body with his. She would be willing and eager, throwing those slender white arms about his neck while he seized one full breast in his mouth to suck and taste . . .

The lurch of the coach dragged him from his mad dream. He glanced out to find that they'd halted. "*Mo chreach*," he muttered, opening the panel.

Jamie jerked upright on the perch. "I'm awake now! I'm awake, sir."

"No, ye're not." Lachlan leaped out onto the road. "I was planning to relieve you soon, anyway. Get in the coach and sleep for a while. I'll drive."

"What about the lady?" Jamie asked as he climbed down.

"Yes, what about the lady?" Venetia echoed, her face framed in the open door, moonlight glinting off her rebellious little chin.

"If the lady's got any sense, she'll sleep, too." Lachlan opened his coat to lay his hand conspicuously on his pistol. "But if she doesn't, she'd best remember that I still have this." He glowered at her. "You hear me, lass? If you so much as make a sound in an inn yard, someone will die. And it won't be me."

Every time he said it, he waited for her to protest that he could never do such a thing. And every time she kept quiet, it peeved him that she believed the lie so readily. Of course, she thought him the worst sort of man, no matter what he said.

"If her nonsense keeps you from sleeping, Jamie," he went on, "I'll tie her up and gag her if I have to." He stared Venetia down. "And enjoy doing it, too."

"No doubt," she countered with a sniff. "You are awfully obsessed with the idea of tying up women." She threw herself back against the seat as Jamie entered the coach and closed the door.

" 'Tisn't women I'm obsessed with tying up," Lachlan muttered, and climbed up on the perch. "It's just you, lassie. Only you."

Although Venetia had done her best to vex Lachlan, nothing had seemed to penetrate his thick skull. He'd acted bored the entire time, staring out the window like a warrior carved in granite, except for the occasional tick of a muscle.

Still, she had to admit that despite his rude comments and surly manner, he'd been a very courteous kidnapper so far. They'd stopped twice more by the road so she could relieve herself. The food he'd brought had been quite tasty, and the carriage was clearly designed for comfort.

She didn't know what to think. Whenever she'd read about the Scourge, she'd imagined some bitter and lazy crofter of Papa's who'd turned to villainy. Her friend Amelia had described the accomplices as pure scoundrels bent on murdering Amelia's husband. And perhaps they had been, given Lachlan's own words about their foolishness.

But Jamie didn't fit that description. She would guess him to be about nineteen and, judging from how he shrank into the corner, a little nervous about being alone with her. He even jumped when his leg accidentally brushed her skirts.

"I won't bite, you know," she said softly, mindful of Lachlan just on the other side of the panel.

"No, milady." Reaching under the seat, he pulled out a folded blanket and handed it to her. "Getting cold now. You might be wanting this." He drew another out and made a big show of spreading it over himself before laying his head back and closing his eyes.

"See here, Jamie, I can tell you're not like your laird. You know that what he's doing is wrong, don't you?"

He cracked one eye open. "Lachlan Ross ain't done a wrong thing his whole life. He's the finest man I ever knowed. So don't speak bad of him to me. I won't listen. And I won't be helping you get away from him, neither."

After that heartfelt speech, he closed his eye, laid his head back, and promptly began to snore.

Well, she couldn't say Lachlan hadn't warned her.

While Jamie slept, she searched for other avenues of escape. The door nearest her had a simple latch—she could easily slip it off if she ever got the chance. But that seemed more unlikely by the hour. And even if she did escape . . .

She lifted the shade to stare out the window. Beyond the road lay the stoic hulks of heathery hills glowing silver in the molten moonlight. Nothing else for miles, not even a cottage. She sighed.

After a while, lulled by the steady beat of horse hooves on packed earth, she slipped into a dreamless sleep.

It was some time later before she awakened to realize that her cheek was pressed against the squabs, the blanket lay over her lap . . . and they'd stopped. Before she opened her eyes, she heard the snick of the driver's panel sliding open.

Feigning sleep, she kept her breathing steady, even

when light from a carriage lamp shone against her face. Only after the panel closed did she look around. Across from her, Jamie snored peacefully, and outside her window, the sky began to lighten.

Then the carriage lurched as Lachlan climbed down. Was he going to make Jamie drive? No, or he would have roused the lad. Holding her breath, she watched through slitted eyes as Lachlan paused outside the window to glance in and confirm that they both still slept.

When he disappeared, she popped up and looked out just in time to see him stop near the road. As he shoved back his coat and rocked back on his heels, she realized what he was doing. With a gulp, she jerked her gaze to the other window.

They were at the edge of a pine forest cloaked in predawn mist. Her blood roared in her ears. This was her chance. In the fog-shrouded woods, she could find a place to hide until she could reach a crofter's cottage.

But she had only a few minutes before Lachlan returned. Keeping an eye on Jamie, she laid her blanket aside and edged open the door opposite the one near Lachlan. Then she leaped out.

The second her feet hit, she lifted her skirts and ran neck-or-nothing for the pines. There she tore through the bracken, ignoring the birch branches that snagged the sleeves of her deplorably bright pelisse robe.

Oh, why had she chosen purple yesterday morning? Once dawn fully broke, her gown would stand out like a beacon against the green bracken. Best put as much distance between her and—

"Damn you, Venetia!"

The cry spurred her on. Frantically she wove through trunks that became more distinguishable by the moment.

Lord save her, the woods weren't very deep. She could now see beyond the edge to where the mist lay heavier over a loch.

Shifting direction, she ran parallel to the loch, praying that the woods stretched all the way around. Instead, the trees petered out into a short swath of bracken that ended in a huge slab of granite stretching right down to the water! And now she could hear Lachlan crashing through the brush behind her. He would catch up to her any moment if she didn't find a place to hide.

Swiftly skirting a rocky foothill, she left the loch, but the way grew harder until she was climbing steadily upward between huge boulders. It was either go up or go back, and she refused to go back to meet Lachlan.

With any luck he'd look for her near the loch. Perhaps the giant boulders would shield her from anyone below. She might even find a cave to hide in.

Suddenly something tawny and fierce dropped onto the path ahead of her and bared its fangs. She nearly screamed . . . until she realized what it was.

Only a tabby, thank heaven. A rather large tabby, to be sure, but still . . . Murmuring soothing words, she approached the snarling creature, probably one of the feral cats she remembered from her childhood.

"Stop right there, lassie," came Lachlan's low voice behind her.

Her heart sank as she turned to see him approach from behind her with his pistol drawn.

Not willing to give up, she edged nearer the tabby. "I am *not* getting back into that coach!"

The tabby growled and she halted, trying to figure out if she could get past it before Lachlan reached her.

Oddly enough, Lachlan paid her no heed. His eyes

were fixed on the tabby as he inched forward. "Move aside so I can get a clean shot at the beastie."

"Beastie! Don't you dare shoot that tabby—"

"That's not a tabby," he said grimly. " 'Tis a wildcat. They still roam this part of the Highlands."

Her breath caught in her throat. She'd heard of the Scottish wildcat, but she'd never seen one.

A fact he probably knew. "That is *not* a wildcat. Look at the poor thing—"

"*You* look at it, damn you, and tell me if ye've ever seen a tabby that big or that vicious."

She stared into the tabby's narrowed yellow eyes. It did seem awfully large for a house cat, and when she took a tentative step toward it, it hissed like a venomous snake.

Then she saw why. Set into the rock beyond it was a cave, and a couple of kittens now appeared in the mouth. Very large kittens, only slightly less ferocious than their mama. One of them clutched a small hare in its teeth.

With a gasp, she fell back, and Lachlan pulled her to his side. But when he raised his pistol, she said, "No, Lachlan, please. It was only protecting its little ones. You'll leave them without a mother."

"Little ones?" he said, then apparently spotted the kittens. Some of the tension left his body. "Ah, that explains it. Wildcats don't usually attack people."

Keeping his pistol drawn, he looped his free arm about her waist. "I'll spare the beastie if I can." He pulled her back with slow, measured steps. "No big motions, ye ken? Nothing that will make her think we mean her harm. She'll be loath to leave her wee ones, so she probably won't follow."

They inched back, keeping the drop-off to their left

and the wall of rock to their right. Only when they were well out of sight of the wildcat did Lachlan turn and break into a swift walk, dragging her along as he shoved his pistol into his pocket.

Now that the crisis with the wildcat was past, it dawned on her that she'd lost her chance to escape. "Let go of me, sir!" she demanded, fighting to get free of his grip on her waist. "You've got what you wanted, but that doesn't mean—"

"Got what I wanted!" He jerked her around to face him, his eyes blazing. "You think I wanted such a fright? To watch you nearly torn apart—"

"I doubt there was any chance of that," she retorted, though the alarm in his face took her aback. "I'd have figured out on my own that the cat was wild."

"Aye, after it mauled you." He swore vilely. "And what did you think to do once you made good yer escape?"

She set her shoulders. "I would have found a crofter's cottage—"

"There are no crofters here, only forest and lochs. The nearest village is twenty miles off. More likely you'd wander the hills until you starved."

She eyed him suspiciously. "Surely I could find sustenance somewhere."

"You know how to fish? To hunt? When was the last time you killed a squirrel, skinned and gutted it, then cooked it over a fire you built yerself?" He made a sound of disgust. "I'll wager ye don't even know which berries are edible."

That he was right annoyed her. "Then I'd simply have to walk until I reached the next village." Turning on her heel, she marched down the path toward the woods. "I could manage twenty miles, you know. No matter what you think, I'm not some languishing, coddled sort of a girl."

"Aye, and that's the trouble," he growled as he hurried to keep pace. "You're just sure enough of yerself to try anything. It will get you killed."

"I should at least like the chance to find out."

"Devil take you, have you no sense?" Catching her by the arm, he shoved her against a boulder. When her temper flared and she hammered at his arms, he cursed and grabbed her hands, forcing them flat against the rock on either side of her hips. "Listen to me! Hold still a bit and just listen, will you?"

She stopped fighting to fix him with an icy glare.

He let go of her hands. "It's not only wildcats and starvation you'd have to worry about. Thanks to the laird's 'improvements' hereabouts, the only people left in the villages are hungry and desperate. They'd take one look at yer pretty gown and yer fine boots, and they'd see a body to plunder, not help."

"I don't believe that," she said stoutly. "The Scots have always opened their hearts to strangers."

"Where? The Lowlands? Edinburgh? In the Highlands, people are suspicious of cultured ladies who sound and look and act English. And there are men who . . ." He swept his gaze down her. "Ye're a pretty lass, an innocent lass. Exactly the sort desperate men want to sully."

"Let them just try," she hissed.

His gaze snapped back to her face. "Right, I forgot," he said with heavy sarcasm. "You'll slash them with yer rapier wit."

His condescension infuriated her. She kicked him as hard as she could manage with her sturdy walking boot.

With a howl of pain he jerked back, and she took off

through the bracken toward the woods. She didn't get far before he caught up to her, pouncing upon her like a beast. Next thing she knew, he had her on her back underneath him.

Rage scored his white features as he pinned her hands above her head. "So you'd fight them, would you?" he snarled. "If some villain tried to harm you, ye'd fight him off."

She struggled to bring her knee up between his legs the way Mrs. Harris had said they should do if some man tried to hurt them, but he anticipated the move, thrusting his thick-as-oak thigh between hers to trap her.

Grabbing her wrists, he held them together in one large fist above her head, then raked his other hand down her neck to her bodice. "Very well, Princess Proud," he taunted her. "Fight! Show me how easily you'd free yerself of some murdering savage who wanted to harm ye!"

She writhed beneath him, but she might as well have been staked to the ground for all the good it did. His weight crushed her so she couldn't breathe, and his single hand was stronger than her two.

Holding her irate gaze with his grim one, he flicked open the top clasps of her pelisse robe, baring the upper swells of her breasts. "Stop me, damn you! Go on! Since you're so ferocious and all!"

He started to slide his hand inside her bodice, and she gasped.

"You see?" He paused with his rough hand lying flat across her breastbone, the fingertips just grazing the inner flesh of her breast. "A moment or two is all it would take, and yer innocence would be gone. Is that what you want?"

She stared up at him, suddenly aware of the strain across his brow and the taut lines of his square jaw. He looked as if he was suffering great pain. Had she hurt him that badly when she'd kicked him?

Or was he simply struggling not to give in to his basest urges? That possibility alarmed her, and she realized how close she'd come to pushing him over the edge. Lord save her.

"Well, lass?" He slid his hand deeper inside her bodice to undo the bow of her corset. "Is that what you want?"

"No!" When he halted his motion, she lowered her voice. "No, Lachlan."

Yet he didn't remove his hand. For a moment, she feared she'd waited too long to stop him. His thigh lay intimately, heavily between her legs, a firm reminder of how easily he'd subdued her. Though the fabric of her corset and chemise still separated her bare flesh from his bare hand, she shivered to feel his fingers inside her bodice, mere inches from the crest of her breast. All he would have to do . . .

"Please," she whispered. "Don't hurt me."

He blinked at her, then yanked his hand free with a curse and rolled off to lie beside her in the green bracken.

At first, the only sound was that of their harsh breaths and the discordant cry of a nightjar. Then Lachlan swore and eased himself up onto one elbow to gaze into her face. "I would never hurt you, you know. Never."

She wanted to believe that. She really did. But she knew how vulnerable she must look to him, lying here with her hair loose and her gown gaping open. And considering the circumstances . . . "That's only because

I'm no good to you if I'm damaged. Papa would never pay you."

Flinching as if she'd slapped him, he stared at her with haunted eyes. "That's not why." The words sounded torn from him. Then his expression softened until he looked less the Highland warrior and more the rangy lad she'd once adored.

"That's not why," he repeated, his voice a husky rumble that made her breath catch in her throat. "And you know it."

Then he lowered his head to hers.

She'd sworn not to let him kiss her again, and a few minutes ago, she would have resisted. But a few minutes ago, he'd been cruel to her. Now . . .

Now he was different. His cruelty had been born of a heartfelt concern for her, a concern now turning into something more. She could see it in his warm gaze, melting to a coppery brown. She could hear it in his indrawn breath when he paused with his lips a mere inch from hers, allowing her a chance to stop him.

She didn't.

So he didn't.

Lord save her.

Chapter Nine

Dear Cousin,

    *What do you know of fortune hunters? Your
every need is met—you've never had to face your
spouse's creditors, wondering if they will take
everything you own. You've never been at the mercy
of a fickle man.*

                    Your testy relation,
                    Charlotte

*L*achlan didn't know what madness possessed him.
He just needed to reassure Venetia—and himself—that
he wasn't the monster he'd probably seemed a moment
ago, a man who would force a woman to endure his
lascivious touch. That's why he'd given her the chance
to refuse the kiss.

But only a chance. Because the minute he'd been
close enough to smell the lavender in her hair and see
the warming of her eyes, he'd had to kiss her. He couldn't
help himself.

And she was letting him. Thank God, or he didn't
know what he might do. He was half drunk from lack
of sleep, with his heart still pumping from the terror of
seeing her at the mercy of a wildcat, and it took all his
strength just to keep his kiss light. Especially when she
melted, her lips parting beneath his own.

After that, there was no keeping it light. He just had
to bury his tongue between those rosy lips. Never mind
that his leg ached something fierce and his ribs throbbed

from where she'd pounded him. Never mind that she could do the same to him again for plundering her lush mouth.

He didn't care; he would take the chance. He kissed her heartily, needfully, wanting everything the bold wildcat of a lass would give him. And she gave him plenty. God help him, she lay in the bracken and kissed him back, drawing his tongue into her mouth, stroking it with hers.

Ever since they'd left Edinburgh, he'd watched her scrap and barter, unwilling to let him win. He'd bullied her at every turn, yet she'd held her own. It intoxicated him, her stubborn ferocity. To have her yielding even a tiny part of herself to him was more tempting than he could resist.

Then her hand crept up to cling to his neck, and his mind blanked to nothing but the taste of her, the sweet silk of her tongue mating with his. Need drove him now, hot and urgent, prodding him to put his hands on her, to explore and caress, to take the edge off his hunger before he lost his mind.

In a fever, he unfastened more ties of her gown and unclasped the belt about her waist, so he could slide his hand inside to stroke her corseted belly. Even that was not enough, for his hand began to roam, up and down, in long, caressing sweeps. But when his fingers brushed the very edge of the swell of one breast, she tore her lips from his to whisper, "What do you think you're doing?"

"I don't know." He skimmed her throat with his open mouth, reveling in the pounding of her pulse beneath his lips. "Something I shouldn't, most likely."

"If anyone were to see—"

"I told you, no one is around for miles." He couldn't

help noticing that she was more worried about not being seen than about what he was doing. "And I ordered Jamie to stay with the horses."

"Still, this is very wicked." But she stated it like a fact, not a warning.

"Aye, very wicked." With his blood thumping high, he pushed her gown open to bare her corset from breast to thigh. "I'm a wicked sort of man. And I suspect you're more wicked than you'll admit." Deliberately, he loosened the gathers that held up the soft cups of her corset.

She swallowed, her gaze dropping to watch him. "Why do you say that?"

"Because of how you were at the ball," he said, careful of his words. He didn't want to spook her. "You went off into the dark with me and took a risk out of sheer curiosity." He bent to kiss her cheek, then tug her earlobe with his teeth. "Admit it, lassie—beneath yer proprieties is a passionate woman aching to thumb her nose at the English rules binding her up so tight she can't breathe."

"Th-that's not true." She gasped when he thrust the tip of his tongue into her ear, then nibbled the lobe. "I . . . like the rules . . . I do."

"Is that why you let me kiss you that night, a pure stranger?" He tugged loose the tie of her chemise. "Is that why you sing so many songs about devilish lords and highwaymen, breakers of rules every one of them?"

She jerked back to stare at him, her hand still gripping his neck. "I sang those ballads to show you the error of your ways."

"Did you now? And why did you bother to learn them in the first place? To prepare for when you met up with a highwayman? No, lass, you learned them because they appealed to your wicked bent." He smiled at her. "You sang them because you've got more of yer rebel Jacobite grandfather in you than ye ken."

Hooking his fingers behind one soft cup of her stays, he drew it down to expose her chemise, then drew down the other.

But when he reached for the chemise, she caught his hand. "I'm not wicked enough for *that*, Lachlan."

Her other arm was trapped at her side; otherwise she probably would've done more than halt his hand. But he didn't let her modesty daunt him. Not now that he had a sight of her thinly covered breasts, rising on either side of her corset busk. Holy Christ, they were plump as pillows, their rosy nipples perking up beneath his gaze through the linen of her chemise.

"A wee bit of wickedness never hurt a body," he said hoarsely as he bent his head to kiss the swell of one breast above the loosened chemise.

Her breath came as quickly as his. "You talk like every seducer I've been warned against."

"Aye, and you like seducers, too, don't you? God knows you sing enough songs about *them*."

"That doesn't mean . . . I don't . . ."

"Your body likes them, anyway." He pressed his luck by thumbing her nipple through the linen. "That's why this little currant is puckering up for me."

She sucked in a ragged breath, and he kissed her, long and deep, a seducer's kiss, until he felt her hand slide up his coat sleeve to his shoulder.

Only then did he pull down her loosened chemise, allowing one of her lush breasts to spill entirely free. He covered it with his hand, exulting in the abundance of it, the way it quivered beneath his caress.

Her hand gripped his shoulder as he fondled and

stroked, his kiss growing more frantic until he couldn't think of anything but how badly he wanted her, how heavy his prick lay in his trews, aching for her.

He finally had her beneath him the way he'd been longing to have her, and for once she wasn't acting like her father's daughter. For once it was just the two of them and she wasn't fighting him. The bonnie lass was lucky he wasn't throwing up her skirts and taking her right here and now.

But he wasn't fool enough for that. A little touching, a little kissing would be enough to hold him until they reached Ross-shire and he could lock her away to await her father.

Or so he tried to convince himself.

He slipped his thigh between her legs, trying to get closer, needing to be closer. With a moan, she wrenched her mouth from his. "Oh, Lachlan, you'll be the ruin of me."

"I won't, I swear," he said, fearing it was a lie and hoping it wasn't.

"You will. Because . . . because I . . ."

"Enjoy this?" he rasped. "You like having my hands on you, do you?"

"Lord, yes."

That was all the invitation he needed to suck her breast, teasing the tip with his teeth, drowning in the female flesh that lay so richly soft beneath him. His other hand dragged down the other side of her chemise, so he could enjoy that breast with his fingers as he laved the first with his tongue.

"Lachlan . . ." she gasped. "You are . . . this is . . ."

Venetia knew she sounded like a babbling fool, but that was how he was making her feel, with his mouth ravishing her and his fingers taking wild, reckless liberties. She shouldn't be allowing it! Why was she allowing it?

"You can't know what you do to me, lass," he whispered against her breast. "You can't know."

"I know what you . . . do to *me* . . ." she rasped as he tugged on her nipple with his teeth, sending sensation screaming along every nerve.

That was why she was allowing this. Because it felt like nothing she'd ever known. And because for once, he wasn't growling at her or cursing her father or turning surly. For once, he was the Lachlan she'd adored as a girl.

So when his thigh rubbed between her legs, startling other sensations to life down below, she didn't even hesitate to arch up against him. The pressure felt so good, so delicious . . .

And curse him if that didn't prod him to take more liberties. Trailing his hand down to the juncture between her thighs, he began rubbing her through her chemise while his mouth continued to suck eagerly at her breasts, one after the other.

Dear Lord, that was astonishing. No wonder girls in ballads were always losing their virtue to rogues. Losing one's virtue had a decided appeal. His tongue was doing the most amazing things to her nipples, while his fingers did a sliding motion down below that made her squirm and arch for more.

How could she have guessed seduction would feel so magical?

And how could he know so well what would excite her? She'd rubbed herself down there a time or two, seduced by the melting pleasure of it, but it felt nothing like this heady . . . delicious . . .

Dangerous . . . unwise— "Curse you, Lachlan, why

are you doing this?" *Why are you making me feel these things?*

He lifted his head from her breast to rake her with a smoldering gaze that set flame to her skin. "I wanted you from the second I saw you." He nuzzled her breast, his whiskered chin wonderfully rough against the soft flesh. "You walked into that ball like a queen dressed as a peasant, and I wanted you."

That seemed a lifetime ago. She'd been so happy to be among other Scots, dancing strathspeys and watching the tartan worn so proudly.

While he plotted her kidnapping.

The thought banished her passion. That's why he'd kissed her then. And probably why he was touching her now. Dear Lord, she was letting him do exactly the things she'd sworn she would never let him do.

Her heart lurching in her breast, she reached down to draw his hand from between her legs. "You didn't want *me*," she accused. She was such a fool. "You wanted Duncannon's daughter."

The sudden uneasy glint in his eyes told her she'd guessed right. "I wanted both. I still do."

She choked down the tears welling in her throat. That was the trouble. He wanted to have his way with her . . . but only so he could strike back at her father.

Then he shifted his thigh between her legs, and she felt the thick bulge in his trousers pressing into her like an iron brand.

Well, perhaps not only to strike back at Papa. Thanks to the harem tales she and the other girls had read at school, she knew what that bulge between his thighs signified. He *did* desire her. Or rather, he desired a woman. She only happened to be convenient.

She fought to ignore the pain that lanced through her chest. He was using her own wishful fancies to get her where he wanted her. Beneath him, allowing him to take shameful liberties with her.

Very well, perhaps it was time she used *his* desire to *her* advantage.

Forcing a smile, she tugged his hand back to where it had been. "So you want me, do you?"

He caught his breath. "Aye. You know that I do."

"You want me. I want to go home." She swallowed. "Perhaps I could earn my release by letting you . . . do things to me." Like let him see her naked or let him touch and kiss her. When a storm built in his features, she added hastily, "Not ruin me, you understand. Just do . . . things."

For a moment, he just stared at her, as if unable to believe what he was hearing. Then to her surprise, he cursed and snatched his hand free to plant it on the ground beside her shoulder.

Fire now glinted in his deep brown eyes as he brought his face down to hers. "So that's what this has been about."

"Wh-what do you mean?"

"Your soft sighs and kisses, your letting me caress and taste you," he gritted out as he hovered over her. "God, what an ass I am!"

Something had gone wrong in her plan, but what? "You're angry."

"Bloody right I'm angry! I thought that you—" He broke off with a foul curse, then shoved to his feet. "Never mind what I thought. I must have been daft. If I'd been using my brain, I would have realized you were just trying out a different ploy for escaping me." Fury lit his face as he paced the bracken beside her. "Because ladies like yerself don't roll in the bracken with thieving Scots like me unless they want something for it, do they?"

If he wouldn't let her bargain for her release by offering him liberties, then it was better he think she had no desire for him at all. Because if he guessed how susceptible she was . . .

That must never happen. He would seduce her so he could turn her into a weapon against Papa, and she'd have nothing left, not even her pride.

"As you say, Lachlan, I am a lady." Quickly, she stood up, too, then began putting her clothing in order. "And ladies do not . . . allow such liberties unless they're . . . desperate."

"Desperate!" He rounded on her. "To do what—save yer lying father's hide?"

"To save my own hide," she shot back.

"I told you from the beginning no harm would come to you as long as your family did as instructed."

Her temper got the better of her. "I know what you said, and it's a lot of rot." She tied up her corset. "Eventually some maid at the inn will notice I'm not sleeping in my bed. She'll tell another, who'll tell another, and the whispers will spread until all of Edinburgh knows. No matter what you say, my future changed irreparably once you abducted me."

He stared her down. "So your solution was to whore yerself?"

"No! I merely thought you might want—"

"To torture myself with a sample of yer delights. What you don't know about men could sink a barge, lassie." He stomped about with fists clenched. "A sample of you has only got me aching for the whole feast."

"Well, you can't have it," she snapped.

"I *know* I can't, damn you! That's what I'm saying! You were taking quite a risk by tempting me the way you were—"

"Tempting *you*? You're the one who started everything!"

"Only because I thought you liked it, too!" He halted a few feet away, his voice turning snide. "I didn't know you were only pretending."

She tied the silk cords of her pelisse robe. "Well, I was," she lied. "I thought it might . . . soften you up some."

A muscle worked in his jaw. "Bloody fool of a woman. Next time try singing, why don't you? It's safer."

"You said you didn't like my singing," she said petulantly.

"I like it a damned sight better than having you beneath me pretending to welcome having me touch yer—" A strange expression crossed his face. Then he stared at his hand, rubbing his fingers together.

When next his gaze met hers, he looked at her as if seeing all her secrets. "So you took no pleasure in our kisses and caresses, did you?"

"No, I didn't," she said in as cold a voice as she could muster. She had to make him believe her. "How could I?"

"And you didn't like it when I rubbed yer privates—"

"Certainly not!" she cried, her face aflame. How could he talk about this so blatantly? "I'm simply not as wicked as you think."

He approached her, his eyes narrowing. "So it was just about softening me up, trying to get me to release you. That's what ye're saying."

Unnerved by his odd intensity, she dropped her gaze to concentrate on fastening her pelisse robe. "That's what

I'm saying." Her hands shook. "I am Princess Proud, after all."

"Aye." He caught her by the chin and forced her to look at him. "You're a princess, all right." He smoothed his thumb over her lower lip, sending a shiver through her despite her attempts to contain her reactions.

A sudden gleam lit his face. "But I'm not so sure about the proud part. More like Princess Machiavelli, ye are."

She blinked at him. "Who's that? Some Italian lady?"

He gave a low laugh. "Machiavelli was a very famous man who wrote a very famous book. About how to be canny. How to get what you want."

She didn't know whether to be flattered or alarmed by that description. "Either way, I'm a princess, aren't I?" She forced some haughtiness into her tone. "And much too regal to be manhandled on the ground like some harlot."

"Unless it's for a good reason," he reminded her.

"Yes, exactly."

With his hand still gripping her chin, he bent close to press his mouth to her ear. "Only one trouble with that claim of yers."

Her pulse quickened. He was too near for her to ignore, curse him. "What's that?"

"A woman's arousal may be deeper hidden, but it's still apparent to any man who touches her in the right place." His breath came hot and heavy against her ear. "You were wet for me, princess. And that's a sure sign that you wanted me."

Wet for him? What—

Ohhh. She'd forgotten about the dampness that had welled against her fingers the few times she'd caressed her privates. It hadn't occurred to her that he might . . . that he would have felt . . .

"You're mistaken," she whispered.

His devilish chuckle sent alarm careening through her. "A man doesn't mistake something like that. But you're welcome to try proving me wrong." Impudent as Satan himself, he nipped at her earlobe. "We can return to what we were doing and see what happens. I'd be more than happy to judge yer arousal—"

"You're a beast," she hissed, jerking back with a glare.

With complete insolence, he scoured her from mussed hair to mussed skirts. When his gaze met hers again, it held an uncanny knowing that made her heart sink. "You may not *want* to desire me, lassie, but you do."

She itched to deny it again, but he knew she was lying now. Yet she'd die before she let him take advantage of it.

Setting her shoulders, she stared him down. "It doesn't matter—"

"Ye're right about that. Flaunt that pretty body of yers as much as you please—it won't get you free of me." Taking her off guard, he snagged her about the waist and tugged her against him. "But that doesn't mean I won't take what you're offering, if you're ever fool enough to offer it again."

He brought his lips to within an inch of hers, his gaze burning brightly. "So if you want to save yer virtue from a low beastie like me, best not be teasing me with tastes and samples. I'm not made of stone, ye know." His eyes gleamed at her. "And neither are you, princess."

For a moment, they stood silent and frozen, then the quiet was broken by someone clearing their throat nearby. "Sir Lachlan."

Jamie. Dear Lord.

Blushing, she tried to pull away, but Lachlan held her tight another moment. "Do we understand each other, lassie?"

She'd never forgive him for prolonging her embarrassment. "Perfectly," she bit out. "Now, if you'd be so kind as to let me go—"

"Certainly, my lady," he said, the faintest hint of humor in his face as he released her. Then he turned toward the woods, and his voice hardened to ice. "Jamie, me boy, ye're supposed to be keeping an eye on the horses."

Swallowing her mortification, she glanced over to find Jamie watching his master with a mutinous expression. "Aye, sir. But you took so long, I thought you might have had trouble finding the lass. I came to help."

"As you can see, no help was needed."

Jamie remained stubbornly silent.

"Now that you're here, you can escort the lady back to the coach."

"You're not coming?" Jamie asked.

"I'll be there in a moment. There's something I want to do first."

"All right." Jamie held out his hand to her. "Come along, Lady Venetia."

Jamie had already taken her arm and was leading her through the woods when Lachlan called out, "And keep a good eye on her this time, will you, lad? I don't need another sprint through the woods."

"Aye, sir!" Jamie dropped his voice to a grumble. "You see what ye've done, milady? I slept through yer running off, and now I'll never hear the end of it."

"You should have helped me when I first asked," she said, unrepentant.

He shook his head. "Ye sure are a spitfire, aren't ye? Nothing like I expected. I thought Duncannon's daughter would be—"

"I wish you'd both stop calling me 'Duncannon's daughter.' I do have a name, you know."

"Aye, milady, sorry." They walked in silence a ways before he spoke again. "It's just that ye're a good sight prettier than we expected. Generally the laird don't lay a hand on the ladies we rob, but with you he seems to be different, and—"

"You don't approve." A sudden hope seized her. Jamie *had* seemed awfully disturbed by how Lachlan held her. Perhaps she could use that.

"Ain't my place to approve or disapprove. I'm just saying that . . . well . . . if the laird did anything he oughtn't, you should . . . that is . . . if you tell me, I'll . . ."

"Protect me from him?" she asked in her most coquettish tone.

"If need be." Keeping his eyes safely on the ground, he helped her over a log.

She allowed her hand to linger on his arm. "And how will you do that?"

Although Jamie flushed bright red, his gaze held all the fierceness she could want. "I'll speak to him, remind him that you're a lady and all."

A fat lot of good *that* would do her. Lachlan had promised to gag her if he heard that she'd tried to turn Jamie against him. "No, please, all I want is to go home." Sliding her hand into the crook of his elbow, she cast him a soft smile. "Surely you can understand that, can't you?"

He blinked, and for a moment, she thought she'd succeeded in tempting him.

Then his face closed up. "Yes, milady, I understand, but I can't help you with that. You're Duncannon's daughter, and the laird needs you to get money—"

"From my father. Yes, I know." With her heart sinking, she snatched her hand from his arm and hurried ahead.

He hastened after her. "But I'll gladly speak to him on yer behalf."

"Thank you, but no, Jamie. There's no need."

They neared where the coach sat by the road, the horses happily grazing. "Are you sure? Sir Lachlan didn't do nothing he oughtn't, did he, milady?"

"He didn't do a thing," she lied.

Except show me how little of a lady I really am. She'd nearly given herself to him, for pity's sake! If she hadn't come to her senses in time . . .

Her eyes narrowed. Yes, she'd stopped Lachlan by offering to let him take certain liberties. And why had he refused? Surely not just because he wouldn't meet her terms and let her go. A true scoundrel would have enjoyed the pleasures, then reneged on his promise. But he'd been insulted by the very idea that she would "whore" herself to gain her freedom.

That wasn't the behavior of a scoundrel.

With a sigh, she stalked through the grass. Lachlan was conscienceless enough to rob people, but not conscienceless enough to force a woman when he had her trapped? Or even to try seducing her?

Who in the dickens was the man, anyway? Was he the wild fellow she'd grown up with, or the courteous soldier she'd met at the ball? Was he the Scottish Scourge, or the responsible chief of the Clan Ross wanting to save his people? And which of them was the ardent lover who'd caressed her sweetly in the bracken?

She wished she knew. Because until she did, she dared not trust herself alone with him again.

They'd reached the carriage, and as Jamie bent to put down the step, she laid her hand on his shoulder. "There is one thing you could do for me, sir."

Jamie straightened to cast her a wary glance. "What is it, milady?"

"Ride with me in the coach from now on instead of the laird."

A stormy look passed over Jamie's face. "So he *did* take liberties—I knew it! I will surely have a word with him."

"No, please don't say anything. He's been a perfect gentleman, and I don't want him to think I'm ungrateful." She forced a bright smile. "I merely prefer your company to his, that's all." *Because you don't make me want to toss my virtue at your feet.*

Jamie searched her face a long moment, then nodded. "I understand, milady. You just leave everything to me."

Chapter Ten

⌒∽⌒

Dear Charlotte,

You know nothing of my life, my dear. If you did,
you would understand that it is not just men who
look at women and see only what they can provide.
Women do that as well. I long ago learned to accept
that the world is full of people who callously use
other people for their own purposes. The question
is—when will you accept it?

Your friend despite everything,
Michael

*L*achlan waited until he was sure that Jamie and the
lass were well out of hearing, and unlikely to return and
surprise him.

Then he unbuttoned his trousers and drawers.
Seizing his rampant erection, he pumped it with frantic
motions. Before he climbed into that torture chamber
of a coach with her, he needed to ease the tension she'd
roused. Otherwise, he'd never be able to behave himself.
He had at least another day of smelling her and hearing
her sing and watching her twin beauties rise and fall with
each of her breaths.

"Holy Christ!" he muttered as his cock spent itself
into the bracken. Just thinking of her breasts made him
come off. How the devil was he to last more days with
her in a coach?

He gritted his teeth. Somehow he must. The
alternative was impossible. Even if she let him lay her

down and bury his aching flesh inside her, he refused to ruin her. That would make him exactly the blackguard she already thought him, the rash idiot his father had always condemned him for being.

It would also mean the end of his hopes for his clan, because if he ruined Duncannon's daughter, there'd be no money for expanding the stills or buying barley seed or anything else. The earl wouldn't rest until he saw Lachlan and Jamie both hanging from the end of a noose.

Unless, of course, Lachlan married her.

Tucking his flaccid cock back into his drawers, he dismissed the very idea. For one thing, she'd never agree. The minute she realized what he was willing to do to her father to get what was owed him, she would never speak to him again.

And even if everything went well between him and Duncannon, even if the old earl finally settled this matter amicably, she'd never belong at Rosscraig. Any lass who considered it "proper" to break her sandwiches up into little pieces would shudder to see the conditions of his estate. Between the whisky mash fumes and the new pigsties, the smell alone would send her off screaming.

All right, so the manor house was well away from that and was handsomely built, too. He'd even managed to keep it from falling down about their ears. But the tattered furnishings needed replacing and the kitchen required a complete redoing, all of which would have to wait until his clan got back on its feet. Or until a woman with more taste than his mother took the place over.

He winced. He loved his mother as well as any dutiful son, but she'd been born a butcher's daughter. She no more knew how to keep up an elegant home than a titmouse would. Before Lady Duncannon's death, that fine lady had helped Mother with setting the place to rights, but once the woman had died, Mother had gone back to her old habits.

Rosscraig was in no condition to support a woman of Venetia's needs and wants. It teemed with boisterous, hardworking men and their scrappy, hardworking women. That roiling lot was no kind of company for a lass who couldn't tell a tabby from a wildcat.

Who begged him to spare its life on account of its wee ones.

He paused while buttoning his drawers. What a tenderhearted lass she was—too tenderhearted for the harsh life of Rosscraig. She was better suited for some London lord who could appreciate her particular talents.

A scowl knit his brow as he finished fastening himself up. He didn't like the thought of that, either, of her in the arms of a puling English dandy. She deserved better, even if her father *was* the worst devil ever to betray his countrymen.

Of course, if she was right that the news about her kidnapping would spread, then she would never have the chance to marry anyway.

Devil take her, she was making him worry about things that weren't going to happen, things that shouldn't concern him! This was about Duncannon, about forcing him to live up to his responsibilities. There was no reason to believe that things wouldn't go as planned, that she wouldn't be returned to her cozy life in London without harm to her reputation or her future.

So why did the other possibilities plague him every

step of his way back to the coach, even more than his stiff leg and his aching ribs? Why couldn't he take any pleasure in the sight of the morning sun dancing its light across the loch or the delicate scent of the honeysuckle twining along the edge of the woods?

And why did anger roar into him with a vengeance to find Jamie sitting in the carriage with her, chatting along like any royal courtier with a princess?

"Out of the coach, Jamie! It's yer turn up top."

He didn't miss the pleading glance Venetia shot the lad . . . or the reassuring pat Jamie gave her hand before he climbed out and faced Lachlan with a stubborn set to his shoulders. "I thought I'd ride inside a bit longer if ye don't mind, sir."

"I do mind. It's nigh on to twenty-four hours since I last slept."

"I thought you didn't need sleep," Venetia taunted him. "I thought you said that soldiers were used to—"

"That was before I had to chase you for half a mile." Before he'd had to endure her beating his ribs and thrashing about beneath him. He fixed Jamie with a stern glance. "Besides, laddie, the lass escaped on *yer* watch, not mine. So I mean to make sure it doesn't happen again."

Bristling at being called "laddie," Jamie crossed his arms over his chest. "And I mean to make sure you don't make untoward advances to the young lady."

"Oh, Lord," Venetia muttered, and threw herself back against the seat.

Lachlan's temper flared right high. What had the scheming wench told the lad? "Are you threatening me, laddie?" he asked, this time deliberately insulting. He strode forward, forcing Jamie to back up against the coach. "Because I'd think long and hard about that if I were you. I can still thrash you with one hand behind my back, and don't think I wouldn't do it, either."

Jamie glared at him. "Do it if you please, sir, but I'm not backing down."

Oh, the lad had fallen hard for the wench already, hadn't he? Lachlan jerked his head toward the coach. "Is that what the lady told you? That I made 'untoward advances'?"

"She didn't have to tell me," Jamie said stoutly. "I saw how you held her. And she had twigs and leaves all over the back of her gown, too."

"Aye, because she went hurtling through the woods like a madwoman and nearly got herself mauled by a wildcat. All because ye slept through our stopping."

Jamie paled, but Lachlan went on venting his temper. " 'Untoward advances' indeed—you wouldn't know an 'untoward advance' if it bit you in yer hairy Scottish arse. She's the only one who talks like that, and you ought to be ashamed of yerself for listening to her when she already got away from you once—"

"Enough!" Venetia said in a commanding tone. Lachlan glanced over to see her glaring at him from the open coach door. "Don't blame Jamie for that. I got away because *you* were off pissing in the bushes."

Jamie's jaw dropped.

Lachlan's was right behind it. "You said 'piss.' "

Venetia flushed. "It seems the only sort of language you understand, you ill-mannered oaf."

A choked sound came from Jamie, and Lachlan looked over to find the lad fighting the urge to laugh. Lachlan's dark scowl took care of that.

"Now, sir," Venetia continued, "if you insist upon riding inside the coach, by all means do so. I don't care one way or the other."

"No, milady," Jamie protested, "I told you I'd look after you, and I will!"

"Silence, lad," Lachlan growled. "She doesn't make the rules around here, and neither do you. I'm riding in the carriage, and that's the end of the discussion."

"But—"

"It's fine," Venetia said firmly. "I've put up with the great lout until now. I'm sure I can put up with him a while longer, laddie."

Jamie flinched to hear her refer to him that way, and Lachlan almost felt sorry for the young idiot. Little did she know she'd done more to harm her cause with Jamie with that one word than with any amount of Lachlan's shouting.

Then Jamie drew himself up. "All right, then. I'll drive." He shot Lachlan a resentful glance. "But I'm keeping the panel open."

Lachlan rolled his eyes but allowed Jamie his bit of rebellion. After all, he could hardly blame the lad for turning into a mooncalf around Venetia. She was the kind of woman a man would die to protect. And no doubt she'd used that to her advantage. But she wouldn't do it with him, Jamie or no Jamie.

As soon as the coach set off, he reached under the seat and pulled out the lengths of rope he hadn't needed until now.

Her eyes widened. "See here, Lachlan, I didn't put Jamie up to challenging you. He did that on his own. So you can't punish me—"

"This isn't about that." He bent down and began to bind her at the ankles. "I need to sleep, and I won't be able to if ye're free to run about." He finished tying her legs and sat up. "Now give me yer hands."

"Please, Lachlan," she begged, tucking them beneath her skirts, "what if I promise I won't try to escape?"

"Don't take me for a fool. You know bloody well that the moment my back is turned, ye'd be running into the woods again." He managed a smile. "It's only for a while, and no harm will come to you. But I've got to get some rest, and you'll make that impossible. Now give me yer hands, lass."

When she just sat there, staring mutinously at him, he hardened his voice. "I see. So you're up for another tussle, are you? Very well."

She thrust her wrists out with insulting swiftness, though her eyes flashed fire. "If you touch me anywhere you shouldn't while I'm like this, I swear to God—"

"I know, princess, I know." He bound her carefully, not wanting to cause her any pain. Then he sat back against the seat. "Now, then, can I trust you to keep quiet? Or will I have to gag you, too?"

She swallowed. "I'll keep quiet."

"See that you do." He lifted one eyebrow. "Because you don't want to be giving me a reason for stopping up yer mouth."

A flush stained her cheeks, wreaking holy hell on his insides. He'd have to stop saying things like that; it just reminded them both of what they couldn't do.

He took up one of the blankets. "If you'll slide into that corner there, I'll cover you. You can probably sleep well enough like that." And with her covered, he wouldn't be tempted to spend his sleeping time staring at her body in a lustful stupor.

She did as he said, but a calculating look was already crossing her face.

He knew that look only too well by now. "I'll be handing my pistol to Jamie while I sleep," he said, "because I can't have you trying to wrest it away."

Her face fell.

"But we both know he doesn't have the heart to kill anyone." He drew out the tartan blanket and covered her with it. Then he moved to sit next to her. "So I want to remind you of one thing before we both try to get some rest," he said softly. "If you scream, it'll just wake me up to stop ye. Then you'll be gagged, and I don't think you want that."

He turned her face up to his, and she stared at him mutely. "But if you do succeed in bringing attention to yerself before I can silence yer mouth, it'll mean a fight at the very least. You might get yerself freed, or you might not, but one thing is sure. If they take me and Jamie and you tell them who we are, they'll hang us."

Brushing back her hair, he locked his gaze with hers. "We haven't hurt you, neither of us, and I swear that you needn't fear that we will. So do you really want our deaths on yer conscience, lassie? All because of some money that's disputed between yer father and me?"

He was taking a chance by trusting her when he ought to be gagging her. But judging from the troubled look on her face, his words had hit their mark.

"I'm going to sleep now, lass. And you'd be wise to spend the time sleeping yerself instead of inventing more ways to escape me."

He settled back against the seat and closed his eyes, but it was a long time before he could relax enough to drift into sleep. The problem of Jamie now plagued him. It would be just like the lad to do something foolish on account of the lady—it grew rapidly apparent that Jamie had a soft spot for her.

So they couldn't go on like this. Once he'd had enough rest to hold his seat on a horse, there'd be a change of plan.

Because the only man he could trust around Venetia now was himself. Even if being alone with her meant he suffered in hell for the rest of the trip.

Chapter Eleven

Dear Cousin,
  How could I ever "accept" the world you describe? The best I can do is teach my girls to navigate it well, while making sure they surround themselves with people less cynical than you.

                                        Your relation,
                                        Charlotte

A rumbling noise rather like distant thunder teased Venetia awake. She snuggled deeper into her bed, then realized that her bed was living flesh and it was speaking to someone in low, muted tones.

She jerked her eyes open to find herself wrapped in Lachlan's arms, with her head comfortably tucked beneath his chin and her cheek pressed to his shoulder. Her bottom lay nestled between his splayed legs, and her bound hands rested on his thigh.

She yanked them up with a blush.

"It's all right, lass," Lachlan murmured. "I've got no feeling left in my legs anyway."

Twisting her head back to gaze at him, she said tartly, "That's what you get for tying me up."

"No, that's what I get for letting you crawl all over me while you slept."

Her cheeks flamed hotter. Shoving against his chest, she scooted onto the seat beside him. "You could have pushed me off your lap if it was a problem," she said, hating that she sounded apologetic.

"It wasn't," he said, though his clipped tone belied his words.

Especially when he flexed his legs and true pain sliced across his features. It was just from having the circulation restored in his limbs, she told herself. It served him right for kidnapping her in the first place— let him suffer.

So why did she have the fleeting urge to take those thick, strong thighs in her hands and massage the muscles until the harsh lines softened on his brow and his eyes slid closed in contentment . . .

Lord, how ridiculous. No lady worth her rank would ever do such a thing. And touching his legs would only lead him to attempt taking more liberties. Which she didn't want. No, indeed.

Strange, though, that he hadn't tried anything while he'd had her neatly trussed. She'd warned him not to, but she didn't flatter herself that he paid her threats any attention. So despite his boorishness and thievery, he must have gentlemanly instincts *somewhere*. Otherwise, he'd have ravished her in the woods when he'd had the chance.

He bent and dragged out the pack he'd kept their food in, then rummaged in it until he withdrew a sheathed knife.

She sat up straight. "Has that been there the whole time?"

"Aye. A pity you missed yer chance to cut out my heart while I slept."

"That would hardly have been practical. Jamie would have shot me if I'd tried." Lord knew the lad hadn't stood firm in the one area she'd asked him to.

"Ah, you're starting to grasp the way of things, I see."

His eyes gleamed at her as he sliced through her bindings with swift efficiency.

As she rubbed her wrists to get the blood moving, he sheathed the knife and shoved it into his pocket. "No point in doing anything foolish. Not that you could have sneaked out the blade without me stirring, but even if you had, you sure as the devil don't have the stomach for murder."

"True. But unlike you, I don't consider that a character flaw."

His gaze grew shadowed. "It's only a flaw when you're fighting for yer life, lass. And I pray to God you never find yerself in *that* position." Then he lifted his face to the open panel to hail Jamie. "How far to Kingussie?"

"A mile at the most, sir. Are you still wanting to stop?"

"Aye, we could use more in our bellies than sandwiches."

"I won't say no to that. But aren't you worried about having to make explanations?"

"It'll be fine. I'll take care of it." When Jamie shrugged, Lachlan added under his breath, "Especially since it can't be helped, laddie."

Lachlan began to tidy the coach. As Venetia watched him fold up blankets and stuff items into the pack, hope sprang to life in her chest. "Does this mean that you intend for us to stay overnight in Kingussie?"

"Would I have needed to spend part of the day sleeping if I had?"

"Well, no, but . . ." Perplexed, she watched as he tied the pack up neatly. "Surely you're as heartily sick of this carriage as I am. I'll do almost anything right now to get out of it for a few hours."

"Now, that's a wish I can grant," he said enigmatically. He dusted off both their hats and handed hers over. "You'll be needing this."

She tied it on, truly confused.

He lifted a shade to stare out the window. "Damn. Looks like rain."

"Poor Jamie."

He slanted a dark glance at her. "Not 'poor Jamie,' princess. Poor us."

Before she could ask what he meant, the coach halted in front of a large wattle-and-daub cottage, scattering chickens in its wake. A milk cow munching grass in the scrubby field nearby looked up, and a burst of barks erupted from an outbuilding. That sent a stout, graying woman exploding from the cottage into the yard, wiping her hands on her apron.

As Jamie jumped down to catch the cottager in a tight embrace, Lachlan leaned over to Venetia. "Look here, lass. Telling the Widow McCain you're being kidnapped won't get you away from me. She won't believe you and won't care about it even if she does. All it'll do is ruin any attempt yer family makes to save yer reputation." He glanced out the window. "And mentioning yer father's name to our hostess would be a very rash mistake."

"Why?" she said acidly. "Because you'd shoot me for it?"

"No." He jerked his head out the window. "But *she's* liable to."

Venetia blinked at him.

"You see, Princess Machiavelli, the only person who hates yer father more than me is the Widow McCain. If you're wise, you'll let me do the talking."

She crossed her arms over her chest. "And how will you explain my being here with you and Jamie?"

"Don't need to. We won't be here long, and Annie knows better than to pry. I'll tell her it's none of her concern."

"But then she'll think that I'm your—"

The word "mistress" was drowned out by the widow exclaiming, "Who is it you have with you, Jamie?" The woman released him to turn her attention to the carriage.

Setting his shoulders as if bracing for a fight, Lachlan climbed out.

The minute the Widow McCain saw him, she froze, the color draining from her features. She looked him up and down, then whispered, "Lachlan Ross, as I live and breathe . . . But you're supposed to be . . . I thought that you were—"

"Dead?" He cast her a rueful smile. "You can't always believe what you read in the papers, Annie." Cocking up his eyebrows in a hopeful expression, he walked haltingly toward her and held out his arms for a hug.

But she was having none of that. She snatched his wide-brimmed hat right off his head, then began to beat him about the head and shoulders with it. "How dare ye let me think you were dead, you big reckless lout!"

"Annie, stop that, will you?" he cried as he dodged her blows. "It's not as if I planned it, you know. Come on, now, that's my best beaver hat ye're mutilating!"

"Mutilating! I'll show you mutilating, you thickheaded clod!" She threw the hat at him, then began looking about the yard. "Where's my broom? Or better yet, my fowling-piece . . . then you'll wish you'd *stayed* dead!"

"Be still, damn you!" Lachlan ordered as he caught

her about the waist from behind. "You know I would've told you if I could. And my life depends on yer keeping it secret, ye ken?" He waited until she'd stopped struggling, then murmured a few words in Gaelic that softened her frown.

At that moment, Venetia would have given anything to understand Gaelic.

"Ye're lucky I don't set the dogs on ye," the woman grumbled.

"I know, I know," he said, his voice gentler than Venetia had ever heard it. "Can I let ye go now?"

The widow nodded, but when he released her, she whirled on him and slapped him hard enough that Venetia heard it in the carriage. "I cried for a week when I heard that you died," she choked out, and as if to illustrate that very claim, tears leaked from her eyes. "Not that I mind learning that it was a sham, but it was cruel of you to let yer friends keep thinking you were dead. Right cruel."

To Venetia's surprise, remorse flooded Lachlan's face before he enfolded Annie in his arms. "Aww, don't cry. I'm here now. That's all that matters."

As Lachlan comforted her, Jamie came over to help Venetia climb down from the carriage. "The widow was Lachlan's nanny when he was a lad," Jamie explained, "and she's looked after him in one fashion or another ever since. Sort of a second mother to him, she is."

Venetia's heart sank. That explained why Lachlan was sure the woman wouldn't listen to her pleas for help. "Lachlan said she doesn't like my father."

"Aye, she was married to your father's—"

"What are you blathering about, Jamie?" Annie pushed away from Lachlan, blotting her eyes with her apron. "Lud, I don't know what came over—" She broke off when she caught sight of Venetia. "And who is this you've brought with you?"

It was rather amusing to see Lachlan at a loss. "Well, Annie, I . . . um . . . you see . . ."

Venetia snorted. So much for his telling his beloved old nanny that the matter was "none of her concern." The man could be such a dolt when it came to women. "Yes, do explain," Venetia told him blithely. "We're all waiting to hear."

"It's complicated," Lachlan bit out, sparing a glare for Venetia. "She's traveling with us, and that's the end of it."

That was more like the overbearing Lachlan she knew.

But apparently that worked no better on Annie. "She's your fancy woman, is she?" Annie's face clouded as she looked Venetia over, taking in her rumpled skirts and shamelessly unbound hair. "I suppose you thought I'd just look t'other way since ye've been raised up from the dead and all?"

That put Venetia's back up. "I beg your pardon. I am *not* his fancy woman."

Annie's eyes narrowed. "Well, aren't we the la-di-da sort of mistress? Ye think because you're English ye're too good for the likes of a clean and decent—"

"First of all, I'm Scottish. Secondly, I'm not his mistress." Without stopping to think, she spoke the only lie that would make sense. "I'm his wife."

Chapter Twelve

Dear Charlotte,
You, of all people, should recognize that cynicism is necessary. Otherwise, your young ladies would head into each season like lambs to the slaughter . . . much as you yourself did all those years ago.
Your decidedly cynical friend,
Michael

*H*oly Christ," Lachlan muttered under his breath. Now he was done for. As Annie gaped at the lass, that scamp Jamie was trying not to laugh.

What had possessed Venetia to say something like that? A wife was permanent, someone he couldn't explain away once this was over, and she knew it.

The light dawned. That was the point, wasn't it? Princess Machiavelli had found a new way to make trouble for him, devil take her.

She offered her hand to the astonished Annie. "Good afternoon, madam. I'm Lady Ross. And I'm delighted to meet any friend of my husband's."

Poor Annie hesitated, then took her hand, her entire manner changing. "Pleasure to meet you, my lady." She made a quick curtsy. "Forgive me for misunderstanding."

"Not at all," Venetia said. "We've had quite a long stint in the coach, and I'm sure I look a fright." She shot Lachlan a triumphant smile. "Besides, my husband should have introduced me properly from the first."

"Indeed he should have." Annie glared at him,

apparently happy to blame him after he'd hid the truth from her. "So this is what you were doing while the rest of us were worrying about you, is it? You were going off to find you a bride?"

Venetia didn't even bother to hide her smirk. Lachlan gritted his teeth. If he called Venetia a liar, then he'd have to explain why she would lie. And despite what he'd said, he wasn't at all sure Annie would approve of his actions.

The lass had left him no choice, had she?

With a sigh, he slid an arm about Venetia's waist. "It wasn't planned, Annie." *That* was certainly an understatement. "We met in London and . . . er . . . decided to marry, despite her family's wishes. That's why we were forced to elope. It was all very sudden."

"Yes, very sudden," Venetia chirped. "And now—"

"And now," he broke in, tightening his arm on her waist, "we're hurrying to the north, which is why we can't stay. I want my wife to meet my mother before the news gets out. I don't want Mother hearing of it from anyone but me."

He was just congratulating himself on finding a way to keep Venetia's little lie from moving beyond Annie when Venetia slumped against him with an exaggerated sigh.

"The man hasn't given me a moment to breathe since we left," she said plaintively. "I do hope you'll convince him to let us rest here a bit."

Mo chreach, so *that* was her plan: wangle an invitation so she could manage an escape. Well, not bloody likely. "We're not staying."

Turning her pretty face up to his, Venetia cast him a sugary smile. "Oh, but my darling, I don't know how much longer I can endure that carriage."

He snorted. She was putting on quite the show for Annie, wasn't she? "Surely, *princess*," he said in a warning tone, "you don't want to wound my mother's feelings by letting her hear of the marriage before we arrive."

Apparently the tone of voice that cowed his men didn't work on Venetia. Her mouth drooped pitifully. "So your mother's feelings matter more than your wife's?" she said, sounding exactly like the pouting miss he'd expected her to be.

Except that she wasn't.

But Annie didn't know it. "I'm sure he doesn't mean that." The widow took Venetia's arm to draw her away from him. "Pay him no mind, my dear. Men sometimes don't think."

"Annie . . ." Lachlan growled.

"Can't you see that the poor woman is all done in?" Annie said. "Ye can't be racing her across the country like one of yer horses."

"Yes, *darling*, I'm not one of your horses," Venetia cooed, throwing him a gleeful glance as she let the tenderhearted Annie lead her toward the house.

He stepped forward after them, and pain shot through his bad leg. Devil take the scheming wench! Bad enough that his leg plagued him something awful from having her resting on it for hours. Now she had to try this. Oh, he'd make her regret it when he got her alone. Just see if he didn't.

"Besides, Lachlan," Annie was saying, "yer mother isn't the sort to have her feelings hurt. She'll be so delighted you found a wife that she'll pay no mind to how she heard of it. She's despaired of yer getting married ever since that silly twit Polly threw ye over."

Venetia shot him a curious glance. "Polly? He never told me of any Polly."

"She was a merchant's daughter in Dingwall," Annie explained. "They started courting after he returned from the war, but—"

"We didn't suit," Lachlan snapped. When Annie started to usher Venetia across the threshold, he caught the widow by the arm. "Now see here, my wife and I won't be staying."

"Don't be ridiculous." Annie snatched her arm free to push Venetia inside. "The lady needs a good night's rest before you go on."

Grinding his teeth, Lachlan followed them into Annie's elegant little hall with its neat staircase and its costly Turkish rug. Unsurprisingly, Venetia gaped at it. He could well imagine what she'd expected after seeing the chickens in the yard.

"We just want a hot meal and a couple of horses," he said tersely as he and Jamie crowded into the foyer.

"You mean, a *change* of horses, right?" Jamie put in.

"No." Lachlan cast Jamie a warning glance. "Horses for my wife and me. We're riding the rest of the way alone." How else could he get rid of Jamie?

"The hell you are!" Jamie cried. Clearly Lachlan had made his decision not a moment too soon. "You can't drag the poor lass over the mountains like that!"

"Of course he can't," Annie said with a stubborn lift of her chin. "Don't be daft, Lachlan." She pointed through the open door to where raindrops had begun splattering the chickens. "You can't take her out in this weather. You'll stay here the night, and then the three of you can go on in the coach in the morning."

"Jamie and the coach are needed elsewhere, for the

shipment in Aberdeen," Lachlan said, having already anticipated Jamie's protests.

Jamie blinked. "That doesn't arrive until next week!"

"And I want you there in case it comes in early. We need the barley, and my wife and I can manage without you." Might as well use the lass's lie to his advantage. "It *is* our honeymoon—surely you won't mind giving us some privacy."

He shot Venetia a gloating look, exulting in her clear panic at being alone with him. It served her right for concocting a story sure to complicate his life.

Then her eyes narrowed. "Don't worry, Jamie." She edged closer to Annie, her new ally. "I'll be fine."

Before Lachlan could set her straight, the rain pelted down with a vengeance, forcing them to close the door.

"You're not going out into that weather, any of you," Annie announced. "You'll have dinner here. Jamie will sleep in the barn and leave at first light."

"Jamie will have dinner and go on tonight," Lachlan countered. "And right now he'll go see to the horses. Won't you, Jamie?"

The young man glared daggers at him, but mumbled an "Aye, sir" before heading out into the rain.

With a disapproving cluck of her tongue, Annie bustled Lachlan and Venetia through the hall and into a parlor where she lit candles to banish the gloom. "You can wait in here while I find my maid-of-all-work to make us some tea. Then we'll see what we have to feed you. I know you'll want to be to bed early—"

"Damn it, Annie, we're not staying the night!" Lachlan snapped.

"Don't be using that language around your lady wife, you big lout." Annie made a fuss over settling Venetia into a comfortable armchair by the fire in her tiny parlor. "I taught you better than that."

"You're not listening to me, devil take you!"

"In the morning, you can rent a gig and horses from the inn in Kingussie. That'll give you some protection from the weather."

"Annie, I swear to God I am not—"

"You're outnumbered, laddie, admit it." She faced him down, every inch the nanny. "You're staying here tonight, and that's the end of it. Because if you don't, I'll send a letter by express to tell your mother of yer new wife. I'm sure it'll get there before you. And you don't want that, do ye?"

He swore under his breath. Mother wasn't supposed to know about Venetia. He'd already planned to stash the lass at the deserted crofter's cottage in the hills that he'd used as the Scourge. If Annie told his mother about her, Mother would throw herself into his battle with Duncannon, and he couldn't have that.

He glanced from Annie to Venetia. "The two of you are determined to force my hand, are ye?" He stared at Venetia, who looked right pleased with herself. "Very well, we'll stay."

A triumphant expression passed over her face, but he didn't allow her to enjoy it. So she wanted to play his wife, did she? Wreak havoc in his life?

Fine, then play his wife she would. He turned to Annie. "Do you still have that extra bedchamber upstairs?"

"I do indeed."

Lachlan shot Venetia a mirthless smile. "As I recall, the bed's not very big."

He watched her gloating shift to alarm. She hadn't thought that far, had she? This wasn't England or the loftier home of a Scottish noble, where a lady could expect a room separate from her husband. This was the Highlands, where a man and his wife lay together in perfect matrimonial harmony.

" 'Tis big enough for two people newly wed," Annie said with a wink.

Venetia's eyes were huge now, and he was having a damned fine time watching her recognize her mistake.

"Oh, I'm sure you're right." He taunted the lass with a smile. "I'm sure my wife and I can make do."

Venetia leaped up to head for the door. "You know, Mrs. McCain, Lachlan is right. We probably should go on."

"Don't be ridiculous," Annie said. "It's pouring outside. And you mustn't let the man bully you. Sometimes a woman has to stand strong against the big oafs."

Lachlan barely restrained a laugh. Stand strong, eh? Little did Annie know.

"Now, you stay here with yer husband while I fetch you the tea. I'll be only a minute." Annie walked out, leaving Venetia to Lachlan's not-so-tender mercies.

"Might as well sit down and make yerself comfortable, princess," Lachlan said acidly. "You've won this round."

"Lachlan, we cannot share a room tonight—"

"Oh yes we can." He approached her slowly, favoring his right leg. "But dinna fash yerself, lassie—after sleeping half the day away, I won't need much sleep." He flashed her a rakish grin.

She groaned, then headed for the door. "I'll tell her that I'm not your wife and we're not staying—"

Lachlan blocked her way. "Ye'll do no such thing. You made our bed, and now you'll lie in it. Besides, the night's rest will do us both some good, and renting the gig is a fine idea. Surely you can pretend to like me for one evening."

As long as I can pretend not to desire you for one night.

"But try to take my advice for once," he went on. "Let me do the talking. We don't want Annie knowing you're Duncannon's daughter, or she might take a broom to *you.*"

"Very well." She twisted to face him. "But why are you sending Jamie away?"

He hesitated, then opted for honesty. "Because he likes you too much." He searched her face, then cocked one eyebrow. "And because you know it. I can't have you using his liking of you to manage an escape."

"Don't be absurd," she said bitterly. "The man may have a soft spot for me, but he's every bit as loyal to you as you said. He'd never help me thwart you."

"You'd be surprised what a man might do for a woman he fancies, princess."

The minute the words left his mouth, he regretted them, for her eyes turned the wild green of the lochs and he suddenly became painfully aware of how near she was, how pretty . . . how irresistible. His head lowered of its own accord as his gaze fixed on that sweet, sensuous mouth of hers—

The door shot open, and Annie trotted in. As they sprang apart, the widow halted, then let out a short bark of laughter.

"None of that now, you two." She waggled her eyebrows suggestively. "Plenty of time for that later."

That was exactly what he was afraid of. Holy Christ, it was going to be a long night.

He wasn't sure who he wanted to throttle more—Annie, for being her motherly self, or Venetia, for being so damned alluring that he had to tuck his tongue between his teeth just to keep from panting after her like a randy hound.

Following them to the kitchen, he ignored the throbbing pain in his leg. He ought to be glad of a night's respite, but in truth he'd prefer the torture of travel to being alone in the dark with Venetia. If he made it through *that,* it would be a miracle.

Thank God Annie was eager to hear the gossip from Ross-shire or he would never even have survived tea. As Jamie joined them and Annie prepared a large dinner of bridies, cold ham, herrings in oatmeal, and cock-a-leekie soup, he was able to control the conversation by feeding her tidbits about the Ross clan. It kept the nosy female from finding out that she had Duncannon's child in her kitchen.

Now he only had to refrain from calling Venetia by her Christian name. He couldn't take the chance that Annie might remember it.

But he was glad they'd stayed. Sitting in the soft lantern light of Annie's kitchen made him realize how bone-weary he was. And how hungry. He devoured everything she put in front of him, and so did Venetia, although she still kept up her laughably prim table manners.

After they'd eaten their fill, Annie held out a platter. "Will you have the last bridie, Lachlan?"

"You trying to fatten me up?" he teased as he took it. "Because you're going about it right, to be sure."

With a frown, Annie brought the platter to the sink. "I wish I could. You're not looking so well, lad." When Venetia seemed startled by that comment, Annie told her, as if in confidence, "He hasn't completely wasted away, mind you—he's still got the shoulders and that brawny build—but he looks thinner and a good deal paler. He never had that stiffness in his limbs before, neither."

"The war was hard on him, no doubt," Venetia said.

"The war!" Annie snorted. "T'ain't the war that's done that, my lady. I saw him less than a year ago, and he was hale and hearty—"

"Jamie, me boy, why are you dawdling around here?" Lachlan broke in. "Ye've got to head out while the rain has let up."

"Aye, sir." Jamie rose from the table with a nod of understanding. "Will ye pack me up some food for later, Annie?"

With a quick glance at Lachlan, Annie reluctantly shifted her attention to Jamie. "I'll pack ye anything ye want, lad."

The young man rubbed his belly. "Well then, I could use some of yer fine oatcakes. Never could get enough of them."

"I can see that," Annie retorted, with a pointed look at the plate he'd wiped clean with one. "Don't you worry—I've got plenty more. You go fetch the laird's bags from the coach, and I'll make up a basket."

Jamie left as she bustled about the kitchen. When he returned with just Lachlan's knapsack, she stared oddly at him. "Where's the rest?"

"That's all," Lachlan put in. "My wife and I eloped, remember? No time for her to pack, and I wasn't expecting to stop anywhere before we got home."

Annie looked outraged as she handed Jamie a basket of food. "So you've forced the poor woman to wear the same gown for days? That's downright cruel, especially for a fine lady like her."

"You have no idea," Venetia muttered under her breath.

"Well, there's nothing for it but to wash her clothes tonight and dry them for the morrow." Annie went to the door and called for Sally, then hurried to the back kitchen door and dragged in a large pot full of rainwater. "Meantime, I think Sally probably has a shift the lass can wear tonight."

Venetia blushed a thousand shades of red as she jumped to her feet. "Really, you mustn't go to any bother—"

"No bother, dearie," she said with a wave of her hand. After hanging the pot on the massive hook above the roaring fire, she headed back to the door leading into the hall. "Sally! Sally? Oh, where has that girl got off to?"

"Shall I fetch her?" Venetia put in.

Lachlan snorted at that blatant attempt to get out of the room and away from her captors. "Sit down, lass. She'll be along soon enough."

Venetia took her chair, avoiding his eyes. As if he didn't already know what she was thinking—that she'd rather be wandering fully dressed through Scotland than trapped in a room with him for the night, half naked.

Not that he could blame her—the thought of sharing a room with her wearing only a shift was sending his blood into a stampede.

"What about you, Jamie?" Annie asked. "Have you fresh clothing?"

"He'll be fine," Lachlan cut in. Thankfully Jamie hadn't heard the part about Lachlan and Venetia sharing a room, but if the boy didn't leave soon, he'd figure it out, and then Lachlan would never be rid of him. "You'd best be going, lad."

"Aye." Jamie cast Venetia a helpless glance. "I'll see you both at Rosscraig soon. And if you need anything before I leave, milady—"

"She doesn't," Lachlan bit out. "Now go on with you." *Before the lass has you down on one knee, begging to be her knight-errant and save her from meself.*

Which might just prove necessary if Annie kept trying to undress them both.

Within moments Annie had the boy out the door and off, then returned to the table. Just when Lachlan was congratulating himself on having dodged a bullet by sending Jamie off successfully, she sat down across from him with a frown. "You'll need fresh clothing as well, lad."

"I don't need anything."

"My late husband was about the size you've become." She crossed her arms over her chest. "Which reminds me, you still haven't told me why you look so ill."

He groaned. He should have known Annie wouldn't let it go.

"I think I can guess why. It's because of that fight you had with the Scourge, ain't it?" With a cluck of her tongue, she eyed him balefully. "You shouldn't have tangled with him. They always said he was a right fierce fellow."

Lachlan bit back a smile. "Well, I survived the encounter and he didn't, so who turned out to be fiercest in the end?"

She shook her head. "Fierce or no, it was foolish. And what possessed you to go against Duncannon's enemy, anyway? You of all people, who hates the earl as much as me. You should have let the Scourge alone. He wasn't hurting nobody."

"What?" Venetia cried, ignoring Lachlan when he

kicked her beneath the table. "The man preyed on innocent travelers! How is that not hurting anyone?"

"Those weren't innocent travelers," Annie countered. "They were Duncannon's friends, and probably every one just like him, turning their land over to sheep and forcing their crofters out."

Venetia blinked. "What do you mean? How could they force the crofters out? Don't the tenants have leases?"

"Aye, but they're yearly. Once the time was up, Duncannon kicked them out of their homes so he could use their land for sheep pasture."

Lachlan silently watched to see how Venetia would react. He'd assumed that she knew of her father's tactics, but perhaps that was a hasty assumption, like all the others he'd made about her.

She looked downright ill. "But in London, they talk of how sheep will save the Highlands. How the improvements on the land will—"

"Improvements!" Annie snorted. "That's a fancy word for eviction, my lady." She turned to Lachlan. "Have ye not explained to her what's going on up here in the north? How the lairds can make twice the money with sheep, so they don't need their crofters? How land that used to support twenty people now supports a hundred sheep and one shepherd? How people are fleeing the Highlands for America by the shipload?"

"I think you're explaining it pretty well," Lachlan said softly.

Venetia glanced from him to Annie, her face pale as ash. "I—I didn't know. They never said what happened to the crofters. I just assumed—"

"That they found work elsewhere?" Annie set her lips in a thin line. "Aye, they did. In America, in Canada. It was either leave or starve. My husband and I were lucky to stay in Scotland after he was turned off by the earl." She leaned back in her chair with a sour frown. "But I still say it's what killed him—not having work, and not wanting to emigrate."

"Annie's husband was the earl's factor," Lachlan explained. "They lived near Braidmuir for some years, until her husband spoke out against the sheep farming and how it was displacing the crofters. That's when the earl had his steward dismiss him and hire that devil McKinley instead."

"That's horrible," Venetia whispered.

Did she mean it? Or was she just trying to soften him up again by seeming to sympathize with his friends?

"My poor love tried his hand at this and that," Annie said, "but nothing much suited him. Got drunk one night, fell off his horse, and broke his neck, he did." She shook her head dolefully. "If I hadn't had an uncle to leave me this lovely house and a wee bit of money, I'd be in America right now meself. Ain't no place for a woman like me in the Highlands anymore."

"Don't be daft, love," Lachlan said, reaching over to pat her hand. "There's always a place for you in the Highlands. I'll make sure of that."

"Oh, go on with you," she said, but her eyes were misting. She wiped them with a scowl. "Now see what ye've gone and done, letting me blather on about the evictions? It only makes me angry, and there's naught to be done about it."

Annie rose and went to check on the pot of water, then called up to her maid-of-all-work. "I've got the water boiling, Sally! Time to start hauling it upstairs for our guests' baths."

Holy Christ, he'd assumed she was boiling water for washing.

When Venetia shot him a panicked look, he groaned. Just the thought of a naked Venetia, water sluicing over her fine limbs, her breasts pink and flushed from the steam . . .

He swore under his breath and rose. "Don't trouble yerself with drawing us a bath, Annie," he said, though he would dearly love to rid himself of the stink of the road.

"It's no trouble, is it, Sally?" she said to the maid as the girl came in.

"Oh, no, ma'am, no." Sally grinned, exposing one missing tooth. "Already hauled the tub into the guest room and put out the towels and soap. And I found some fresh lavender and rosemary in the garden to sprinkle in it, too." She cast Venetia a shy glance. "For the lady."

Lachlan clenched his fists. Wonderful. Venetia would not only be naked and clean, but sweet-smelling, too. As if he didn't already have enough trouble keeping his hands off her.

"You don't mind sharing the water, do you?" Annie asked as she poured it into two buckets for Sally, who headed up the stairs with them.

Venetia had risen, too, and was looking to him for help in getting out of the awkward situation.

"No, of course not," he said. "But . . . er . . . I'll head into town and arrange for the gig, so my wife can have a nice long soak. I'll bathe when I return. Cold water's good enough for me." Right now cold water was *exactly* what he needed.

"Yes, that's an excellent idea," Venetia chimed in cheerily.

Too cheerily. *Mo chreach,* what was he thinking? He couldn't leave her alone here. She'd steal a horse and head off to London before he was half a mile away. He was already forgetting she was his captive, not his wife.

"I'll go to town and take care of arranging for the gig," Annie said, thankfully. "Ye're both tired and in need of a hot bath and a good sleep."

Sally popped into the kitchen and Annie added, "Why don't you take Lady Ross upstairs and help her undress while Lachlan and I bring in more water to put on for the washing?"

"Yes'm," Sally said, and headed for the door with Venetia following after.

Only after they were gone did Lachlan realize his error. He'd let Venetia go off alone with Sally.

Cursing under his breath, he strode for the stairs. "I've got to ask my wife something," he muttered. "I'll be back to help you with the water in a bit, Annie."

But first he had to make sure his "wife" didn't bring yet another new ally over to her cause.

Chapter Thirteen

❦

Dear Cousin,

*Teaching ladies to be wise isn't the same as
teaching them to be cynical. Is it cynical to make
sure that a man isn't just out for what he can get
from a woman? I think not. Only if I taught my
heiresses not to trust any man could you call me
cynical. But in the times we live in, a woman must
learn to protect herself from scoundrels.*

Your perturbed relation,
Charlotte

*V*enetia surveyed the guest room as Sally ushered her
in. Tucked beneath the eaves, it was dark and not overly
large, with a tiny coal grate set into the wall. Aside from
the tin tub dominating the room, the other furnishings
were a washstand, a sturdy walnut chair, and a beech
bedstead scarcely large enough for one person, much
less two.

Worse yet, the bedchamber had only one small
casement window. Even if she could squeeze through it,
she'd never survive the fall to the ground. That left her
only one alternative—enlisting the maid's help. Because
Venetia was *not* spending the night with Lachlan in that
skinny bed.

'Tis big enough for two people newly wed.

She groaned. Even if Lachlan proved more a gentleman
than she'd initially thought, she dared not lower her

guard. Any man who hated her father so much would never marry her. She'd end up ruined and unwed, and her life would be over.

No, she mustn't spend the night alone with him here. She'd take her chances with wildcats on the road back to Edinburgh before she'd do that.

"How well do you know the laird?" Venetia asked. If Sally shared Annie's fondness for Lachlan, she wouldn't be much help.

Sally blinked at the unexpected question. "This is the first I've met him, my lady. But I must say he's a fine-looking gentleman, fine-looking indeed."

"That fine-looking gentleman is not who he seems. Yesterday—"

"—we traveled so hard and fast that we barely had time to think, much less bathe," Lachlan finished as he swung open the door. His scar stood out in high relief against his ashen brow, but his eyes were as dark and angry as the wind-sculpted rocks near Braidmuir. "So we vastly appreciate your going to so much trouble for us, Sally."

Venetia's stomach roiled. Leave it to Lachlan to guess what she would try.

"I didn't mind a bit. The water's nice and hot for you." Sally smiled at Venetia. "If you'll take off your gown, I'll help you with your corset."

Venetia frowned at Lachlan, who cast her a thinly veiled smile that told her she had no chance of getting him out of the room now. But at least he had the decency to turn his back and head for the window so she could undress.

Hastily Venetia undid her gown, wondering if he

meant to stay in the room the entire night. She'd go dirty rather than sit naked in a tub with him present. Yet she dearly wanted to bathe. Just the sight of the steaming water made her skin tingle with anticipation.

"Is there a key to this room, Sally?" Lachlan asked from where he stood at the window, holding the dimity curtain aside to gaze out.

"Yes, sir." Sally cast Venetia a puzzled glance as she took Venetia's gown.

"My wife has a tendency to walk in her sleep." The blithe lie rolled off Lachlan's tongue with ease. "So if you'd fetch the key, I'd be most grateful. I can't have her falling down the stairs in the dark, can I?"

Curse the man. He thought of everything.

"No, sir, of course not."

When Sally hesitated, glancing at Venetia, Lachlan faced her, his jaw set. "Thanks, lass. And bring whatever nightclothes you can find for my wife. I can take care of her corset."

Bobbing her head, Sally slipped out. In two strides, Lachlan was behind Venetia.

"Lachlan—"

"Quiet!" He began to undo her laces with a swift efficiency that gave her pause. Clearly the man had performed this service for other women, curse him.

"Here's what we'll do," he went on. "When Sally returns with the key, I'll make an excuse for sending her off. Then I'll step outside, you can hand me the rest of yer clothes, and I'll take them down to Annie so you can have yer bath."

She twisted her head to look up at him. "Alone?"

"Alone." He met her gaze coolly. "Though I'll be locking the door, ye ken?"

"Fine." She stifled her disappointment. At least she'd get a private bath.

Her corset fell away, and he caught it, then held it out to her. But as she took one end of the padded fabric, he held the other end fast. "You have to promise, though, that you won't try to escape through the casement. Even if you get through, there's nothing below to cushion yer fall, so you'll break yer damned neck."

"I already determined that for myself, thank you very much."

He arched one eyebrow. "Good. At least you've got *some* sense."

Sense, but not much clothing at the moment. Fortunately, he kept his gaze fixed on her face. That bit of gentlemanly consideration gave her hope. Perhaps sharing a room with him tonight wouldn't be too awful, after all.

"I'll give you an hour to bathe while I help Annie," he went on. "That shouldn't rouse her suspicions." He released her corset. "But when I return, I'll expect you to be out of the tub and dressed, do ye ken?"

Clutching the corset to her chest, she nodded quickly.

"Then you can turn yer face to the wall while I undress and bathe."

Dear Lord, he meant to bathe, too? What a tempting image *that* conjured up, of him sliding naked into the steaming tub, slicking soap over his taut muscles.

"If you don't mind, that is," he said.

He was eyeing her peculiarly now, and she realized she'd been running her gaze over his body with shameful thoroughness.

"No ... I don't ... that is, if you want to bathe ..."

At his knowing expression, she forced herself to stop babbling. "I was just wondering . . ." How to ask this? "We're not really going to share the bed, are we?"

The minute his eyes deepened to that luscious chocolate brown, she knew she shouldn't have asked. "I ought to *make* you share it with me, princess, since ye're so eager to be my wife." The soft burr of his brogue resonated in the pit of her belly, especially when he added, "Might as well carry the pretense to its logical end, wouldn't you say?"

She swallowed, wishing that the very idea didn't send a thrill chasing along her every nerve. "You know perfectly well that I didn't mean—"

"Dinna fash yerself, lassie," he bit out. "I'm not fool enough to put myself within two feet of you when ye're dressed like that. I'll sleep on the floor."

"That's fine, then," she said, relieved. Or so she tried to convince herself. "Thank you."

"Don't be thanking me yet," he grumbled. "The night is young, and I still mean to make you pay for upsetting all my plans."

Realizing he was just blustering to save his pride, she teased, "And how will you do that, pray tell?"

"Mayhap I'll take a page from yer book and sing you to sleep." He shot her a glance of mock menace. "That'll show ye, won't it?"

"I wouldn't mind hearing you sing," she admitted.

That seemed to unsettle him, for he turned his gaze away with a frown. "You say that now, but when my voice sets the dogs to howling, you won't be so eager."

Just then Sally returned with a fresh chemise and the key to the room. True to his word, Lachlan sent her off on some errand, then went to stand outside while

Venetia finished undressing and handed her clothing out to him, wrapping the dimity coverlet about her for modesty. Only after he'd locked her in and headed downstairs did she abandon the coverlet to climb into the tub.

She sank into the water with a sigh of pure pleasure. A bath was lovely enough, but to be left alone to enjoy it was bliss. It seemed like ages since she hadn't had Lachlan or Jamie looking over her shoulder every minute.

She scrubbed her hair and her body with the soap, the familiar scent of lavender and lye bringing tears to her eyes. How long before she saw home again? Would she ever? Somehow she couldn't see Lachlan handing her over to Papa without getting what he wanted in return. And she couldn't see Papa giving it to him.

This entire thing couldn't end well.

As soon as she bathed to her satisfaction, she dried off and donned Sally's chemise, which was rather snug in the bosom. Then she climbed into the bed, pulled the cover up to her chin, squeezed her eyes shut, and turned her face to the wall. If she could fall asleep before Lachlan returned, there'd be no talk between them, and perhaps he wouldn't be tempted to do anything.

Oh, what was she thinking? *He* wasn't the one she should worry about. Despite his grousing, he'd been a perfect gentleman in nearly every instance.

Meanwhile, *she* was softening toward him to a dangerous degree. She'd always prided herself on her ability to see past a man's handsome face to the character that lay beneath. Flattery had never swayed her, for she could spot insincerity even beneath the smoothest compliment.

Yet when Lachlan spoke of wanting her, she turned

into a puddle of pudding. She sighed. Why was that? Why did she keep forgetting this was just about him and Papa, and she was only a tool for Lachlan to get what he wanted?

Perhaps it was because he'd been forthright about his aims after he'd kidnapped her. He'd stated his case baldly and let her determine the truth for herself. Even the sad tale of the Highlands at dinner had been brought up by the widow, not him. He hadn't attempted to use it to gain her sympathy.

And what a shock to discover that Lachlan wasn't the only person who hated Papa. All that talk about sheep and forcing out the crofters ... could it be true? She'd heard her father's Scottish friends expound upon how they'd improved their land with sheep farming, but she'd never considered where that left the tenants who'd tilled it. Somehow she'd thought both were living together in harmony.

But now snippets of things she'd heard in London came back to her. One of Mrs. Harris's good friends was a newspaperman named Charles Godwin, who'd often written about "injustice in the Highlands." Venetia had paid his essays no mind, since everyone said he was a wild-eyed radical. Now she had to wonder. And there'd been one lord who'd complained of trouble with his crofters.

Unfortunately, whenever she'd stumbled upon such conversations, she never got to hear the rest, for the gentlemen didn't discuss such matters before ladies. So she'd had trouble piecing together what was really happening.

Lord knew Papa never talked about it, except to rail against his backward countrymen. But since he was always railing against something, she pretty much ignored him. Now she wished she'd paid closer attention.

Punching up her pillow, she tried not to think about tonight's discussion. But Lachlan's words rang in her ears. *Annie's husband spoke out against the sheep farming . . . That's when the earl had his steward dismiss him.*

Surely Papa could never be so unfeeling. He'd always prided himself on treating his employees well. He'd pensioned off their servants and kept others in service as long as they desired to work. It didn't seem like Papa to turn off a factor who'd worked for him for years. Perhaps the steward had acted on his own.

A soft knock sounded at the door. "I'm coming in, lass," Lachlan murmured.

He was back to bathe. Dear Lord.

Pretending to be asleep, she kept her face to the wall as he entered. She heard the telltale snick as he locked the door, then the rustle of clothing as he undressed. Apparently her pretense was convincing, for he said nothing to her.

But the lack of conversation made everything worse. Because as she heard the sounds of splashing, curiosity got the better of her. What would he look like in the bath? Would his shaggy hair curl up at the ends or trail damply down his neck? Would his chest and back prove as broad as they seemed, or was it just the cut and thickness of his clothing that made him seem brawny?

And would it be so terribly awful if she peeked to find out? He was concentrating on bathing; he probably wouldn't even notice. One little look to assuage her curiosity—how could that hurt? Then she could sleep.

Turning onto her stomach, she tilted her head just

enough so she could view the tub. It sat perpendicular to the bed, and his back was to her, fortunately.

Or unfortunately, since it meant she saw very little, just his upper back and shoulders. But what a back and shoulders. Rough-hewn as the rocky crags he'd climbed in his youth, they looked nothing like the smooth alabaster statues in the museum in London. His skin was tanned and sinewy as a laborer's, the surface marred by scars, probably from the war.

He dunked his head in the water, and when he came back up, his hair streamed in brown rivulets down his neck. She was still taken off guard when his large hands grabbed the sides of the tub and he pushed himself to a stand, bringing her eye to eye with his pale-skinned bottom. His very tight and nicely rounded bottom.

So *this* was how a naked man really looked—the muscles bunching in his haunches as he leaned over to snatch up a towel, his strapping shoulders rippling as he dried himself, then turned slightly sideways to reveal . . .

An ugly and jagged scar that stretched from his knee to mid-thigh. She gasped. It was clearly recent, for it still glowed an angry red, as if the water had roused its temper.

"Oh, my word," she whispered.

Lachlan tensed. Too late, she realized she'd said it aloud. Before she could look away, he glanced over, his gaze locking with hers. "What is it, lass?"

She should have muttered some excuse and averted her gaze, but now that she'd seen the thing, she had to know about it. She pointed to his leg. "Who did that to you?"

A muscle flicked in his whiskered jaw. Still standing in the tub, he tied the towel about his waist before pivoting to face her, glowering at her like some Highland warrior in a white kilt. "Who do you think? 'Twas your father's men."

She sucked in a breath. That wasn't the answer she'd expected.

And he knew it, too, for he met her gaze with a belligerence that dared her to refute it. Now she could see smaller pink scars along his ribs and a gash on his arm similar to that on his thigh.

"What did they do to you to make such a horrible wound?" she whispered.

His face looked carved from stone. "After they wrestled my knife away, two of them held me while the third beat me with a cudgel. He broke my thigh so badly that the bone came through the flesh, tearing the muscles and tendons."

Reaching for the chair next to the tub, Lachlan braced his hand on it so he could lift his leg over the lip.

She could see how even that effort cost him, for when he continued speaking, his breath came harder. "Mother was able to set it, but with me pretending to have died of my injuries, we couldn't risk bringing in a physician from town to look at it. So the flesh is taking its sweet time healing."

"I can see." Horror filling her, she rose from the bed. "How many other places did they strike you? What other bones did they break?"

He gave a harsh laugh. "I'm not listing off my weaknesses so you'll know where to hit me the next time you try an escape, princess."

"I would *never*— I couldn't possibly—" But she *had* hit him, hadn't she? Not intentionally, of course, but probably enough to bring him to his knees.

Her heart lurched in her chest. "That's why you didn't tell me, isn't it? So I wouldn't use the knowledge to hurt you." When he conceded the point with a shrug, remorse flooded her. "I'm sorry. I'm so sorry."

"Don't be. I went through worse than this during the war. I didn't suffer overmuch."

"The devil you didn't." She scanned him with an eye trained from years of volunteering at the hospital with her friend Lady Draker. A hard lump caught in her throat at the sight of his scars. "Tell me where else they hurt you. I swear I won't take advantage of what you say."

His gaze flicked over her, as if determining her sincerity, before he released a heavy sigh. "It doesn't matter, lass."

"It matters to me." She glanced around and spotted the key on the floor, where he'd placed it while he bathed. Before he could react, she snatched it up, then clenched it in the fist she held behind her back. "Tell me where else they hurt you, or I'll make you wrestle me to the ground to get this."

He swore vilely.

"Or perhaps," she said, backing away, "I'll just unlock the door and make good my escape. Then you can run after me in your towel—"

"The ribs," he said tersely.

She halted, one eyebrow raised.

"They broke five ribs, two on one side, three on the other."

How many times had she elbowed him in the ribs? Oh, Lord. "And the scar on your forehead," she whispered, "was that from them?"

He sighed. "When we wrestled for the knife, yes."

"You're lucky you didn't lose an eye." Blinking back

tears, she gazed at the puckered scar on his forearm. "I suppose they were the ones to break your arm, too."

"No, that came when I fell from the bridge after they brought the cudgel down on my head." He gave a dark smile. "Fortunately I have a very thick skull. The blow only stunned me long enough to realize I wouldn't survive the next one, so I pretended to be knocked unconscious, and I rolled off the bridge."

She gazed at him in amazement. "How far did you fall?"

"Twenty feet or so. A jutting rock broke my arm, but probably saved me, for it shifted my fall enough so I hit the water instead of the rocks. Fortunately, I had the presence of mind to stay under and let the current carry me until I could grab some rushes with my good arm and drag myself out to hide in the bracken. Since it was near dusk, the men never found me."

A broken arm and leg and ribs . . . a knife wound . . . a blow to the head. It was a miracle he'd survived at all.

Tears stung her eyes. It was yet another thing he'd kept from her that would have garnered him her sympathy if she'd known.

Instead, he'd endured her blows without revealing a thing. How many times had she kicked at him and beat at him while he'd cursed and moaned and groaned? He'd probably been in agony, the poor, suffering man!

But she would make it up to him by easing his pain now. She could do that much, at least.

Chapter Fourteen

Dear Charlotte,
Scoundrels aren't as prevalent as you assume.
Most men are simply looking for someone to listen
to their tales, cast them an admiring glance from
time to time, and hold them through the long,
dreary nights. I suspect most women are looking for
that as well.

Always your servant,
Michael

$\mathcal{L}$achlan was touched by the seeming sympathy in Venetia's face. Then she darted to the door, proving that it had been just a ruse. Holy Christ, she'd taken him off guard with all her questions, and now she meant to escape him!

He dashed after her as fast as he could with wet feet and his bad leg, but she got the door unlocked before he could reach her.

"Sally, Sally!" she called out through the door. "I need you!"

Halting just behind the door, he gaped at her. He could hear the maid rushing down the hall. Sally's room was up here, too, if he remembered correctly.

"Damn it, lass, what are you doing?" Lachlan hissed at the same time as Sally asked her, "What is it, milady?"

"My husband has a war injury that is paining him," she told the maid calmly, "but I lack the proper ointments to help him. Might you have any horse liniment?"

What the devil—

"Aye, miss. I'll fetch it for you at once."

"And a bowl and some clean cloth for bandages, if you please. Oh, and if you have any comfrey root in your garden—"

"The missus has some downstairs. I'll be right back, milady."

After Sally rushed off, Lachlan leaned against the door to shut it, his heart in his throat. It appeared that Venetia's sympathy hadn't been pretend after all. "Horse liniment, lass?" he said softly. "What are you up to?"

"I used to give aid at a hospital with my friend. A physician there swore that the best thing for healing damaged muscle was horse liniment." A sad smile touched her pretty lips. "It does work for horses, doesn't it?"

"I'm not a horse."

She raised an eyebrow. "You might be. A beating like the one you endured would have killed a mere man."

"Like I said before, I'm hard to kill."

Dropping her gaze, she fingered the scar on his forearm, her voice an aching murmur. "I can't believe my father would countenance something like this."

He stiffened. As always, she thought the best of Duncannon. "Sikeston said very plainly that the message was from yer father. That he'd ordered them to beat some sense into me. Into the Scourge—so that I'd stop my thieving."

"Sikeston?" The blood drained from her face.

"That was the name of the man in charge. One of the others called him that."

She turned away from the door, as if in a daze.

"What is it, Venetia?" he demanded.

"Nothing. It's just . . ." Her brow knit up in a worried frown.

"You know something," Lachlan growled.

"I'm not sure."

"Damn it, tell me what you know—"

"I've brought the things you asked for," Sally announced from the door.

Venetia took the items, then dismissed the girl.

As soon as Sally was gone, Lachlan snapped, "What is it that you know about your father's men?"

Her lovely eyes looked darkly anxious. "They're not my father's, I don't think. Not really." Wandering over to the washstand, she set down the bowl she'd got from Sally. "But three men did meet with him a few months ago."

Three men. The ones who'd assaulted *him*?

"Papa wouldn't let me anywhere near them," she went on, "but I gathered that they weren't the sort of men . . . that is . . ."

"They were killers."

"No!" She concentrated on using the bottom of the liniment bottle to crush the comfrey root with fierce, hard strokes. "I don't know. I'd never met or heard of them before, however. I didn't get the idea they were friends of Papa or even people from the estate."

Did she mean the men who'd attacked him or not, damn it?

Avoiding his gaze, she wiped off the bottle. "I asked Papa if they were there because of the Scourge, and he told me it was none of my concern."

"So why do you mention them?" he asked impatiently.

She turned toward him, her expression wrought with pain. "A week after they came was when I read about your supposed death. And——" She hesitated, as if reluctant to reveal something that might implicate her father in any wrongdoing.

"And?" Lachlan prodded.

"Their leader's name was Mr. Sikeston."

Lachlan released a pent-up breath. He'd been sure all along that they'd been sent by Duncannon, but he'd only had his memory to rely on for that belief. "You realize you've now given me proof that yer father ordered the attempt on my life."

Alarm suffused her cheeks. "No, I've only given you proof that my father talked to the men who attacked you."

"Don't be a fool. What other business would Sikeston have with yer father so soon after my attack in Scotland?"

He could see from her face that she knew he was right; knew it and hated it.

"Ye're forgetting that they told me they had come with a message from him. Then they went straight back to him, probably to get paid for killing me."

"If they'd meant to kill you, why bother to give you a message?"

That bit of logical reasoning annoyed him. "They brought a cudgel down on my head, damn it!"

"I know. I know." Anguish shone in her eyes as she headed toward him, the bottle of horse liniment in one hand and a cloth in the other. "It hardly matters what they intended. What they *did* was unconscionable."

"That's not what you said before," he taunted her. "You said I deserved being damned near murdered because I'd been robbing people."

Her cheeks flushed, but she didn't flinch. "I was

wrong. No one deserves such a beating." She dragged the chair over by the window, where the light, though fading, was still strong. "Sit. Let me at least try to make it better."

"Why?" he asked, though the sympathy in her face made it clear enough.

"Because I'm sorry for what they did. What Papa probably asked them to do."

At least she was acknowledging the earl's part. "You've got nothing to be sorry about. You couldn't have stopped it."

"But that doesn't mean——" She let out an exasperated breath. "Consider it a kindness between . . . neighbors, all right?"

Neighbors, not "friends." But could they ever be friends? He wasn't sure. Still, what could it hurt to let her doctor him if she had a mind to it?

He took a seat on the chair, and she glanced down, then turned a healthy shade of red. "Um, you may want to cover yourself a bit better."

He followed her gaze to where his towel gaped open, exposing parts of him better left unexposed to a maiden. He stifled a laugh. "Sorry, lass." He readjusted the towel. "But given yer experience with doctoring, you ought to have a passing knowledge of what a man looks like."

Cheeks aflame, she examined his arm. "At the hospital, they were always careful not to allow women to deal with cases involving naked men."

"Ah," he murmured. "More's the pity for the naked men."

She ignored his comment, turning his arm toward the light so she could see his scar better. "Is the area tender?"

"A bit."

She pressed her thumb against the spot where that bone had also torn his flesh. The never-ending ache exploded into agony, making him grind out a foul curse.

"If that's 'a bit,' " she said dryly, "then I hate to see what you'd consider real pain." She poured liniment on the cloth. "This will burn at first, but it will feel much better later."

"Burn?" he queried. She rubbed the liniment on his arm, and his wound seemed to catch fire. "Holy Christ Almighty! You trying to kill me, are ye?"

He grabbed for her cursed liniment, but she stepped nimbly back. "Stop that!" Standing well out of reach, she doused her cloth with more liniment. "If I'd wanted to kill you, I would have hit you over the head with the bottle." She cast him a chastening glance. "Behave yourself, or I still may."

Bloody heartless wench. But he had to admit that once the flames subsided, they became more like a heat, a soothing heat that took the edge off the ache in his flesh. That was the only thing that kept him from protesting when she ordered him to lift his arms so she could doctor his ribs.

Now he had a different torture to contend with. Bad enough that the most seductive wench this side of the English border was rubbing his bare skin to heal his aching flesh. Must she also be wearing a shift that concealed hardly anything?

When she bent over him, his cock roused unmercifully. Even the sudden fire of the liniment on his ribs didn't dampen his arousal, for her low bodice now gaped open so he could plainly see the fulsome swells of her breasts.

Worse yet, he only had the damned towel to cover himself with, and it rose right up like a camp tent. Oh, and he could camp here forever, he could, drowsy with the scent of liniment and lavender, her hair drifting silklike over his chest.

"I'm afraid this next one is really going to hurt," she murmured. "And I ... um ... will need to lift the towel a bit."

She reached for the towel, and he caught her hand. "Let me do it." He wasn't sure he could trust himself if her hand brushed his erection.

Somehow he managed to wrestle the towel up high enough on his thigh to expose the scar without exposing the rest of him. He should have just told her to leave it be, but already he craved the soothing warmth the liniment had given his other wounds. And his leg *had* been plaguing him something fierce.

Still, the searing pain when she spread the ointment on his worst one made him gasp and clutch at her arm until he caught his breath. That took a few moments. "All right. Do the rest. I'm ready."

With a nod, she continued her ministrations, but her shoulders shook, and next thing he knew, a wet drop landed on his upper thigh. Then another and another. Tears. *Mo chreach*, the lass was shedding tears over him.

"Here now," he said softly, "what are you crying for? It's not so bad as all that, is it?"

"It's awful," she choked out. "What you must have suffered..."

In all this time, he hadn't seen her cry once, not over the kidnapping or his crude remarks or anything. But here she was, crying for the pain he'd suffered. It was too sweet to bear. "Sh, sh, lassie," he murmured, looping his arm about her waist to tug her down onto his good leg so he could comfort her. "I've had worse, trust me."

"I-I know," she choked out, "but I can't b-bear to think of you . . ."

She trailed off into sobs, and he wrapped his arms about her, touched beyond words by her sympathy.

God help him, but the lass surely could cry. As she buried her face in his neck and sobbed, he stroked her back, helpless to know how to ease her tender heart. "It's all right, princess, I swear it is. I've been walking on the leg for weeks, dancing on it even."

The mention of dancing sent her into another bout of sobs. "I-I *made* you d-dance on your b-bad leg—"

"No, you didn't." He held her close, nuzzling her hair. "If you want to blame it on somebody, blame it on yer aunt. She's the one who started talking about my death and got me worried that you'd recognize me."

Venetia gave a little hiccup against his shoulder. "She did, didn't she?"

"Aye." Tipping her chin up, he brushed her tears away with his thumb. "And I wasn't about to have her resurrecting me from the grave before I was ready, you know. Dead men aren't supposed to appear in kilts at fancy balls."

That garnered him a watery smile. "You didn't look a bit dead, either," she managed.

"I certainly didn't feel dead." Taking the cloth from her fingers, he used a dry part of it to wipe her eyes, then let her blow her nose into it before he dropped it on the floor. "Especially not when we were alone."

She was staring at him now, her pretty green eyes huge in her flushed face, and it felt like that night at the ball. Only this time she knew what and who he was. But instead of flailing at him as she ought, she was gazing at him as if seeing him for the first time—not as a villain but as a man caught between the devil and the sea.

"I know it doesn't mean much," she whispered, "but I *am* sorry for every time I kicked you and hit you and crawled over your poor leg while you slept—"

"Don't think on it," he growled, unable to bear another word. Especially the part about her crawling over him. "You didn't know. It wasn't yer fault." And having her look at him like that, perched all fresh and clean on his lap, was already more temptation than he could stand.

He told himself to put her aside, to get her away. He even set his hands on her waist. But then she slid her arms about his neck, and he knew he was in trouble.

"Let me make it up to you," she whispered, the sound turning his resolve to jelly. "Let me show you that I'm not like my father." She stretched up to kiss the scar on his forehead, and something gave way in his soul.

"I know ... you're not like ... yer father," he said hoarsely. "You smell better, for one thing." He'd meant the joke to keep him from doing something daft, but her throaty laugh had the reverse effect.

So did the kisses she scattered across his collarbone. He'd never felt anything so dear. Yet he blundered on, fighting to ignore his rapidly stiffening cock. "You look a damned sight better in a gown than he ever could, too."

"I'm not wearing a gown just now," she pointed out.

The unnecessary reminder made him half lose his

mind. He lost the rest of it when she trailed tender kisses down his chest, her lips lingering to caress his nipple.

"Holy Christ, lass, you have to stop that," he ground out.

She jerked back. "Am I hurting you? Because I didn't mean—"

"Ye're making me take leave of my senses, that's what ye're doing."

Her kittenish smile sent a jolt of heat to his groin. "I told you, I want to make up for hurting you all those times I hit you." She slid her hand up his chest.

He groaned. "And how do you mean to do that—by tempting me into ruining you?"

Her smile faltered, yet she persisted. "Isn't there some way I could give you enjoyment without ruining myself?"

The very words put ideas in his head that bloody well shouldn't be there. He ought to ignore them. So of course he promptly answered, "Aye, there is."

Her face brightened, and he groaned.

"But you can't be doing things like that, you know," he added hastily, trying to reverse his dangerous admission. "It isn't wise. It can only lead to trouble."

"And lying alone together in a room all night when we desire each other *won't* lead to trouble? Show me how to give you enjoyment without ruining myself, and I swear it will end there. It has to."

"*Mo chreach,*" he muttered under his breath. He was done for.

"Is it kissing that you like best?" she murmured, pressing her lips, her luscious lips, against his throat. "Should I kiss you here?" She dusted kisses over his chin.

"Or here?" She delved into the corner of his lips with the tip of her tongue.

That was all it took—a few sinful kisses from her very proper little mouth—and his control snapped. With a growled curse, he caught her head in his hands and kissed her back, thrusting deeply, hungrily inside. Her mouth held a profound warmth he could lose himself in, opening easily beneath his urgent tongue to let him plunder and plunge.

Reveling in how she twined her tongue with his, he skimmed his fingers down her throat to caress the twin pulses that beat and throbbed wildly beneath his thumbs. Then he slid his hands further to the ties of her shift, untying them in one swift jerk before shoving the linen off her shoulders so he could fill his hands with her bountiful bare breasts.

"Wait, Lachlan," she tore her lips from his to murmur, "I'm supposed to be . . . giving *you* pleasure."

"Touching you gives me pleasure," he rasped, thumbing her nipples until she gasped. "Giving you pleasure gives me pleasure."

"But . . . I want . . ."

"Here," he said, seizing her hand and dragging it down to his rearing cock, "if you want to please me, stroke me here."

Her minxish smile as she grabbed hold of his flesh was almost more than he could bear. This could get very dangerous very fast, with his curious little virgin trying out her innocent wiles on him for God knew what reason.

"Stop." He caught her hand to stay it, and she cast him a startled glance. "If we're to do this, lassie, then we must have rules, ye ken?"

"Rules?" she whispered. "Why?"

"Without them we're sure to end up rolling about in that bed over there, and I know you don't want that."

Nor did he. Because nothing would destroy his plans faster than ruining the daughter of the Earl of Duncannon.

Chapter Fifteen

◆⟡◆

Dear Cousin,

*Are you so familiar with what women want
that you can make pronouncements about it? I was
under the impression that you are a bit of a recluse,
that you do not like to go out into society. Or am I
mistaken?*

*Your curious friend,
Charlotte*

Rules are good, the sane part of Venetia argued.
*Remember Mrs. Harris's main rule—if you think you
shouldn't do something, you probably shouldn't.*

Rules were good *if* you could follow them. Clearly,
she'd lost the capacity. Because she was fairly certain she
shouldn't be perched on a man's lap half naked, with her
hand on his privates, contemplating the unthinkable.

And all for an apology that he said she didn't owe
him. He was probably right. It had been his choice to
kidnap her, his choice not to tell her of his injuries, his
choice to put himself in a situation where he got hurt in
the first place.

But those perfectly logical thoughts vanished
whenever she saw his scars and remembered the agony
coursing over his face. Then it was hard to think of him
as anything but incredibly brave for surviving his ordeal.
Surely it wouldn't hurt to reward such bravery with a bit
of pleasure.

All right, so that was just an excuse. The truth was,

the walls of rules she'd erected to keep him at bay were crumbling down around her, and she couldn't shore them up. She'd clung to them for a long time, thinking they would protect her, yet it hadn't stopped her from being kidnapped.

And why? Because Papa had been breaking the rules, not honoring his debts, ruining people's lives even as he pretended to be an honorable man.

Well, Papa could go to blazes. And so could the rules. "I don't think we need rules." She fingered the damp curls at the nape of Lachlan's neck. "I've had enough of them to last me a lifetime."

His troubled gaze burned into her. "You say that now, when the heat is upon you, but in the morning you'll regret throwing them aside. Then you'll hate me."

Knowing he might be right only made it worse. Oh, why couldn't he just kiss her and let her forget who he was and how much he despised her family? Why couldn't he lose himself in her the way she lost herself in him?

Despite his grip staying her other hand, she could feel his flesh swell against her. Clearly he wanted her. What had happened to the wild Lachlan who took what he wanted with reckless abandon?

Why must he behave wisely now, when she just wanted to be reckless? He only balked because of his cursed plans for her father. Well, if it took her all night, she would banish from his mind any thought of what lay between their families. She would banish his soldierly control.

Defiantly, she lifted her mouth to his, tugging at his lower lip with her teeth, then soothing it with her tongue. Though he still kept that iron grip on her wrist, she was rewarded by his heartfelt groan, followed by his mouth opening over hers to deepen the kiss. Soon their tongues were entangled again and their mouths warmly locked, and she felt herself sliding down into that place where it was just the two of them, nothing more.

But when she tried to shrug her hand from his grip, he drew back to stare at her. "One rule, then," he said hoarsely. "Only one. To keep us from going too far."

She cast him an exasperated glance. "What rule is that?"

"You don't leave my knee. As long as you remain there, I can't take yer innocence. But we can still use our mouths and hands to pleasure each other." He leaned her back against his arm so his hot gaze could pour over her naked breasts. "We can still enjoy each other. Like this." Lowering his head, he sucked her breast, tonguing and teasing the nipple until she moaned.

"Lachlan, oh, my word . . ."

"Do you agree to my rule?" he demanded, in between tormenting her breasts with his deft mouth.

Desire pooled low in her loins. She would agree to anything if he would just keep doing what he was doing. "Yes, yes, I swear." She brushed a kiss to his hair. "Now let me . . . touch you, too."

With a growl of satisfaction, he released her wrist, only to close her hand around his thickening shaft. She glanced down to see her fingers partly obscured by rich, dark curls. The sight startled her. "I-I never knew that a man had hair down there."

Squeezing her hand into a stroke along his shaft, he gasped, "Didn't you?"

"How could I?" She brushed his hand away so she could stroke him on her own. "My only experience of naked men comes from statues, and they have smooth, grapelike privates."

"Statues and ballads," he groaned as she fondled him. "Had you no real men in yer life to learn from, lassie? No kissing cousins? No brothers of schoolgirl friends to dally with in the woods?" He tugged on her nipple with his teeth, sending sensations shooting through her.

"None to teach me anything naughty." Or delicious. She blew out a labored breath. "Although there *was* a book . . ."

A choked laugh erupted from him. "Of course there was. To go with the naked statues. What sort of girls' school did you go to, anyway?"

"A fine one," she said haughtily. "Naked statues are art, you know."

"And the book? Was that art, too?"

"Hardly. It was about a harem, but it wasn't terribly detailed about . . . well . . . something like this. So I don't know . . . that is . . ." She caressed him tentatively, hesitantly. "Am I doing it properly?"

"There's nothing proper about what you're doing to me, lassie."

"I mean, am I doing it right? Does it please you?"

"It pleases me something fierce." He arched against her hand. "But if you could hold a bit tighter and squeeze a bit harder . . ."

She did as he said, marveling at the silkiness of his skin and rigidity of the flesh beneath.

After a few of her long pulls, his eyes slid closed and he hissed a breath through his teeth. "For a woman . . . who got her knowledge from statues and ballads . . . you sure know how to . . . arouse a man. Ye'll be the death of me yet."

"That's my plan. To kill you with pleasure so I can escape."

"Good plan," he choked out. "Wish you'd thought of it sooner."

"So do I."

With a dark chuckle, he seized her mouth again, his tongue delving deeply as her hand worked his flesh. But kissing her wasn't enough for him, oh no. Rogue that he was, he soon had her chemise lifted and his hand inside her drawers so he could stroke her between the legs, softly at first and then more firmly.

She liked it. A lot. Far more than she'd have expected. Which only proved he'd been right when he'd accused her of being secretly wicked. Every time he touched her, he seemed to rub off more of the lady's veneer that Mrs. Harris had striven hard to cover her with.

A hysterical giggle bubbled out of her, making Lachlan jerk back with a frown. "And what do you find so amusing, lassie?"

"I was thinking . . . Mrs. Harris should add . . . *this* to her curriculum," she managed to gasp, although what he was doing to her was muddling her mind. "She'd get lots more . . . pupils."

His eyebrow arched high. "Do you like it, then?"

"T-too much . . . yes . . ." she stammered as she tilted her pelvis against his practiced hand.

With a gleam in his heated gaze, he slid a finger inside her.

"Lachlan!" she cried, shocked by the bold maneuver. "You can't do that!"

"Ah, but I can. As long as you stay on my knee, we'll be fine." He plumbed her flesh with a knowing smile. "Better than fine, if I've anything to say about it."

His hand certainly had a lot to say about it. It was devilishly witty, too, fondling her below with a deftness that had her squirming for more.

Suddenly he fingered a particularly sensitive spot, and she practically leaped off his lap. "Lord save me!"

"Too late for that, lassie." He stroked her senseless, making her writhe and wriggle on his knee. "No one's saving you from me now. I mean to see you find your bliss before the night is gone."

"My bliss . . ." She stared up into his heavy-lidded eyes as the word provoked a memory. "So *that's* what it means!"

He blinked, but didn't pause in his caresses. "What?"

"A-a naughty ballad I read. It talks about . . . bliss. I never understood it before . . . it says Darby wants to seize on the lock . . . that lies in Oonagh's moss of curls between two red lips . . ."

A rasp of a chuckle left his lips. "I know the ballad. And you, princess, must be wickeder than I realized, if that's the sort of ballad you collect."

She tried to glare at him, but how could she when he was touching her so wonderfully? "It was merely . . . an academic interest," she said, then shamelessly belied the words when he thrust another finger deep inside her, and she grabbed at his forearm to guide his motion. "Oh, my . . . that is . . ."

"Aye," he said, his voice low and husky. "Perhaps you'd care to . . . share that academic interest with me."

His fingers drove into her below with a rhythm that beat through her like a gypsy's tambourine, drowning out conscious thought. "What?"

"You're not doing *yer* part, princess," he reminded her.

Only then did she realize she'd stopped fondling him, too caught up in what he was doing to her to notice. "Oh! Right . . . sorry . . ."

She returned to stroking him, and he let out a sigh that soon turned to gasping. "Ah, lass . . . yes . . . keep doing that . . . until I say to stop . . . harder now . . . faster . . . aye, like that . . . God help me . . ."

After that there were no more words, for they were straining together, each intent on the other's enjoyment, working their hands in counterpoint, caressing heated skin and slick flesh as their need drummed higher and higher, crescendoing to a roar and then a scream—

Her scream as pleasure pierced her, sharp and sweet, driving her beyond her senses. Lachlan swallowed her scream with his hot, searching mouth even while his own body went taut, his flesh spasming beneath her fingers.

As she reeled from the unfamiliar shocks of sensation, he yanked his hand from between her legs to grip the towel tightly around her hand. Then a warm fluid poured out of him, over her fingers and into the cloth.

He dragged his mouth free of hers. "Holy Christ! Holy Mother of God . . ."

Her pulse sang in time to his oaths. Dear Lord, what a feeling! What on earth had he done to her?

Whatever it was, he must have felt the same, for he clutched her tightly against him, burying his face in her neck, breathing hard into her hair as he shook against her.

It took a moment for the clamor in her loins to subside, and another for his body to slump, as if drained of substance.

Then he murmured, "That was . . . a damned sight better than . . . academic."

"Yes," she said, half laughing. "Yes, it was."

They panted together, like pipers finishing a reel. The steady drumbeat of rain on the window and the hiss and pop of the lantern were the only sounds beyond their heavy breathing. Slowly the chill of the unheated room seeped into her limbs.

Yet she hated to leave his knee. She bent her head to his. "So this is why Oonagh says she'd 'part with life for joys like this.'"

"Joys like this are rare, princess." He nuzzled her cheek, her ear, her hair. "Beyond rare. And thus all the more to be treasured."

His words gave her hope. Until now she hadn't dared to think past this moment, sure that his desire for her wouldn't outweigh his desire for vengeance against her father.

But what if it could? What if he was willing to put his revenge aside for *this*, for passion . . . for marriage? She was well past twenty-one—she could marry whom she pleased. And if they did it before Papa reached Scotland, he wouldn't be able to prevent it. She also had a fortune, which might sway Lachlan if his quarrel with Papa was just about the money.

Sadly, it wasn't. Her heart sank. The feud between them went beyond that—as Lachlan's wounds amply demonstrated.

She clutched him to her fiercely. No, there had to be a way. Perhaps she could make up for the rash acts of Papa's men. Perhaps if she offered him her help and her fortune, he might listen. Perhaps if she offered him her body . . .

She drew back to stare at him, taking hope from his tender smile. "One should enjoy rare pleasures as often as possible, wouldn't you say?" Running her hands up his strong arms, she gave him what she hoped was a seductive glance. "The night is young and—"

"Och, no, lassie." His smile faded. "Rare pleasures are meant to be rare."

Her mouth went dry. "They don't have to be."

"Aye, they do." Eyes solemn as an eagle's gazed darkly at her as he wiped her hand clean on his towel. "You have to go back to bed now. Alone. Before I'm tempted to do the part of the ballad that we skipped."

She slung her arms about his neck. "And what part is that?"

His gaze flicked to her naked breasts, and he sucked in a harsh breath. "You know what part. Where Darby enters Oonagh and they jointly 'oil her lock' with 'showers of bliss.' That part."

"That sounds intriguing," she whispered, leaning up to kiss his mouth.

He stopped her before she could. "No. I will not ruin you."

An admirable sentiment before, but surely not now. "Would it be so awful if you did?"

"Aye. I'd have to marry you then, and I cannot."

I cannot. Nothing like the bald truth to ruin a good seduction.

But she wouldn't let him throw this away so easily. "Why not?" she whispered, trying not to let his words wound her.

Dropping his gaze, he concentrated on pulling her chemise back up to cover her breasts. "Even if yer father would allow it," he said, "and even if he and I can settle this matter between us, you wouldn't be happy at Rosscraig."

"How do you know?"

His cold glance struck her to the heart. "Because ye're too fine a lady for that sort of life."

Odd how he could turn what should be a compliment into an insult. Her breath burned her throat as she rose, trying to gather the shreds of her pride about her. She noticed he made no move to stop her.

"Too fine a lady?" Her fingers shook violently as she tied her chemise. "Surely I have just amply demonstrated that I'm not remotely a fine lady."

"That's not what I'm talking about, lass." He stood and the towel fell away, but she got the merest glimpse of him naked before he turned his back on her and scooped up his drawers. "Even the finest ladies have desires. But it doesn't change what they're born to. And once the heat of desire cools, they have to live in real houses and endure real hardships. Desire doesn't make up for that."

Not for a woman like you. He didn't have to say the words.

She watched despairingly as his lovely behind disappeared beneath the stockinette. He meant for this to be the only time they were intimate, didn't he? He'd allowed it because she'd pressed him, but he would never take it further.

"Let me see if I understand you. The fact that I desire you doesn't matter. Nor the fact that I enjoy your company—"

"Enjoy my company?" With a bitter laugh, he faced her. "You've spent the past two days calling me a vulgar scoundrel. None of that has changed."

"Everything has changed," she whispered. "You know it has."

"I know nothing of the kind." He set his chin the way he set his shoulders, with a warrior's belligerence. "You felt sorry for me, felt responsible for the wounds yer father's men inflicted. And we got . . . carried away. But that doesn't mean we could make a life together. You know better."

She only knew that his hatred of her father ran deeper than she'd dreamed, that it stretched even to her. He was perfectly happy to play with her "in the moment," but marrying Duncannon's daughter would never be acceptable.

Until now she'd never been ashamed of who Papa was, who *she* was. And the fact that he could make her ashamed angered her. "You despise my father that much, do you?"

"It has naught to do with him." But he wouldn't meet her gaze, turning instead to scoop up his clothes.

"Really? And if I weren't his daughter, you'd still spurn me?"

"Spurn you!" He whirled on her. "You'll be the one to spurn me when yer father comes after you, and I'm forced to—"

When he broke off with a curse, her heart plummeted. "Forced to what?"

He didn't reply, just strode into the hall to deposit his clothes for Sally to wash, then reentered and slammed the door before grabbing a pillow from the bed.

"Answer me, Lachlan." Foreboding clutching at her chest, she followed him to where he tossed the pillow to the floor. "I asked you before what you'd do if Papa didn't give you the money, and you evaded the question. I'm asking again, and this time I want the truth. What do you mean to do?"

"Stay out of it," he growled. "It has naught to do with you."

"If that were true, I wouldn't be here. Tell me what you mean to do. I'll give you no peace until you tell me."

"Fine!" He faced her, eyes ablaze. "You saw what yer father's men did to me just for robbing McKinley. And now I've gone and kidnapped his daughter. If he comes here without the money, it'll be because he wants my head. It'll be him or me, don't you see? It must end one way or another, and it's damned sure not going to be because I let him get away with treachery."

She didn't understand. "So if he refuses to give you the money he owes—"

"Then I'll call him out. And if you're married to me, you'll end up either a widow or the wife of yer father's killer." With a rigid tilt to his jaw, he crossed his arms over his bare chest. "Devil of a choice, wouldn't you say?"

Chapter Sixteen

∽⬥∽

Dear Charlotte,

Why must you ask questions you know I won't answer? This I will say: although I don't much enjoy society, I don't stay locked away, either. If I did, how could I gain you the inside information you need to help your girls? Careful, friend; if you don't stop pestering me with questions about my identity, you may find me much less eager to pass on my gossip.

Your determined-to-remain-anonymous friend,
Michael

𝓛achlan faced Venetia down, wishing desperately that she didn't look so fetching in a shift, that her earlier cries of pleasure weren't still echoing in his ears. Because her expression of horrified disbelief turned all his previous enjoyment to ashes.

"So that's why we won't be marrying," he snapped. "This battle between me and yer father isn't a game for ladies. It's hard and cruel, and it won't end to yer satisfaction, of that you can be sure."

"Only because you're both stubborn as the devil," she said in a hollow voice.

"Aye, I'm stubborn, but I deserve justice, damn it! And justice doesn't mean letting him get away with what he did."

"You'd fight him in a duel? That's not justice. He's an old man, not a soldier. We both know you'd win. It would be murder, pure and simple."

"It was damned near murder when he set his men on me, but I don't see you crying over the unfairness of that," he spat.

"I did," she said softly. "I do."

There it came again, that sympathy in her face, that heart-wrenching sympathy that made him yearn.

Damn her! There was no place in his plans for yearning.

"The point is," he bit out, "marrying you won't solve a damned thing. It'll only force you into a terrible situation. And that's assuming you could be happy with me in the Highlands at all, which is doubtful."

"It certainly is," she said haughtily, "if you're meaning to kill my father."

"I don't want to! I want only what's owed me." He dragged in a heavy breath. "But if he refuses to pay, I'll annihilate him, do ye ken?"

The vitriol in his voice made her recoil.

He struggled not to care. "I want the money. Failing that, I want to be sure he won't send more men to kill me, and I can't be sure of that unless he's dead."

"According to your image of him, you can't be sure of that even if he pays the money."

"Why would he kill me, then? He wouldn't get the money back. But until the matter is settled, I can't go back into the world. I refuse to spend my life hiding. One way or the other, this ends when he comes to Scotland."

"What if you married me?" A look of desperation crossed her face. "That would settle it. Surely he wouldn't expose you if you were my husband. And my dowry is almost as large as his debt. You could forget about the loan."

"Are you daft, lassie?" Opening his knapsack, he dragged out the tartan he used for warmth when he had to camp in the hills, then spread it on the floor where he'd thrown the pillow. "Have you forgotten who controls yer dowry?"

She paled. "Oh."

"If we marry before yer father arrives, you'll lose yer fortune and I'll lose my chance at getting the money my clan needs. Besides, killing me would appeal to him even more if it was the only way to free you from my evil clutches."

"He's not this monster you make him out to be. If I could just talk to him, make it clear that I *want* to marry you, that I'm happy—"

"He'll do a jig and forgive all, eh? Give us yer fortune, pay me back what he owes, welcome me into the loving arms of the family? Not bloody likely."

"At least let me try."

"No! I'm not taking the chance that he'll cut you off and me in the bargain. My clan needs that money, do ye ken?"

She curled her arms about her stomach and sank down onto the bed.

The haunted look on her face cut him to the soul. He hated destroying whatever romantic fairy story she'd been spinning for the two of them, but it was best to halt it now, before she started dreaming of how to paint Rosscraig and what color to weave the cloth for their baby's blankets.

He snorted. Weave the cloth, indeed. That was too practical. Fancy ladies plied their needles to ornament useless fripperies like dancing slippers and reticules.

He couldn't afford reticules or slippers for her. He

could barely afford the copper for the whisky stills he hoped would make all their fortunes one day. The copper that Duncannon's money would provide.

But not if she tangled herself up in it. And for what? Because he'd given her pleasure, and she'd taken the notion that it boded well for their future? Damned fool female. What if she saw his manor and balked, as any woman of sense would? Then where would he be? Married to a woman whose father would kill to free her.

He wasn't risking his head, nor his clan's future. He needed that loan repaid, even if it meant he couldn't have her. Even if it meant he'd never get to take her to bed, never get to make her his, never get . . .

He swore foully. Life wasn't fair. He'd have to get used to it. "You understand now, don't you, princess?"

She nodded mutely, tucking her legs up beneath her with the look of a wounded doe. Holy Christ, how that killed him.

"I have responsibilities to my clan and my crofters. I can't just throw them away because I happen to fancy kissing Duncannon's pretty daughter."

"Stop calling me that, curse you!" Anger sparked in her eyes. "You've made it quite clear you have no desire to fit me into your life—don't belabor the point."

This time he made no attempt to apologize. Best to leave it this way. Then there'd be no confusion between them.

And no more kisses or caresses. No more fondling in the dark.

He gritted his teeth. This was how it had to be. He would never have dallied with her if he'd realized that she didn't see it, too.

Right. He would have ignored the soft delicacy of her hands nursing him, the gentle caring of her smile . . . her half-naked form bending over him.

Don't think about that, laddie, or you'll never last the night. "Well, then." He tried for a tone of nonchalance. "Best we get some sleep."

She rose abruptly. "You should take the bed. It's not good for you to lie on the floor with your wounds still healing."

That she could still care about his suffering made a lump lodge in his throat. "I slept on the ground on the way to Edinburgh," he said. "This is no different. At least I've got a pillow this time."

"Lachlan—"

"No, lass, I'm not letting you sleep on the floor. Take the bed. That's the end of it."

As he turned to where he'd left his pillow and tartan, she hurried over to the bowl she'd left on the washstand. "At least let me finish dressing your wounds. I haven't put the comfrey on them."

"I don't need—"

"I won't take no for an answer." She picked up the bowl, added some water, then worked the mixture with her fingers. "The crushed comfrey root is the most important part. It hardens on the wound, healing it over time. You must have it."

Mo chreach, would this night of tantalizing tortures never end? "All right," he ground out, though he didn't know how he'd survive another bout of her tender ministrations. "But be quick about it."

Not only was the lass quick about it, she was downright unfeeling. With her face set, she plastered his worst wounds with the thick sludge and used some linen to bandage them. Then, cool as any physician, she washed her hands and trotted off to bed, leaving him staring after her.

So that was how it would be, eh? No more kind smiles for him, oh no. She was done with that.

Fine. He didn't care.

He stretched out on his back on the hard floor, throttling his moans in his throat rather than have her hear them. He didn't need her to nurse him, anyway—he'd done well enough until now without such a thing.

Never mind that it felt good having her fuss over him. He wasn't a lad anymore to need petting and such; he could take care of himself.

That was the unconvincing litany he recited as he fell off to sleep.

On the night after Venetia's kidnapping, Maggie dined with Colonel Seton in the common room of the Edinburgh inn, wishing she didn't feel so conspicuous. Surely people were wondering where her charge was. No one would believe for long the tale they'd spread about her niece being ill, not after how well Venetia had looked only two nights ago.

Quentin would never forgive her for this. She could never forgive herself. Just the thought of what Venetia might be enduring . . .

She moaned aloud.

"It will be all right, I swear." The colonel gave her hand a reassuring squeeze, then held it a moment longer. Though she knew it was wrong of her to encourage such behavior, she let him. She was so worried, and he was so understanding, the poor, dear man.

Though it *was* scandalous that they should sit so, with their gloves off and their bare hands joined so shockingly.

"So your men have sent you no report?" she asked, trying not to notice that his strong grip made her tremble like a schoolgirl.

"Not yet." He threaded his fingers with hers, his gaze a sharp, glimmering blue before he dropped it to their hands. "You know how wild the Highlands are. You can travel miles without seeing a village. And it's only been a day—"

"A day and a half," she corrected him.

He smiled indulgently. "Aye, a day and a half."

"But the men left that very night?"

His smile faded. "I told you they did."

"I would have felt better if I could have spoken to them first."

"And how would that have kept your niece's identity a secret?"

She'd forgotten about that stipulation. Nonetheless . . . "At least tell me whom you hired. Then when my brother-in-law arrives here, I'll be able to tell him."

The sudden flummoxed look on Colonel Seton's face gave her pause. Until he began to cough and wheeze, and his cheeks turned a ruddy hue.

"Colonel Seton?" she asked. "Colonel? Are you all right?"

"Water," he whispered. "Need . . . water . . ."

She poured water from a pitcher, then held it to his lips. But he was coughing so hard, he couldn't manage more than a few sips.

Alarmed, she called for a servant. "My friend

seems to be having an attack of some sort. Might you have a private parlor where he could rest for a moment?"

"Yes, my lady, this way," the servant said.

Supporting the colonel with her arm about his waist, Maggie helped him stumble into the private room. Worry seized her heart as she sat beside him on a settee and stroked his back while he coughed. Strange how quickly she'd come to care for the man. She wished she could say it was only because he was helping her with the kidnapping, but she knew down deep that was a lie.

After a few moments, his coughing subsided. "Better?" she asked.

"Much better," he wheezed. Grabbing her hand, he cradled it against his chest. "Sometimes I have coughing fits. Bad lungs, you know." He flashed her a warm smile. "Thanks for soothing it."

"I did nothing really." She fought the little flutter of her heart.

"Oh, you did plenty, lass. Plenty." He lifted her hand to his lips and kissed the back of it, then each knuckle, then turned it over so he could kiss her wrist.

"Colonel," she said in a breathy voice, "perhaps you shouldn't . . . that is . . ."

"Call me Hugh, at least." His beautiful eyes played over her face. "And perhaps, if I might call you Maggie?"

"Yes," she said, hardly realizing what she'd answered.

"Sweet, beautiful Maggie." He leaned close as if to kiss her.

The door opened, and the innkeeper hurried in.

"Are you all right, Colonel? My servant said you were unwell."

The colonel—Hugh—let out a sigh. "I could be more right," he said under his breath, his gaze dropping to Maggie's mouth.

Her heart began to race in a most dangerous fashion before she shifted her gaze from him to the innkeeper. "Yes, he's fine. But I'm sure he'll feel better once he's home." She glanced at Hugh. "After all, the hour *is* late, sir."

His brow darkened, but he nodded. "I suppose ye're right. I should be going." He stood and started to turn away.

"Wait, you said you'd tell me what men you hired," she said.

With a furtive glance at the innkeeper, he murmured, "I'll bring you a list in the morning, all right? We can have breakfast together."

"Thank you, yes. That would be lovely."

After he left, she spent most of the night wishing he'd stayed. So her first reaction when he didn't come for breakfast the next morning was disappointment, followed swiftly by worry, since his note said he still felt unwell. She'd hoped he would at least send the list, but there was nothing with the note. He did, however, promise to attend her for dinner.

Except right before dinner he sent his regrets and promised breakfast the next morning. And still, no list. That's when her suspicions became thoroughly roused. For a robust-looking soldier, Colonel Seton had more health problems than seemed normal: his bad foot, his lungs. Indeed, wasn't it odd that a man with lung trouble would undertake a climb such as the one they'd gone on with Venetia?

And why did his health difficulties always crop up at

the most inopportune times—that day on the mountain, and now when she wanted to know more about what he was doing to help her niece? It could be nothing, of course, but still . . .

Perhaps it was time she learned more about the colonel.

Chapter Seventeen

Dear Cousin,

*You should take care, too, or I will call your bluff.
Be fair—I've never worked very hard to uncover
your identity, because I knew that our agreement
didn't allow for such. But if it soothes your temper, I
will refrain from annoying questions for the nonce. I
wouldn't wish to lose so valuable a friend for such a
frivolous reason.*

Still your relation,
Charlotte

The new day had scarcely dawned when Venetia awoke.
It was hard to sleep when your heart was breaking.

Her heart? No, she wouldn't give that over to a
stubborn devil like Lachlan, no matter how lovely his
kisses or how wounded his soul. She'd been foolish last
night, but she wouldn't be so in the light of day.

Her cheeks flamed, just thinking of how she'd
practically begged him to marry her. How many times
had Mrs. Harris said that a man could desire a woman
without wanting her for his wife?

*Once the heat of their desire cools, those ladies have to
live in real houses and endure real hardships. Desire doesn't
make up for that.*

Tears stung her eyes. She knew when Lachlan was just
making excuses. He'd heard her speak of the Highlands,
seen her endure difficulties on the road, yet he could still
say that?

Yes, because of who she was. And because it didn't suit his plans to marry her. He wanted to confront her father, and she got in the way of that.

Still, she could hardly blame him for his anger at Papa. She stared across to where Lachlan had finally found a comfortable position on his side. With his hands tucked under his head, he looked almost boyish, his scar hidden by a thick lock of chestnut hair and his dark lashes fringing cheeks that for the first time in days had a healthy color. Perhaps the comfrey and horse liniment had done him some good. He didn't seem to be moaning anymore.

She fisted her hands beneath the covers, trying not to think of how he'd groaned in his sleep earlier in the night whenever he'd shifted position. Every groan had been a nail in her conscience. How could Papa order that a man be beaten so awfully? What kind of monster must he be?

No, Papa's hirelings were the monsters. Surely he couldn't have commanded anything so brutal. Papa was a gentleman, for heaven's sake! They didn't do such things to other gentlemen, not even gentlemen thieves. Did they?

Unable to bear her thoughts, she sat up. No point in trying to sleep anymore. She kept seeing pictures of Papa fighting Lachlan, of Lachlan being shot or Papa bleeding to death—

No, it mustn't happen. She had to stop it. She would return and convince Papa to repay the loan, argue on Lachlan's behalf. Because if Papa confronted Lachlan in person, there was sure to be bloodshed. With two men so proud and stubborn, neither would ever back down.

Edging from the bed, she scooped up her corset and

shoes, then crept to the door, where the key still lay in the lock. Both she and Lachlan had forgotten about it last night; indeed, until now she hadn't realized how easily she could escape.

She glanced at him, at the bandages on his arm and leg, and regret knifed through her. Who would change them? Who would crush fresh comfrey and plaster it on his flesh? What if his wounds worsened?

Her sigh blew a strand of hair from her face. Better wounded than dead.

Careful not to wake him, she turned the key and slid the door open. Then she locked it again on the outside to slow his pursuit.

She headed down the stairs on cat feet. First she had to find her clothes, which she prayed would be dry. After dressing, she would walk into town. Annie had already arranged for a gig—Venetia would just claim to be fetching it.

With plans churning in her brain, she snuck into the kitchen ... then froze. Annie was kneading bread dough at the kitchen table with her back to the door, and Venetia wanted to cry. She could see her clothes draped over chairs by the fire just beyond Annie, but they might as well have been in China.

What should she do now? Ask Annie to help her leave? Rummage for clothes elsewhere in the house?

That was decided for her when Annie turned and spotted her. "Ah, my lady, you're up early." She beckoned to Venetia to enter. "Come in, come in."

As Venetia padded into the kitchen, Annie caught sight of her bare feet. "Heavens, you must be freezing! Come sit here by the fire and warm yerself."

"I came to get my clothes," Venetia said, her mind

racing with how to broach the subject of Annie helping her return to London.

"Ah, yes. They should be dry enough to wear by now."

"If you could help me put on my stays," Venetia said, aware of time slipping away, "I would vastly appreciate it."

Annie shot her a veiled glance, but went to get it. "I suppose you're hoping to be dressed before yer husband rises."

The comment brought Venetia up short. Had Annie guessed—

"I know how it is for newly married couples," Annie went on. "Sometimes men can be such randy beasts in the morning, and they don't realize how difficult that can be for an untried young woman."

Venetia blinked. Annie thought . . . she'd assumed . . .

But perhaps that could be used to her advantage. "Exactly," Venetia said, not having to feign a blush. "I'd rather he didn't awaken to find me in my shift."

As Annie came over with the corset, Venetia drew a heavy breath. "That's not the only reason, however. The truth is, I'm thinking that I might . . . well . . . I'm very anxious about my family, you see. Lachlan and I fled so suddenly, and now there's some sign that my father is in pursuit."

"Oh, but you and the laird are married now, so there's naught yer father can do to stop it." Annie laced her up, then went to get the other clothes.

"He could kill Lachlan." Or Lachlan could kill him, the more likely scenario. "He protested the marriage most strenuously. So I think I should go back and reason with him." Which was very near the truth.

"That would do no good, dearie." Annie clucked her tongue in sympathy as she held out a petticoat for Venetia to step into. "If you leave your husband, it'll only convince yer father that you're unhappy." She cut her eyes slyly up at Venetia. "And you're not, are you?"

"No," she said hastily, "but I'm afraid that if Papa catches up with us, I'll end up a widow. They are both so stubborn, you see. I only want to soothe Papa's temper, assure him that I'm happy."

"That's all you want, is it?" Annie looked skeptical as she went to shove a loaf into the dutch oven. "Then I advise you against going back. Lachlan wouldn't take well to having his wife run off so soon after the wedding."

Venetia forced a smile. "I'm not running off—"

"And you've got no money, no transportation."

As she pulled on her gown she fought for calm. "What about the gig you arranged?"

"They'll not let it go without my word. So unless you mean to walk back—"

"I'll do what I must," Venetia bit out.

"Don't be a fool," Annie snapped. "You'd get no more than a mile out of Kingussie before yer husband caught up to you. The whole idea is daft, it is."

Frustration tinged Venetia's voice with impatience. "Daft or not, I have to go, don't you understand? And you have to help me get away before Lachlan awakes." She tried a pleading tone. "I wouldn't ask if it weren't important."

Setting her hands on her hips, Annie pierced Venetia with a sharp glance. "This isn't about soothing yer father's fears, is it? You're just unhappy with Lachlan. I know he can be a rough man, but you have to give him a chance—"

"I don't have to do anything, curse it!" Venetia burst out.

Then she forced herself to take a calming breath. In ballads, it was always easy for a woman to run from her husband; she just took off with the tinker man. A pity that life wasn't more like ballads. "You don't understand."

"Oh, but I do," Annie said in a cold voice. "Here I was thinking you might be better for him than that Polly. But you're the same as her, only worse."

The words stung, which was simply absurd. Lachlan didn't even *want* to marry her, for pity's sake! What did it matter if Annie thought her a horrible wife?

But now that Annie had raised the ghost of Lachlan's former fiancée, she couldn't rest until she knew about her. "What exactly did this Polly do?"

"Abandoned him, that's what, and with little more cause than you've got." Annie cast Venetia a considering look. "Or mayhap you just don't realize what he went through with her."

Venetia sighed, feeling her chance to escape evaporating.

Annie dragged out a chair. "Sit down, and let me tell you about yer husband. After I'm done, if you can still walk out on the man, I'll help you. I'd rather see you break his heart quick and easy than fracture it a bit at a time like Polly."

The mention of Polly was too intriguing to resist. And it wasn't as if she had a choice. Annie was right—without help, she wouldn't get far before Lachlan caught up to her. "Very well." She took a seat.

Her brow beetling in a frown, Annie strode over to turn Lachlan's clothes in front of the fire. "They met right after he returned from the war. She was a merchant's daughter and set her cap for him—and his new baronetcy—right away. She wanted to be Lady Ross something fierce, she did."

Annie shook her head. "Lachlan couldn't see that scheming part of her. Men hardly ever do, though I daresay a beauty like her would have dazzled any weary soldier fresh from battles and blood. They had a quick courtship while he was still taking stock of his father's properties, but as cattle prices fell and the place wasn't earning what it ought, he had to keep putting off the wedding."

Venetia caught her breath. How painful that must have been for him—to be setting up a life of a certain kind for himself and realize it wasn't to be.

"Even a fool like Polly began to see she wouldn't have the fancy life of a baronet's wife she'd hoped for." Annie scowled. "Then after he came back from a trip to London and told his people they'd have to tighten their belts, she grew downright cool toward him."

Venetia winced. That must have been when he'd tried getting Papa to repay the loan.

Annie's hard gaze bored into her. "Lachlan made excuses for her, but his heart was starting to crack even then. He started spending time away from the estate, going who knows where at night. She wasn't getting coddled like she wanted, so she up and took off with some jumped-up knight's son with piles of money. Broke Lachlan's heart right proper, she did."

And further fueled his hatred of Papa.

Venetia stared down at her hands, remembering his words. *You wouldn't be happy at Rosscraig . . . ye're too fine a lady for that sort of life.*

Could she really blame him for assuming she would

never belong in the Highlands? Especially after she'd been so missish at first.

"So if you run off now . . ." Annie began.

"I'm not running off." Venetia shifted her gaze to stare out the mullioned cottage window at a rooster strutting among the hens. "I just didn't . . . I couldn't stand the thought of him getting hurt by Papa."

"They'll have to come to terms with each other eventually, lass," Annie said, her voice softening. "The sooner the better, I say."

Annie didn't understand, and Venetia couldn't explain without revealing who her father actually was. She doubted Annie would be so keen to champion the marriage if she knew. But neither would she want to help Venetia escape.

"I don't want you thinking he's got no prospects, though," Annie went on. "The whisky is selling right well, I understand, and Jamie says they're starting to grow their own barley—"

"Whisky?"

"Aye, that's how yer husband is keeping his crofters working—with whisky stills." Annie's eyes grew alarmed. "You knew about that, didn't you?"

"Oh, yes, I merely forgot," Venetia said quickly. "But I thought most stills in Scotland were illegal?"

"So is his, but a man's got to make a living somehow. And there's thousands of them. Until England stops taxing them so heavily that a man can't afford a licensed one, there will be thousands more. So although the laird can take care of you, it ain't going to be fancy and it ain't going—"

A roar, then a pounding from upstairs made them both flinch.

"What the devil?" Annie cried.

"I believe my husband is awake," Venetia said, her heart thundering. "I locked him in, you see."

"Ah." Annie gathered up Lachlan's clothes, then approached Venetia. "If you still want to leave him—"

"No." Venetia rose, her mind made up.

This was probably insane, but she couldn't leave—not now. Lachlan deserved to have his day. He'd gone through fire to get here; she'd just have to pray that once Papa reached Scotland she could make him recognize that.

Flashing Annie a wan smile, she took the clothes from her. "I'd best let him out before he breaks down the door." She started to leave, then paused to look back. "Thank you. He would never have told me those things himself."

"I know. Stubborn as the very devil, he is."

That was the trouble. She raced up the stairs. His stubbornness could very well get him or her father killed. But which was better for *her*: go home and risk that Papa would lock her up while he continued north to murder Lachlan? Or stay so she could try to stop it?

She must see this to the end, must be there for any confrontation. It was the only way to make sure nothing awful happened.

Pausing outside the door, she wondered if she was making a huge mistake. The door shook with the force of his blows, and the thought of facing his anger again was rather daunting.

But really, she had no choice. Setting his clothes aside, she unlocked the door with shaky hands, then jumped back as it swung open to reveal Lachlan in his drawers, looking like the devil himself as he sprang forward.

Then saw her standing there. That cleared the scowl from his scarred brow. "You're here," he said inanely. His breath came in heavy gasps. "You didn't leave."

"I considered it," she said archly. "After all, I don't particularly like being dragged about the countryside with my hands bound." She gestured to his bandaged arm. "But who would dress that? Who would torment you with hour after hour of ballads? And who—"

Jerking her to him, he gave her a thoroughly wanton kiss that sent her traitorous pulse thumping. Then he drew back, instantly contrite. "Forgive me, lass. I had no right—"

"It's fine," she said, breathless after such a show of ardor, even knowing it was only borne of relief. "I understood the sentiment." Bending, she picked up his clothes and held them out. "You'll need these. Leave the bandages in place until tonight. Then I'll dress your wounds again."

As she turned toward the door, he asked, "Where are you going?"

"To help Annie with breakfast."

"Ask her if she'll pack a lunch for us, too. I'll pay her for it. Or if you'd rather, we can stop at an inn to eat."

Hiding her surprise, she said, "What I would like even more is not to have to relieve myself by the side of the road."

"All right." His voice softened. "We'll stop whenever you need to, wherever you want."

"I would appreciate that." She turned to smile at him. "In exchange, I promise not to sing at the top of my lungs."

His eyes warmed. "I don't mind the singing." Then apparently realizing he was being too nice, he added gruffly, "But do you *have* to sing about hangings and jilted ladies?"

A laugh escaped her. "And what would you rather, sir? A ballad about dauntless Highlanders?"

"Or fearless Highland lasses." He captured her hand, then stared at it pensively. "Why didn't you leave?" He rubbed his thumb over her bare knuckles, warming more than just her flesh. "The real reason, not your teasing ones."

She swallowed, wondering how much she dared tell him. She was already too vulnerable to him, and letting him inside her thoughts would give him another way to hurt her.

Best to stick to the barest facts. "I want to determine the truth for myself: about Papa, about the loan, about what has happened in the Highlands. If I go back to England, I'll never find out."

She couldn't stand living her whole life not knowing the full story of how Lachlan and Papa had come to despise each other. If Lachlan was reluctant to have her as a wife, she should at least find out if his reasons were sound.

"So you'll go with me willingly now? You'll see this to the end, no matter what happens?"

"No matter what happens," she echoed.

She'd just have to pray that what happened didn't break her heart.

Lachlan stared blindly ahead as he drove the gig, with Venetia sitting silent at his side. She'd stayed. She'd had a chance to escape, and she'd stayed.

God help him, why'd she have to go and do that? He would've preferred having to drag her back to his side. At least then he could have nursed his anger at her. But how could he be angry when she was so accommodating?

It had been hard enough to resist her when she was fighting him. Now that she wasn't, it would be even worse.

The sweetness of it tempted him a good deal more than her half-clad body last night, and that made her dangerous as hell. Because naught had changed—if he married her, her father would never give Lachlan what was owed him.

"I would have found you, you know," he said, trying to convince himself that her actions didn't matter. "You would never have made it to London alone."

"I know."

"I would have caught up to you on the road within an hour, and we'd still be here, driving north."

"I realize that."

Now she was trying to soothe his pride, devil take her. Or had she really abandoned her plan to escape because she thought she couldn't do it? No, not the fearless Venetia. He began to wonder if she mightn't be able to handle life in the Highlands after all.

Damn, what was he thinking? She was used to silks and satins, marble floors and fine paintings.

"Do you ever hear anything about Polly?" she asked. "What has happened to her and her husband?"

"Polly?" He glanced over to find her watching him with latent sympathy. Damn. "So Annie told you about her, did she?"

"Yes. I wanted to know."

"You're too nosy by half," he grumbled. "But just so you won't keep plaguing me with questions, I heard she has two young ones and a husband with a roving eye. Though I don't guess that bothers her none, since he's rich as Croesus and buys her all the pretty gowns she'd ever want."

"I seriously doubt that pretty gowns make up for an adulterous husband."

"From what I hear about London lasses, pretty gowns make up for a lot of things," he muttered, uncomfortable with this conversation.

Suddenly, they rounded a bend to find their way blocked by a milling herd of Cheviot sheep. He pulled up on the reins, his already taxed temper exploding. "Get out of the way, you bloody bastards! Now you're filling the roads, too, are ye?" He stood up and flapped his arms. "Go, go, damn you!"

A shepherd ran down the hill. "I'll have them out of yer way in a minute, sir!" the boy cried, scarcely bigger than the sheep himself. "I'm sorry, I am, sir."

"And well you ought to be," he muttered, though his temper ebbed at the sight of a child given such responsibility. "Tell me, lad, who owns these sheep?"

"MacDonell of Keppoch, sir."

He gritted his teeth. "And how many people did he serve with writs of removal to get his pasture-land, eh?"

The lad blinked. "I-I don't know, sir."

"I'm sure you do. It's never a secret. They serve the writs, come for the people, drag them begging for mercy from their homes, and then burn their houses down around them—"

"Lachlan," Venetia said in a low voice as the shepherd paled. "He's just a boy. Leave him be."

When she laid her hand on his arm and tugged, he

stiffened, but sat down and took up the reins. "Well, then, get those bloody beasts out of the way, will you?" he barked at the boy. "We don't have all day."

As the young shepherd cleared the roads, Lachlan could feel Venetia's eyes on him. After the sheep were headed once more down the slope, she said, "Are people's homes really being burned?"

He snapped the reins, and the horse started. "Why don't you ask yer father?"

When she uttered a noise like a wounded deer, he regretted the nasty comment. But he wouldn't take it back. What he'd said was very near the truth. Even if her father hadn't resorted to such measures, plenty of other lairds had.

They traveled a while in silence. Then she drew herself up. "I want to see."

"See what?"

"What you and Annie keep talking about." She sat rigidly beside him, her hands folded neatly in her lap, even though that took some doing in the turns. "The abandoned crofter's cottages. The sheep taking over the land. All of it."

He stared grimly ahead. "I can show you that easy enough, lass. It's everywhere."

And he proceeded to prove it. The road led beside many an estate overrun with Cheviots, those bloody animals who devoured every blade of grass, whose fat flesh and rich fleece coaxed the owners into throwing out their tenants. He showed her cottage after abandoned cottage, many of them roofless and crumbling now.

At every posting stop, her mood became bleaker, her face longer. After a while, he couldn't bear to look at her, and their conversation grew strained. During a long stretch past Inverness, she asked, "How long has this been going on?"

"Years," he said. "Many crofters left before you and I were even born. The rest have been shipping out daily by the hundreds. They go because they've nothing left, or because the lairds convince them that things will be better in Canada." He clenched the reins. "But not everyone survives those long voyages. A ship that left last year arrived in America with forty less people than when it sailed."

With every word, he felt an abyss opening up between them. When, during the late afternoon, she fell into a nap, it was the side of the gig that she rested her head upon, not his shoulder. It was probably just as well. Otherwise, he'd have spent that hour futilely aching for her.

Since it was still daylight when they entered the part of Ross-shire where he might be recognized, he was forced to meander along back roads. By the time they reached the thatched cottage on his estate where he meant to keep her, it was nearly sunset. "We're here, lassie."

She jerked awake, her face soft from sleep. "What?" Sitting forward, she surveyed the area. "This isn't Rosscraig."

"No. I told you—I don't want my mother involved, and she doesn't know this place. So until yer father comes, we'll be staying here."

"Together?" she said, alarm evident in her voice.

"There's two bedchambers."

"Oh." She didn't look reassured.

"I've got estate matters to occupy me," he continued hastily, "so you won't see me much anyway." Not if he could help it. Many more hours in her company, and he'd soon be considering how to manage the impossible.

"If you tell me what you like to read, I'll have books fetched for you. And I'll send the lads to Dingwall for needlework things and whatever else you like to occupy yer time."

Gazing about the clearing, she murmured, "I've never been good with a needle, I confess. But books would be wonderful. And I should like some herbs and a few items from the apothecary." She cast him an accusing glance. "If you and Papa insist upon shooting each other, I need to be prepared for patching you up."

He ignored her tone and the lurch in his gut at the thought of her wanting to take care of him after all he'd put her through. "I'll see what I can do."

Hopping down from the gig, he came around to help her. The minute his hands clasped her waist, she sucked in a breath, and the faint sound did something wicked to his insides. So did the flash of awareness in her eyes, the luminous glow of her face in the light of the dying sun, the trembling of her body beneath his grip.

He set her swiftly on the ground and released her before he could do something he'd regret. Like kiss her again. Like lay her down here in the secret woods and take her in slow, easy strokes—

A door slammed behind them, and he stepped back. But when he turned to greet the intruder, it wasn't one of his clansmen who met his gaze with steely eyes.

It was his mother.

Chapter Eighteen

Dear Charlotte,

Forgive me if my letter sounded sharp. Family
difficulties presently cause me concern. But I
understand your curiosity. I just prefer you don't
indulge it.

Always your servant,
Michael

Since Venetia was still trying to contain her wildly
veering emotions after Lachlan's hungry look, it took her
a moment to register who'd come to greet them.

Then she recognized the wiry auburn curls, velvety
brown eyes, and strong jaw of Lachlan's mother, and
realized it was Lady Marjorie Ross who regarded her
with a wary gaze. Which turned angry when it moved
to Lachlan.

"So you went and done it," she bit out. "You took
Duncannon's daughter."

Duncannon's daughter again. Didn't *anyone* use a
person's name in Scotland?

"You shouldn't be here, Mother," he said, every inch
the Highland chief, though the stiffening muscles in his
neck betrayed his unease. He gestured to the cottage.
"How did you even know—"

"About this place? I'm not the fool you take me for,
you know."

"I've never taken you for a fool," he said, his voice
placating.

"No?" Hurt twisted her tone. "They drag you from the bracken half dead, beaten to a bloody pulp, and you spout a tale about fighting the Scourge, thinking to pacify me like I'm a slack-jawed idiot." She clapped her arms over her chest. "I didn't press it, not while I fought to keep you alive through that fever, and not afterward. I told myself that after nearly dying, you'd surely give it up."

Lachlan eyed her warily. "Give what up?"

"Riding the roads. Robbing Duncannon's friends."

Lachlan looked as if someone had just walloped him with a whisky jar. Venetia rolled her eyes. So Lachlan's mother *did* know of his activities. She wasn't terribly surprised.

Anger flared in Lady Ross's thin face. "In the past few years I've often wondered if the Scourge might be you, but I convinced myself you'd never do such a thing. Until the beating." Her voice hardened. "I shouldn't have told you about that loan. 'Twas foolish of me." She set her chin. "I wanted you to *talk* to the man, shame him into paying us back. Not take yer life in yer hands."

Her gaze swung to Venetia. "And now this. Kidnapping a lady. I never thought to see a son of mine behave so."

"It's not a kidnapping," Venetia said, though she wasn't sure why she bothered to defend him. "I came willingly."

"Quiet, Venetia. As she says, she's no fool." Lachlan's voice turned brittle. "And no doubt one of my clansmen blathered the truth."

"Aye," Lady Ross snapped, "Jamie told me the whole thing."

"Damn that insolent pup, he's supposed to be in Aberdeen!"

Lady Ross sniffed. "He thought I should know what you were doing, on account of the lady and her reputation. And he was right." She stepped to Venetia's side. "That's why I'm taking charge of her."

"Over my dead body." Fury swelled visibly in Lachlan, pulsing from him in waves. "The lady and her reputation are *my* concern. I won't have you interfering."

"And I won't have you ruining her," she told Lachlan stoutly. "If I could, I'd take her back to her father"—she held up her hand when he started to interrupt—"but since he's probably already on his way here, it's best to wait until he arrives. In the meantime, we have to protect her reputation. Bad enough you traveled alone with her for two days. You'll not live unchaperoned with her, too. She'll stay at Rosscraig. And you'll stay here at the cottage."

"The devil I will!" Lachlan cried. "I'm not letting her out of my sight!"

His resistance perplexed Venetia. "Why not? Surely you don't fear I'll escape. If I didn't leave this morning, I certainly won't run off now."

She felt Lady Ross's gaze measuring her, but it was Lachlan's, hot with temper and a wild intensity, that made her blood pound in her ears. "You said you care only about getting the money your clan needs. And I understand that, I do."

Especially after seeing the sad situation of other lairds' crofters. At least Lachlan refused to bow to the methods of those "improvers."

"But you also said you didn't want me ruined," she continued. "And if I stay alone with you, I surely will be." Who knew what might happen in the wee hours when they were both lonely? She dared not risk it. If he bedded her, he'd feel honor-bound to marry her, and he'd already made it clear how he felt about that.

"Despite what you think, son," Lady Ross put in, "people do notice your comings and goings. I'm not the only one who knows about this cottage. Some of your clansmen know and Jamie and—"

"And I'll thrash them senseless if they talk," he growled.

When his mother's brows lowered in a frown, Venetia laid a hand on Lachlan's arm. "Be sensible. There's no reason for me *not* to stay at Rosscraig if your mother is willing." Unless he didn't want to be parted from her because he actually cared about her.

The muscles in his arm bunched beneath her hand. "Your father could try to sneak men into Rosscraig to rescue you," he said sullenly.

Lady Ross snorted. "How could anyone manage that? Yer men patrol every roadway, watching for excisemen. When Duncannon comes, you'll know it."

"I'd feel better staying at the manor," he ground out.

"You're supposed to be dead, remember? It's easier to keep up the pretense when you're not there. If word gets round outside the clan that you're alive and well and holding a woman prisoner in yer manor, you'll have more than Duncannon to deal with."

"Damn it, Mother—"

"We'll do this right proper, we will." Lady Ross squared her shoulders. "You'll stay at the cottage as you've been doing, and Lady Venetia will stay with me at Rosscraig as my guest. I'll tell people she's yer father's London cousin."

With a black scowl, he rubbed the back of his neck. "Damn you both," he muttered under his breath. His angry gaze fell on Venetia. "So this is what you want, is it, lass? To be well away from me?"

Strange that he'd put it like that, if he only cared about his plans for Papa. "I want to preserve my reputation as best I can." *Since you refuse to marry me.*

Now was his chance to speak. If he felt more for her than some inconvenient desire, if he considered her more than just a tool to get what he wanted from Papa, then he'd have to tell her so.

"Fine," he clipped out, "stay with my mother. I don't want you in my hair anyway, complaining about yer accommodations. Let Mother deal with it."

That wasn't fair, and he knew it, but the fact that he'd made the insult at all cheered her. He really wasn't taking this well, was he?

Pasting a brilliant smile to her lips, Venetia moved to his mother's side and drew on every rule of ladylike behavior she'd been taught. "I'm sure I'll be quite comfortable at Rosscraig. As I recall, it was a perfectly lovely little house. I'm looking forward to visiting there." Leaving him glowering, she turned to Lady Ross. "Shall we go? I'm tired and should like a cup of tea by the fire."

"That you shall have, and a good meal, too," Lady Ross said.

As they walked away, Lachlan called out, "Venetia?"

Hope leaped in her heart as she turned to him. "Yes?"

He looked as if he wanted to say something of great import. Then his face went carefully blank, and his voice turned distant. "If you need anything—"

"I'm sure your mother will take excellent care of me," she said, hiding her disappointment. He was such a stubborn lout, curse him.

Well, she had pride, too. And she wasn't about to throw

it aside on the slim evidence of his veiled comments and hungry looks.

Her hostess led her to a curate cart waiting out of sight of the cottage. It was only after they'd driven off that Lady Ross spoke again. "My son didn't . . . hurt you any during these past few days, did he?"

"He was a perfect gentleman." It wasn't much of a lie. She'd been as much to blame for their intimate encounter last night as he. And while he'd bruised her heart and certainly trampled her pride afterward, she could recover from that eventually. Though she now cherished a hope that she wouldn't have to.

"He's a pigheaded fellow, he is. But I never imagined he would carry this battle with yer father so far." She patted Venetia's hand. "Well, dinna fash yerself over Lachlan anymore. I'll see that he leaves you alone until yer father arrives."

"You don't have to do that," Venetia said. "He doesn't bother me."

"He needs to learn he can't just go about kidnapping young innocents. If he means to plot trouble, he can plot it elsewhere. I'll bar him from the house, I will."

"Really, Lady Ross, you needn't—"

"Do you want to catch the lad, or not?" Lady Ross said, flicking the reins.

The comment caught her off guard. "I-I don't know what you mean."

"I saw how the two of you looked at each other. And you were ready to defend him, even after what he did. Besides, Jamie told me . . ." She glanced at Venetia. "You care for my son, don't you? I can tell he cares for you; I've never seen him look at a woman as he looked at you. Not even Polly."

Though the words warmed her, they didn't change anything. "Yes, I care for him. But he made it quite plain he won't marry me."

"No, not as things stand now." Lady Ross brooded as she guided the cart horse up a rutted dirt track. "He's letting his pride rule him. He'll never go hat in hand to ask the earl for his permission, and yer father won't give it with anything less, if he'll give it at all. And if you marry without your father's blessing—"

"Lachlan won't get the money you need. I know."

"Money. Faugh! We'll manage somehow. But I want grandchildren. I want someone to look after him." Her voice shook. "I want him to stop doing things that'll get him killed. You and I have to settle this muddle without bloodshed."

A chill skated down Venetia's spine. "You know what Lachlan is planning?"

"I know my son. He won't be satisfied with aught else but the loan repaid." She slid a worried glance at Venetia. "I know yer father, too—he won't be satisfied with anything but the Scourge's head on a platter."

"I don't believe that. And I don't know why you both see him this way."

"You forget that Alasdair and I and yer parents were once good friends. I used to know Quentin very well, which is why I don't understand why he refused to honor his debt. But he changed in that year before yer mother's death. He even had Lachlan—" She caught herself. "It doesn't matter. The point is, you must persuade the two men to settle this matter amicably. That would be easier if you and Lachlan were to wed."

"Lachlan is rather set against that idea," Venetia said

dryly. "And it's not as if you can *force* him to marry me, you know."

"You'd be surprised what a determined mother might accomplish when it comes to getting a good wife for her son."

Venetia eyed the older woman speculatively. "What makes you think I would make him a good wife, when he's convinced himself otherwise? You haven't seen me since I was a child. I could be a shrew or a featherhead—"

"A featherhead wouldn't have tried to escape her captors so cleverly." When Venetia blinked at her, Lady Ross cracked a smile. "Jamie told me how you stood up to Lachlan on the road."

She guided the horse into the broadening drive that Venetia recognized as leading up to Rosscraig. "And any other young lady would have arrived here screaming her outrage, complaining about her treatment at my son's hands. You showed up ready to defend him and eager to set matters right. That alone told me you'd suit him."

Venetia sighed. "A pity he doesn't feel the same."

"Oh, he will." Lady Ross drew the cart up before the house. "By the time we get through with him, he will."

"What do you mean?"

"I've got a plan. But first, you'd best be sure you want him." Grimly, she pointed at the manor. "Because *that* is what comes with marriage to my son."

Her heart in her throat, Venetia gazed at Rosscraig. The whitewashed, L-shaped manor that stood out in her memory as a shining tribute to Scottish successes was anything but that now. Sections of chimney were missing bricks, several roof slates were cracked, and the short stone wall skirting the gallery crumbled off to the ground on one end.

After they disembarked and entered the manor, she discovered that the inside was even worse. Tatters of once beautiful damask curtains hung from rusting rods, and a layer of coal dust coated the high ceilings. The carpets desperately needed replacing, and every room cried out for new paint.

"Lachlan kept up with the major repairs fairly well until the beating." Lady Ross scowled. "Now even those have gone by the wayside, and we can't afford laborers. It takes all of the men distilling, hiding, and transporting the whisky just to keep the clan in food, clothing, and coal. I do what I can to keep the manor house in order, but you need a man for some things."

She ducked her head guiltily. "And I've always been handier with a gutting knife than a dustpan and linens. My father was a butcher, you know."

"I understand." Venetia forced a smile, though the state of the once glorious Rosscraig broke her heart. "You should see my needlework—I have two left thumbs when it comes to sewing a stitch."

"Forgive me for being blunt, but if you live here as the laird's wife, you won't have time for needlework. Or much of anything else."

Lady Ross eyed her expectantly, and Venetia realized this was a test—a far more important one than any Lachlan could have thrown at her.

Little did the woman know that Venetia had spent her entire life waiting for the moment she could return to the Highlands and settle into a lovely house of her own. A few crumbling bricks and tattered draperies weren't about to cow her.

Lachlan was the larger obstacle. Could he ever see her as someone besides "Duncannon's daughter"? Did he even want to? And if he did, would he be willing to put aside his quarrel with her father in order to have her in his life?

There was only one way to find out. It was time that Lachlan Ross learn exactly what sort of woman he was dealing with.

"Well?" Lady Ross said. "What do you think?"

"I think," she said, linking her arm through Lady Ross's, "we have a great deal of work to do. Now, about that plan of yours . . ."

Chapter Nineteen

Dear Cousin,

I'm sorry for your difficulties. You know I am willing to help however I can. I even promise not to ask for details beyond what you are willing to disclose.

Your friend,
Charlotte

"What do you mean there's no breakfast?" Lachlan glared at the poor Ross relation his mother must have installed as a butler at Rosscraig. After Lachlan had held back an entire day before riding over here from the cottage to see how Venetia fared, *this* was the reception he got?

What had happened to their housekeeper? And why had she added a butler, anyway? It was one more mouth to feed—apparently one that was eating all the breakfast. "Cook always has it on the table by seven. It's only seven fifteen now."

The man shrugged. "The ladies was up at dawn this day and last, sir, and done with breakfast by six. Been working like two fiends, they been."

He'd expected to find Venetia languishing of boredom, not working, of all things. "Doing what, pray tell?"

"Don't rightly know. They just send me to fetch things from time to time."

That sounded downright suspicious. "Where are they now?" Removing his hat, he tried to hand it to the man.

The butler wouldn't take it. "Forgive me, sir, but they said they wasn't to be bothered by anybody, even you."

His temper flaring, Lachlan hooked the hat on the rack himself. "It's *my* house, damn it!" He loomed over his clansman with a dire expression. "So I can bloody well bother anybody I bloody well please. Now *where are they*?"

"In the drawing room, sir," his new butler squeaked.

Stomach rumbling, he marched upstairs, which was easier to do now that he'd been rubbing his wounds with horse liniment. He had Venetia to thank for that.

But he wouldn't thank her for *this*. Devil take it, he'd been looking forward to a hot breakfast at the manor—black pudding and potato scones and rashers— something other than cold oatcakes. Instead, he was met with no breakfast and some butler trying to keep him out. What the devil was going on?

Venetia must be stirring up trouble. This was what he got for staying away to avoid her temptations. *Leave the lass to Mother*, he'd told himself. *You've got urgent business languishing.*

He snorted. It still languished. Because whether he was examining the barley on the malting floor or cutting the peat for the kilning, Venetia invaded his thoughts. The germinating barley smelled enough like the comfrey she'd plastered on his wounds to rouse memories of her tender doctoring. And when he and his men tramped through woods to the peat bogs, he thought of how he'd laid her down in the bracken to put his mouth and hands on her soft, yielding flesh—

With a curse, he hastened his steps. She plagued his thoughts only because he worried about how she and his mother were getting on. If he satisfied his curiosity, then he could put her from his mind.

A thump sounded from the drawing room, followed by feminine laughter and a low male voice he couldn't make out. He scowled. It had better not be some tradesman his mother had called in at Venetia's request. What if Venetia had taken it into her head to turn his manor into a fancy showpiece he couldn't afford?

He hastened his steps. Mother wasn't one to buy on credit, but he'd left the ladies alone together for a day, and that might be something the lass would do just to torment him. Damn, damn, damn, damn.

"What is going on up here?" he demanded as he burst into the drawing room.

Several pairs of eyes swung his way, mostly belonging to Rosscraig's few maids and the housekeeper. But Lachlan only cared about the pair belonging to Venetia. Who didn't look the least bit bored.

She scarcely even looked like a London lady anymore. In a borrowed gray gown with frayed cuffs and a stained apron, she fit right in with the servants, a lock of her glorious hair drooping over one eye and her cheek marred by a streak of blacking. None of it dimmed her attractions one bit.

"Lachlan?" His mother moved from behind the other lasses, her gaze cold on him. "Go away, for heaven's sake!"

That response from his mother, who was always begging him to keep her company, flabbergasted him.

"Go do . . . whatever it is you and the lads do all day," she went on. "You're not supposed to see this until it's finished!"

"If I'm paying for it, I'll damned well have a say in

what's done," Lachlan barked as he spotted Jamie perched atop a ladder, hanging curtains he'd never seen.

"Paying for it?" Mother said. "What are you talking about?"

"The new drapes." He flicked his hand toward the sofa. "That new settee. And whatever else you've been buying on credit."

"Don't be a fool—that's our same old settee. We just covered it with the good parts of our old curtains. And the new curtains are our old bed canopies." She smiled fondly at Venetia, who watched him with those green eyes that never gave him quarter. "Being up away from the light, the fabric stayed fresh-looking, so the lass here suggested we use it for curtains and take down the canopy rails of the beds. Don't need canopies anyway."

"We were fortunate that the colors match," Venetia put in, "and we were able to salvage most of the curtain fringe, too—it looks lovely on the settee."

"We" apparently included the clanswomen cheerily engrossed in scrubbing floors and beating rugs and God knew what else.

"Looks nice, don't it?" Jamie chirped from atop the ladder. "Brightens the room right up. You should see what the ladies did with the dining room, sir, fixing it up and arranging things all proper. Did that yesterday. Even cleaned the ceilings with a special mixture Miss Ross invented."

Miss Ross? Oh, right, Venetia was supposed to be a London cousin. And judging from Jamie's besotted smile, the lad had forgotten she was too lofty for the likes of him.

Lachlan fought the urge to drag the lad down and smack the smile from his lips. "Aren't you supposed to be taking care of the barley floor? The malting is still going on, you know."

"Yes, sir," Jamie mumbled, and started to descend the ladder.

"Pay no attention to Lachlan," Mother told the lad. "He's only complaining because he wasn't consulted. He can spare you for a while."

He could, but why should Jamie get to stay here, seeing Venetia with her cheeks flushed and her eyes shining with enthusiasm, while Lachlan spent his days at the stills, pining after her?

"If you need a man helping you, I'll do it," Lachlan said, though in the past he'd have sooner dragged his naked body over hot coals than fool with drapes and such female foolery. "Let Jamie go back to the stills."

"No, indeed," his mother retorted. "If you spend yer days here, you risk being seen by anybody who visits from town." Her eyes gleamed at him. "Besides, it won't do to have you hanging curtains when the earl arrives. You'll need to look fierce and manly if you want to cow him into giving us our money, won't ye?"

Was that sarcasm he heard? From his *mother*, of all people? He looked to Venetia, who seemed to hide a smile as she blacked an andiron.

That smile provoked him even more. "Duncannon won't be here for a few days yet," Lachlan persisted. "And if anyone comes, that new butler you hired without consulting me will warn me so I can duck out of sight."

His mother clapped her work-worn hands on her bony hips. "You've got more important things to do than hang about here. Lord knows ye've told me that often enough in the past five years. We wouldn't dream of keeping you from it." She strode toward him. "Jamie will do us fine. Now go on with you, and let us do our work."

Reluctantly, he headed toward the door. "Perhaps I'll see you at dinner," he said as he reached the hall.

"We're too busy to take regular meals." His mother smiled at him from the doorway. "I'll have Cook send a nice dinner to the cottage for you, all right?"

"But . . ." But what? He glanced beyond Mother to where Venetia paid him no mind at all, too busy setting the andiron in place.

A hard knot formed in his gut. He wanted more than dinner. He wanted to talk to Venetia, to see her, to be with her. But he wasn't about to say that. Because he had no right to any of it, not when he'd be handing the lass over to her father in a few days.

If he didn't end up killing the man.

"Yes, send dinner," he mumbled, then left.

The next morning, after a night of restless dreams about Venetia, he swallowed his pride and went early for breakfast, but either they'd seen him coming or they really were at a crofter's house seeing to a sick child, as the butler claimed. No one was home.

The butler didn't know which crofter. He didn't know when they'd return. He didn't know a bloody thing that might keep Lachlan from howling his frustration to the skies.

He told himself that was the end of it. They didn't need him at the manor, and he sure as the devil didn't need them. He'd often spent weeks away with the malting or the kilning, making sure the excisemen didn't find his illegal stills. How was this any different?

Because Venetia is there.

That was absurd. He'd never missed having a woman

about before; why should he miss it now? He didn't want Venetia singing to him, annoying him . . . coddling him. No, indeed. He could slather horse liniment on his own wounds. Never mind that she had a way of doing it . . .

He had to stop thinking of her!

It didn't help that he had to listen to his clansmen prattle on over the next few days about the changes at the manor and how Venetia and his mother were getting on so well. Every other minute, somebody was saying things like "You should have heard your London cousin singing 'Gypsy Laddie'" or "You should have seen the lass teaching the wives how to make their silver shine."

Apparently his "London cousin" could come and go as she pleased, while he was forced to stay away so nobody outside the clan would learn he wasn't dead. He tried twice to see her, but the one time he actually caught them home, Venetia excused herself at once, leaving him to visit with his mother, who chided him for coming.

That glimpse of the lass was like a few drops of water dribbled in a parched throat. Not nearly enough.

He could demand to see her, but then both she and Mother would know he yearned for her. That would only raise impossible expectations.

But by the third afternoon after their arrival, when the butler told him they were out walking, probably in fairyland somewhere, he couldn't take it anymore. Determined not to be put off again, he planted himself in the woods outside the manor house where he could watch both entrances. If they really were walking, they'd have to come past him, and she wouldn't be able to make an easy exit.

He felt like a besotted idiot, lurking out in the woods, but just as he'd decided that the horse liniment must be going to his head, the kitchen door opened and Venetia slipped outside.

Just as he'd suspected—they'd been in the manor all along.

Heart hammering foolishly in his chest, he crept through the trees toward her. Where was she going alone? And dressed like that, too, with a country lass's tartan *arisaid* draped about her slender form and belted right proper?

After a furtive glance about, she tugged the excess over her head like a hood, then walked away from the house.

She cut off across the field separating the Ross estate from the Duncannon one, and his eyes narrowed. Ah, she was headed to her father's house. To find shelter and beg whoever lived there to help her return to London? No, she could have done that before.

He hesitated, wondering if he should follow. If Duncannon's people recognized him, it would raise questions about his miraculous resurrection. Next thing he knew, folks would be traipsing onto his estate to find out what was going on. Then he'd never keep this matter between him and the earl private.

Still, he couldn't let her roam Braidmuir alone; it wasn't safe. She might run afoul of rough men who didn't know who she was. He'd just have to be careful, stick to the woods and stay out of the parts where people were.

That's what he told himself as he set off after her.

Unsure what to expect, Venetia crossed the bridge over the burn separating Lachlan's land from her father's. She'd asked Lady Ross to bring her here, but the woman had worried about anyone recognizing her.

Given how many years Venetia had been away, she found that highly unlikely, but just in case, she'd borrowed an *arisaid* from a servant to cover her head. She had to see what had happened in the years she'd been away. Especially after Lachlan's comments about burned-out cottages.

Lachlan. No, she wouldn't think about him. Their three days apart made her miss him too much . . . and realize she'd probably read too much into his kisses and caresses. Although he'd visited the manor, he'd never once asked to see her. He'd inquired about their whereabouts and taken any rebuff in stride, as if his inquiries had been motivated only by politeness.

His mother said that his pride kept him from showing that he cared. Venetia wanted desperately to believe her, but she'd begun to lose hope. By now, Papa had received Lachlan's letter and was heading to Scotland. If Lachlan never relented . . .

A band closed around her chest. How could she blame him for not wanting to marry the daughter of a man who'd ravaged his countrymen? That was how the people at Rosscraig saw Papa. Thinking she was a Ross cousin, they'd spoken freely of how the earl allowed his factor, McKinley, to toss people off the land with cruel abandon.

And now as she wandered Braidmuir, careful to avoid the groundskeeper or occasional shepherd, she quickly saw the results. There were no burned-out cottages, but there might as well have been. Of the twenty-two crofters' huts, only four appeared inhabited, probably by sheep farmers.

What had happened to the red-faced potato farmer who'd given her rides on his plow horse when she was a child? Where was the toothless granny who'd sat in front of the pink cottage, churning her spinning wheel every fine day?

Gone, all of them. Tears trickled down Venetia's cheeks. Only the Ross estate nearby bustled with life. Clansmen tilled land, coopered whisky barrels, and tended the stills. Women did their washing while their children swung from branches and gathered heather. Lachlan had struggled to keep his people in their homes, to make sure they were provided for, even when it meant risking his life.

Even when it meant this foolish kidnapping. Now that she knew why he'd done it, she could hardly bear to remember the insults she'd hurled at him. Especially when she saw Papa's land lying silent except for the bleating sheep.

She brushed tears from her eyes. The Cheviots were everywhere, clogging every pasture, jostling up every hill. They'd overtaken even the grassy glen near the burn that bounded the property, the one Lachlan had always liked to fish.

Must they take this bit of her childhood from her, too? Temper flaring, she began shooing the flocks, trying to force them to leave the glen, but they only stumbled off a few feet before returning to grazing.

"There's no point, lassie," said a low voice from the woods behind her. "Even if you empty this glen of them, they'll fill others. And it's not really their fault anyway, is it?"

The band around her chest grew painful as she whirled to find Lachlan watching her while leaning against the same gnarled oak he used to favor. With his hair tousled and his trousers grimy from his work, he looked exactly as he'd looked sixteen years ago. It made her want to throw herself into his arms.

It made her want to cry. He was no longer the endearingly wild Lachlan of her childhood. Thanks to her father, he wasn't allowed to be.

"No, it's not the sheep's fault," she said, her heart in her throat. "But neither is it mine."

He pushed away from the tree. "I didn't say it was."

"You shouldn't be here, you know. Someone might see you."

He shrugged. "Someone might see *you*, but that didn't stop you from wandering among the crofters' cottages."

"You've been watching me the whole time?"

"Mayhap." His expression veiled, he approached her. "Why?"

The question seemed to unnerve him. "No reason."

She wanted to scream. He'd followed her over here, and he couldn't even tell her why? "Very well." She headed up the hill behind the crofters' cottages. "Then you have no reason to stay."

He kept pace easily with her. "You shouldn't be here alone."

"I'm not alone." Gathering up her skirts, she hastened her steps. "I've got the sheep for company." She paused at the top to stare at him. "Why do you care what I do, anyway, as long as it doesn't affect your plans?" A sudden suspicion made her stomach roil. "You think I'm trying to escape, don't you?"

"Don't be daft," he growled as he approached.

"Why else would you risk coming here where you might be seen—"

He cut her off with a kiss, a hard one meant to quiet her. It stunned her so much that for a moment she allowed it. Until she remembered that this was how it always started—with him kissing her and pretending things could be different between them, then reminding her afterward that they couldn't.

She'd had enough of *that* game. When he tried to deepen the kiss, she tore her mouth free. "Don't you dare!" she bit out, then strode down an alley between two cottages, struggling to hold back tears.

"Why not?" Hurrying after her, he caught her again, this time about the waist. His eyes searched her face. "It's only a kiss I'm wanting, lass."

That was exactly the problem. He wanted a moment's dalliance. "Two days ago, you couldn't be bothered even to ask how I was doing." She glared at him. "And now you expect me to *kiss* you?"

Frustration lit his features. "I didn't . . . I wanted . . . How *are* you doing?"

"Perfectly fine. And you?"

Her remote tone made him scowl. "I'm not fine at all, damn it!"

"I hardly see what that has to do with me," she said primly.

"I didn't say . . . Holy Christ, why are you acting like we never—"

"Is someone there?" said a voice from beyond the alley.

They froze. Glancing about, Lachlan spotted the side door into a nearby cottage at the same time as she. He shoved her inside, then eased the door closed behind them. They held their breaths as someone walked down the alley and then, apparently satisfied that no one was around, left.

Lachlan reached for her with clear intent, but she

skittered off before he could touch her. When she then nearly stumbled over something, she glanced around to see piles of fluffy-looking muslin bags behind her. Apparently the cottage was used to store the cursed fleeces from her father's sheep.

Skirting the edge of the pile, she headed for the other door in front. If he thought he could come over here just to dally with her, he could think again.

But she should have known the arrogant wretch wouldn't give up so easily. He was behind her in two strides and dragging her back against his body.

"Let go of me!" she cried as she pushed at his restraining arm.

"First I want my kiss, lass," he said hoarsely.

Wriggling free, she whirled to face him. "I'm sure any of your young clanswomen would be delighted to kiss the laird." Her voice grew brittle as she backed toward the front door. "And you don't hate their fathers, either."

In the dim light filtering through the windows, Lachlan seemed even larger, his hair nearly dusting the low ceiling as he stalked her. "I don't want their kisses. Only yours."

"Have you forgotten I'm 'Duncannon's daughter'?" she said sweetly. "I'm the last person you want kisses from." She'd nearly reached the door, thank heaven.

"I don't care about that," he said, his tone mutinous.

"Seems to me that's *all* you care about. You certainly don't care about me."

She grabbed the door handle behind her and pulled, but he was upon her now and shoved the door closed.

"I care enough to want a kiss from you." He braced his hands on either side to trap her. "One kiss, lass." His eyes glittered down at her. "Give me that at least."

"Why?" She shoved against his massive chest, which didn't do her any blessed good. Why must he be so big, so overwhelming . . . so persistent? "You've already said you don't want to marry me, that we have no future together. So why would you want to kiss me?" She lifted an eyebrow. "Unless you've decided that debauching Duncannon's daughter would be the ultimate revenge."

"No, damn you," he growled, eyes ablaze. "I'd never—"

"Ah, so *that's* why you followed me," she taunted him, determined to get the truth out of him, even if it meant making absurd accusations. "To ruin me."

"I wanted to protect you!" he said with a hint of belligerence.

"From what, the sheep?"

With a curse, he glanced away, clearly debating what to say. She ducked under his arm and ran for the other door. She'd nearly got it open when he called, "I wanted to see you, all right?"

Her hand froze on the door handle.

"I wanted to be with you." When she turned, shocked by what he'd said, he approached her with eyes the warm, rich color of chocolate. "To talk to you." Reaching her, he drew her into his arms. "To hold you. I missed you, damn it."

"You certainly had a funny way of showing it," she said tartly, though her heart felt as if it would slam right out of her chest. He cared. He'd missed her. He'd actually admitted it. "Any time in the past few days, you could have—"

"Been put off by the butler or my mother while you merrily slipped out the back way?" The tension in his voice was unmistakable. And unwarranted.

"Asked to speak to me. Simple as that."

"I'm here now, aren't I?" He nuzzled her brow, his hot breath branding her skin. "And you won't even give me a kiss for it."

"Because I know why you came here." She wasn't ready to give in yet. It was fine for him to miss her, but that didn't mean he wanted more. "You thought that without your mother nearby, you could dally with me to your heart's content. Well, if that's what you're after, you can just head right back—"

"What if I were to say I want to marry you?" he rasped.

Her gaze leaped to his. She couldn't believe she'd heard him right.

Though surprise lit his own face, he steadied his shoulders. "Aye. What if I were to marry you?"

Hope stole through her, despite her efforts not to be too hasty. "I thought you said we couldn't marry because of Papa and the money."

"We'll work it out somehow. Just say you'll marry me."

She stared at him. He'd changed his mind. The word "yes" flew to her lips, but she caught it just in time.

What about the hurtful things he'd said? Or how she'd practically had to bludgeon him into admitting he missed her? He finally mentioned marriage as a possibility, and now the cocky lad thought that should have her falling at his feet?

Well, he could wait a bit longer for that. She'd suffered for three days, uncertain of his feelings—she was *not* going to give in easily. "I don't know if I *want* to marry you anymore," she said with a lofty sniff. "I think you should just trot back to your stills and your bachelor's cottage and—"

This time his kiss gave her no quarter. His mouth sought the secrets of hers with an intensity that left her breathless . . . aching . . . hungry. She must have shown it, for when he drew back, he wore a decidedly self-assured expression.

"Mayhap you'd like to reconsider that answer, lass," he taunted her.

He was so blessed sure of himself, wasn't he? Worse yet, he was sure of *her*. And that simply wouldn't do, or she'd never be able to live with him.

Ruthlessly, she quelled the thundering in her chest and forced a blithe smile to her lips. "Rethink it? Why? I hardly think one kiss changes anything."

His self-assurance vanished. "So you're going to be stubborn, are you?" He moved forward, walking her backward. "Going to try and make me slobber after you like one of yer fancy London suitors. Make me beg."

"Absolutely. You're the one who said I'm too fine a lady for life in the Highlands." She thrust out her chin. "Perhaps you're right. Perhaps I'd be better off finding an English husband with pots of money and a grand title—"

The next thing she knew, he'd pushed her down onto the soft fleece bags. She was so stunned, she just gaped at him as he shed his coat and waistcoat, then removed his shirt. Surely he didn't mean . . . he wasn't planning . . .

"So you seek an English husband, do you?" The amber light of the setting sun turned his hair a rich mahogany and burnished his tanned chest a fine gold hue that made her hands itch to touch it. "Then I know what I have to do, lassie." He yanked off his boots, then stripped off his trousers in one swift jerk.

The little thrill that coursed through her veins sent the blood right to her head. Lord save her. "Wh-what do you mean?" she whispered, though she was pretty sure she knew.

Her mouth went dry as he threw himself down beside her and unbuckled her belt, then drew her *arisaid* aside to reveal the servant's gown she'd donned since nothing else at Braidmuir fitted her.

He didn't seem to mind the worn seams or the ragged fabric. Tugging loose the fichu that barely made the too tight bodice respectable, he ran his hot, hungry gaze over the breasts practically spilling out of her bodice.

"Can't have a Scottish lady as lovely as you falling into the hands of a Sassenach. I have to save you from that." His eyes met hers, and a slow seducer's smile spread over his lips. "If you won't be sensible, you leave me no choice but to ruin you. Then you'll *have* to marry me."

Chapter Twenty

Dear Charlotte,

 *Think no more of my difficulties. I've heard
disturbing news for you about Lord Duncannon.
Apparently he left for Scotland rather suddenly
yesterday. No one seems to know why, but I fear it
has something to do with your former charge, Lady
Venetia.*

Your friend,
Michael

*L*achlan wasn't entirely surprised when Venetia scowled at him, then said, "Of all the arrogant, presumptuous—"

He kissed her hard, gripping her head so he could take her mouth fierce and deep, the way he knew she liked it. He wasn't about to lose his chance with her just because she'd turned missish about his methods.

And though she dug her fingers into his shoulders as if to push him away, she opened her lips to him, her body straining against his.

Thank God. He hadn't come here meaning to offer marriage, and he sure as the devil hadn't come to ruin her. But after he'd seen her wandering her father's estate with tears streaming down her cheeks, losing her temper at the sheep . . .

What self-respecting Scot wouldn't want a wife like that? One who saw the land for what it could be, was meant to be: a place for nurturing families? Clearly he'd been wrong about her never belonging at Rosscraig.

She'd already seduced half his clan into accepting her.

The way she was seducing him now with her generous mouth. Hungering for more than kisses, he covered her breast through the gown.

She froze, then broke the kiss to stare up at him. "I haven't yet said I'd *let* you ruin me, have I?" she chided as she stayed his hand.

"Oh, but you will, lass, you will." Shrugging off her grip, he kneaded her breast shamelessly.

Her breath quickened, and he could feel her nipple hardening through the worsted wool. "What makes you so sure?" she asked in a throaty whisper that clutched at his heart.

"Because I know yer deepest secret."

A wary light shone in her eyes. "And what is that?"

With a grin, he reached beneath her to undo her buttons, then bent to whisper against her lips, "Ye're not as much a fine lady as you pretend."

That got her dander up something fierce, for she shoved him back, then rose to cast him a haughty glance. "I'm certainly too fine a lady to be letting you tumble me in the fleece, Lachlan Ross."

"Are you now?" With a laugh, he grabbed her gown as she tried to stalk off. He didn't mind her playing Princess Proud when he knew he could demolish the sham with one kiss.

Well, not *one* kiss, mayhap, since she fought to jerk her skirts from his grip.

"Now, lassie," he said as he reached beneath them with his free hand to grab her foot. "I have the greatest admiration for yer expensive schooling and yer fine bloodlines and yer fancy London accent, I do."

Ignoring her snort, he dragged off her shoe, tossed it aside, then seized her stocking foot and brought it to his lips. "And I realize I'm scarcely fit to kiss yer feet." Though he did it anyway—twice.

As he rose to his knees, she stopped fighting, staring down at him with eyes turned the sultry green of lush fields. He had to favor his stronger leg while kneeling, but that didn't keep him from sliding his hand up her stocking-clad calf with lascivious intent. Or from following the caress with kisses that traced the same path, up the inside of her leg to her knee and the garter tied above it.

"But there's times even a fine lady should put aside her pretty ways," he said hoarsely. Inching her skirts up her lovely long legs, he gazed at the twin swaths of smooth white thigh above her garters, and the blood rushed rampant through his veins. "Times she should let a rough Highland laddie do what he does best."

"And what is that, pray tell?" she asked in a voice turned breathy and low.

He lifted her skirts high enough to bare the silky black triangle of hair beneath, for she wore no drawers. "Make her ribbons reel."

"Ribbons re— You stole that line from one of my ballads!"

"Aye. I'm not much good at wooing with my own words." He grinned up at her, then parted her curls to expose her dewy flesh to his gaze. "But this, lassie, *this* I can do right well." Then he covered her tender parts with his mouth.

With a sharply indrawn breath, she caught his head as if to push him away. But as he began to caress her with his mouth, she curled her fingers into his hair, then drew him closer. "Lachlan . . . my word . . . that is . . . very naughty."

"Can't help myself, lass." He laved her with his tongue, relishing her sweet smell of aroused female. Her thighs trembled as he caught them to hold her still for his caresses. "You *taste* naughty."

Half drunk with need, he fondled her with his mouth, inside and out, strafing her delicate pearl with his tongue until he thought he'd go mad with wanting. She was such a heady treat after days of fasting, he feared he'd come off just from tasting her.

Her hands dropped to grip his shoulders hard, and she moaned low in her throat. For all her proprieties, his London lass was a quick study in the enjoyment of pleasure. No doubt it was those naughty ballads and books she read.

Then he glanced up at her blushing face and noticed she wouldn't meet his gaze, though her eyes were open. He chuckled against her hot, satiny skin. Mayhap not so quick a study after all. "Tell me, lass," he murmured between quick licks, "is this how a fine lady likes to be caressed? Because if I'm not pleasing you, I can always stop."

When her answer was to arch herself against his mouth, he exulted. He drove his tongue deep inside her silky flesh, delighting in the urgent gasping breaths she gave as he stroked strong and sure, his blood afire with the thrill of watching her find her pleasure.

Soon he was clutching her hips and driving her on and up until her fingers dug fiercely into his shoulders and she uttered a soft cry, staggering a little beneath the release, rocking her limbs.

He savored the taste of her a moment longer, changing his caresses to feathery kisses scattered over her delicate curls. But he gave her no more time than that to come down, too aroused to wait any longer.

He wanted to be inside her, wanted to make her his before she came to her senses and refused him again. So while she was still reeling, he rose and circled behind her to finish undressing her.

"You ought to be . . . ashamed of yourself . . ." she whispered, though she let him unfasten her gown and stays.

"For what?" He shoved them off before turning her to face him.

"For being so good at tempting a lady into ruin."

The petulance in her voice made him laugh. But his laughter died when he reached for the ties of her chemise and she clutched at them protectively.

He raised an eyebrow. "You've got too many clothes on still."

"What if someone comes by and sees us?" she whispered, with a furtive glance at the bare glass windows that fronted the alleyway.

"It's nigh on to sunset and supper," he assured her, prying the ties free of her hold. "They won't be lingering about here, trust me."

"But if they do?"

"Assuming they don't recognize you and set the dogs on me, they'll just send us packing." He cast her a teasing smile as he untied her chemise. "Unless they decide to watch."

"Lachlan!" She looked thoroughly scandalized. "Surely they'd *never*—"

"They'd be mad not to." He tugged her chemise off,

then caught his breath. What a vision she was. "Any sane man who got a glimpse of you in the flesh would keep looking as long as he was able and then some."

Though her cheeks turned the ruddy hue of autumn leaves, she suffered his gaze as he took in her heavy breasts and dusky nipples, her dimpled waist and shapely hips. "Ye're a wonder of nature, lass, a wonder of nature."

A hesitant smile touched her lips. "My dressmaker says my bosom is too large for the current fashions."

"Your dressmaker is a fool." Enjoying the mere sight of her, he took his time about unbuttoning his drawers. "And I don't know about fashion, but there's no such thing as a woman with breasts too large." He shoved his drawers off and kicked them aside. "I'm told that some women feel the same about a man's . . . er . . . privates."

Judging from the alarm suffusing her face as she saw his cock spring free, Venetia wasn't one. Not yet anyway. "Oh, Lachlan, I don't know about this."

He dragged her down into the fleece with him. Thank God she let him. "About what?"

"That!" Lying there looking wary, she pointed to his cock. "It's too . . . and I'm not . . ."

"You'll be fine, trust me," he said with a choked laugh.

"Do you promise?" she whispered as he slid his thigh between her legs to part them. "Do you swear it?"

"I promise." But the question brought him up short. He'd never deflowered an innocent. What if he did her serious harm? No, that didn't usually happen, did it? "It'll take adjustment—always does—but even with you being a maiden, you'll come out of it whole and healthy, I swear."

Her eyes narrowed. "What do you mean, *always does*?

How many women have you bedded in your lifetime, anyway?"

Uh-oh, he shouldn't have mentioned that. "A few," he mumbled, then covered her mouth with his to take her mind off it.

Because he was itching to go on. Just having her beneath him, open and willing, turned his cock painfully hard. The lavender smell of her intoxicated him more surely than whisky, and he could feed on her butter-soft mouth for a lifetime. But first . . .

He shifted to lie between her legs, all the while caressing the warm flesh of her honeypot until she relaxed. When she lifted her arms to encircle his neck, he knew she was willing. Careful not to alarm her, he replaced his fingers with his cock, pressing in, pushing inside her, restraining the urge to thrust all at once.

But Holy Christ, that took some doing. She was wet and tight, better than anything he'd imagined. And she was his, all his at last, his princess . . . his wife-to-be. The thought made him swell inside her.

"Oh, Lord," she whispered. "Are you sure—"

He tore his lips free as he braced his hands on either side of her shoulders. "I'm sure," he said, though he'd give anything to be able to spare her this part.

She was trying so bravely not to flinch, his bold lassie, but her taut lips showed the strain of that effort.

"I'm taking it as slow as I can," he murmured, brushing kisses over her lips, her cheeks, her brow, "but being inside you is the sweetest thing I've ever known."

A tentative smile touched her lips. "And those are the sweetest words a man has ever said to me." She relaxed a little, and he slipped inside her another inch.

Relieved, he managed to smile, too. "I can hardly

believe that. Don't yer fancy London lords whisper compliments at the balls . . . about yer pretty hair and yer sparkling eyes and yer fine mouth . . ."

"Occasionally."

He'd said it to tease her, but the ready admission made him frown. "Do they now? And did you ever let them kiss that fine mouth?"

Her eyes lit up with mischief. "Occasionally."

He came up against the barrier of her innocence. "How many times?"

With a laugh, she pressed her breasts up against his chest and echoed his answer. "A few."

Oh, she thought she was so witty, did she? "Well, they won't be doing it anymore," he vowed. Then, seizing her mouth with his, he plunged his cock deep.

When she moaned against his lips, he prayed that was the worst of it. He stayed still inside her, though it took an act of will. She encased him like a hot glove, making him ache to press on.

But he didn't. He just kept kissing her and holding her and caressing her wherever he could reach. It humbled him that she'd given herself to him so trustingly—he wasn't about to ruin that.

After a moment, he felt her relax, and he drew back to murmur, "All right?"

"I think so." She wiggled her hips. "It's not . . . it wasn't too bad."

A groan escaped him as her motion wrung his cock. "It will be, if you don't stop doing that," he said hoarsely.

She blinked at him. "Why?"

"Because I want to go on, but I need to be slow and easy—and I can't when you're driving me mad like that."

"Like what?"

"Moving like that."

She wriggled her hips again. "Like this, you mean?"

"Now, lass—"

"I could move like this instead." Eyes alight, she rubbed her breasts against his chest. "Or like this." She shifted her lower body so that his cock sank in deeper.

"So you mean to drive me mad, do you?" he rasped as he began to move. "You want me to take you hard and fast, I suppose."

A minxish smile touched her luscious lips. "Could you, please? It sounds perfectly . . . delicious."

Just the way she said "delicious," all proper-like, was doing things to his insides no woman ever had. "Ye're a teasing wench, lassie," he growled as he drove into her again and again, dizzy from the feel of her wringing his cock. "A proper-speaking, princess-walking wench with a body made in heaven."

"Am I?" she whispered, but her eyes slid closed and her face flushed.

He'd never seen anything prettier . . . or more arousing. "You like that, do you?"

"Yes," she breathed. "Yes . . . yes . . ."

"*Mo chreach.*" He'd heard that some women took naturally to lovemaking. No surprise she was one of them, given how well she'd pleasured him in Kingussie.

Now if only he didn't die of *this* pleasuring . . . She shimmied beneath him like a gypsy dancer, her full breast ripening beneath his questing hand and her hips rolling, sucking him in deeper, rising in time to his thrusts until he couldn't think, couldn't breathe, couldn't hear for the blood roaring in his ears.

Princess Proud was his at last, his forever. His to hold, his to protect, his to defend even from Duncannon.

No, he wouldn't think of that devil now. Not with his release hard upon him, dragging him on like a team of horses pounding recklessly down a steep hill . . . not with her sweet honeypot tensing and convulsing and her body straining beneath him.

Not when the woman he'd coveted night upon sleepless night was giving herself to him at last.

"Lord save me!" she cried as her release hit her. "Heavens!"

"Aye . . . princess . . . aye . . ." He came with one final thunderous thrust, his heart pounding fiercely. "Holy Christ!" He clutched her to him as his seed gushed out of him like a mountain spring. "Holy Christ . . ."

It had the sound of a vow, and that was fine. Because now that he had her, he meant to keep her. No matter what happened between him and Duncannon.

Chapter Twenty-One

Dear Cousin,

Your news about Lord Duncannon is disturbing indeed. His daughter said he swore an oath never to return to his homeland. If he's willing to break it, then something dreadful must have happened to Venetia. Can you use your sources to find out what it might be?

Your alarmed relation,
Charlotte

Venetia rested her head on Lachlan's chest as she lay naked in the fleece, completely content, his breath ruffling her hair and his arms wrapped about her. The strong beat of his heart comforted her, as did the tender way he brushed kisses over her hair. He was her strong Highland lover, and no one could take that away from her now.

He hadn't said he loved her, true, but then she wasn't sure she loved the pigheaded fellow, either. Until she knew what he meant to do about Papa, she dared not give him her heart.

She probably shouldn't have given him her body either, but his words had lifted her hopes. If he'd been willing to propose marriage, he must have changed his plans for Papa.

Sounds of activity outside the cottage penetrated her sensual haze, though whoever was out there quickly passed on. But it reminded her that lying about on her father's estate with Lachlan wasn't the best idea, especially with the sun setting.

She sighed. "Your mother will wonder where I am. We should go back. Besides, we'll soon have trouble finding our way back in the dark."

"Then mayhap we should stay until morn," he said, his voice a contented rumble.

A laugh bubbled out of her. "You are perfectly wicked, do you know that?"

"Aye, that's why you like me. I remind you of those fellows in yer ballads—the ones always meeting their lovers in bowers and barns and fields, taking their pleasure amidst the flowers or hay. You ought to leap at the chance to spend the night upon the fleece, like one of the people in yer songs."

Sadly enough, she would. She just couldn't. "Don't tempt me. We're not married yet, you know."

"Oh, but we are, lass."

Propping her chin on his chest, she eyed him quizzically. "How on earth do you figure that?"

"Scottish law says that as long as we agree between ourselves and speak 'mutual consents' to marry, then we're married, at least in the eyes of the law."

She gaped at him. "Surely there'd have to be a minister present."

With a grin, he shook his head no.

"Witnesses?"

"None of it. Why do you think Englishmen always carry women to Gretna Green to marry? Because it's so easy. They do it in front of witnesses in case anyone contests it, but the law says you don't need that. Just mutual consents."

"Except that we didn't speak any consents," she pointed out.

"True. But here's where the law gets tricky. It allows for three kinds of irregular marriage—you can live in sin and have your marriage considered legal by 'habit and repute,' you can exchange present consents to marry, or you can exchange future consents and then consummate the marriage. We just did the last."

"That's absurd."

"Aye, that's Scotland for you." He twined a lock of her hair pensively about his hand. "But truth is, while irregular marriages are legal, most everyone frowns on people not having a proper wedding in the kirk. My mother will expect one. As will yer father, I imagine."

"He certainly will. Especially since I haven't yet consented to marry you. Which means we're still unwed, Scottish law or no. Because the consummation came before any promises to marry."

A frown touched his brow. "Did it? I could have sworn you said—"

"No." She cast him a teasing smile as she traced the curly whorls of hair about his nipples. "If you'll recall, I told you I was too fine a lady to marry you."

With a black frown, he caught her hand. "Well, then, we'll have to remedy that oversight, won't we?" When she remained silent, he said, "You *are* going to marry me, lass. I ruined you. At the very least, yer father will demand it."

Much as she wanted to lose herself in this moment with Lachlan, it was time to settle a few things. "First I need to know what you plan for him."

His face darkened. "I expect him to pay the money. That hasn't changed."

"Of course not." She pushed up from him and reached for her chemise. "But if he ... well ... refuses and turns stubborn about it? Will you call him out?" He was silent so long that her heart began to pound in her chest. "I'm not saying he doesn't deserve it, mind you, but ... well ..

"He's yer father."

"Exactly."

He muttered a curse under his breath. "And you'd never forgive me if I murdered him, I suppose."

"Never," she whispered.

"Very well." A sigh escaped his lips. "I won't call him out."

She let out the breath she'd been holding.

A scowl knit his brow as he watched her rise and pick up her corset. "But that doesn't mean I'll let him get away with not paying the money."

"Of course not."

"And if *he* tries to kill *me*—"

"He won't, I promise," she said hastily.

But what if Papa *did* try to kill Lachlan? Or challenged him? Even if Papa came prepared to be reasonable, their discussion of the money might escalate into a battle that ended in bloodshed anyway.

Lachlan rose and seized her corset to help her lace it. "Now will you agree to marry me?" he murmured, his breath warming her neck.

She thought of what Lady Ross had said about how bloodshed might be prevented. "Only if you'll make me one promise."

His fingers froze on the corset ties. "I already promised not to call yer father out."

"I know." But that didn't solve the problem of Papa,

who had a tendency to come roaring into any situation with his mind made up. "Before you say anything to him, before you even see him, I want to meet with him."

"No," Lachlan said flatly.

Her heart lurched in her chest as she faced him. "Hear me out. I know how to get around Papa better than you do. If you'll just give me the chance to explain the situation to him in a rational manner—"

"No, never." Eyes glittering, he drew on his drawers, then his trousers. "I'm not having my wife do my dirty work for me."

She blew out an exasperated breath. "It wouldn't be like that. Think of it as sending in a negotiator. Because I know once I set everything out for him, he'll see things properly."

He scowled as he pulled on his shirt and fastened the buttons. "Ye're mad if you think I'll stand back and let you offer him concessions I'm unwilling to make."

"I won't do that!"

"Aye, you won't. Because the only talking you'll be doing is to tell him that we're married, that you were willing. He and I will settle the rest between us."

If they even got that far. "You don't understand—"

"Oh, I understand right well, lassie." His eyes darkened to a smoky black. "You want to smooth it all over—coax yer father into giving me yer dowry, instead of making him admit to his responsibilities. Then you'll come tell me that the dowry is enough, and that'll be the end of it for you. Only it won't be the end of it for me. It never can be."

"What does it matter how the money comes to you?"

"It matters, damn it!" He dropped to the floor to draw on his boots, then swore as he landed on his leg badly.

"Look at me—I still can't even sit down without making an ass of myself, thanks to yer father! And you want me to let the whole thing pass?"

"I didn't say that!"

"But that's what you think. I'll be giving yer father a piece of my mind no matter what, lassie." He jerked on his boots. "I won't stand by and let him bully me and mine before my clan ever again."

She blinked. "Again? When did my father ever bully you?"

A flush touched his cheeks, and he dropped his gaze to his boots.

"There's something you haven't told me, isn't there? Something else between you and my father."

"Nothing of any importance," he said, though he wouldn't look at her. "Not compared to the money."

Well, she'd find out about it somehow. "You're forgetting that I want to make sure you get the money."

"Aye. By taking me out of the discussion." He crossed his arms over his chest. "I won't allow it, and that's an end to it."

Oh, he was such a proud fool! "I'm just trying to avoid a fight between you and Papa. Why can't you see that, curse you?"

"I told you I won't call him out. That'll have to be enough."

She wrapped the *arisaid* about her and belted it, then strode up to lay her hand on his arm, gentling her voice. "And will you promise not to fight with him at all, no matter what he says or does?"

Anger flared in his face. "You can't expect me to promise something as foolish as that, lass. I have to defend myself if he attacks me."

That's exactly what she was afraid of. "So the result will be the same as if you *did* call him out. You'll argue, tempers will get hot, he'll go for your throat, and before I know it, you'll be beating him to a bloody pulp."

"Would you rather he beat *me* to a bloody pulp?"

"No!" She read skepticism in his face, and hurt scored her heart. "How could you even think that? I don't want *anyone's* blood shed!"

"Too late for that, lassie—blood has already been shed." He nodded to the pile, where her virgin's blood stained the fleece. "And that blood ties you to me, damn it, *me*. So you'll let me, yer husband, decide how this is handled."

She gazed up into his anguished features. "And what about your clan? Don't they get a say? They need the money, but they need *you* more. What will happen to them if you're arrested for murder? Or worse yet, are murdered yourself?"

He scrubbed his hands wearily over his face. "They'll get on. Besides, that's not going to happen."

"Can you promise that?" When he hesitated, she pressed her advantage. "Because I swear that if you let me speak to Papa first, there will be no bloodshed." That much she was certain of. If she could only get Lachlan to agree.

For a moment, she thought that appealing to his protective nature had done the trick, that he would be sensible about this whole thing.

Then his body stiffened, and his eyes hardened. "You ask too much of me."

She stood there stunned, watching him become the Scourge once more, a man whose uncompromising principles were sure to be the end of him.

"So nothing has really changed," she whispered. "I'm still Duncannon's daughter to you."

Temper flared in his face. "I don't think of you that way, and you know it."

"Don't you? You're still certain I'd take my father's side in any discussion. You still can't put aside your vengeance for me."

"It's justice I want, not vengeance!"

"The trouble is, I want neither. I want peace. For you *and* your clan. And peace won't be found if you and my father go at each other with daggers drawn."

"You don't want peace, lassie," he said, eyes glittering. "You want peace at all costs. Sometimes peace isn't worth the cost. Not if it means a man doesn't have justice. I will have my justice, and yes, I will have it at any cost."

"Then I can't marry you." She turned for the door so he wouldn't see the tears starting in her eyes. "Because I fear I will lose you to your justice."

"You won't lose me." He hurried up behind her and, catching her by the arm, swung her around to face him. "I won't let you go, lass. At the very least, I mean to give you my name before yer father comes."

"Why? So I can live as your widow? That's how I'll end up after you're murdered by my father. Or if you kill him—" She broke off with a sob. "I'd rather take my chances being ruined and alone, thank you."

"Venetia," he said hoarsely, trying to draw her back into his arms.

"Don't." She resisted his pull, and when that made him only more determined, she added, "I'll scream, I swear I will. I'll scream until my father's men come running, and then I'll tell them that Sir Lachlan Ross is alive and well and trespassing on my father's property."

She held her breath, praying he didn't call her bluff. She could never risk anything happening to him at the hands of her father's men, but she had to do *something* to make him leave her right now. Because if he began kissing her again, she didn't know how long she could hold out.

He released her with a curse. But as she reached for the door, he murmured, "Don't be thinking I'll let you go that easily again, lass. I know you need time to sort things out. But I mean to have you as well as my justice. You can be sure of that."

With those words ringing in her ears, she drew the *arisaid* over her head and hurried out the door.

But she'd gone only a short way before she ran into two Scotsmen. They looked as startled to see her as she did them. Then one demanded, "Who are you and what are you doing here?"

"I'm sorry, I got lost," she mumbled, aware that Lachlan was probably on the verge of leaping out of the cottage to protect her. "I'll be leaving now."

The man lunged toward her as if to stop her, but just then a racket erupted from the cottage loud enough to alarm even the sheep. As the nearby flock scattered, the men rushed inside to investigate, leaving her to run neck-or-nothing for the bridge.

She only had time to glance back and see Lachlan slip from behind the cottage and melt into the woods before the men dashed back outside and began looking around for her. Fortunately, she'd reached the bridge, and within seconds she was safe again on Ross land.

But as she hurried up the road toward Rosscraig, thanking heaven for her narrow escape, she wondered if she'd ever really feel safe again.

I mean to have you as well as my justice.
That's precisely what she was afraid of.

It was long after midnight in Edinburgh when Maggie
hesitated on the steps of the colonel's town house. No
lady ever went alone to a gentleman's abode, and certainly
not this late. But if what she suspected about Hugh was
true, she dared not twiddle her thumbs at the inn.

After a few quick raps with the knocker, she awaited
the servant impatiently. But the colonel himself
answered, lacking coat, waistcoat, or cravat, with his
shirt unbuttoned and the tails hanging free. The sight
of him with tufts of chest hair showing and his manly
chin jutting free of collar points and cravat was most
unsettling. Hugh was even handsomer in dishabille than
fully dressed.

Though a faint odor of brandy clung to him, it wasn't
unappealing, especially since his eyes were clear as he
gaped at her. "What in blazes are you doing here at this
hour? I told you—"

"You told me a great many things, Colonel Seton," she
snapped as she pushed past him, forcing herself not to
notice his virile appeal. "About the men going after my
niece, about the daily reports—"

"Yes, yes, and they haven't arrived yet. I explained all
that—the men may not be able to find a postmaster very
easily. Such things take time, you know."

She whirled around to find him stuffing his shirt into
his trousers and trying to make himself look presentable.
The gentlemanly gesture further infuriated her. She'd
begun to consider him a man she might actually care
for—until she'd found out that all his understanding
and sympathy had been a lie.

She stiffened. "Yes, things take time, especially when there are no men. No riders. No reports. When the entire mission is concocted from thin air."

His head shot up so fast that she knew she'd hit on the truth. And the look of panic in his eyes told her that it was probably even worse than she'd feared.

"I thought so," she said, turning for the doorway.

He grabbed her arm, holding her in a surprisingly powerful grip while he thrust the door shut. "Now, Maggie, don't be a fool just because ye've got some daft notion—"

"Don't you dare call me Maggie, you sly bastard!" she hissed as she broke free of him. "I allowed it when I thought you were a gentleman, but I shan't stand for it now that I see what you really are!"

Eyes the color of rain-drenched slate stared her down. "And what is that?"

"A liar. A blackguard. An accomplice to that scoundrel, the Scourge."

He let out a low oath, then seized her arm again. "It appears you and I need to have a discussion, Lady Kerr. But not where the servants might hear."

He marched her down the hall with an officer's brisk command, ignoring her attempts to get free.

Perhaps she shouldn't have been so hasty in rushing over to accuse him without her manservant to protect her. Her alarm intensified as Hugh forced her into what appeared to be his study, then shut and locked the door behind them.

This wasn't the blundering colonel she knew. This man was used to ordering soldiers about . . . and forcing women to do as he pleased. Good heavens.

She backed away, glancing about for a weapon as he

strode past her to light more candles on the mantel. Two were already lit on the desk where he'd obviously been sitting when she'd knocked at the front door, and beside them lay a letter opener. It wouldn't do much good, but it was something.

Keeping a wary eye on him, she edged in that direction. "I should warn you that I instructed my servant to go to the authorities if I don't return shortly," she lied. "He knows all my suspicions. If I go missing, this is the first place he'll come looking for me."

"I see." He flexed his jaw angrily as he set the lit candles into their holders. "So you've got yer mind set about me, have you?" As he turned from the mantel, he fixed his gaze on her mouth, his voice softening. "How could you even think I could hurt you, after last night?"

Last night, when she'd foolishly allowed him to kiss her in the hall outside her inn room. She'd told herself it was just to allay his suspicions until she heard her manservant's report, but that was a lie. Hugh had a way of touching her that made her feel youthful and full of energy. She found that quite hard to resist after her years alone. Indeed, they'd kissed rather shamelessly until someone had come up the stairs, forcing them to break apart.

It horrified her just to think of it now.

Standing before the desk, she seized the letter opener behind her back. "Last night was only your way of taking my mind off what you were really up to."

"And what might that be?"

"Aiding and abetting the Scourge in kidnapping my niece."

"Ah, yes, of course. You've decided I'm a villain." With

a forced smile, he came toward her. "But if you'd give me the chance to explain—"

"Halt right there, Colonel Seton!" she cried, brandishing the letter opener. "Or I'll gut you like a fish!"

He flinched, then swore under his breath. Altering his direction, he went behind the desk, opened a drawer, and pulled out a knife the length of her forearm. Then, seizing it by the blade, he offered her the hilt over the desk. "If you mean to gut me, at least use a weapon that'll do some damage. That pig-sticker will scarcely draw blood."

As she gaped at him, he said, "Take it, damn you! Or put that toothpick down so we can discuss this rationally."

His flinty gaze didn't waver, but she took comfort in the fact that he'd offered her a blade. With a sniff, she laid down the "toothpick," then planted her hands on her hips. "How long have you been the Scourge's accomplice?"

He slid his knife back in the drawer. "What makes you think I am?"

"I had my manservant investigate to discover who you sent after the scoundrel." She choked down the anger roiling in her belly. "He visited every regiment situated in the area, then informed me tonight of what he'd learned. No one has been tapped for any secret missions. No one."

He visibly tensed. "The men I sent weren't soldiers."

"Then give me the names of the men you did send."

Feathering his fingers through his graying hair, he muttered a curse.

"You can't, can you? Because there are none."

"It isn't what you think," he growled. "I didn't want to risk your niece's life by doing what the Scourge said not to."

"Try another excuse, sir." She glowered at him. "My manservant learned that until a few days ago, you'd been seen several times in the company of two Highlanders. You told me that day on the mountain that the kidnappers had gone north to the Highlands."

"An idle speculation, nothing more," he said.

"One of the men you were seen with was scarred in the same fashion as that fellow at the masquerade ball. The fellow you claimed not to know, who made a point of dancing with my niece before disappearing mysteriously later."

He groaned.

"So who is he? Who *is* this ruffian who is probably at this very moment debauching my poor niece?"

"He wouldn't," Hugh protested. "He's a gentleman." When she stared at him, shocked that he'd actually admitted his culpability, he sighed. "If I tell you everything, will you muzzle yer manservant before he does more harm than good?"

"It depends on what you have to say," she retorted, her heart aching. After years of protecting herself from bounders and cads, how could she have been swayed by a scoundrel? "I shan't let some villain hurt Venetia." She leaned over the desk to scowl at him. "*Who is he?* Tell me, or I swear I will go straight to—"

"Enough!" His heavily whiskered jaw flexed spasmodically. "The man is Sir Lachlan Ross. Chief of the Clan Ross."

Shock kept her motionless. "Alasdair Ross's son? But he's dead!"

"No, though not for want of Duncannon's trying."

She blinked. "It can't be . . . how can . . . young Lachlan is the Scourge?"

"You know him?"

"Of course I know him. The boy's parents were my brother-in-law's friends for years. I saw them often when I visited." She shook her head, unable to fathom it. "Lachlan always was a wild one, but for him to become a thief . . ."

"He only wants what Duncannon owes him. That's why he takes it from the man's friends."

"Owes him?" She frowned. "I don't understand."

"Don't you?"

"No, I can't imagine what you're talking about."

He stared at her, seemingly perplexed by that. "Well, then, perhaps we'd better puzzle it out together." He nodded toward a chair. "Sit down, lass. It'll take me a while to tell you the whole of it."

She did as he asked, her chest tight with apprehension.

He paced his study, relating a tale of deception and broken promises. When he was done, she sat back in the chair, stunned. She'd never heard of the loan between Quentin and Alasdair, but it explained so much— Lachlan's becoming the Scourge, Quentin's odd refusal to hunt the man down, everything.

Thank heaven for one thing: Lachlan wasn't likely to hurt Venetia. He knew her and had even seemed to be fond of her when she was a girl. Besides, if he meant to get what he wanted, he didn't dare harm a hair on her head.

Maggie glanced at Hugh, who'd halted near her chair. "Are you sure that Lachlan doesn't know why Quentin never repaid the loan?"

"I'm sure. Duncannon brought all of this on himself, in my opinion, and—"

"Yes." She squeezed her hands together to quell her sense of impending doom. "Unfortunately, I think I *do* know why Quentin never repaid the loan."

"Why?"

She rose. "No time to explain. I must reach Rosscraig before Quentin does."

"Now see here, lass, I promised Lachlan—"

"Do you want your friend to die? Because that's what will happen if I don't stop this nonsense before Quentin gets to Lachlan. Quentin will never pay that money to any son of Alasdair Ross. He'll see Lachlan dead first."

The colonel gave her an assessing glance, then nodded. "Very well. But I'm going with you." He tied his cravat hastily about his neck, then went searching for his waistcoat.

"We cannot travel together, for heaven's sake!" Panic seized her at the very thought of spending days alone in Hugh's company. "It wouldn't be proper."

He cast her a wry smile as he donned his waistcoat. "We've gone far beyond proper, don't you think? Bring along yer manservant if it suits yer propriety. But I'm not letting you travel across Scotland alone, and I'm sure as hell not letting you get in the middle of this thing with Duncannon and Ross. It's not safe."

"As if you care," she said in a low voice, turning toward the door.

Catching her by the arm, he pulled her close. "I *do* care, no matter what you think. I hated having to hide the truth from you, do ye ken? I never expected it to be so hard. You were so trusting, so concerned, so—"

"Foolish," she finished, with a hard little smile. "A silly

old fool who thought that a man might want her despite her short temper and fading looks."

With a heavy sigh, he bent his head close enough that she could feel the heat of his breath on her hair. "The only thing fading about you, Maggie, is yer good sense. Do I seem like a man who could pretend to fancy a woman when he doesn't?"

She couldn't look at him. "I don't know."

He muttered an oath, then released her to drag on his coat. "Then you've got plenty of time to figure it out. Because ye're not traveling to the north without me."

Chapter Twenty-Two

❦

Dear Charlotte,
I'll do my best, but gathering information about
Scottish affairs is more complicated than passing on
trivial bits of gossip about gentlemen in society. It
will take me some time. But do try not to fret over it
as you are wont to do.

Your humble servant,
Michael

After his fine afternoon with Venetia soured so abruptly, Lachlan spent a long, restless night kicking himself for not securing the lady while he'd had the chance. He should have made her promise to marry him before he'd bedded her. Or somehow tricked her into speaking present consents.

Why was she balking, anyway? He'd taken her innocence, damn it! That alone should have made a proper lady like her beg him to marry her.

But no, she had to have everything her way, the meeting with her father especially. He scowled as he rose and did his morning ablutions. She was mad if she thought he'd let her give away what he'd fought for. Crying over empty crofters' cottages was one thing, but she wanted to bargain with Duncannon for his clan!

Never, not while he had breath. The meeting would take place between him and her father, and that was that. She'd just have to trust him to keep his temper.

And what did she mean, he didn't trust *her*? She didn't

trust *him*, blast it. She talked as if he were the same rash youth as when she was a girl.

You did kidnap her. And tell her you'd shoot people if she tried to escape.

But that had been at first, when they were at odds. Surely she didn't consider him such a hot-tempered lout anymore.

You told your mother three days ago that you'd thrash your clansmen senseless if they talked about Venetia.

He winced. That didn't put him in the best of lights, either. Nor did the sneaky way he'd gone about seducing her. Why *should* she trust him? She hardly knew him except as a villain.

Very well, then he'd have to show her his gentlemanly side. He had a few more days before Duncannon arrived—he'd use them to court her.

Because he wasn't letting Venetia go back to London ruined and unmarried, no matter what fool notions she'd got into her head.

He glanced at the table and saw the plate of stale oatcakes that he'd been eating for the past couple of days. The courtship would start this morning. He didn't care how Venetia and his mother protested—he was having a proper breakfast, with them.

Time to put an end to this sly behavior from his mother and his wife-to-be, their sneaking about to avoid him. And he knew exactly how to do it: he would blackmail her. It would set off Venetia's temper at first, but he couldn't court her if she avoided him, so he had to deal with that before he could go on.

He didn't enter through Rosscraig's front door this time. He slipped in through the servant entrance, tamping down his annoyance at having to sneak into his own house. He was rewarded by the looks of shock on his mother's and Venetia's faces when he sauntered into the dining room and took a seat at the table.

The maid who was serving the ladies started. "Good morning, sir. We didn't expect . . . that is . . ." She trailed off with a helpless glance at his mother.

"Fetch the laird some breakfast, girl," his mother said, quickly recovering her aplomb. She cast him a sweet smile, then rose. "Since you're here, you might as well eat. But I'm afraid that Miss Ross and I have some matters to——"

"Sit down, Mother." He glanced at Venetia, who'd also risen. "You, too, lass. Unless you want to have a long discussion about the fine properties of yer father's fleece."

Venetia paled.

"Fleece?" his mother asked, while she stubbornly remained standing.

Though Venetia's expression of alarm tweaked his conscience, he ignored it. He was only playing the same game she'd played last night by threatening to scream and bring her father's men running.

Besides, if he'd wanted to be truly underhanded, he could have told his mother what they'd done, then sat back and let *her* pressure the lass into marrying. But he didn't want Venetia that way. He wanted her willing.

"Well, lass? Shall we talk about fleece?" Leaning back, he tucked his thumbs in the band of his trousers and stared her down. "Because I'd rather stay around and have you show me what you and my mother have been doing."

"We're not finished," his mother broke in. "Come back in a couple of days——"

"No, I think we should show him." Tearing her gaze from his, Venetia sat back down and ventured a smile for his mother. "We've done enough to give him an idea of how it will look in the end. And this way we can get his opinion on our other plans."

Venetia's sudden willingness made his mother eye him with suspicion, but when he merely arched an eyebrow, she took her seat, too. "So you want to see what we've done, do you?" his mother said.

"Aye."

"Did you even notice all the changes in *this* room?"

No. He'd been too busy making sure they didn't run off so he could begin his courting. But he pasted a smile on his lips and lied. "I did indeed."

Mother's eyes narrowed. "And what do you think?"

He gave a quick glance around, as if trying to form his opinion. The oak paneling had been newly cleaned and polished. The tablecloth he remembered as tea-stained and ugly had been dyed a pretty dark green so that the spots were hardly noticeable, especially when the table was set with sparkling silver.

He started to ask where they'd found such expensive tableware, then realized that the pattern looked familiar. Damned if it wasn't the same stuff he'd eaten off of for years. He'd just assumed that the dull gray metal was pewter.

"It's very nice, all of it. My compliments to you ladies."

The maid brought in a plate of fried black pudding, toast, and rashers and set it before him. As he fell upon it eagerly, Venetia picked up a shining silver pot.

"Some coffee, Lachlan? Or do you prefer tea in the morning?"

Her prissy tone reminded him that this wasn't a regimental camp, or even his slovenly cottage. Mindful of his manners, he slowed his eating. "Tea, no milk." He glanced at his mother. "When did we start serving coffee at breakfast?"

"The lass likes it," his mother said. "She says they drink coffee in London a great deal. Chocolate, too, though we can't have that, seeing as how it's so dear."

"So you like chocolate, then, do you, lass?" he asked.

Venetia handed him his tea without looking at him. "I fancy a cup from time to time, yes."

"Then I'll send a lad to Dingwall to fetch you some. And anything else you might require."

Her gaze flew to his, startled.

"Before my overzealous mother came and whisked you away the other night," he went on, "I told you I wanted you to be comfortable. So if you fancy chocolate or books or ribbons or whatever else a lady needs, just say the word, and I'll make sure you get them."

"How about twenty yards of muslin for curtains? And some lime for washing the floors?"

He frowned. "I was speaking of things for *you*, not Rosscraig."

"I'd rather see the money spent on your lovely home," she persisted.

"And why is that, pray tell?" he asked in a husky voice. "Have you got a sudden itch to feather yer future nest, lassie?"

He ignored his mother's gasp at this clear evidence of his intentions, focusing his gaze on Venetia.

Two spots of color formed high on her cheeks before she dropped her gaze to her plate. "I'm trying to help your mother, that's all."

He let that pass, but the conversation cheered him enormously. Mayhap she wouldn't be so hard to court after all. Especially when his mother's beaming face showed she was more than willing to help.

He finished eating, then pushed his plate away. "Well, then, let's take that tour now. I've a fierce hankering to see what you ladies have been doing."

"And what of the muslin?" Venetia asked. "Can you get it for me . . . us?"

With a lazy smile, he rose. "Write down everything you're wanting, and I'll send Jamie over to Dingwall for it." If the way to her heart was with curtains and lime, then he'd find a way to get them for her, even if he had to buy on credit.

Rounding the table, he offered her his arm. "Shall we go?"

An uncertain look crossed her face, but she stood and took his arm. He suppressed a grin as they left the dining room, with his mother walking behind, her delight obvious.

Let the courtship begin.

It was the third morning after she'd lost her innocence to Lachlan, and Venetia was even more rattled now than she'd been then. She'd expected him to remain absent from the manor. Indeed, she'd hoped for it, so she could avoid the temptations he presented.

But no. He'd not only spent every waking hour here, he'd behaved as courteously as any London gentleman. He'd climbed ladders on her behalf, despite his stiff leg. Ignoring his mother's sly smiles, he'd fetched cushions and, yes, even held curtains.

So she was disappointed to discover that today he'd

left after breakfast, with no word as to where or why he was going and how long he'd be gone. All she could learn was that he'd taken the coach, which was unusual, according to Lady Ross.

At first Venetia simply missed his hanging about. But by late afternoon, she started to worry about him. So when the butler said the laird had returned and was wanting her in the dining room, she practically flew there, not bothering to find out if his mother was there, too, to chaperone.

When she entered, Lachlan rose from the table, which held a steaming pot, two cups, and some fresh scones. It was the first time she'd ever seen him in anything but rough attire or regimentals, and she had to admit he looked quite fine. His waistcoat was embroidered silk, and his coat of fine, dark green merino made her think of shaded glens and sheltering oaks. His buff trousers fit his muscular build to perfection, reminding her just how fine his thighs were.

Her cheeks heated. "The butler said you asked for me?" she said formally, trying to keep her emotions in check.

"Aye. I brought you something." He pulled out a chair for her next to his, and that's when she saw the sheaf of broadsides stacked up on the table.

Her gaze flew to his. "Where did you ... how did you ..."

"I rode over this morning to Inverness. I'm not known there, you see. We do most of our business in Dingwall."

That was because Dingwall was a few miles away, while Inverness—a town eight times larger, with libraries and an academy and lots of shops—was a good two hours' ride each way. She walked to the table in a daze, then stood leafing through the pages, acutely aware of Lachlan watching her.

"Will they do?" he asked.

"They're lovely," she said in a choked whisper, then sat down to examine them further. No one had ever given her such a thoughtful gift. Not only were there unusual versions of ballads she already owned, but three of the broadsides contained lyrics to ballads she'd never encountered, and one was even in Gaelic.

She couldn't believe he'd ridden four hours to obtain these. The very thought of it brought tears to her eyes. She brushed them away quickly, before they could fall and ruin the ink of her precious copies.

He poured her a cup of what was in the pot. "Can you read Gaelic, lass?"

That's when she realized she was staring at the one in Gaelic. "Not as well as I'd like," she said evasively.

Shortly after her arrival, she'd determined that the Ross clan held in contempt any Highlander who didn't speak Gaelic. She wasn't about to call attention to her lack, especially in front of Lachlan.

She darted a quick glance at him as he handed her the cup and sat down beside her. "You must have had a difficult time locating such a wide variety," she murmured.

"It took a bit of doing, but I managed." With a smile, he pushed the cup at her. "See how this tastes. Cook wasn't sure she made it properly."

Blinking, she stared down into the cup and caught her breath. Chocolate. He'd got her chocolate, too. She sipped some, then promptly burst into tears.

"Here now, lass, don't be doing that!" he cried, laying his arm about her shoulders. "Surely it can't taste that bad."

"No, no, it's perfect," she said, feeling like a fool as she dabbed at her eyes with a napkin. "That's the trouble. It tastes exactly like the chocolate at home."

He tensed. "London, you mean."

With a nod, she drank some more, relishing every velvety-sweet drop. Heaven. Pure heaven.

"Do you miss the city very much?" he asked in a strained voice.

She glanced up to find him staring at her with an unfamiliar vulnerability. Forcing a smile, she set the cup down. "Only when I drink chocolate."

His gaze locked with hers. "Then I'll never buy you chocolate again."

When he lowered his head toward hers, she didn't stop him. How could she, when he was being so adorable? He kissed her, and it was better than before, better even than chocolate. His tongue dipped inside as if to test her resistance, then plunged more boldly.

She probably shouldn't let him do this. She doubted that he'd changed his mind about the meeting with her father. But didn't he deserve at least one kiss after he'd ridden all the way to Inverness for her? Just one . . . sweet . . . unending . . .

Someone cleared his throat nearby, and the two of them sprang apart to find Jamie watching from the doorway.

The poor lad wore a look of betrayal that cut her to the heart. She'd known he was nursing an attachment to her, but she'd thought it nothing more than a boyish crush. She'd certainly done nothing to encourage it. Still, judging from how he clenched his hat in two bony fists and glowered at her, that didn't matter.

He thrust out his chin, then turned his scowl on Lachlan. "Yer mother sent me to tell you to stay out of sight, sir. Some of the lads saw McKinley headed this way with ten men or more."

McKinley? Papa's factor? That couldn't be good.

In an instant, Lachlan turned from ardent lover to chief of his clan. He rose and strode to the doorway. "Is Duncannon with him?"

Venetia held her breath, praying that Papa hadn't come. She wasn't ready.

"No sign of him yet," Jamie said. "And McKinley is coming from the estate, not Dingwall. Probably just wants to make trouble again about the lads taking the short way through Duncannon land when they head to the main road."

"I hope that's all it is," Lachlan said tersely. "Where's Mother?"

"Out front, pretending to be gardening. She figured it was best if McKinley didn't see what we've been doing inside the house. He might wonder what has got her started with fixing up the place."

"Aye, he might. God knows she's never done it before." Lachlan rubbed the back of his neck. "All right. Go up to the north field and tell the lads to come down. Tell them to bring their sickles, but not to be seen unless things turn ugly."

He strode out into the hall, still barking orders at Jamie. "Send Roarke to warn the fellows doing the mashing to stay out of McKinley's sight. He'll use any excuse to make trouble for us. The last time the bloody devil reported seeing an illegal still near Duncannon land, we had excisemen plaguing us for days after."

Curious to see this "devil" she'd heard so much about, Venetia wandered to the front of the house to peer out the window near the front entrance.

"Venetia!" Lachlan called out. "Stay inside, ye ken?"

"Of course."

A voice from outside arrested them all. "Good day, Lady Ross."

"Mr. McKinley," Lachlan's mother answered. "And what brings you to Rosscraig this fine morning?"

"Go!" Lachlan hissed at Jamie, who disappeared through the servants' entrance. Then he turned to Venetia and whispered, "Come away from the window."

Mouthing the words "in a minute," she carefully drew aside the heavy velvet drape just enough to give her a view of the front drive.

Lady Ross stood near a badly overgrown rosebush that she'd apparently been hacking to death in her zeal to look like she'd been gardening. Facing her was a burly man with a coarse reddish beard who sat atop a beautiful bay mare that would rival any costly one in London.

Venetia scowled. Where did a factor get the money for such exquisite horseflesh? She couldn't imagine that Papa paid him enough for that. The factor probably lined his pockets by throwing tenants off the land they loved, then filling it with sheep. She began to wonder if Papa actually knew. He paid so little attention to his Scottish property.

The rude Mr. McKinley didn't even bother to climb down from his mount. "I was at Braidmuir to collect the quarterly rents, where I was informed that your people have been trespassing on the earl's land."

The factor's smoothly sinuous voice was that of a man who sowed discord wherever he went. If she hadn't already been predisposed to dislike him, she would hate him just for that.

"My men encountered a woman leaving a cottage where we store fleece," he continued. "When they counted the bags, they discovered one missing."

Venetia's gaze flew to Lachlan.

"Yer blood stained it," he said softly. "It didn't seem right to leave it there for anyone to find."

Wincing, she returned her attention to the drama outside.

"And what makes you think the thief is one of *my* people?" Lady Ross asked, though her voice shook. Venetia wondered if she was remembering Lachlan's mention of fleece.

"The woman fled here, my lady. And you know better than anyone that Lord Duncannon doesn't tolerate thievery on his land, even by a neighbor. I heard about the punishment administered years ago to your own son after an incident of thievery. So I don't imagine he'll regard this with any kinder an eye."

Her heart sinking, Venetia glanced to Lachlan again, who was glowering at the front door so blackly, she was surprised it didn't erupt into flames.

Is *that* what Lachlan had meant about being humiliated? What had Papa done to him, for heaven's sake? And why hadn't she heard of it? It must have occurred before Lachlan joined the regiment.

"My employer is sure to demand restitution for the stolen fleece," Mr. McKinley went on. "That's why I'm here. We can either handle this between us, or I can go to the authorities."

"Now, Mr. McKinley, do not be hasty—"

"I have with me the two fellows who saw the culprit.

They're sure to recognize the female. So we'd like to search the property and talk to all the women."

"I'll be damned if I let them!" Lachlan hissed. "He's just looking for an excuse to find our stills so he can report them to the authorities."

When Lachlan started for the door, Venetia made a split-second decision. She could handle Mr. McKinley's sort. She'd seen Mrs. Harris do it often enough with bullying gentlemen who came to the school making outrageous demands. What she *couldn't* handle was Lachlan being seen before Papa arrived.

So before Lachlan could reach the door, she stepped outside and closed it firmly behind her. "Ah, Lady Ross, there you are. I was wondering where you'd gone off to. I wanted to show you the painting I'm working on."

Beyond Mr. McKinley, Venetia could see Ross men gathering, their faces resolute and their hands gripping scythes and sickles and poles—anything that might serve as a weapon. They weren't about to allow their property to be searched and their women harassed by the likes of Mr. McKinley and his band of rowdy fellows.

Venetia ignored Lady Ross's startled look, focusing instead on Mr. McKinley, whose gaze had swung instantly to her. She wished she were wearing something other than a paint-splattered gown that was too tight for her. Then again, perhaps that would work in her favor, since it displayed her bosom nicely. With a silky smile, she thrust her breasts out for the man's perusal.

"Forgive me, sir, for being so bold, but I'm shocked to realize that we have not met. I mistakenly thought I'd already been introduced to all the gentlemen of the area." Using a languid walk that oozed gentility, she trailed down the steps. "I'm Miss Ross of London, a cousin of Lady Ross's late husband. And you are . . ."

"Mr. McKinley, miss. Factor to the Earl of Duncannon." He tipped his hat, appreciation flickering in the eyes that followed her every step. "My employer's estate, Braidmuir, borders Rosscraig to the east."

"Oh, yes, that delightful place! I stumbled upon it quite by accident a couple of days ago when I took a wrong path. What beautifully rustic cottages it had. And the sheep were too adorable for words."

"You were at the estate, were you?" Mr. McKinley asked, casting an uneasy glance at the two men she recognized as having accosted her.

"Aye, she's the lass we saw," one of them said. "But she had something over her head to cover her face—"

"To cover my face!" she protested with a tinkling laugh. "I was wearing a costume, as it were. An *arisaid*." She smiled at the factor. "I know you're a man of fashion, sir, and probably do not bother with such things, but I confess I find the local dress quite deliciously colorful. I just had to wear the traditional tartan while I explored the countryside."

Mindful of Lachlan's men, who stood warily observing the interchange, she clapped her hand to her chest. "It made me feel so daringly Scottish, a veritable Highlander. I cannot wait to tell Papa of my adventures. He's a barrister, you know, and a great lover of Walter Scott's novels."

Noting how his face paled at the mention of her father's supposed profession, she went on babbling. "Indeed, he wanted to stay and observe the same Highland customs that have so captivated me, but after he delivered me here last week, he was forced to return to

London—some emergency at Parliament, I believe. The Duke of Foxmoor is one of his close friends, you see." Louisa and the duke would surely forgive her that little white lie.

Mr. McKinley began to look decidedly ill. "Yes, I see."

"But I'm sorry," Venetia went on, struggling to hide her enjoyment at unsettling the unctuous Mr. McKinley, "I believe I interrupted some business you were conducting with Lady Ross?"

"No, no, a slight misunderstanding is all," he said with a quelling glance at the two men who looked as if they might gainsay him. "We'll be going now."

Lady Ross approached him wearing an expression of sheer glee. "But yer fleece, sir—aren't you wanting yer fleece? As you say, the earl doesn't approve of thievery. Though if you go to the authorities, I'm sure Miss Ross's father—"

"My men undoubtedly miscounted," he said hastily, dragging out a handkerchief to mop his forehead. "Nothing to worry about. It will turn up." He nodded to Venetia, twin lines of panic deepening his brow. "Do give my regards to your father, miss."

She gave him a regal nod. With any luck, her tale would get the man dismissed.

Waving amiably, she stood on the steps while Mr. McKinley and his men rode off between two glowering lines of Rosses. As soon as they were gone she was besieged by Lachlan's clansmen, who surged up the steps, carrying her before them into the house while Lady Ross practically danced along behind them.

Inside, Lachlan awaited them, watching with gleaming eyes as at least twenty men and women crowded into the entrance hall around him.

"Did you hear yer cousin rout McKinley, sir?" one of the clansmen cried. "Oh, what a lass, what a lass!"

"Aye," Lachlan answered, the glittering promise in his gaze making her breath catch in her throat. "She *is* quite a lass."

"I thought McKinley would melt into a puddle, I did," Lady Ross chimed in. "He was that nervous at the thought of having a barrister breathing down his neck."

"Does yer father really know the Duke of Foxmoor?" asked one voice from among the crowd.

"Is he even really a barrister?" asked another.

As she was wondering how to answer that, another voice spoke from behind the others. "No, he's not a barrister."

She turned to see Jamie staring at her, his eyes resentful as he pronounced the words that would make them all hate her now.

"Her father is the Earl of Duncannon himself."

Chapter Twenty-Three

Dear Cousin,
I fret because I lack your talent for uncovering
the truth. Certain things a woman cannot discover,
no matter how many female confidantes she
possesses. You men tend to be a closemouthed sort,
you must admit.

Your fretting relation,
Charlotte

Lachlan groaned as a stunned silence descended. Damn the jealous lad! Angry about that kiss he'd seen, Jamie apparently now meant to take it out on Venetia.

Judging from the look of betrayal etching her face, he'd chosen the best way to do it, too. "You don't know what you're saying, lad," Lachlan began.

"Don't lie to them, sir." Jamie's voice held a challenge. "They'll find out the truth when Duncannon comes for her. I say we might as well tell them now."

"Oh, you do, do you?" Lachlan growled. "I don't recall asking for yer advice in the matter, and I sure as the devil don't remember giving you permission to—"

"It's all right, Lachlan," Venetia said, her voice low. "Jamie has a point. It's not as if we can keep it secret much longer."

Roarke, Lachlan's right arm on the estate, stepped in front of her, his ruddy face wary. "So it's true then? You're the earl's daughter?"

"Yes." Venetia tried for a smile and failed.

Jamie pushed in amidst the crowd. "Me and Lachlan took her from Edinburgh for the ransom and brought her here. When Duncannon arrives, she'll be going back with him to London, assuming he pays the money."

"Took her!" Roarke said. "You mean, you kidnapped her?"

When all eyes turned to Lachlan, he swore under his breath. Once he got Jamie alone, he would wring the scrawny lad's neck. "Yes, we kidnapped her. After the man tried to have me killed, we figured it was the only way to get the money he owes my mother." The men knew about the money—he'd told them after he'd confessed to being the Scourge.

One of the clanswomen looked confused. "But Miss Ross . . . I mean, Duncannon's daughter . . . just talked to McKinley. If she's being held against her will, why didn't she—"

"Lady Venetia is not being held against her will," Lachlan's mother snapped. "Aye, my son took her— without my knowledge, I might add—but she's been a guest in my home ever since, and she'll remain one until the earl comes to fetch her. So that's enough talk of kidnapping. She can leave anytime she wishes, and she knows it, don't you, lass?"

"Of course." Venetia ventured a smile. "I went over to Braidmuir, after all; I could have stayed there. But I only wanted to see what has been done to the land." Her voice broke a little. "It's a terrible shame. I remember when I was a girl and so many people made their living there."

"Aye," agreed his clansmen, shaking their heads.

"And I mean to see that something is done about it," Venetia persisted. "I can't believe Papa knows what that awful factor of his has been doing. When he realizes what his land has become, I'm sure he'll change his ways."

Lachlan snorted, but no one paid him any mind.

"Well, I for one don't care if the lass *is* Duncannon's daughter," a clanswoman said. "She could have told McKinley who she was and had the laird carted off to jail. Instead, she routed the bastard right well. I say that proves where her loyalties lie."

The other women nodded their agreement.

"And look at the work she's done for the manor. Made it right nice. She didn't have to do that after what the laird done to her." The woman planted her hands on her hips. "She's been one of us, and I don't see why that should change."

"Yes, but her father is on his way, did you not hear?" Roarke put in. "What will happen to us when he arrives?"

All eyes turned to Lachlan.

"I'll talk to him," Lachlan said, a bit defensively. "I'll demand my money, and if Duncannon has any sense, he'll give it to me."

"We're in trouble now, we are," muttered a woman at the back of the crowd.

When others started mumbling much the same, Lachlan drew himself up. "And what's that supposed to mean?"

Roarke cast him an uneasy look. "No offense, sir, but you aren't exactly the negotiating kind."

"He's got a temper, he does," one of the ladies murmured.

"Aye, especially when it comes to Duncannon," said another.

"We'll be lucky if we're not *all* carted off to prison."

"Now see here," Lachlan snapped, ignoring Venetia's smug smile, "I'm perfectly capable of having a reasonable discussion with the earl."

A sullen silence made it clear they didn't share his opinion.

He scowled. "I've been your chief for five years, damn it! Haven't I taken as good care of you as I could?"

"We know you have, sir," a clansman said. "You've been a good chief, and a good laird to Rosscraig."

Only slightly mollified, Lachlan asked, "And have I ever landed any of you in trouble with the law?"

"No." Roarke sighed. "But you haven't had to deal with Duncannon directly until now. You're a reasonable fellow most of the time, but you have to admit that the very mention of his name turns you into a raving madman."

"A madman, aye," murmured other voices.

Holy Christ, his whole clan was against him. "So what do you lot want me to do? Lie down and let him trample us? Give up the money I know he owes us?"

"Beggin' yer pardon, sir, but you could have the lass talk to him," said one of the women helpfully. "She's already said she'd speak to him on our behalf, and if she goes in first to soothe his temper like she did with McKinley—"

"Aye, a good idea," said the others among themselves. "Let the lass speak to him. Why not?"

"*Mo chreach*," he muttered. If he didn't know better, he'd think Venetia had put them up to it. But she looked too surprised by the show of support from his clan for that to be the case.

"It's a good idea, Lachlan," his mother chimed in, as bad as the rest. "It will soften Duncannon's temper to see that his daughter hasn't been harmed."

"And you know she'll be on our side—look how she was with McKinley," Roarke said.

He gazed around at his clan, his gut twisting to see their anxious faces. They really didn't believe he could confront Duncannon without losing his temper. Just like Venetia, they thought he'd make things worse and spawn a battle that would lead to bloodshed. That would deprive them of their laird, one way or the other.

They need the money, but they need you *more.*

As he hesitated to answer, they began to look hopeful. And the hope they embraced revolved around her, God rot them.

"Very well," he said. "I'll consider letting the lass speak to him. *Consider* it, mind. But that's all I'm saying for now."

Apparently that was enough, for the traitorous wretches let up a cheer. Meanwhile, Venetia was beaming at him as if she'd already won what she wanted, and just the sight of her so happy roused his blood.

He'd been losing this battle since the minute he'd kidnapped her, the minute she'd started worming her way under his skin and into his heart. She'd already entranced Jamie and enlisted his mother to her side. If he weren't careful, she'd soon be running his clan, too.

One of his rascal clansmen called out, "Admit it, sir, you know you can trust Lady Venetia to do right by us. We can tell you're sweet on the lady."

"Aye, and she's sweet on you, too," called one of the women.

At Venetia's blush, Lachlan's pulse thundered in his ears. "Are you sweet on me, lass?"

"I might be." A teasing smile touched her lips. "If you weren't such a thickheaded, stubborn lout sometimes."

His clansmen suddenly tensed, and the women caught their breaths as they watched to see how he would react. No one had ever said such a thing to his face.

But then, no one had ever been Venetia.

He laughed. "Aye, lassie, I suppose I am."

The tension broke, and everyone else joined his laughter.

Then the comments flew fast and furious through the hall. "I told you he was sweet on her," said one. "You can tell from how he looks at her," said another. Cook even revealed, "He rode all the way to Inverness to fetch her chocolate."

It was starting to be downright embarrassing when someone cried, "This calls for a celebration. The laird and Duncannon's daughter are courting!"

That they could make the leap from his being "sweet on" Venetia to courtship didn't surprise him, but the poor lass looked a little stunned by it.

"We should have a ceilidh dance!" said a woman, and the cry was echoed all around. "A ceilidh! A ceilidh!"

That was all it took to have the men pour into the drawing room to shove furniture aside and roll up rugs, while someone sent for the clan piper and fiddler, and his mother directed the action with clear delight. Some of the women headed down to his cellar to find the best whisky, while others hurried to the dining room to lay out refreshments.

Venetia stood in the midst of the flurry, looking overwhelmed. He pushed through the melee to her side. "Have you ever been to a ceilidh, lass?"

"It's the Scottish equivalent of a ball, isn't it?"

He laughed. "A ceilidh is far more than a ball, I assure you, and nothing like that silly thing in Edinburgh. It's a rowdy, thundering affair, with loud music and louder dancing. Are you sure ye're ready for that?"

She gazed up at him, eyes alight. "I can handle anything you give me, Lachlan Ross. Just see if I can't."

"I don't doubt it," he said, then slid his arm about her waist and hurried her into the room.

The fiddler had already started up, and in seconds they were sucked into the maelstrom of sound that was a ceilidh in a small space. Feet were stomping, the fiddler was sawing, and the whirl of dancers was a maddening rush.

She caught on quickly to the steps, since it was mostly plain dancing of the sort she'd find at any country ball. But the Rosses performed them with greater enthusiasm than any puling English lords, so it took her a while to loosen up enough to match the other women.

By the time the piper arrived to add the drone of bagpipes to the mixture, Venetia had become downright lively. Her cheeks shone pink, her eyes sparkled, and her limbs fluidly executed the steps. With his heart lodged in his throat, Lachlan danced a couple of sets with her before his leg started to pain him too much. Then he sat on the sidelines sipping a glass of whisky while he observed her.

She was a wonder to watch, a shimmering, kicking glory of a woman in paint-stained skirts and a bodice that showed too much of her bosom for his comfort. Not that any of his men ventured to stare at her ample charms. In their minds, she already belonged to the laird, and that was enough to keep them polite, even if she hadn't been Duncannon's daughter.

He shook his head. Duncannon's daughter. She was

no more that than she was a fairy. She was herself, and he began to fear he would do anything to have her.

The only clansman who seemed immune to her appeal just now was Jamie, who sulked in the corner, angry that his pronouncement hadn't got the reaction he'd wanted. Apparently, she noticed him there, too, for she left the floor to approach the lad. To Lachlan's surprise, she smiled at Jamie and offered him her hand.

The pigheaded fool looked as if he might refuse, but she said something and the anger on his face dampened. Within minutes, she had him grudgingly joining her on the floor.

Lachlan shook his head. She couldn't stand to make an enemy of the lad, could she? It must be peace at all costs for members of the clan, even if one of them was being an ass.

Time passed, and the evening turned into night. The fiddler began to tire, and the dancers' feet grew sore. He'd lost sight of Venetia half an hour earlier, so he wandered into the hall and then the dining room, where he found her surrounded by some unmarried clansmen.

The instant kick of jealousy in his belly caught him off guard. They were only doing what all young men did, flirting with a pretty lass, but damned if it didn't annoy him something fierce.

As he neared them, he realized they were doing something worse than flirting. They were pressing her to drink from a glass. And she was doing it, too.

"Here, now," he barked as he approached. "Don't be giving her whisky, for God's sake. She's a lady. She's not used to it."

"It's not their fault," she told him, her eyes overly

bright. "You make whisky—I want to see what it tastes like. So I asked for some."

He leveled a glance on Jamie, who of course was part of the pack. "How many glasses has she had, lad?"

"That's her second."

Striding up to her, he started to take the glass from her, but she raised it and said loudly, "Let's have a toast!"

That brought the rest of the clan crowding in to join the laird and his sweetheart in the dining room.

"Very well, a toast it is." He smiled down at her as people scrambled to find glasses and pour themselves whisky. "And what should the toast be, lassie?"

"Something fitting for a ceilidh," she said brightly.

Wedding vows would be fitting for a ceilidh.

Even as he thought it, his blood began to race. This would be the perfect time for him and Venetia to speak present consents. Though they didn't need witnesses, it was convenient to have them. And perhaps with her tipsy, he could convince her to speak her part.

Lachlan eyed her closely. No, she didn't look drunk enough to let that pass. She wasn't slurring her speech or weaving on her feet, so he'd never get her to say the vows. Unless . . .

She'd claimed to know Gaelic, but he'd lay odds that she'd lied.

Oh, that was a wicked idea. But she was just foxed enough that it might work.

Ignoring his nagging conscience, he murmured, "How about a toast in Gaelic. That's fitting for a ceilidh, don't you think, princess?"

"In Gaelic, yes," she echoed, a smile splitting her face.

He tested his theory. "We give toasts in twos in

Scotland. Why don't you give it first, then I'll repeat it? You did say you speak Gaelic, didn't you?"

Her smile slipped a little, but she nodded. "I-I did. I do. But you should give the toast. It's your house and your ceilidh. Then *I'll* repeat it."

She was making it so damned easy. Princess Proud just couldn't bear to show herself lacking before other Scots. "All right."

Looking round to see that everyone had got their glasses, he raised his own, then began to speak. *"Tha mise Lachlan Ross a-nis 'gad ghabhail-sa Venetia Campbell gu bhith 'nam bhean phòsda, gus an dèan Dia leis a' bhàs ar dealachadh."*

The crowd sucked in a collective breath as they recognized the words: "I, Lachlan Ross, take you, Venetia Campbell, to be my wife, until God shall separate us by death."

They all looked at her expectantly, as did he.

"Now you say it, lass," he prompted. If she didn't understand the words, she would never remember the entire thing, and that's what he was counting on.

"I . . . I . . . could you repeat it, please?" she said. "I didn't catch it all."

Jamie glowered at him. "She doesn't understand what you're saying."

"Yes, I do!" she said petulantly. "I just want to make sure I get it right."

His mother and the rest of his clan all looked pleased as could be. Either that, or they were conveniently ignoring the oddness of his insisting upon speaking the vows in Gaelic.

He took a deep breath, then said, "Repeat after me, lass: *Tha mise Venetia Campbell . . .*

She repeated it.

"*A-nis 'gad ghabhail-sa Lachlan Ross . . .*"

If she'd realized that he'd switched the names this time around, she gave no indication of it, for she said exactly what he'd said.

"*Gu bhith 'nam fhear phòsda . . .*" he went on, then held his breath to see if she noticed he'd changed "wife" to "husband." Apparently not, for she repeated every word.

"*Gus an dèan Dia leis a' bhàs ar dealachadh.*" He could hardly suppress a grin while he said those words. If she said these, it was done.

The minute she finished the last bit, the crowd erupted into cheers, more than ready to take the wedding vows at face value. It didn't hurt that Venetia herself reinforced the deception by beaming up at him before drinking her whisky.

That smile drove a stake into his conscience. And it now dawned on him what a vexing dilemma he'd landed himself in.

The minute he told her they were married—or any of his clan mentioned it—she would figure out how he'd manipulated her. He could protest all he wanted that he'd thought she knew Gaelic, but she was no fool, his Princess Machiavelli. And the fact that the vows were legal, that his whole clan would loudly proclaim in court that she'd known what she was saying, wouldn't matter a whit to her.

At least they were married, and he'd no longer have to worry about her returning to London ruined, without the protection of his name. But he held a wildcat by the tail, to be sure. So what the devil was he to do about it?

Chapter Twenty-Four

Dear Charlotte,
   If men are closemouthed, it is because we cannot trust women with our secrets. Once a woman hears them, she wants to wheedle her way into every part of the man's life, and most men prefer their privacy.

Your cousin,
Michael

After Venetia repeated Lachlan's toast, the evening took a strange turn. One minute she was enjoying being part of the clan, and the next, he was bustling the guests out. Though it was late, why must he be so rude about it?

Then Roarke clapped Lachlan on the shoulder, congratulated them both—for what, she wasn't sure—and started to talk about her marriage to Lachlan. For no good reason, Lachlan abruptly suggested that the two men have another drink in the dining room. Alone.

Left to her own devices, she sought out Lady Ross, who was straightening things in the drawing room. As Venetia began to help, the woman said, "No, don't you bother with that. I'm just doing a bit before I go to bed."

"Actually, I wanted to ask you about what McKinley meant this afternoon," she said. "He mentioned Lachlan being punished, and my father and thievery."

"Oh, that." Lady Ross nervously stacked up dirty plates. "I don't know what he meant. The man's mad. Surely you could see that."

"I'll grant you he's a scoundrel, but I daresay not a

mad one. And everyone else seemed to know what he meant, too."

With a sigh, Lady Ross faced her. "You'll have to ask Lachlan."

"I tried while we were dancing, but he just changed the subject. And no one else will tell me, either. What was so horrible—"

"He doesn't want it spoken of, that's all. He'd never forgive me if I told you myself. Besides, it's only proper that he tell you, seeing as how you're his wife."

"His wife!" Venetia exclaimed. "What do you mean?"

Lady Ross blinked at her. "You didn't know?" She sighed. "I suppose Lachlan didn't explain about irregular marriages in Scotland. Those vows you spoke were enough to make it legal here." She shook her head. "He should have told you, damned fool, before he went into it before God and everybody. It's a good thing you talked to me first, or you'd have quite the surprise when he came to yer bed . . ." She trailed off as she saw the look on Venetia's face.

"What marriage vows?" Venetia said hoarsely.

Lady Ross blanched. "You said you understood what the Gaelic meant."

The toast. That she'd repeated word for word . . .

Had Lachlan realized she didn't know? She replayed the incident in her head. Oh yes, he'd realized it, the devious wretch, or he wouldn't have insisted on saying the vows in Gaelic.

Her temper exploded. The scoundrel had tricked her! And she'd fallen right into it, too, like a witless fool!

Lady Ross grabbed her arm, alarm showing in her face. "You *did* understand the vows, didn't you? Because if you didn't, it isn't legal."

Venetia stared at Lady Ross, her mind awhirl. She could deny that she'd meant to marry him, but Lachlan had a whole clan eager to gainsay her. Lady Ross might take her side, but Venetia would look like a fool, and she might not be able to change anything anyway.

Besides, she'd wanted to marry Lachlan—just not until she could be sure he wouldn't get himself killed confronting Papa.

Her eyes narrowed. She could still do that, couldn't she? Lachlan didn't know she'd guessed the truth. That's why he was behaving so oddly, hurrying people out of the house, taking Roarke off to drink away from her.

She had the upper hand. And she meant to use it, too. For this little deception, she would make Lachlan dance to her tune. That's what wives were for, after all.

"Venetia!" Lady Ross demanded. "Did you know what you were saying or not?"

"I did." Venetia pasted a smile on her face. "I'm sorry, the whole business about irregular marriages has taken me by surprise. I thought Lachlan and I were entering a betrothal with that toast, not a marriage. But it's fine. I did want to marry him, as you well know. I just . . . didn't quite understand."

Lady Ross let out a breath, then impulsively hugged Venetia. "It's glad I am that you're his wife. Glad indeed."

Venetia held the woman close. "Me, too," she said, entirely sincere.

But that didn't mean she'd let her devil of a husband run roughshod over her.

She headed back to the dining room, but Lachlan was still drinking with Roarke, and it was probably prudent not to talk to him while he was in his cups. She would go

to bed and await him where they'd have some privacy.
If he wanted his wedding night, he'd find her. And then
she'd have a merry time watching him try to explain why
he had the right to share her bed.

If she didn't have him begging her forgiveness and
promising her the moon before the night was out, then
she was no wife at all.

Lachlan awoke to complete darkness. His head lay
cradled in his arms on a table, and he sat in a chair . . .

Right, he'd been drinking whisky with Roarke. He
lifted his head, surprised to find himself nearly sober. He
must have been sleeping off the whisky for quite a while.
He hadn't drunk that much anyway; mostly he'd been
putting off the moment when he'd have to tell Venetia
what he'd done. After Roarke had left, he'd lingered a
while longer, then must have fallen asleep.

That's why it was black as the devil's heart in here.
He'd let the candle burn out. Damn.

He cocked his head to listen, but the house was quiet.
Everyone had gone to bed, including his lovely new wife.
Who didn't know she was his new wife.

When he rose, the chair fell over. All right, so he was a
bit unsteady on his feet, but he only had to find the flints
and light a candle.

That proved harder than he'd thought. Once he left
the table, he got disoriented. Despite his attempt to
be quiet, he kicked over things while searching for the
fireplace, and even after he stumbled into the mantel by
accident, he couldn't find what he needed. Devil take
Mother and Venetia and all their fancying up the place
and moving things about.

"Where could they have hidden the flints?" he

muttered as he felt along the mantelpiece, knocking off a candlestick in the process.

"They're in that silver box on the other end," said a voice behind him just as a finger of light stabbed into the room.

He whirled around, shoving the hair out of his face so he could better see who'd come in bearing a candle. Venetia herself.

She wore a nightdress and a robe, and her hair tumbled about her shoulders in wild waves of ebony. She looked as if she'd just come from bed. He wanted to carry her right back.

Then he saw her stern expression as she surveyed the scene. Three chairs had been knocked over, and a silver tureen careened beside a pewter platter. Next to the burned-out stub of candle on the table lay the empty jar of whisky and the glasses, still miraculously erect.

"Good even, princess," he mumbled, not sure what to say. "I didn't mean to wake you. I was just looking for flint to light a candle."

"Thank heaven you didn't find any, or I'd be putting out fires as well."

"And what's that supposed to mean?"

She scanned him with a contemptuous glance, and he became painfully aware that he wore no coat or cravat, his waistcoat was unbuttoned, and his shirttails hung half out of his trousers. He probably looked like he'd just left a tavern.

"It means you're obviously foxed," she said.

"I'm not!" He stepped toward her and landed on the base of the candlestick instead. It shot up to bang him in the shin. "Holy Christ Almighty!" he swore as he kicked it aside.

"Stop that!" Hurriedly lighting candles in a nearby sconce, she went over to set her own candle on the table, then began picking up chairs. "I won't have you destroying the dining room while you're drunk."

"I'm not drunk, I tell you," he said sullenly, though he figured it was probably best just now if he stayed still.

She eyed him askance. "There's an entire jar of whisky gone, Lachlan."

"Roarke downed most of it. Besides, I've been drinking whisky since I was a lad. I should hope that by now I can hold my liquor."

He bent forward to pick up a chair.

"Don't move!" she commanded as she flew to his side.

But he'd already righted the chair and fallen heavily into it. "I only need a moment to get my bearings." *Before I take my wife to bed and make love to her.* But he couldn't do that without admitting what he'd done. And this probably wasn't the best time for such a confession. "Let me just sit here a bit."

"Good idea. We don't need you falling into any lochs on your way back to the cottage."

His eyes narrowed. "I'm not going back to the cottage."

"Why not?" she said in a suspiciously sweet voice. "That's where you sleep."

Damn. "I . . . um . . . well, there's no reason I can't sleep here for one night, is there?"

"For one night," she repeated, her tone cold.

She started to move away, but he caught her hand, then tugged her close. "You could put me to bed, lassie."

"Why should I want to do that? I'm not your wife yet, you know."

He ought to tell her the truth. But he just couldn't. No, what he needed was to seduce her again. Then, when she was sated and feeling tender toward him, he'd tell her they were married. Aye, that was a good plan.

He hauled her onto his lap. "But you can still put me to bed, seeing as how we're courting." He slid his arm about her waist.

"Courting?" she said dryly.

"They say you're sweet on me." He brushed a kiss over her hair. "They say I'm sweet on you, too." When that didn't soften her temper, he slipped his hand inside her robe to caress her belly. "Do you remember the last time you sat on my lap?"

She tipped up her chin. "The only time I remember being on your lap was when I had my hands and feet tied for hours."

Testy wench. "That's not when I meant, and you know it. Mayhap you just need a little reminder." Pulling her head close, he sealed his lips to hers.

Holy Christ, she tasted good, of whisky and woman, both tart and sweet. For a moment she responded like a woman ought, opening her mouth and drawing him into her silky softness. Her tongue danced with his, and her body relaxed beneath the strokes of his fingers.

Until his hand covered her breast.

"Lachlan," she whispered, tearing her mouth from his, "are you trying to seduce me?"

"If I can." He fondled her brazenly.

"Even though we're not actually married yet?"

He ignored a stab of guilt. "That didn't stop us before," he said evasively.

"Only because you took advantage of me in a weak moment."

"So why don't you take advantage of *me* when I'm foxed and can't protest? Tit for tat, turnabout is fair play."

She snorted. "A real tit for tat would be me tossing you into a carriage, tying you hand and foot, and hauling you about Scotland. Though I daresay you're not foxed enough to allow *that*."

Guilt skewered him again. "If it'll make you happy, I swear that when this is over, you can tie me up and haul me about as much as you please."

The sudden gleam in her eyes gave him pause. Then she shifted on his lap, slipping her arms up about his neck with a sultry smile, and he forgot about everything except the feel of her in his arms.

"That does sound intriguing," she said in a husky voice, "especially the part about tying you up. In fact, I rather fancy doing it right now. Then I could 'take advantage of you' as much as I wanted."

Just like that, his blood began to thunder. "You fancy that, do you?"

"Oh yes." With a seductive glance, she bent forward to kiss his chest through the open V of his shirt, then ran her tongue up along his collarbone. "It's a pity that you want to wait until 'after this is all over.'"

His heart started pounding something fierce. "I don't suppose we'd have to . . . wait. If you don't want."

She pressed her mouth to his ear. "What I want is to have you at my mercy, Lachlan Ross. You're so masterful and overwhelming that I can't entirely relax with you. Especially since we're not married."

Her arch tone made him jerk his head around to stare at her, but she'd already dropped her head and had begun to suck and lick her way down his neck. "But if you were bound so I could be free to touch you all over, kiss you all over"—she slid her hand between them to cup his stiffening cock—"run my tongue over every part of you . . . I know I'd feel much more comfortable."

The very thought of her tongue laving his cock and ballocks turned him stiff as a pike. For that alone, he'd let her tie him up.

All right, so this knowing temptress on his lap wasn't quite the Venetia he knew. But he liked this Venetia. He liked her a lot. And he'd go mad if he had to wait much longer to have her again.

He reached for the tie of her robe, but she caught his hand. "First, I bind you," she said. "Then the clothes come off."

Her persistence about tying him up gave him pause. "Ye're not planning to bind me and leave me here for the maids to find in the morning, are you?"

"Lachlan!" she said with a pretty pout. "I could never do such a thing!" She rose from his lap with a disappointed sigh. "You don't trust me, that's what it is. I only wanted to have a bit of fun, but—"

"I do trust you, lass, I do!" He grabbed her hand before she could walk away, then pulled her to stand between his legs. "If tying me up is what you want, then I'm willing to oblige." Especially if that was the only way to share her bed tonight.

"And you'll let me do as I please with you once I've got you tied up?" she said with a kittenish glance. "Anything I want, no matter how wicked?"

God help him, yes. "Whatever you want."

Her blazing smile sucked the breath right out of him. "Good," she said, then untied her robe and dangled the tie in front of him. "I'll use this."

As she circled behind him, he quickly shed his waistcoat and shirt, leaving him naked from the waist up, then tugged off his boots. He would let her do the rest. A smile touched his lips. He wouldn't mind that a bit.

The smile vanished when he felt her tying his hands. She was tying them tighter than he'd expect of a lass who'd never tied anybody up before. When she then secured them to the chair, he felt a twinge of unease. He'd counted on being able to leave the chair if he wanted.

By the time she returned to stand before him with a dark, sly smile, his heart was thumping madly in his chest. Her robe gapped open just enough to show her translucent shift and the curves it teasingly hid. But to his annoyance, she didn't remove it.

She just stood there surveying him—her eyes scouring his shoulders and chest and belly until they fixed upon his splayed legs with the bulge between them. The bulge that swelled beneath her gaze.

"Your robe," he rasped, so aroused he thought he might explode. "Take it off. You promised."

She planted her hands on her waist and cast him a glance that was right devilish. "All in good time, husband, all in good time."

He'd already opened his mouth to protest when the word "husband" registered. "Husband?"

Her laugh was most wicked. "Come now, Lachlan, you know perfectly well that we spoke our marriage vows earlier this evening. In Gaelic, no less. How could you forget, after you worked so hard to trick me into saying them?"

Holy Christ, she knew the truth. And he was done for, if he didn't play this very carefully. "Trick you?" he said, trying to sound innocent when he felt oh-so-guilty. "How did I trick you? You said you knew Gaelic."

"And you knew I was lying."

"I didn't—"

"You didn't correct me a while ago when I said we weren't married, did you?" Her eyes glittered at him. "I said it three times."

She'd set a trap for him, and he'd stumbled right into it. "How did you . . ."

"Your mother told me. Imagine my shock upon hearing that we were married without my realizing it." She sidled up close, then leaned down to whisper in his ear, "And without my having the opportunity to refuse, either."

With a light nip of his earlobe, she drew back again, and he groaned. *Mo chreach,* he was in trouble now. He tried to rise, but she'd not only tied his hands to the chair, she'd tied the chair to the table.

"Don't bother to get up, husband," she said in a silky voice. "You're going to be sitting there a while yet. At least until I have what I want from you."

He fell back into the chair, cursing himself for not seeing the trap until it was sprung. "And what might that be, lassie?" he rasped, though he feared he knew.

"Everything, my dear." She bent to run one long finger up his inner thigh, slowly, sensuously, rising to just short of his ballocks before she took her hand back, leaving him hard and heavy and aching. "I mean to have you offering me everything I want."

Then she flashed him a merciless smile. "Because you won't get what *you* want until you do."

Chapter Twenty-Five

Dear Cousin Michael,
If you have a wife, I feel vastly sorry for her. In
my experience, men only prefer their privacy when
they want to use it for devious purposes.

Sincerely,
Charlotte Harris

Now *this* was more like it, Venetia thought, savoring the moment. It was thrilling to have the arrogant wretch bound and at her mercy. Trick *her* into marriage, would he? She'd make sure he never tried anything like that again.

Though Lord knew he looked too delicious for words like this—the well-crafted chest with its smattering of curls, the lean waist whose scars appeared markedly improved . . . the strong thighs parted just enough to display a very obvious arousal beneath his trousers. She could barely resist the urge to smooth her fingers over those finely hewn shoulders, gleaming in the firelight.

But she dared not do so yet, or she might find herself sucked into the sensual pull he exerted on her whenever they were alone. As it was, the longer she stared at him, the more he lost his alarm and regained his arrogance.

"Can I assume from what you just said that I will eventually get what I want out of this?" he asked with a taunting lift of his eyebrow.

"Depends on what you want."

A scowl darkened his brow. "You *know* what I want, damn it." He scoured her body with a hungry gaze that told her exactly what he meant to do to her if she ever got close enough for it. "I want you in my bed. I want my wedding night."

"Then you'll have to meet my demands."

She slid off her robe, delighting in how his eyes drank her up. Dangling the threadbare cotton wrap from one finger, she strolled over to trail it up between his legs, right over the aroused flesh swelling his trousers to breaking point. Thank heaven for those harem tales and her friend Amelia's descriptive letters about houri dances in Morocco, where she lived with her American husband.

"It appears you were right about me," she said in a throaty murmur as he moaned. "I do have a wicked bent."

He swore foully. "I won't be tied up forever, ye ken?" His gaze burned into her. "Once I'm free, there's naught to stop me from taking my wife over my knee."

"I wouldn't be making cocky threats just now, if I were you." She dragged the flimsy fabric of her wrap up and down over his arousal, knowing it couldn't possibly be enough to satisfy him. "Besides, all it would take is for me to explain that I don't understand Gaelic, and you won't have a wife."

His eyes narrowed. "My clan will protest that you claimed to know exactly what we were saying."

"And I will protest otherwise. Then there will be a nasty dispute in court." She threaded her fingers through his hair and drew his head back until he was glaring up at her. "Tell me, Lachlan, who do you think the magistrate will believe? An earl's daughter? Or the rough Highlander who kidnapped that earl's daughter? After pretending to be dead for six months?"

He closed his eyes with a groan. "Very well, lassie, ye've made yer point. So what are yer demands?"

Releasing him, she started with a small one to lower his guard. "First, I want a real wedding, one performed in the church before a minister and witnesses. I shan't risk anyone disputing our marriage once our children are born."

His eyes lit up at her mention of children. "Of course, a real wedding. Yer father and aunt will want the same, anyway. I have no quarrel with that."

"Good." Now came the important things. "Second, I want information that no one else seems willing to tell me."

"About what?"

"What McKinley was talking about today, what you referred to once before. That Papa had you punished years ago for something. I want to know why and how and for what."

A flush touched his cheeks as he squirmed in the chair. "I can't imagine why you'd need to know such a thing."

"Because once Papa arrives and I go to speak to him, I need to have all the facts before me. I need to know what I'm dealing with."

He glowered at her. "I already told you I'm not letting you speak to yer father for me, so if you're thinking to keep me tied up until I promise—"

"I'm thinking that by the time I'm through with you, Lachlan Ross, you'll promise me anything," she said, feeling a wild surge of power at being in control of *him* for once. She pulled loose the ties of her chemise, then opened it just enough to expose the swells of her breasts and the dark valley between.

His gaze shot there like an arrow to a target. "*Mo chreach,*" he said hoarsely.

"Tell me what McKinley meant, and I'll not only remove the chemise, but I'll let you taste what's underneath."

The bulge between his legs swelled. "You're a more devious female than I gave you credit for."

"I learned it from you."

He gave a choked laugh. "Aye, that's probably true."

She dropped the chemise off one shoulder. "So will you tell me?"

"Take off yer shift," he ground out. "Then I'll tell you."

"No, you'll tell me first." She came up close and bent to rub her clothed breast over his cheek.

Quickly he turned his head and seized it in his mouth, sucking it through the fabric. She let him . . . for just a moment. Then she drew back. "Tell me, Lachlan."

A muscle worked in his jaw as he glared up at her. "I'd never have let you tie me if I'd known you could be so cruel."

"But you did, and this is what I want from you. The truth. All of it."

"And you won't stop plaguing me till I tell you, will you?"

"No."

He sighed. "Fine." Squaring his shoulders, he glanced away into the flames of the candles. "When I was sixteen, a groundskeeper at Braidmuir saw a pack of boys running off from the orchard with bags full of apples. Since they were my friends, he told yer father that he thought I was among them."

Anger flared in his eyes as they swung to her. "It wasna true. Back then, I'd never have stolen apples or anything else from yer father. I was wild, not a thief."

His brogue had turned heavier, thicker, as if the past years of travel and soldiering in the British army had melted away to leave him just a Highland lad again. "But yer father seized on the idea I had a part in it and stormed over to demand of *my* father that something be done, that I be brought before the magistrate and made an example of."

She shook her head, incredulous. "Because of apples?"

"He said 'twas the principle of the thing. He was sure I'd persuaded the other boys to do it. And even after my friends said I wasn't with them, he believed they were just protecting 'the laird's son.'"

A rough sigh escaped him. "So my father called me in. I swore I had naught to do with it—I thought he believed me, too. But instead of taking my side, he proposed to yer father a punishment. He said it was to keep me from being brought before the magistrate, but . . ." He looked away again, shame spreading over his features. "I would rather have said my piece in court than endure what Father suggested; a public caning."

She stared at him, shocked. "My father didn't agree to it, surely."

"Ah, but he did, lass. The earl was furious about the thieving, and my father wanted to appease him, God only knows why." He tensed. "So Father brought me before the entire clan and yer father's people, made me pull down my trews, then gave me the twenty strokes he and yer father had agreed upon."

"Oh, Lachlan," she whispered, her stomach roiling to

think of the humiliation he must have suffered. For a boy as proud and defiant as Lachlan had been, even at sixteen . . .

"He caned me like a dog. Or a thief." His voice grew belligerent. "I wasna a thief, no matter what yer father said."

Then it dawned on her. Sixteen. "That's why you left the Highlands." She came up to lay her hand on his shoulder. "That's why you joined the regiment."

"Aye." He swallowed convulsively. "After that, I couldn't . . . face anyone. I couldn't stand how they looked at me, whether with contempt *or* pity."

"It was a horrible thing for your father to do," she said hotly. "And a horrible thing for my father to agree to."

"It wasn't the strokes that bothered me," he said, his face aflame. "God knows Father caned the devil out of me often enough when I was a boy, and he honestly thought he was saving me from a worse time with the magistrate. But that was what made it so awful—him thinking my only choices were jail or a caning. Him thinking I would actually—"

"Do such a thing. It hurt that he didn't believe you," she said, stroking his hair to soothe him. "It hurt because you didn't deserve it."

He nodded grimly, then shot her a startled glance. "How do you know I didn't deserve it?"

"You just said you didn't do it."

"Aye." He thrust out his chin. "But my own father didn't believe me. Why should you?"

"Because I know what kind of man you really are," she said tenderly.

"You mean, the kind who would ride the roads to

steal from yer father and his friends, and kidnap a young innocent—"

"You did those things on behalf of your clan, something I well understand."

He snorted. "If you did, I wouldn't be tied up here so you could make yer demands on me. Why do you think I never told you about the caning? Because I knew it would make you distrust me even more. Because I knew you could never understand."

The words tore at her. He was right—she *hadn't* understood. When she'd asked that he give up his right to confront her father, she hadn't known how much she was expecting him to give up. He'd waited sixteen years to get his due, to learn why his father had bowed to Papa's will even though Papa had owed him money. To find out why Papa never paid, and why Alasdair Ross hadn't made him.

He'd waited sixteen years for his justice, and she'd expected him to throw it aside for her. That wasn't fair.

"So what's yer next demand?" he said dully. "I suppose it's that I do what you please with yer father. Ye're going to prance about driving me insane, trying to make me say—"

"No." She pressed her finger to his lips. "Not anymore." This game had taken an ugly turn she'd never intended. "You win. Do as you please with Papa, though I hope you'll remember that I prefer a live husband to a dead one."

He gazed up at her, relief showing in his face. Then his eyes darkened and he caught her finger in his mouth to suck it. Her breath quickened. She drew out the finger and bent to replace it with her mouth, kissing him slowly, deeply. He tasted of smoke and malt, the bittersweet tang of whisky adding to the growing fog of need and desire overtaking her brain. As his tongue delved and stroked, toying with hers, she felt her heart fill with love.

Love? Yes, love. She loved him. It probably wasn't wise, but she couldn't help that. She loved that he cared so fiercely for the land and its people, she loved his stubborn pride, she loved that he had come to treat her like one of his clan.

Did she dare to tell him? Dare to give him that much power over her when he already had more than was wise? She would die if he didn't feel the same.

Unsure and vulnerable, she drew back only to hear him murmur, "Take off the shift, lass. I told you what you wanted, so now I get to see you. And taste you."

She would show him instead. For now, she would simply show him how she felt. She shimmied out of her chemise, then leaned on his good leg to thrust her breast against his mouth. With a hungry growl, he caught the nipple between his teeth, then sucked it in so he could flick his tongue over it repeatedly.

Throwing her head back, she uttered a sigh of sheer delight. Lord, he did that so well. Eager for more, she sat down across his lap and pushed the other breast in his face so he could pleasure that one, too. Greedily he took it, licking and nipping it until she thought she'd go mad.

She spread her hands over his chest, reveling in his slick skin, his flexing muscle, the heat coming off him like that off a thoroughbred after a race.

"Lower," he said hoarsely. "Please, lass . . . touch me lower, I beg you. Touch my cock . . ."

The coarse word startled her, but she'd been acting less than a lady, so she could hardly expect him to act like a gentleman. In keeping with her newfound pleasure in wickedness, she not only unbuttoned his trousers and his drawers to allow his "cock" to spring free, she left his lap to kneel on the floor between his legs.

When he caught his breath, his shaft thrusting forward like an impudent rogue, she smiled up at him. "I did promise to lick you everywhere, didn't I?"

"Lass!" he said, looking shocked as she closed her mouth around him. Then a sigh of pure pleasure slid out of him. "Lass . . ."

Remembering how he'd liked her to stroke him that night in Kingussie, she tried to do it with her lips and tongue. And she must have done it partly right, for he was muttering, "Oh yes . . . Holy Christ, yes . . . like that . . . yes . . ."

But it was awkward, and her mouth didn't seem large enough to hold him.

"Come here, princess," he rasped, confirming her fears.

She released his flesh to shoot him a pained glance. "I . . . I'm doing it badly, aren't I?"

He choked out a laugh. "If that's how badly you do it with no knowledge whatsoever, I shudder to think what you'd be like with experience." His voice lowered to a heavy thrum. "I want to see you while you make love to me, all of you, your pretty breasts, your fine mouth. Come ride me, wife. Before I go mad."

Drunk from the sweet liquor of his words, she rose. "Shall I untie you first?"

He arched one eyebrow. "Only if you think I've atoned for having tricked you. I couldn't survive another night like this."

"You know perfectly well you'd never let me tie you

up again, anyway." With a laugh, she stood between his legs and stretched over his head to reach the carving knife she'd left on the table while tying him. It put her breast in close proximity to his mouth, and he seized it, sucking it with eager fervor.

That made it difficult to stay properly still to slice his bonds. "I'd stop doing that if I were you," she muttered. "Unless you want me to slice off a finger."

He froze. But the second she'd cut him free and tossed the knife onto the table, he grabbed her. Shoving his thigh between hers, he widened her so he could force her astride his lap.

"Take me inside you," he ordered, his eyes hot and needy in the candlelight. When she blinked, he softened his voice. "Lower yerself onto me, ye ken?"

"Ohhh," she said, and did just that, reveling in his throttled groan as her flesh met his, groin to groin.

"That's it . . . ah, princess . . . ye're a wonder, you are . . ."

There were no more words then, just her all over him, him all over her. His hand kneaded her breast, her hands clutched his shoulders. His mouth razed her flesh with openmouthed kisses while they began to move together, her up and down, him in and out.

Soon the glory was building inside her, coupled with a sheer, dark pleasure that had her writhing atop him and begging him in half-coherent words. "Oh, my darling . . . yes, Lachlan . . . take me, my love . . . make me yours . . ."

She reached her pinnacle in a thrilling rush, her body screaming its joy as she shot over the edge into ecstasy. With an answering growl, he thrust hard and poured his warm seed deep inside her.

As they strained together to wring every drop of

delight from their union, a sudden hope consumed her. Heaven grant her that his seed would take root, that they had just now created a life on this, their wedding night.

Because as she cradled him close and he clutched her fiercely to him, burying his face in her neck, she felt more than just part of his flesh. She felt part of his soul, the wild and tender soul that was Lachlan. Her Lachlan. Forever.

Before she could stop herself, she murmured, "Love me, Lachlan."

Lachlan nuzzled her neck and said hoarsely, "I do, wife. I do."

And her joy was complete.

She had little chance to enjoy the moment before sounds of the servants at the back of the manor warned of the approaching dawn. Laughing like children, she and Lachlan scurried about the dining room to scoop up clothes and hide the evidence of their intimacy.

Once they'd crept up the stairs and into the master bedchamber, they quickly stripped down to nothing and crawled into bed and each other's arms.

Venetia's heart leaped as she gazed into the face that became dearer to her with every hour. "Did you mean it?" she whispered.

"I did," he said solemnly, brushing a kiss over her brow.

The fact that he didn't have to ask what she was talking about touched her more than anything.

"I started falling in love with you when you actually discussed with me what lay beneath a man's kilt. Then after Kingussie, when you doctored me . . ."

He shook his head. "Do you know how hard it was for me to let you go to bed alone that night? How little I slept for imagining you beneath me, murmuring yer ladylike sighs while I showed you how badly I wanted you? It damned near killed me to refuse you. 'Tis a miracle I resisted you as long as I did."

"Indeed it is," she teased. "But think how much longer I had to resist you." She cupped his whisker-rough cheek. "I've loved you ever since I was seven and you climbed an oak to fetch down my kite."

He frowned. "I don't remember that."

"I'm not surprised. You only did it because I plagued you about it, and there was no one else around to help me. Back then I was just a pest to you. But to me you were the most wonderful fellow in the world." Tears clogged her throat. "And if I'd had even an inkling of the awful thing Papa made your father do to you—"

"Shh, lassie, shh. Let's not speak of that." Rolling onto his back, he pulled her into his arms.

"I know it embarrasses you, but it shouldn't. You were brave to endure that caning, even when you knew it was unjust."

"Right before I ran off and abandoned my family."

"Who can blame you? You felt betrayed. Besides, the important thing is that eventually you came back." She propped her chin on his chest. "Why?"

He looked pensive. "This is my home, my clan. No matter how far I traveled, I could never escape the longing for it. Especially after what I saw at the Battle of New Orleans. We lost half of our men that day. Our British commander wouldn't give the order to retreat, despite the lack of ladders to climb over the American bulwarks."

A muscle worked in his jaw. "So we had to stand there and let the Americans cut us down one by one, with musket and cannon. Discipline, you know. We Scots are nothing if not disciplined in battle."

He shook his head. "After you see a thing like that, hear your fellow countrymen crying out for home as they die, it makes you crave what you've lost. Or what you've thrown away out of pride."

Her heart twisting for him, she pressed a kiss to his chest. "And then you came home to nothing."

A shadow crossed his face. "Father died without my ever making my peace with him. Without his ever telling me—"

"Why he behaved as he did. I know; it's very odd. If Papa owed him so much money, why did your father agree to such outrageous demands for your punishment? Why should he?"

"Do you still not believe me about the loan?" he said, tensing.

"I'm not saying that. It just seems a vexing puzzle."

"Aye," he said, relaxing. "But not one we're liable to solve just now."

"Did you ever ask your mother if she knew why?"

"Once. She said Father thought it would be good for me. Put the fear of God into me."

"And she didn't try to stop him."

He arched one eyebrow. "Don't you remember what I told you about Highland women?"

"Yes," she said dryly. "And I hope you know I will never be the kind of Highland woman to stand meekly by while you do as you please."

A chuckle escaped his lips. "No, I don't expect that, to be sure." He began to stroke her back. "Otherwise, why would I be letting you talk to yer father on behalf of me and the clan when he comes to fetch you?"

Her gaze flew to his. "You don't mean . . . you haven't decided . . ."

"You're my wife," he said with a rueful smile. "If I can't trust you to argue for us, then who *can* I trust?"

"Oh, Lachlan!" she cried, moved to tears. "Thank you, thank you! You won't regret it, I swear!"

She stretched up to cover his face with kisses. That became one long and sensual kiss that drove every thought but him out of her mind. And before she knew it, he was rolling her beneath him, settling himself between her legs, kissing his way down to take her breasts in his mouth.

And she forgot everything but the delicious maelstrom of making love with her husband.

Hours later, with sunlight flooding the room, Venetia awakened to the murmurs of servants in the hall, probably debating if they should disturb their master and new mistress. She considered ignoring them and going back to sleep, but she was hungry. And knowing her husband, he would be, too, once he woke up.

As she rose from the bed to draw on her shift, she glanced to where Lachlan lay on his back in a sound sleep, his forearm slung over his eyes and the sheet covering only half his body. Hard to believe he was her husband in truth now.

Hard to believe he loved her. She might die from the joy of it.

With her heart full, she covered the rest of his body before dropping a tender kiss on his tousled head and taking her clothes into the adjoining dressing room. There, she closed the door and summoned a maid through the dressing room door to help her finish dressing.

"Oh, milady," the servant exclaimed. "I was just coming to wake you. We've guests in the drawing room, and they're demanding to see you."

"My father?" she said, her heart dropping to her stomach.

"No, milady. It's a Colonel Seton. And he's got a Lady Kerr with him."

Aunt Maggie. How on earth had she found out that Venetia was here?

Dressing hurriedly, Venetia flew down the stairs, eager to head off her aunt before Lachlan awoke. When she burst into the drawing room, she found Lady Ross trying to calm her anxious aunt while Colonel Seton looked on grimly.

"Aunt Maggie!" Venetia cried, overcome at the sight of the familiar face.

"My dear girl!" Her aunt rushed over to enfold her in a hug so strong it left Venetia breathless. Then to her shock, the woman began to cry.

Venetia smoothed her hand down her aunt's back, crooning softly. "It's all right. I'm fine. You can see I'm fine."

"I was so worried . . ." her aunt choked out.

It took Aunt Maggie another moment to gain control over her tears. Then she drew back to wipe her eyes. When Colonel Seton hurried over to offer his handkerchief, it was impossible to miss the warm glance that passed between him and Aunt Maggie.

When the woman returned her attention to her niece, her blotchy face held so much worry that Venetia felt a twinge of unwarranted guilt. "I've come to take you back," her aunt went on. "If we leave at once, we can meet your father at the docks in Inverness, for I've no doubt Quentin will come by ship—it's the easiest and quickest way."

"I'm not leaving," Venetia protested. "Lachlan and I are married now."

"Yes," her aunt said as she seized her hand, "Lady Ross has told me that you married the scoundrel, but—"

"He's not a scoundrel."

"He kidnapped you! You know he's the Scourge, don't you?"

"I know a great many things about Lachlan, including why he chose to masquerade as that person," Venetia said firmly. "Most of all, I know I love him."

"And I love her," said a voice from the doorway. With a black scowl, Lachlan strode in to stand beside Venetia, slipping his arm possessively about her waist. "We're married, and there's naught you can do about it, Lady Kerr. You're sure as the devil not taking her from me."

He turned a hard gaze on the colonel. "Why did you bring Lady Kerr here, damn it? You were supposed to keep her in Edinburgh."

"I tried!" Colonel Seton shot back.

"You told me he wasn't part of your plot," Venetia said under her breath to Lachlan.

"I wanted to protect him," Lachlan snapped. Then he glared at the colonel. "Clearly, he didn't feel the same loyalty."

"Damnation, man," the colonel snapped, "Maggie's no fool. She figured out what I was up to and threatened to ruin everything. I had to tell her. I had no choice." He thrust out his chin. "Besides, I'm glad I did. And you will be, too, once you hear what she's got to say."

But Aunt Maggie was now pacing and thinking aloud. "Perhaps we can still fix this. You haven't had time to marry in the church; no bishop would give a special license to a dead man." She halted to cast Lachlan a pleading glance. "So you must have had an irregular marriage. And that can be overturned in court, depending on the circumstances."

When Lachlan tensed, Venetia said hastily, "Our vows were spoken before a roomful of witnesses, Aunt Maggie. It can't be overturned."

Her aunt sank onto the settee, her face ashen. "Then your father will kill him, my dear."

"He won't!" Venetia hurried to take a seat beside her aunt and lay her arm across her shoulders. "I know Papa is liable to be angry, but—"

"Angry!" Aunt Maggie shook her head. "You have no idea. If he arrives here to find Alasdair's son married to his only daughter, he's liable to commit murder."

"But why? Papa is the one who never repaid his loan."

"And with good reason. A reason that Alasdair clearly accepted."

"But I am not my father," Lachlan said sharply. "My clan needs that money. I won't stand by and let Duncannon run roughshod over my people because Father was too much a coward to demand what was owed him!"

"A coward? That's not what it was at all," Aunt Maggie protested.

"Then what was it?" Venetia pleaded with her.

Aunt Maggie wrung her hands, her gaze darting first to Lady Ross, then to Venetia. "I'll explain it to Lachlan, and Lachlan alone. I'll say no more with Lady Ross and you in the room."

"If my husband had something to do with this mess,"

Lady Ross broke in, her gaze fierce, "then I'll be hearing what he did, no matter how bad."

"And since this affects my husband, it affects me," Venetia added. "You have to tell us all."

"You don't want to know, my dear," her aunt said, her voice plaintive. "Please don't make me tell you. Just come back with me—"

"No." Venetia rose and went to Lachlan's side. "Not without my husband."

"Fine, but don't say I didn't warn you." Aunt Maggie remained silent a long moment. When she began to speak again, her voice had taken on a tragic tone. "Whatever financial agreements may have been made between Alasdair and Quentin were overturned the summer my sister died."

"This has to do with Mama? But how? Why?"

"Because as far as Quentin is concerned . . ." Aunt Maggie paused, pain flashing over her face. "As far as your father is concerned, Alasdair Ross killed your mother."

Chapter Twenty-Six

∞

Dear Charlotte,

We must stop this foolish argument. I will never say what you want to hear—that all men can be painted with the same brush. I've lived long enough to learn that plenty of fine fellows are forced into seeking rich wives by the necessity of doing their duty. And plenty of scoundrels hide their perfidy behind their supposed morality. Life is not simple, and neither are people.

Your true friend,
Michael

Lachlan stared at Lady Kerr, a horrible premonition seeping into his bones.

"But Mama died in childbirth," Venetia said.

Her aunt nodded. "Yes. She was bearing Alasdair Ross's child at the time. Your half brother."

"Half brother," Lachlan said in a whisper. "Please tell me that Venetia and I are not . . . we were never . . ."

"No!" Lady Kerr hastened to assure him. "No, you're not related. The affair between your father and my sister happened long after Venetia was born. It barely lasted a year."

Lachlan's gaze flew to his mother. He'd been about to ask if she'd known, but one look at her stunned expression told him she had not. Damn.

Lady Kerr shot his mother a pleading glance. "I'm so sorry, Lady Ross. You were never supposed to know of it. Quentin doesn't even know that my sister told me before she died." The woman's gaze returned to Lachlan and Venetia. "Neither of you were supposed to hear of it. They never meant for any of you to be hurt."

"They?" Lachlan still couldn't quite take in this new development.

"Quentin, your father, my sister," Lady Kerr explained. "Your father and my sister took the secret to their graves. Quentin would have done so, too, if not for—"

"Me," he choked out. "If not for the Scottish Scourge stirring up trouble about that loan."

Venetia laid a soothing hand on his arm, but he shrugged it off, going to gaze blindly out the window. All these years and he'd never guessed, never once realized that such an ugly family secret lay at the root of their troubles. His father. And Venetia's mother.

No wonder Duncannon had refused to repay the money he owed. What man with any spine would repay the man who'd cuckolded him?

Lady Kerr rose from the settee. "I never knew about the money, I swear. My sister never mentioned it, and back then women of our rank were rarely told such things, anyway. If I'd known, perhaps—"

"That's why Alasdair didn't press the earl for repayment," Lady Ross said in a hollow voice. "Out of guilt. He'd killed Duncannon's wife."

"I don't see why you two keep saying that," Venetia burst out. "Mama died in childbirth. It was no one's fault, even if she had been carrying Sir Alasdair's child. She could just as easily have been bearing Papa's."

"I'm afraid not, my dear," Aunt Maggie said gently. "After you were born, the surgeon told Quentin that another childbirth would kill her. Your father loved her and he wouldn't risk her life. So they didn't share a bed from then on."

Lachlan turned to see Venetia quietly crying, the tears streaming down her face. Anger at his father swelled in him. Father was responsible for ripping the lass's mother from her. God help him. God help them all.

"Don't think too badly of your mother," her aunt said, putting her arm around Venetia's shoulders. "She was terribly lonely. She begged Quentin, pleaded with him to ignore the surgeon. She said it was worth the risk. He refused. So Susannah turned for companionship to the only other man she saw as a friend. Lachlan's father."

"Companionship!" Lachlan's heart grew heavier by the moment. "He seduced her, you mean. My father, the high and moral clan chief, the man who spent my childhood lecturing me for my wicked urges, seduced her. He was an adulterer, plain and simple."

His mother went ash-white. "Lachlan, please—"

"No, Mother, I won't defend him! He took Duncannon's wife, and he did what he always did to everything he touched. He destroyed her." His gaze fell on Venetia. "He destroyed your mother, lass. I'm sorry. I'm so sorry."

"It's not your fault," she whispered. "Everyone at fault is dead."

He gave a hollow laugh. "Ah, but what happened afterward is my fault," he said in an aching whisper. "I made it worse by demanding my due when all your father wanted was to forget. And then I kidnapped you—" His voice broke. "Oh God, what have I done? My father took the earl's wife, and now I've taken his daughter."

"It's not the same, Lachlan!" She hurried across the room to grab his arm.

He looked down at that small, defenseless hand, and shame washed him anew. "No, don't, lass. Don't." Removing her hand, he backed away. He glanced to his mother, then to Lady Kerr, then whirled for the door. "I have to think on all this . . . I have to figure out what to do. What's right."

What must be done if he was to be able to live with himself.

Venetia gave a little cry and started after him, but her aunt stayed her. "Let him go, my dear. Give him time."

He heard the words dimly as he strode from the manor, but they barely registered. Because his mind was drifting back long years to a childhood he'd never wished to examine too closely before.

One event burned in his memory: the time he'd startled his father crossing the bridge from Braidmuir. Lachlan had received such a tongue-lashing that it had kept him from wondering what his father might have been doing on the Duncannon estate in the wee hours of the morn.

Now that he thought of it, there'd been other signs. Duncannon's surprising behavior in the months after the impending "blessed event" had been announced. Even now, Lachlan remembered seeing rage on the earl's face every time his father entered a room. His father had said they'd quarreled, but no mere quarrel could have produced such anger.

And Venetia . . . His breath caught to remember Venetia, a little slip of a thing, worrying herself sick over how her parents argued late at night. He'd made light of her concerns, telling her that married people always argued.

How wounded to the heart she must have been after

her mother's death. Of course, he hadn't been around to see *that*. Oh no, he'd already run off to become a soldier, because his father had betrayed him.

His blood ran cold. That finally made sense, too. His father, the adulterer, had served him up to Duncannon, who'd probably been mad with worry over his wife's pregnancy. His father, the coward, had lacked the courage to support his son in the wake of his own awful sin. Easier to let Lachlan suffer, in hopes that throwing Duncannon that sop would reduce his own responsibility.

But that wasn't the only sop he'd thrown, no. Father had let the loan slide, and in the process had let his entire clan suffer. His clan and his wife and his son. Because he'd taken what wasn't his own. Because he was too much a hypocrite to admit it. A self-righteous ass, that was Alasdair Ross.

Lachlan wandered blindly down the path to Braidmuir. But Father wasn't the only one, was he? Lachlan winced to remember the self-righteous nonsense he'd blathered at Venetia to justify the kidnapping. Duncannon had shown him mercy at every turn, never seeking to have him hanged, never pursuing him as a criminal, and only sending men to beat him after Lachlan had driven him too far.

So it wasn't guilt over not repaying the loan that made Duncannon reluctant to stop him. No, it had probably been fear—that any investigation into Lachlan and the feud might expose his mortifying secrets. Duncannon had simply not wanted to destroy his daughter's fond memories of her mother, and an innocent lady's fond memories of her husband. Even Lachlan's own memories. In his own bullheaded way, Duncannon had been protecting them.

And Lachlan had repaid him by stealing his daughter, taking her innocence, and tricking her into marrying him.

The guilt threatened to choke him.

He looked up, startled to find himself in the glen where he and Venetia used to see each other so often as children. Where he would fish and she would skip around pronouncing him too scruffy for a baronet's heir.

The memory shot a shaft of pain through his chest. She'd been right—he was too scruffy, too unscrupulous, too hasty to pass judgment without determining all the facts. Too eager to ruin a man's life without just cause.

He'd thought he'd changed, grown responsible, changed his wild ways for more sober ones. But he hadn't. Just like Father, he'd hidden a dirty hand beneath a clean glove.

Well, no more. The battle between him and Duncannon ended now.

Even if he had to tear his heart out of his chest to ensure it.

"Did you find him?" Venetia cried as Jamie entered the drawing room.

He gazed at Venetia, Lady Ross, Aunt Maggie, and Colonel Seton, then sighed. "He told me not to tell you where he is. He wants to be alone for a while. That's what he said."

"But why?" Venetia rose to pace the room, her heart twisting in her chest. "What good does it do for him to sit brooding?"

"He probably just needs time to think things through." But worry etched lines in Lady Ross's brow. "I'm sure he'll be fine. Lachlan's not the kind to do anything foolish."

Venetia looked at Lady Ross and her throat constricted. The woman had been dealt quite a blow to her memories, yet here she was, clearly anxious over her son.

And with good reason. "Yes, but Lachlan has rather rigid ideas about justice and right and wrong. The longer he sits brooding, the more it will settle inside him like a cancer. We both know how he is—he takes things more to heart than anyone realizes."

More even than she. Though it still hurt to think of Mama, her sweet, laughing mama, lying in another man's arms, it didn't strike her as deeply as she'd expected. After the initial sting, she'd realized that she'd barely known her mother. Venetia had always remembered her as the perfect lady moving in perfect circles through a perfect manor, almost like a fairy tale. Or a ballad.

But life wasn't either one, and people could have two faces. She'd learned that from Lachlan when he'd stripped her lady's facade from her to unearth the woman beneath. Being a lady didn't mean being dead inside.

She wasn't surprised that Papa had thought otherwise. Or that once he'd discovered the flaw in his fairy-tale wife, he'd turned to hiding from it, hiding the secret away. He'd turned to loathing Scotland and Highlanders and everything associated with that part of his life. He'd abandoned his people and his land.

Although that was no answer, she could understand it. His memories must have plagued him sorely. To live here would have meant seeing Rosses every day beneath his very nose. And now that she was married to one . . .

She caught her breath. How would she ever make Papa easy with that? Would she have to give him up to have Lachlan? Or give Lachlan up to soothe Papa's pride?

No, she wouldn't do it. This could be settled. There

could be peace. It had been sixteen years, for heaven's sake! It was time to lance the boil that had been festering for years. Time to heal.

Lachlan would surely see that. He had to. Somehow she'd make Papa see it, too.

But as the hour grew late and there was no sign of her husband, she began to despair. She understood his anger, but not his need to be alone. They could comfort each other if he would only come home.

She spent the evening pacing, worrying. And it didn't help when she blundered upon Aunt Maggie standing outside in the dark, wrapped in Colonel Seton's intimate embrace. They sprang apart, but not before she'd seen them kissing.

"I was looking for Lachlan," she murmured, embarrassed.

"He hasn't come this way, lass," the colonel said. Then he seized her aunt's hand. "I know this isn't the time, but I thought I should tell you . . . when this is done, I intend to marry your aunt." He stared fondly down into Aunt Maggie's face. "The foolish woman has actually agreed to have me."

The sight of them in love drove a stake through her chest. "Even though you helped Lachlan kidnap her only niece?" Venetia snapped, then became instantly contrite. "I'm sorry, I didn't mean that. I'm glad he did it, or I would never have met him." She stared out into the night. "I'm just so worried about him."

Her aunt came to her side. "It will be all right, my dear. I know it will."

Venetia wished she could believe that. But later, after everyone had retired and she lay alone in the master bedchamber they'd shared for only one night, she began to despair again. If Lachlan, the randiest fellow in creation, wouldn't even come to her bed, what hope was there? And why wouldn't he come?

The next morning she awoke with a dull ache in her heart, only to find that one more person had arrived for their little party.

Papa.

He roared into the yard of Rosscraig like a typhoon. She could hear him all the way upstairs, riding his horse back and forth before the manor, shouting, "Venetia! Damn it, Venetia, where are you?"

Throwing her wrap over her nightdress, she went to the window and thrust her head out. "I'm here, Papa! I'm here!"

When he looked up to see her leaning out, the relief flooding his haggard face brought tears to her eyes. If she'd ever doubted that her father loved her, such doubts were put firmly to rest now. He'd ridden recklessly into his enemy's camp without any of his own men. She didn't know if that meant he was mad or brave, but she didn't care. She was just so amazingly glad to see him.

"Hold on!" he cried, his expression fierce. "I'll find a ladder to get you out!"

She laughed. "Stay right there—I'm coming down. I'm not a prisoner, for pity's sake."

Not even bothering to dress, she hurried to meet him in front of the manor, while the news spread through the estate and people rushed out to see the reunion. He jumped down from his horse to catch her up in his arms, his body shaking as violently as if someone had just snatched it from the icy cold loch.

She drew back to look at his dear face, taking in his

poor color and the dark circles under his eyes. Tears clogged her throat to see how frail he'd become in just a few weeks. "Oh, Papa." She smoothed back his gray hair with a trembling hand. "You haven't been taking your tonic, have you? Or eating enough or—"

Her breath snagged on her sobs, and she clutched him to her again, vowing she would do whatever it took to make this right for him. To keep him from hurting more.

This time he was the one to pull back, his eyes searching for any little evidence of harm. "You look better than I dared hope to expect. Ross didn't . . . hurt you, did he?"

"No, Papa. He was a perfect gentleman. And ever since we arrived, I've been staying here with his mother. Lady Ross has taken very good care of me." She glanced beyond him to his horse. "Did you ride all this way alone?"

"From Inverness only. I came by ship. We docked there late last night, and I had a devil of a time finding a horse to rent. Ross said come alone, so I did." His jaw tightened. "Brought the ransom, too, though it's hidden at Braidmuir. He won't see a penny of it unless he lets you go."

"You brought the money," she said.

"And myself, the two things he wanted." He flashed her a wan smile. "Because all I wanted was you safe."

"That's what you have, Duncannon," came a voice from the beech grove beside the manor.

Her heart in her throat, Venetia turned to find Lachlan striding toward them with Jamie behind him. He looked even worse than Papa, if that was possible. He wore a hastily donned shirt and trousers, a rumpled coat, and boots, nothing else. His hair was wilder than usual, and his beautiful eyes were shadowed with guilt. She'd seen many emotions on her husband's face, but never guilt. The sight of it made her ache down deep.

"So, the scoundrel himself has slunk out of hiding, has he?" Papa's face glowed with an unholy anger as he looked upon Lachlan. "I suppose you're here to collect yer money."

"No," Lachlan said as he approached. "I don't want the money."

That seemed to bring Papa up short. Then he scowled. "I'll be giving it to you all the same. I want you to leave my family alone, you blood-sucking divil, and for that I'll pay the ransom. But we'll be clear on this, Ross—'tis money extorted from me, and naught else. I dinna *owe* you a damned thing."

As the blood drained from Lachlan's face, Venetia wanted to rush to his side and hold him. But first she had to deal with her father.

"Papa," she murmured. "I know about the loan and why you didn't repay it." When his startled gaze flew to hers, she whispered, "I know about Mama and Sir Alasdair."

Horror and shame filled his face. "Ross told you? But how did *he* know—"

"No, Aunt Maggie told both of us and Lady Ross last night. She thought it best that we hear the truth before you came."

Looking stunned, he glanced at her aunt, who'd just rushed out to join the group, with Colonel Seton not far behind. "You knew?" he asked.

She nodded. "Susannah told me before she died. Quentin—"

"You had no right to speak of it!" he cried, heedless of the other people crowding around. "It was private, none of yer concern!"

Venetia laid her hand on his arm. "I'm glad she did. Now we can put this nastiness behind us."

Her father ignored her, whirling on Lachlan. "You! This is all yer fault. You couldn't leave well enough alone, could you? You had to go digging into the past, uncovering things that should never have seen the light of day—"

"I know," Lachlan said hoarsely. "That's why I'm here now, my lord. I ask no mercy. You have a right to yer justice. I'll accept any sentence, suffer any indignity for kidnapping Venetia. If I'd had any idea of what Father did, I would never have—"

He stopped, his voice thick with emotion, then steadied his shoulders. "But now that I know, I mean to take whatever punishment you dole out. Do what you will with me—have me horsewhipped, arrested, and put on trial for being the Scourge, whatever you will. I won't fight you."

His speech started an angry murmuring among his clan, who didn't know the circumstances, but it broke Venetia's heart. Lachlan shouldn't take so much upon himself. He'd acted to right what he perceived as a wrong. Did it really matter so much that his perception had been flawed?

"I ought to have you hanged," Papa said in a low, fierce voice.

Lachlan didn't even flinch. "Aye. Kidnapping is a hanging offense."

"No!" She threw herself in front of Papa. "I won't let you!"

"I said I ought to, gel," he grumbled, "not that I would." He paused to scan the yard where Rosses stood about in confusion, not sure who was the enemy now and who the friend. "His mother and clan depend on him. Why do you think I haven't tried to have him arrested before? I knew he was only doing what he thought was right." Anger flared in his face. "Though you went too far when you took Venetia, Ross."

"Your men nearly killed him, Papa." She turned to gaze upon the man she loved. "They beat him half to death. Months after it happened, he still can't walk without pain."

Shame etched her father's wrinkled brow. "Aye, and that was wrong. I never wanted that." He slid his arm about her waist. "I don't want you punished, Ross. I don't want anything from you except my daughter. And to be left alone."

Lachlan took a shuddering breath, then said in a low rasp, "That I can give you, sir."

A horrible foreboding seized Venetia. "You can't give me back, Lachlan. You're my husband."

Her father's shocked gaze swung to her. "Your husband?"

"Yer daughter is mistaken, my lord," Lachlan said in the same toneless voice he'd used that night in Kingussie, when he'd tried to put her out of his heart.

With her belly churning, she left her father's side, hardly able to believe what he'd just said. "I'm your wife. Why would you deny it?"

He wouldn't look at her, and that alone was a blow to her heart. "The wedding wasna legal, my lady, and you know it."

As a low grumble started again among the crowd, her father said, "What do you mean, it wasn't legal?"

"We spoke the vows in Gaelic, sir."

"My daughter doesn't know Gaelic," Papa said.

Lachlan arched his eyebrow. "Exactly. I tricked her into repeating the words. No court would ever uphold the marriage."

A stunned silence fell upon the others. Aunt Maggie sighed, and Lady Ross began muttering under her breath about foolish men with pigheaded ideas.

Like this one. Lachlan was throwing her away, devil take him. Because of some misplaced notion that he'd be giving her father justice. How could he? "You can't prove I don't know Gaelic. Everyone in that room heard me say that I did."

For the first time all morning, Lachlan shifted his gaze to her. "Can you repeat the vows now, Lady Venetia?"

His formal manner hurt almost as much as his rejection.

"Lass?" her father prodded.

She drew herself up. "This isn't a court. I don't have to repeat them or prove anything. My word should be enough."

Her father grabbed her arm. "Damnation, daughter, if he did trick you into saying vows, there's no reason you have to—"

"We consummated the marriage," she said with a blush. "I should think that's reason enough."

Papa stared at her, stunned, then glowered at Lachlan. "You bedded my daughter, you black-hearted ass?"

"I did not," Lachlan said calmly.

Venetia could only gape at him. He would deny that,

too? He would wipe out every precious moment they'd shared? How dare he!

"She says otherwise," her father growled, "and why should she lie?"

"Because she feels sorry for me and my clan; she thinks to help us by marrying me and giving me her fortune. Yer daughter has a tender heart and a canny mind. She's figured out that you would never agree to a marriage, never agree to give me her dowry, unless she was ruined."

"Damned right, I wouldn't!"

"Fortunately, she isn't ruined, sir." His gaze swung to her, unmistakably tender. "No mere man could possibly ruin such a perfect creature as yer daughter."

Tears stung her eyes as she caught the twist he'd given to "ruin"; he was trying to soften his rejection of her. Did he actually think he was doing her a favor by releasing her from the marriage? Did he really expect her just to go along?

The devil she would. "Yet you're calling this perfect creature a liar."

He paled. "Not a liar. Just overzealous in yer eagerness to help my clan."

She approached Lachlan. "And the fact that I love you means nothing to you? That you claimed to love me?"

The sudden flicker of something in his eyes, something needy and dark and desperate, gave her hope.

Then his face went blank again. "I claimed a lot of things with you." He swallowed, then continued in that cool, awful voice she was rapidly growing to despise. "They were only villainous attempts to get what I wanted—yer dowry, the money I thought yer father owed. That doesn't mean the things I said were true."

Now, *that* roused her temper. She marched up to him, face alight. "So you don't love me? That's what you're saying."

He stared down at her, his expression conflicted. "Go home, lass. You don't belong here in this ruined place, scraping and saving for a few curtains."

She noticed he couldn't bring himself to say flat out that he didn't love her. "I don't care about any of that! And I *do* belong here, I do! Ask anyone in your clan, and they'll say the same."

"You belong with yer family. I thought I had just cause to take you, but I was wrong, do ye ken? I had no right at all."

Her eyes narrowed. "That's what this is about? You've transgressed against your own rules of right and wrong, so now you mean to atone for that by doing something foolishly noble?"

"I'm not going to be like my father, damn it!" he shouted, then caught himself and lowered his voice. "My father stole what didn't belong to him from a man who was his friend, who'd done naught to hurt him. Father never had to pay, and thanks to that, I've gone and done the same, rubbing salt in a man's wounds who didn't deserve it." He crossed his arms over his chest. "Well, no more. It ends here."

"You mean, you plan to atone for your sins by trampling *my* heart."

Pain flashed over his face before he masked it. "I'm sending you back where you belong. Where you always belonged, if I'd had the sense to see it." He glanced away, a muscle throbbing in his jaw. "Once ye're safely back in London, you'll see that I'm right. Ye'll find a man worthy of you, and you'll take yer place in society where you belong. You'll forget this, all of this."

"You must think I'm quite the fickle female, if you believe that."

"I think ye're caught up in the romance of yer childhood home. But it won't last."

He'd said something like that before, but back then he hadn't known her well, so he'd had reason to believe it. He didn't now. That he could convince himself that he did infuriated her.

"What if I find myself with child?" she asked, heedless of who else heard.

With a glance beyond her to where her father jerked upright at the mention of children, Lachlan stiffened, then returned his gaze to her. "Ye're only saying that to force yer father's hand. Because you and I both know that if you found yerself with child, yer father would make me marry you."

"And you would marry me then?"

"*If* you ever found yerself with child. Which you won't."

So that's how he was going to justify this . . . this insanity. He would send her back to London ruined but free to take another husband if she pleased, figuring that her dowry would smooth over any man's objections to an unchaste wife.

But if she should happen to bear his child . . . well, that was a different matter. He would have to claim her then—it was the right thing to do. Keeping her now that he'd married her wasn't right, oh no. Letting their love heal the rift between their families wasn't right, oh no.

But if a child came into it, then and only then he could forget his cold and lofty ideas about justice.

Well, he was in for a surprise. She had a sense of justice, too. He might have spent years away from the Highlands because of his pride, but she wasn't about to let him spend years away from her because of some foolish ideas about atoning for his sins. So she'd have to force his hand.

"Fine," she said, tipping her chin up. "If you don't want me, I'll leave."

He gritted his teeth. "I didn't say I didn't want—"

"But listen to me, Lachlan, and listen well." She walked up close until she was nose to nose with him. "I'll give you three days to come to your senses. Then my father and I will leave for London."

He just stared at her, his face as rigid as his justice.

She scowled. "Once we do, I'll be gone from you forever, do you understand? You'll know nothing more of me, ever. If I should happen to find myself with child, you'll never know. If I marry some other man and let *him* raise your child, you'll never know."

His jaw grew taut. "Yer father would tell me—"

"Not if *he* doesn't know. And if I have to move to another country to ensure that, I will." That seemed to shake him, so she went on relentlessly. "If I leave here without you, then my life is my own. Who knows? I may just join my friend Amelia in Morocco for a long visit and never return."

That made alarm flare in his face, and she said, "If you're going to shut me out of your life, Lachlan, then I'll shut you out of mine." Her voice broke. "So you'd better think long and hard about your justice. Because once I'm gone for good, you'll get to spend the rest of your life wondering where I am and how I'm doing and whether you have a son somewhere with another man's name."

When he just continued to stare at her, hollow-eyed, she stifled a sob. She'd counted on such a threat bringing the stubborn lout around, but what if it didn't? Would she really walk away from him, to leave this place forever in three days?

No, never. But she wasn't about to tell him that. It was time Lachlan Ross learned that life didn't always go according to his plan. That right and wrong weren't as easy to define as he believed.

"Here's one more thing for you to think on over the next three days." Tears burned in her throat. "Consider this while you're sitting in the master bedchamber where we confessed our love, while you're doing the 'right thing' and atoning for everyone's sins."

She reached up to cup his cheek. "The greatest sin of all is to deny love. And there's nothing in this world you can do to atone for that."

Then, with her heart breaking, she turned, took her father's arm, and left Lachlan to his cold and lonely atonement.

Chapter Twenty-Seven

~∞~

Dear Cousin,

*I am willing to call a truce between us, if you'll
agree with me on one matter. A man hunting
for a wife ought to admit his situation from the
outset. That way no woman can ever accuse him
of treachery. Surely you'll admit that the best
marriages are built on honesty.*

Your relation,
Charlotte

*L*achlan spent his first day away from Venetia in a
blessed numbness, checking on the stills and going into
Dingwall to let people know he wasn't dead. It was sober-
ing to find himself the object of such great concern. His
flimsy story that he'd played dead only until the Scourge's
men could be routed met with astonishing acceptance.
They were apparently so glad to have him back, they
weren't going to quibble over how it had happened.

At least *someone* wasn't angry at him. His clan members
were furious that he hadn't pressed Duncannon for the
money. They couldn't understand his reasons, since they
didn't know what his father had done, and he meant to
keep it that way. Duncannon deserved not having his
secrets widely known.

Mother deserved her privacy, too. He cringed every
time he thought of how mortifying it must be to discover
that your dead husband had taken your friend into his
bed. Lachlan didn't know how to comfort her.

Not that she would let him. Refusing to speak to him, she stomped about the house telling the maids what a pity it was that Venetia couldn't be there to help. She referred to him as "my idiot son" with a frequency that began to annoy him.

Of all people, Mother should understand. Couldn't she see that the lass deserved better than a life in the Highlands cut off from her family?

Guilt clutched at him anew. It had been one thing to hear Venetia speak of her aging, ill father, and quite another to watch her worrying herself over the shattered relic of a man. She needed her father; the man needed her. She certainly deserved better than a lifetime chained to the scoundrel who'd ripped her from him.

Never mind that she didn't seem to agree; she would in time. It would be selfish of him to keep her here. What did it matter if the thought of her leaving Ross-shire, never to return, stripped the very flesh from his heart? Letting her go was the right thing to do.

Then why did it feel so very wrong?

That night he couldn't sleep. And in the morning, he awoke to the realization that he had only one more day before she would make good on her threat. God help him. The thought of her bearing his child without his knowing it . . .

No, that at least must never happen.

He went to find his mother. "I need you to pay Venetia a visit at Braidmuir."

Mother arched an eyebrow at him.

"You must beg her to write you from London if she finds herself with child."

His mother crossed her arms over her chest. "And why must I do this?"

"Because it would be yer grandchild! Surely you care what happens to it."

"Aye, but you gave up my right to care about the bairn when you denied the marriage. Which you said you didn't consummate anyway, remember?" Her eyes held an unholy glint. "So as you told Duncannon, there won't be any grandchild."

He scowled at her. "You know damned well that I bedded Venetia on the night we said the vows. Half the servants in Rosscraig probably saw her leave my bedchamber in the morning. And they'd never keep something like that from you."

She shrugged. "I still don't see what that has to do with me. You had yer chance to keep her; you threw it away and the bairn with it."

"It's not any bairn I care about!" he cried. "I just can't stand the thought of her bearing one alone, ye ken? What if something happens?"

Her face softened a fraction. "Seems to me you gave up the right to worry about that, too."

He rubbed the back of his neck in sheer frustration. "What if she goes to Morocco like she said? Do they even have doctors in a place like that? She'll be forced to use some foreign fellow, who'll most likely kill her in his ignorance."

"That could happen, I suppose."

He glared at her. "And if she stays in London and has a child, she'll be branded a whore by society. She'll have to live in seclusion." He shook his head. "Venetia wouldn't be happy in seclusion. She likes being around people."

"I didn't think you cared what she liked," his mother said with a cool smile.

"Of course I care! That's why I'm doing this. For

her. So she can have the decent life in society that she deserves."

"Has she said that's what she wants?"

He let out an oath. "The lass doesn't know what she wants. How can she, when I've tricked and seduced her at every turn?" He paced restlessly. "She hasn't even considered that marriage to me means leaving her sickly father, since I doubt Duncannon will ever wish to return to the Highlands."

"Perhaps. Still, it's her choice to make, isn't it?" She eyed him closely. "Besides, you didn't care about any of that *before* you learned about yer father and Lady Duncannon."

"I did care. But I was a selfish ass, willing to run roughshod over what she needed if it meant I could have her."

"Aye, because separating her from the villainous Earl of Duncannon seemed just to you. Separating her from the wronged Duncannon only seems cruel."

"When you put it that way . . . well, yes." A lump lodged in his throat. "Look at the havoc Father wreaked on the lass's life by sending her mother to the grave. I'm no better." He crossed his arms over his chest. "Father didn't set his wrong right, but I can. I have to."

"First of all," she said tersely, "yer father didn't send Lady Duncannon to her grave. She sent herself. She could have refused to lie with him. God knows I wish she had." A sad smile touched her thin lips, and he felt a lurch of sympathy for what she must be suffering. "But she didn't. And while I know you gave Venetia no choice when you kidnapped her, she had plenty of choices to leave afterward. She didn't take them." Her eyes gleamed at him. "She didn't say no to sharing your bed either, did she?"

"Only because she was worried about her father and wanted to soften me."

"You don't really believe that, do you? What about her words of love? Those were just lies?"

Instantly, he saw Venetia's face, her look of betrayal, when he'd pretended not to love her. "I don't know," he whispered. "All I know is that if I hadn't meddled where I shouldn't have, she'd be back in London where she belongs." The thought of how heedlessly he'd wrenched her from her life tortured him. "I did what I had no right to do and shattered her life. Hers and Duncannon's."

"Aye, that's true. Trouble is, like some wee bairn who's knocked a jar off the table, you think you can fix the broken glass by fitting all the pieces together and setting it back up where it was. You think you can pack her off home with her father as if nothing ever happened between you. That won't work, my son."

Touching a hand to his cheek, she gentled her voice. "But that doesn't mean you can't melt down the pieces to make a new jar. Oh, you'll have to figure out the new way for you and her and her father. So whatever glass you blow won't be the same as the first, because nothing in life stays the same." She smiled indulgently at him. "But it can be just as good. Or even better. If you're willing to try."

He pulled away from her, unshed tears clogging his throat. "If I keep her with me here and she ends up miserable, missing her father, missing her home, I'd never forgive myself. After everything I've done to her family—"

"She doesn't care—she said that. So why won't you at least try? Don't you love her?"

"I love her more than my life," he whispered.

"You love her, she loves you, so . . ." She trailed off as she searched his face. "Ah, that's what you're afraid of. That she won't *keep* loving you. That once you're not controlling everything and she can really know you, she won't like what she sees."

Startled by that oddly truthful remark, he stared at her, his heart pounding so heavily he could hardly stand it.

"Did you actually believe that nonsense yer father always spouted, about how wild and irresponsible you are? It's not true. It never was." Her voice grew choked. "Ye're not the only one who's been thinking about things these past few days. I realize now why Alasdair was always so angry at you."

A ragged sigh escaped her. "Because he was terrified that you'd guess the truth—that one day you'd see beneath his discipline to discover *he* was the wild and irresponsible one. So he drove you away. He was a coward who couldn't face having you find out about him."

She rubbed tears from her eyes. "Don't be a coward, driving away anyone who cares enough to see you for yerself. It's easy to live yer life alone, son. It takes courage to live with another. But in the end, yer life can be so much richer for it."

He could hardly breathe for the tears choking him.

"At least give the lass the chance to know who you really are. If you don't, you'll surely regret it." Then, with another soft pat of his cheek, she walked off.

Give the lass the chance to know who you really are. Aye, the thought of that *did* terrify him. What if she came to hate him, hate his rough ways so much she left?

He gave a choked laugh. If she left then or left now, what difference was it? Either way he'd be without her.

And a couple of days without her had already shown him he'd ne'er survive a lifetime.

Gazing around at Rosscraig's newly painted walls, he remembered the pride shining in her pretty face when she'd taken him round to show the work she'd done. Mayhap that pride wouldn't last. Mayhap she would tire of the harsh Highland life.

But he had to give her—and himself—the chance to find out. Because if he didn't, his life would be too awful to endure.

Quentin stared down at the ledgers before him, a tightness in his chest. Venetia was right. Things had fallen apart at Braidmuir. McKinley had been dipping his hand into the profits deeper by the day, from the looks of it. And Quentin had let him do it because he couldn't be bothered to oversee him properly.

He could blame it on his health or bad memories, but the fact was, it had been sixteen years since Susannah had betrayed him with his closest friend. That was a damned long time to hold a grudge.

And a damned long time to let other people do his dirty work. He still wasn't sure he'd done wrong by bringing in the sheep farmers, no matter what Venetia might think about it. But he did know that he'd once had what Ross had now on his land: people who cared about each other, who looked out for each other. Something was lost when that was gone, no matter the reason.

He sat back to stare about him as the afternoon sun streamed in the window. His daughter meant to restore what had been lost, didn't she? Everywhere in the house, dust covers were coming off tables and chairs, silver was being brought out of storage, beds were being made. When he asked why she was doing it even though they'd be leaving for London shortly, she just cast him a sad smile that told him she was still waiting for Ross. Then she went back to her work.

Leaving him with a chill in his heart.

What was he to do about Ross? The man had kidnapped his daughter, yes, but he wasn't the reckless idiot that Quentin had assumed. Quentin had spoken to the people in Dingwall—they'd sung his praises. And God knows Ross had managed to hold his estate together when any lesser man would have given up.

Still . . .

The sound of horses in the drive made him start. It couldn't be Lady Kerr and that colonel fellow. They'd already left for London, eager to tell the man's daughter about their impending wedding.

A few moments passed before the housekeeper knocked at the door of his study. "Sir Lachlan Ross to see you, my lord."

Damnation. This was all moving too quickly.

But Venetia would have his head if he turned the man away. "Send him in."

Ross entered, hat in hand, unease written all over his face. "Good evening, sir." He thrust out his chin. "I've come to fetch my wife."

Quentin's eyes narrowed. "As I recall, you said you don't have a wife."

"I said a lot of things. Because I thought she deserved a better husband than me."

"Aye, she does."

That made Ross scowl, looking as if he were about to choke to death on his pride. But Quentin had to hand it to the man—he didn't back down. "The thing is, sir . . . whether I deserve her or no, I love her."

"Do you?" he said skeptically.

"I do." Ross set his shoulders. "Mayhap that's hard for you to believe with everything that's happened between you and me, but it's the truth. I know you don't want me for a son-in-law—God knows I don't blame you—but I think she loves me, too. So if she'll take me back, I swear to you I'll spend the rest of my days trying to make her happy."

Quentin dragged in a heavy breath. The moment he'd been dreading had come, the moment when he had to decide. The divil of it was, now that it was here, the choice seemed easy. Because he and the laird wanted the same thing—to make the lass happy. And she'd spent the past two days making it clear she could only be happy with Lachlan Ross.

He sighed. "So what is it you want from me?"

"Yer blessing. It would mean a great deal to her to have it."

"And I suppose you want her dowry, too."

A mulish pride flared in Ross's face. "No, my lord, I won't take yer money."

Quentin sat back in his chair. "Then I won't give you my blessing."

That drew the man up short. "It just doesn't seem right—"

"I won't have my only daughter 'scraping and saving for a few curtains' when a tidy fortune is to hand. You'll take the money, or I won't give my blessing. That's an end to it." The fact that he even had to argue such a thing banished whatever other misgivings he'd had about handing Venetia over to Ross.

Ross let out an oath, his fingers working the brim of his hat something fierce. Then at last he sighed. "Fine. I'll take her dowry. But it'll be pin money for her and a settlement for our children, do ye ken?"

"Whatever you say. Though I imagine she'll have quite a bit to say about it herself." He picked up the decanter of whisky on his desk. "Sit down, and we'll have a drink to seal the agreement."

With a terse nod, Ross took a seat, his gaze flitting around the study. "Are you meaning to stay at Braidmuir?" he asked as Quentin poured the glasses.

"I'm thinking on it. Venetia is making me think on it."

A smile touched Ross's lips. "She has a way of doing that to a man."

Quentin handed Ross a glass. "She says I've neglected my property enough." He picked up his own glass with a rueful smile. "And she wants me around to dandle any grandchildren on my knee."

Ross stared into the glass. "What does McKinley think of yer staying around?"

"I don't know. I dismissed him this morning."

The man's head shot up.

"I didn't like what he'd done to the place."

A new respect showing in his face, Ross sipped his whisky, then blinked. "Where did you get this?"

"From some fine fellows in town. Told me it was the best whisky round, even if it was from an illegal still." Ross's flummoxed expression brought a smile to Quentin's face. "If you see the man who makes it, you might tell him what I've been hearing in London: that the Duke of Gordon means to propose an excise act so that whisky making will be affordable in Scotland again. Whisky this fine deserves a wider market."

"I'll tell him."

Quentin sipped more whisky, preparing himself for one more onerous task. "Ross, I never meant for Sikeston and his men to beat you so badly. I sure as the divil never ordered them to kill you."

Looking distinctly uncomfortable, Ross shook his head. " 'Tis all in the past now. No point in speaking of it."

"But it wasn't the first time I had you endure a beating, so let me say my piece." He took a gulp of whisky. "Years ago, when I accused you of stealing, I really did believe that you'd put those lads up to it. I'd just learned about . . . yer father and Susannah, and I would have believed anything bad of you."

He turned the glass round in his hand. "I took it out on you, because I couldn't take it out on him, and because I thought that striking at you would strike at his heart."

"Except that he didn't have much of a heart, did he?"

"Seems that way, I have to say." He gazed at Ross. "I did find out later that it wasn't you, but by then you had run off. So . . . I want to say I'm sorry for that, for thinking ill of you, for having you—"

"Thank you, sir," Ross muttered. "It was a long time ago."

"Aye."

They drank together a moment in silence, then Ross set his glass down. "I don't mean to be rude, sir, but—"

"You're wanting to see my daughter. I know." He nodded toward the door. "You'll find her in the glen by the woods. God only knows why she likes to walk there so much."

Judging from how Ross colored, *he* knew. Quentin tried not to dwell on why that might be.

But as the laird hurried to the door, Quentin called out, "Ross?"

The man paused in the doorway to look back. "Yes, my lord?"

"If you hadn't come for her within the three days, I would have hunted you down and cut your heart out, do ye ken?"

To his surprise, Ross gave a faint smile. "You wouldn't have found anything to cut out, sir. The lass stole my heart long ago."

As the man headed down the hall, Quentin downed the rest of his whisky and leaned back to survey his domain. Perhaps coming back to Braidmuir wouldn't be such a trial after all. Good whisky, a hardworking son-in-law . . . grandchildren.

Not to mention that Lady Ross was looking surprisingly fine these days. Age sat well on the woman, carving character into the face that he'd remembered as plain. He could use a woman about the house, now that he was going to lose his daughter to that rascal Ross. And the lady *was* a widow, after all.

That thought kept him smiling for quite a while.

Chapter Twenty-Eight

Dear Charlotte,

A truce is an excellent idea. Only remember,
my fine cousin, that an expectation of honesty and
truth goes both ways. And one day soon I shall
expect to see some of that from you. For I sometimes
wonder if you're as honest with yourself—or with
me—as you pretend.

Your impatient friend,
Michael

Venetia wandered through the glen before halting
at the patch of white daisies near the large oak. She'd
planted them as a child, thinking to please Lachlan
with something pretty for him to look at while he was
fishing.

She snorted. The big lummox hadn't even noticed
them.

That should have taught her that the man was
incapable of seeing certain things, even when they stared
him right in the face. If something didn't concern his
clan or his manly pride or the Highlands, it was beneath
his notice.

Tears stung her eyes and she squelched them ruthlessly.
She wouldn't cry anymore, she wouldn't. Why should
she cry over that obstinate fool?

All the same, she couldn't resist picking a daisy and
doing what she'd done so often as a girl, ripping the

petals off as she chanted the litany that so many girls had chanted before her. "He loves me. He loves me not."

"He loves you."

She froze at the familiar voice coming from the hill behind her. She didn't look. She couldn't. What if she'd only imagined it?

Then she heard the heavy boot-steps descending. "He loves you," the voice repeated, thick with emotion. "I love you."

A thousand times in the last few days, she'd prepared herself for what she'd say if this moment ever came. But she couldn't remember a word of it as she faced him. Though he was dressed in his finest, he looked uncertain of himself, even nervous. She'd never seen Lachlan nervous about anything.

"I love you," he said again.

"How can I believe you," she whispered, "when just two days ago, you practically denied it to my face?"

"Two days ago, I was an ass."

"Yes, you were." When he looked at a loss for words, she let out a breath. "I can understand your saying the wedding wasn't legal, because it really wasn't." She stared down at the hapless daisy. "And I can almost understand your not wanting to admit before Papa that you'd bedded me." Her voice broke. "But how could you deny that you loved me?"

"I know. That was very wrong." As he neared her, she could see the dark circles beneath his eyes, the pallor of his skin. "I have no idea how to make this right. You said that there's no way to atone for denying love, but I'm praying hard that you're wrong. Because I'll do whatever it takes for you to forgive me."

She wanted to throw herself at him and tell him she

forgave him now, but she wasn't going to make this easy for him. Not after what he'd put her through.

"And why *should* I forgive you?" she said hoarsely. "You only came after me because you're worried that I'll have your child and you'll never see it."

"No." He stepped closer. "I'm worried that you have my *heart* and I'll never see it. Like I told yer father, you stole my heart long ago. Without it, without you, I'm an empty shell of a man."

The words were so sweet, she wanted to cry. Then his other words registered. "You spoke to my father?"

He nodded. "To ask for his blessing. He gave it, too."

A frown touched her brow. Had Lachlan only come after her because Papa had absolved him of his foolish guilt? "What would you have done if he'd refused to give you his blessing?"

His dark eyes burned into her. "I would have sent my regrets that he couldn't join us when we repeat our vows in the kirk. But whether we speak them again or no, you're my wife. Nothing yer father can say will change that."

Her heart soared. He really did love her. He really had come just for her.

"Please, lass," he choked out. "You have to come back to me. If you don't, you'll force me to do something drastic."

"Like what?"

"Kidnap you again. I brought the coach." He looked amazingly solemn as he reached in his pocket and pulled out something he dangled before her. "And rope. And I'll use both if I have to."

She bit back a smile. "I hardly think that's the way to get back into my good graces."

He handed the rope to her. "Then you can tie *me* up with it and leave me here for the sheep to trample a while. Is that what you'd rather?"

"Actually," she said, taking the rope from him, "I'd rather use the rope for something else entirely."

"What?"

She looped the rope around his wrist, then hers. "To tie us together." Tears of joy filled her eyes. "So we can never be apart."

He took her in his arms. "We never will be again, I swear," he whispered.

Then he kissed her with all the tender care a woman could possibly want. There, in the midst of the glen where she'd first learned to adore him, he kissed her, and it was even more wonderful than she'd imagined in her girlish fantasies.

It had taken her years, but she'd finally gained her ballad hero. And this time, she meant to hold on to him for the rest of her life.

When he drew back, his eyes shone and his breath came in sharp, impetuous gasps. "Shall we go home, wife?" he said in that seducer's brogue she loved so well.

She glanced up the hill to the cottage where he'd made her his, then cast him a teasing smile. "We could. Then again, it seems a shame to let all that lovely fleece go to waste . . ."

With a laugh, he looped his arm about her and they hurried up the hill.

The daisy fell unheeded to the ground, one petal left on its stem.

He loves me.

Forever.

Epilogue

❦

*V*enetia returned from the retiring room at Colonel Seton's town house in Edinburgh, to find his ballroom filling with guests from his wedding to Aunt Maggie earlier in the day. An orchestra was tuning up, but she noticed no pipers. Aunt Maggie must have won *that* argument with the colonel. She'd been adamant that her wedding celebration be an elegant affair— no strathspeys, no Scottish reels, no pipers, and no whisky.

Venetia sighed.

"That sounds ominous," said Mrs. Harris, who came to join her.

She smiled at her old schoolmistress. "I've been meaning to ask what possessed you to leave the school in the middle of a session. I'm sure the colonel could have found some other person to bring Lucy up here."

"Ah, but then I wouldn't have had the chance to meet your husband. It's not often that one of *my* pupils ends up eloping with a Scottish laird of little fortune and no connections."

Her gaze shifted to where Lachlan helped the colonel move some chairs. "But I must say I begin to understand why you felt compelled to toss aside every rule I taught you. He's quite a strapping fellow in his regimentals, isn't he?"

"You have no idea," Venetia said, laying a hand on

her belly. She'd waited to say anything to Lachlan until she could consult a doctor here in Edinburgh. But now that she was sure, she meant to tell her husband just how strapping a fellow he was, the minute she could get him alone.

"You know," Mrs. Harris said, "of all my girls, you were the one I felt sure would snag some very rich, very titled gentleman."

"Sorry to disappoint you," Venetia murmured, though she wasn't in the least.

"Don't be ridiculous—you seem happy, and that's the most important thing." Mrs. Harris cast her a fond glance. "You're different here. More relaxed."

She laughed. "No one married to Lachlan Ross could be anything else. He has a way of making a woman forget entirely about propriety." When Mrs. Harris frowned, she said, "You seem different, too . . . agitated. And you're never agitated. Has Cousin Michael been alarming you with his gossip?"

Mrs. Harris's frown deepened. "You might say that. Or you might say that he's arrogant and opinionated and secretive, an annoying trial of a man."

Venetia bit back a smile. "I said much the same things about Lachlan. Indeed, my aunt said much the same about the colonel. Perhaps you are developing a more than cousinly interest in your 'cousin.'"

"Bite your tongue!" Mrs. Harris fluttered her fan furiously. "I don't even know who the man is, for heaven's sake. He's probably seventy years old at least, and though I'm past thirty, I'm not yet in my dotage."

"I'm only saying—"

"Look lively, my dear, someone's coming."

That effectively ended the conversation. With a

little leap in her pulse, Venetia turned to find Lachlan approaching.

Bestowing a polite nod on Mrs. Harris, he offered his arm to Venetia. "I was hoping to persuade you to dance with me." His eyes twinkled. "I'm afraid it's just a dull old waltz, nothing you could sing to, like 'Tullochgorum,' but you might find it enjoyable."

"Very amusing," she said as she took his arm. "Behave yourself, sir, or I'll sing 'Tullochgorum' all the way back to Rosscraig tomorrow."

"There are worse ways to pass the time," he said as he led her to the floor. "At least it will keep Mother from plaguing us with her snoring."

"Didn't I tell you? Your mother is riding back in Papa's carriage."

Lachlan scowled. "Oh, she is, is she? And whose fool idea was that, a widow and a widower traveling alone together—"

"They're not traveling alone, Lachlan," she said with a laugh. "We'll be in the carriage behind. Besides, you, of all people, have no room to complain about a man and a woman traveling alone."

He took her in his arms as the music began. "I can't say I like it, though. Grant you, yer father has done fine things at Braidmuir, bringing back some of the crofters and trying to manage both the sheep and the farming, but that doesn't mean I want him courting my mother. It doesn't seem proper somehow."

"Proper!" She nodded over to where his mother danced stiffly with Papa. "You don't get much more proper than that."

"Only because Mother has never been to a fancy ball."

"I hadn't thought of that—she's probably more comfortable at a ceilidh."

His arm tightened about her waist. "And you, lass? Where are *you* more comfortable?"

She stared up into his dear face. "Wherever you are."

He seemed to like that answer, for his gaze smoldered and his hold turned decidedly lascivious. "So you won't mind leaving the city tomorrow?"

"Certainly not. I'm eager to be home." She hesitated, but this seemed like the perfect moment. "I'm eager to begin work on our nursery."

"Nursery! We don't have a—" He halted on the dance floor to gape at her, then dropped his gaze to her still-flat belly. "Are you . . . are we . . ."

"Aye, sir." She mimicked his brogue. "I'm expecting a bairn, I am."

He let out a whoop more fitting for a battlefield than a ball, then lifted her and swung her about.

"Lachlan!" she protested with a giddy laugh. "Put me down, for heaven's sake! People are staring!"

"Let them stare," he said, though he lowered her gently to the floor. "It isn't every day a man receives such news from the woman he loves. Anyway, these city Scots need a little shaking up, don't you think?"

She glanced around at Aunt Maggie's "elegant" friends, who all had the look of pinch-faced Englishmen compared to Highlanders like Jamie, who was dancing happily with a new sweetheart. "Oh, I do." As Lachlan took her in his arms and began waltzing again, she added, "They're much too stuffy."

"Too rigid."

"Too English. We really ought to shake them up. It would do them good."

His eyes gleamed at her. "And what do you have in mind?"

"We could send for a piper and a fiddler. I wouldn't mind dancing a strathspey or two." She grinned. "They could play 'Tullochgorum.' "

"I brought some of my finest whisky for the colonel. It's in our room at the inn. I could send for that, too."

"We could turn this ball into a regular ceilidh."

"Aye." He sighed. "But yer aunt would never forgive us, and you know it."

She sighed, too. "I suppose if we're to keep peace in the family, we shouldn't do it."

"I don't think so." They danced a moment. "But I tell you what, princess."

"Yes, my love?"

"When we return to Rosscraig, we'll throw the ceilidh to end all ceilidhs. And you and I"—he paused to look down at her belly—"and the bairn will dance as many strathspeys as you please."

"Or . . ." She trailed off with a coy smile.

"Or?"

"We could have our own private ceilidh in the colonel's study."

He got that look on his face that never failed to send delicious shivers dancing over her skin. "Now?"

"That depends." She dropped her gaze to his kilt. "Are you practicing the 'old traditions' tonight?"

"Why?" he asked, his face reddening.

"Because, my dear husband," she leaned up to whisper, "that would make it much easier to do it in a chair."

And with his laughter ringing in her ears, he waltzed her right out the side door.

Author's Note

◈

𝒯he Scottish Clearances of the eighteenth and early nineteenth centuries have had a lasting effect on the Highlands. To this day, the area is underpopulated because of the "Improvers" who filled their land with sheep, forcing their crofters to emigrate. It's the reason the east coast of the United States and Canada is filled with people of Scottish heritage, the reason Scottish Highland Games abound in those areas. While we've reaped the benefits of assimilating that rich culture into ours, it devastated the Highlands, which hasn't been the same since.

Whisky, however, played a large part in salvaging the economy. After 1823, when the Duke of Gordon's Excise Act made it profitable to license a still, legal operations sprang up all over the Highlands. The Glenlivet distillery began as an illegal still on the duke's land (which is why he championed the act in the first place). I like to think that Lachlan went on to found a great scotch whisky.

Entire books have been written about the king's visit to Edinburgh, but one thing most scholars agree on—Sir Walter Scott's novels and his orchestration of the pageantry of the king's visit changed how the outside world viewed Scotland forever. The kilt became the universal symbol of Scottish attire instead of just a Highland custom, and the culture was romanticized.

And yes, the laws for Scottish irregular marriages (recognized by civil authorities, though not by religious ones) were exactly as I described them. They remained in place until 1940, when the laws were reformed.

Last, there are still wildcats in Scotland, although some people dispute whether they're true descendants of the breed or mixes of the original Scottish wildcat with domestic cats. Certainly, they existed during the period of my book. And they do indeed look just like large tabbies. Except when they snarl.

POCKET BOOKS
PROUDLY PRESENTS

Sabrina Jeffries'
next delightful
School for Heiresses novel

Coming soon
from Pocket Books

Turn the page for a preview. . . .

Anthony followed the schoolteacher down the hall to allow him a good look at her shapely bottom. How would it feel to cup it in his hands? Perhaps *that* would rouse a blush in her fair cheeks—

Stop that, you randy bastard! he told himself. *You can't seduce Miss Prescott.*

She was probably a virgin, and he hadn't lied when he'd said he didn't debauch virgins. That was too unsavory even for him.

Still, her lack of blushes made him wonder. So did her forthright manner. You never knew what secrets a woman hid beneath a cloak of respectability. He'd learned that long ago.

As if she'd read his wicked mind, the young lady turned to him before they reached the office. "Lord Northcourt, if you want your niece enrolled here, you'll have to mind your tongue around my employer. With every rash remark, you make it more difficult to persuade Mrs. Harris to keep you."

"*Keep* me!" he said, smothering a laugh. "You seem to have mistaken me for a lapdog, sweetheart."

"I am not your sweetheart, drat it!" She cast a furtive glance in the direction of Mrs. Harris's office. "And that's precisely the sort of remark I'm talking about. My employer is generally amiable, but men of your kind annoy her."

"My 'kind'?"

With a sigh, Miss Prescott continued down the hall. "You have to understand," she explained as he kept pace with her, "in her youth, she eloped with a soldier who turned out to be a rogue. Not only did he waste most of her fortune at the gaming tables, but she found out later that he often frequented ladies of the evening. Is it any wonder she dislikes rakehells?"

"And how do *you* feel about rakehells, Miss Prescott?" he said, watching to see her reaction.

She hastened her pace. "Having only met my first one today, I can hardly voice an opinion."

"That doesn't stop most people."

"Most people have seen a rakehell in his natural habitat. I have not."

"Natural habitat?" He laughed. "You really *are* a lover of science." Stepping in front of her, he blocked her from going farther. "But you must have an opinion. You won't wound my feelings if you admit it."

A sigh escaped her lips. "Very well, then."

Ah, now we get to the lecture on morality.

"From what little I know of rakes, they seem a fascinating species, well deserving of study." Sidling neatly past him, she continued down the hall.

He managed to close his slack jaw long enough to hurry after her. A "fascinating species"? "Deserving of study"? Was she serious?

Seconds later, they emerged into the foyer where he'd earlier been admitted. Sounds of girlish chatter cascaded down the impressive central staircase. The Elizabethan-era building had apparently been a private residence before being adapted for use as a school, and the high ceilings only amplified the noise.

Miss Prescott halted outside a door painted white. "Why don't I show you the dining room before the girls come down for their afternoon tea?" She spoke as if she hadn't just made the most bizarre pronouncement about rakes that he'd ever heard. "Then I can bring you upstairs to see the classrooms while the girls aren't engaged in lessons."

"All right." He followed her into a spacious room with a mahogany dining table that easily seated twenty. "Tell me, Miss Prescott. Why in God's name would you think we rakehells deserve study?"

With a shrug, she began straightening chairs. "Because of your reckless way of life, I suppose."

"Why do you think it reckless?" he countered, not sure if she was trying to insult him.

"Don't you fight duels?"

"Absolutely not. You have to get up at dawn for those."

Her eyes narrowed. "Don't you race your phaeton?"

"I don't own a phaeton." He did race his curricle from time to time, but no point in mentioning *that*.

"And I suppose you don't drink strong spirits, either."

"Well, yes, but—"

"That isn't good for the constitution. It makes otherwise healthy men suffer from headaches the morning after, or cast up their accounts in the street. Such reactions tax the body unduly."

He held out his arms. "Do I look as if I'm teetering on the edge of death?"

Miss Prescott skimmed him with blatant nonchalance. "Not now, but I daresay you look quite different on the mornings after your carousing."

"I can handle my liquor perfectly well, I assure you," he snapped, unaccountably peeved by her logic.

"Fine." She strode off toward a door across the room. "Do you gamble?"

"Of course."

"Surely you consider *that* reckless. You could easily lose your estates and your future. Given the odds of winning versus losing, it's rare for someone to increase their annual income by gambling, yet rakes insist upon taking the risk."

"It isn't a risk if you know the mathematical odds and play accordingly."

She looked skeptical. "I suppose you're going to tell me you know how to avoid heavy losses."

"I know that the odds of winning at loo are about 5 to 1. Of course that depends on whether you play three- or five-card loo and how many players you have. When you factor in whether the Eldest Hand plays a King or an Ace to start, the odds can vary from 5 to 1 to 10 to 4—according to my calculations."

The quick flare of admiration on her face warmed him as no woman's ever had. He'd always excelled at mathematics—that's why he'd been able to augment his small allowance so effectively with investments—but women weren't usually impressed by a man's mathematical skill.

To have her look at him so, through new eyes full of interest, roused every one of his rakehell instincts. He suddenly realized how easy it would be to step close and kiss that enticing mouth.

Now *that* would be reckless. "My point is, Miss Prescott, I'm well aware of the odds, so I never risk more than I can afford."

Setting her hand on the door handle, she frowned. "But why risk anything at all? You don't have to gamble to enjoy playing cards."

He laughed. "I'll inform them of that at my club and see if they agree."

A thundering noise overhead made her start. "The girls are coming. Quick, through here. We don't want to be inundated by questions and curious glances."

With a nod, he followed her into a spacious ballroom. He paid no mind to the lightly polished oak floors that stretched an impressive distance beneath a crystal chandelier, or the rows of simple white chairs that flanked walls covered with elegant green fabric.

He was much more interested in why Miss Prescott, with her apparent disapproval had proposed that he give cautionary rake lessons to her charges.

"We teach dancing three times a week in here," she said, acting the impersonal guide. "Every Saturday night we hold an assembly, and once a month we invite local boys to attend so the girls can practice their skills with gentlemen."

"Do you dance, Miss Prescott?" he asked, hoping to learn more of her background.

"When I can." Circling the room, she headed out two open French doors onto a gallery that afforded a magnificent view of well-laid-out gardens teeming with lilacs and roses. When she halted beside the marble balustrade, the afternoon sun cast a sheen of gold over her glorious curls.

"I'm surprised that you don't find dancing to be reckless," he said, trying not to imagine her lush hips swaying and her even lusher breasts rising and falling with her exertions.

"I suppose it can be." She tipped up her chin at him. "If it leads a man and woman to do other things."

At *last* they got to the heart of the matter. He had known she would eventually raise the subject of morality, especially in relations between men and women. Her sort always did.

"What 'other things' do you mean, Miss Prescott?" he drawled, the devil in him determined to force her into speaking the words aloud.

She eyed him as if he were a fool. "You know what I mean. Swiving."

"*Swiving?*" He burst into laughter. "You have an interesting vocabulary for a schoolteacher."

"The word comes from Shakespeare," she said defensively. "It's perfectly acceptable."

"Perhaps for a tavern in Spitalfields, but gentlewomen aren't supposed to talk about swiving."

"Oh, but they should! Then they'd learn the dangers to be had from it. Indiscriminate swiving is the *most* reckless activity of a rake. It spreads disease, it provokes characters like that Harriette Wilson with her *Memoirs* to blackmail gentlemen with the threat of ruin, it can result in the siring of illegitimate children—"

"Disease," he broke in, incredulous. "Blackmail and illegitimate children—*these* are what concern you about the indiscriminate swiving of rakehells?"

"Of course." She eyed him with clear surprise. "What else?"

"Virtue? Morality?"

She snorted. "Those are the very things that make it so reckless in the first place—especially for a woman. Aside from losing her position and possibly her home, she risks finding herself with child and cast out by a society that dismisses her as 'immoral' to excuse its not taking care of its women."

Her bleak assessment unnerved him. Yes, women could plummet from respectable to disreputable in society's eyes very easily, even when the man was to blame for it, but that little inequity hadn't bothered him before. His lovers had either been soiled doves, or widows who knew how to have their fun without losing their heads. Neither needed much protecting.

With his young niece's future to consider, however, he couldn't look at the average woman's prospects in quite the same way. And that disturbed him. Deeply.

Which in turn annoyed him. "Some people, even women, find the pleasures of 'swiving' well worth the risks, Miss Prescott."

"I can't imagine why." She surveyed him with a wary eye. "You were *sincere* about your intention to reform, weren't you?"

That brought him up short. "I don't have much of a choice."

"Everyone has a choice, sir."

"Perhaps." He cracked a smile. "Though it's harder for those of us who are born wicked."

"Don't be silly," she chided. "Wickedness is a habit cultivated over time."

"And habits are hard to break." He searched her face. "You don't believe I'm capable of reform, do you?"

She dropped her gaze. "As you say, habits are hard to break. But you can break them if you really want to."

"Whether I want to is immaterial. I must. And when I set my mind to something, I generally succeed. So, yes, I am sincere about reforming."

At least until he had Jocelyn married and well settled.

After that, he wasn't sure. He fully planned to restore

the family fortunes, but he refused to follow in his father's footsteps by making estate affairs the center of his life. And though he must eventually marry to produce an heir, he was in no hurry to yoke himself to the sort of respectable female he *ought* to marry, who would suffer his touch only to have children.

At the same time, his brother's death had cast a pall over the dissolute life he'd been living for some years. He'd always thought he had plenty of time to settle down and marry. Now he knew otherwise.

"Good," she said as she met his gaze. "I need this position, you know, and if you were to attempt to seduce one of my pupils—"

"Or you?"

For the first time that afternoon, uncertainty deepened her amber eyes. She masked it with a shaky laugh. "You may attempt to seduce *me* as much as you please. I'm afraid it would be pointless. I'm not reckless by nature, and I'm too aware of the risks. Besides, such things don't tempt me."

The bloody devil they didn't. "I could prove you wrong in that," he said softly.